OF ABRASION

THE ALTERED EARTH TRILOGY

Of Friction

Of Abrasion

Of Imperfection

OF ABRASION

ALTERED EARTH SERIES
BOOK 2

S.J. LEE

PEW BOOKS

Library of Congress Cataloging-in-Publication Data is available.

ISBN (paperback) 979-8-9892965-2-1
ISBN (ebook) 979-8-9892965-3-8

Cover design by Jason Arias

CONTENTS

OF ABRASION

A CALL TO ARMS

WHEN MIRIAM TANNER arrived in the North, death laid out its passengers on display, their broken bodies scattered amongst the devastation of a calculated blow. No one knew the numbers yet, but marines were missing and many had met their demise amid early-morning dreams.

A combat medic, Miriam let years of training and experience drive her muscles and motions as she joined others to stem the bleed of casualties. She was exhausted, but she had a job to do. The ones still breathing were the priority, not the dead.

So, horror kept her company as she moved from one injured to another, bandaging, medicating, and adjusting tourniquets where she could. Fix this, treat that, and race against time. It was all a game, a morbid but efficient dissociation, and she was good at it.

Except for the one she had already lost.

Miriam hadn't shared her discovery with Razor-Echo, her team from Special Operations Group, and as she stood outside a triage station, it hung as a heavy weight. When Kai Wester joined her, Miriam wanted to say it, relieve the secret burden imprisoning her.

Sam Ryan. Callsign "Valkyrie."

Dead.

Sam was dead.

The three words rolled up her tongue, but she clamped her mouth shut. She couldn't bear saying it, or hearing it, out loud. If those words formed beyond her lips, it'd be real. Final. And Miriam was grasping at a thread of hope that the tattooed and scarred flesh she had found was only a dream, a terrible figment of her terrible imagination.

A fraying thread.

She swallowed, but the three words lodged in her throat like a lump of lead.

Sam was dead.

But it wasn't real.

Not yet.

A marine panted as he jogged toward them, perspiration glistening on his chestnut skin. Saif Nasiri, or *Nas* as he preferred, thrust a wrist forward, his metallic cuff illuminating. "Look."

Kai tutted and deftly swiped two fingers across his outstretched device, projecting a network broadcast onto a larger and extended holodisplay. On it, a white-haired man gestured emphatically.

"What is this? Turn it up," another teammate demanded as he stepped forward, his frame shadowing the others. Benjamin Fox swiped at the sheen of sweat below his shadowed jaw.

Miriam could detect the hints of alcohol on his breath and skin. Or maybe it was all of them combined, including her. Most of the team had been celebrating at the compound bar in Station the previous night, hours before everything happened.

The same night she had been kissed and kissed back.

Regret spiked in Miriam's chest and her breath hitched. She could still feel Sam's lips, soft against hers. If she had let that moment in the corridor unfold... If she hadn't pushed Sam away, would the woman have stayed in Station City with her? Would Sam still be alive?

"Today, we say no more—"

Miriam blinked. Sam wasn't dead. What she had seen wasn't real. Someone else could've had that scar and that circle tattoo. It could've been someone else. It wasn't Sam.

"No more to the falsifiers sitting in their palace—"

It *had* to be someone else.

"No more to the unjust, criminal tyrants. No more to the oppressors. We shall restore our freedom, our rights to this world *we* cultivated!"

Colorful eyes pierced through the holodisplay's distortion, their flecks of green, blue, and brown glowing, and an icy shiver ran up Miriam's spine. In the feed's background, a sizable crowd roared, and she folded her arms, gripping her triceps in a self-embrace.

Kai pulled at a strand of her dark hair. "Who—where is this?"

"Their capital, Arshangol. Him..." Nas trailed off, his head wobbling uncertainly.

The volume and display cut out as Fox palmed Nas's cuff, and the four watched a group of injured marines pass and enter the triage station.

"No one knows who he is. At least not yet." Nas shook their teammate's hand away, and the feed continued.

Kai's eyes grew, then narrowed. "Wunbies?"

The question was almost rhetorical. It had to be. The wunbies—*Apostates,* as the other genetically engineered Altered called them, or the *Promised,* as they called themselves—were terrorists following the old Sovereign's fervor and campaign against humans. Like most of the population, Miriam knew about the Altered supremacists, but the wunbies had never been at the forefront of Station's mind. The city's politics, domestic issues, and general tensions with the *alties* often overshadowed the one-off lone-wolf attacks in the border regions.

But now the wunbies were relevant. The attack on the

United Military Federation's northern outpost came less than two days after an attempted siege of the humans' southernmost base a continent away. Miriam and Echo had been at the epicenter of it all.

"Where did you get this?" asked Kai.

"Jace. BigInt. This is circulating on every feed in alty territories."

"Live?"

Nas rubbed his forehead. "No, I don't think so. The original broadcast must've been a couple hours ago."

Fox gestured impatiently, and the group quieted.

"The Royals and their cronies have committed heinous acts against their own. They obsess over their blood and hoard their science, but all this—this city, this wealth—was built on our backs. They have forgotten that we are the many, we are the people, and we are their strength. *We* are the power."

Muffled shouts and cries rang up in a chorus. A stomping rhythm stirred in the feed's background, and it wrapped in the device's static as it grew louder.

"We are one blood. We are the Promised, and our time is now. Your time is now! Your future is in your hands."

Pain lanced in Miriam's arms and she looked down, her fingers curled into her skin. She forced her hands to open, but the sting continued along each crescent where her nails had dug in.

"Take back what was promised!"

PROLOGUE

GUNFIRE STUTTERED *into her ears before a bellowing roar followed, and she flinched back, a hand shielding her eyes as night became day. Heat simmered against her face, and then it was gone. Giant flames burned bright as they rushed around her, their legs skittering this way and that. Their shrieks curdled and the silence that followed clawed at everything within her.*

And then monsters broke through the gates.

She wanted to run. Couldn't.

It was too late, anyway.

Glowing eyes leaped out and consumed her.

PART 1

EPIDERMIS

1

———————————

LOST AND FOUND

"THERE'S SOME BLOOD ON YOUR..."

Miriam drew the back of her sleeve across her face in a feeble attempt to remove a stray hair from her eyes. It stuck rebelliously to her forehead and she gave up, wiping at the line of sweat along her neck instead. She ignored the dark-haired man dressed in Station military grays next to her. She loved Yuri Gregov, her best friend and teammate, but it was a stupid comment. Blood stained her clothes and exposed skin in layers, fresh crimson tints over oxidized browns.

She pushed past him and through the tent flap, hoping for fresh air. Each step away from the triage area brought a less constricted breath, but the scent of rubbed iron followed, hovering around her. Miriam tugged at her disheveled outer frock, crumpled it between gloved hands, and dropped it into a nearby barrel.

"They've set up cots at the south gym. We can drop our packs, maybe grab a quick bite before shuteye. The others are taking first shift."

Only partially listening, she peeled off her gloves and added them to the growing pile of trash. She took a deep breath, but it cut short at the inhale of metallic tang. Even if she could shower and change, she couldn't do much about the smell. That butcher's scent would linger, seeping into her skin like a reminder, a brand.

Miriam pulled at her collar, wanting to strip her sullied uniform off as well, but she restrained herself. For now, she'd accept the relief of physical distance from the frantic arena of wounds, burns, and casualties under the tarp and tents. It had been a nonstop shift of patching holes, pushing critical care, and delaying what she could until more advanced specialists or outbound flights were available. Still, guilt regurgitated now that she was outside. She could do more, help more.

"The others are saying something interrupted the systems. At least from what they can gather. It'd make sense, you know, why defenses were down. Hell, I can't imagine."

In the distance, the last trails of daylight dissolved behind a skeleton of a building, its protruding frame exposing the bones and sinews of a military's daily machinations. Miriam and Echo had started their morning in Station City, a flight away. Only two or three days before, they had been much further south, and now here they were, stuck in an unexpected and never-ending day at the opposite end of human civilization.

Mobile generators whirred behind her, and she squinted as more white lights flickered on. They spotlighted the worst-hit buildings, their blown-out cavities staring like empty eye sockets and their broken surfaces like cracked smiles.

"Comms mentioned the network should be back up. Well, more stable at least, so that's good... We'll hear from Mute and Valk. I know it."

Miriam kneaded a thumb into her palm.

The tattooed circle and the scar.

"It's a big outpost. They're probably busy with recovery or defense efforts. I heard SOG pieced together some units and pushed out to observation posts toward the other coast. We'll hear from them soon."

The detached arm.

Miriam's stomach twisted, and she rushed to the barrel but then recoiled at the sight and concentrated smell. She scrambled away and doubled over, but nothing came out. She hadn't eaten since they left Station, not on the airship nor the entire time Echo scraped through their assigned search quadrant. Their location had been one of the worst hit; the on-compound residences lay partially leveled with living quarters exposed, concrete and metal splintering around impact sites.

"Whoa, hey, take a breath. Deep breath." Yuri rubbed slow circles into her back. "It's okay."

Nothing was okay.

Miriam tried to spit, but it caught on her lower lip—a dull reminder she hadn't been hydrating either, not with all the work set out. There were too many casualties, too many bodies, too many parts still lying around.

A specific part.

Of a specific person.

"It's a lot. Take your—"

"Yuri." Miriam wiped her mouth with the back of her hand. "I need you to stop talking."

He froze, then pulled away, an apology under his breath.

Part of her ached and wanted that comforting touch back. In its absence, Miriam missed it more. She considered telling Yuri, considered letting go of the words pulling her under the surface. Perhaps by saying it, the burden would lift, or at least spread its weight. But the moment passed. Her stomach gave another warning flutter.

Saying it would make Sam's death real. If she didn't, Miriam could still entertain the impossible idea of rewinding time, going back to that shared memory in that dingy back corridor of Duncan's. The kiss, the touches, it'd all felt so right. If she could change anything, she'd erase the fear before she pulled away—or had she *pushed* Sam away? Would it have changed anything if she hadn't?

Miriam retched again.

◊

She ran, her arms pumping, but her boots stuck in the mud, slowing with each step. She didn't know what was behind her—didn't dare look—but the wet and guttural growls nipped at her back and drove her forward. The path narrowed ahead, and her heart pounded. Despite the panic rising in her throat, she shimmied herself along a ledge.

Their leers and gnashing teeth fell behind as she stepped further, pressing her body to the rock wall. A few more steps and she'd be free. A few more steps and she'd be safe. A hand offered out, and she reached for it, a fingertip away.

And then she was falling, a severed arm above her as she plummeted.

Miriam woke with a start, her blood coursing through her stiff body with each thumping heartbeat. Her gaze shifted from the high ceiling to the side where she could make out shadows.

Monsters.

She flinched but then squinted. Not monsters, but large equipment, weights, and machines. Stale sweat filled the air, and soft coughing peppered the surrounding space. She was in a gym. In the North. Ursus. She squeezed her eyes shut and turned on her side, curling her knees in.

When her breath calmed, Miriam peeked out just enough to see the haze of a figure next to her. Its silhouette brought her to a different time, a different place, but then it was gone, followed by disappointment—only tossed clothes and an assault pack on an otherwise empty cot. Exhaustion settled back in as her body crashed against the blip of adrenaline. She had already forgotten the nightmare, but the fear lingered.

Miriam pressed her wrist to her forehead, her commcuff illuminating brightly before her skin smothered its display. The network was up and running, having been restored the previous day. Communication and organization were the military's large muscles and had been one of UMF's first priorities. It ran on information—even if that information came in the form of official updates and pending investigations, completing a worsening picture with its quantifiable destruction and damages. It emboldened more questions than answers, one specifically more than the others. Had they been complacent?

With the confusion of the wunby attacks in the South, no one had expected another hit, especially not one as blatant as this. And the attack on Ursus was different from the one at Temunco Outpost. Something had jammed the communications and security systems, but there were no alty assailants, at least none left to be identified. Chaos had come in the darkness of a waking dawn.

The siblings, reconnaissance specialists, had only just returned from a grueling mission. Had they—had Sam lived on compound? Miriam couldn't remember if it had been mentioned during their short time together.

She raised her hand and stared at her commcuff, its display on the last-opened window: a private channel from days prior.

> M. TANNER: Are you guys okay?
>
> M. TANNER: Sam, ping me when you can.
>
> M. TANNER: We're on our way.
>
> M. TANNER: We're here in Ursus.

The messages remained an unbroken block.
Delivered.
Unread.
Unanswered.
Sam "Valkyrie" Ryan was dead.
Miriam clenched her jaw and swallowed. The others probably suspected it as well, but they didn't bring it up or press in their brief interactions. She was thankful for that small respite. Only Yuri continued to elicit hope from his eternal optimism. She loved her friend, but it was too much.

By the time she had dressed, Miriam was running late. She found her way to the exit, where daylight came in through the seams of a thin metal door, and crisp northern air greeted her unkindly.

"Morning."

Miriam blinked into brightness. Echo's lead, Vallen Krill, stood with Yuri, Nas, and Kai next to a four-seat rabbit, and steam wafted from the cups in their hands. Her teammates looked a ragged bunch, sporting days-old bandages from their last encounter with the alties. As the team's medic, Miriam normally would've checked on their recovery progress several times by now, but she had arguably been busy. They all had.

Yuri picked up another cup off the vehicle's dashboard and offered it forward. "Figured you'd need some coffee."

He knew her well. As she took it, Miriam mumbled her gratitude, then breathed in its fumes. The drink itself was bitter and diluted, but she didn't care. It was fuel. Her nightmare had negated any rest, and she'd take energy in any form.

To her relief, no one tried to make conversation. Even Nas and Kai, who regularly discussed some kind of technology, politics, or current event, were respectful of the morning grim. She felt the weight of Yuri's stare, but Miriam kept her gaze low, unwilling to meet his dark eyes and their undesired concern. His attention turned away as heavy boots crushed on gravel. The last member of SOG Razor-Echo nodded an acknowledgment as he neared. Stubble graced Fox's jaw and chin, dark rings pocketed his eyes, and a crease had somehow become a fixture between his brows.

Somewhere in the distance, a muffled explosion broke the silence, and all but Krill turned in its direction.

"Second one today," Nas said. "EOD and Intel have been working nonstop. That has to be one of the last sectors they're clearing. Duds, I guess."

Kai scratched the skin above her heavy-lidded eyes. "I'm glad there *were* duds. Do we know how it happened yet?"

"Some are saying it was an EMP, drones maybe, but there's no way, not with all the countertech we have. Others are saying they breached the compound somehow, suicide bombers or couriers delivered—"

"How would wunbies have gotten through?"

Nas shrugged. "It's just RUMINT. It's early. We won't know the full details until they analyze everything."

"Hell, but that'll take weeks."

"More."

"They're still trying to figure out what happened at the southern border," Kai said.

"But do we know why yet?" Yuri asked.

"Duds? Wunbies must've rushed the job."

"No." Yuri shot a look, then softened. "Why they attacked Ursus."

Nas shook his head. "Why did wunbies attack the South? Territory? Ideology? I have my theories." He moved his weight from one leg to the other and winced. "But does it matter? They hate us; they think we're an infestation."

Take back what was promised.

Miriam stared into the dark liquid inside her cup. She could still hear the passion in those rallying words.

Krill cleared his throat. "Let's stick to official information for now, see what UMF and City Center say in the coming days. Jace mentioned some Royals have already sent their condolences—"

Fox spat to the side. "Don't want their condolences. They sent *condolences* for Temunco, for Matam, and New..." He didn't finish the settlement's name, the hometown of Junpei, the young marine who had been their guide in the South. Though Echo had only known him a week, Jun had grown on all of them, Fox in particular. The two had bonded, only for the teenager to be killed alongside countless others by the alty supremacists.

"Well, Command's trying to work with City Center and the Royals to confirm what exactly is happening. Alties are having their own issues on their turf right now, and the last report said comms with them have been spotty."

Miriam doubted it was because of their communications equipment or the difference in their technology. Humans and alties never worked together, not with their tensions and history.

"Wunbies declared war. Ursus must've been a show of power," Nas said.

Kai rubbed her eyes. "On us? Or their own government? Either way, I can't believe we've actually established some kind of communication with the Royals. I know it's not much, it's late, and under terrible circumstances, but we needed this for peace, or whatever peace we could've had…"

The group stilled.

After a moment, Krill stifled a yawn. "Let's focus on getting this place back up and running." His voice shifted. "Any news on…?"

Miriam stiffened. She knew what and whom he was referring to.

Yuri glanced over and Miriam intently watched her coffee, wondering if she could drown herself in it. Her lips cracked open, but then she tongued her cheek and closed her mouth firmly.

"Not yet. I tried Mute, but there're several reasons why they might not be up on comms," Yuri offered. "Gonzalez from Foxtrot mentioned another ragtag group pushed out to the border. Just in case…"

Just in case the wunbies stormed into human territory again. This time from the North.

"And?" Krill prodded.

Yuri shook his head. "Nothing. Not over our comms, at least."

Krill scratched at his arm cast and made an indifferent sound. "We should turn in," he said with a nod at Kai and Fox. To the others, he gestured with his head. "They set up an alternative ops center. Make sure to stop by and do your comm checks. And Tan, they're consolidating assets over to the east clinic. I know you've been at the satellite site..."

"Yeah, got it," Miriam acknowledged.

"I'll double-shift," Fox grumbled. "Foxtrot's in the north sector and they need warm..."

Bodies. He was about to say *bodies.*

The man's upper lip twitched. "They're still pullin' marines from the rubble. Plus, I can't sleep. Might as well keep workin'."

Krill didn't argue, and Yuri offered his unfinished coffee. Fox tilted its contents into the back of his throat as Kai and the team lead bade their goodnights.

"Can't sleep? You doing alright?" Yuri asked.

"That's a *really* stupid question," Fox muttered. "Think the local dive's still standin'? Need something stronger than this." He raised the empty cup, tiny in his hand.

Careful of the liquid inside, Miriam pressed hers forward. "Here. I should get moving," she mumbled. Her new work location was well across the compound, and without another word, she walked away.

"Everythin's fucked," Fox said behind her. "Is *she* okay?"

Miriam kept moving, one foot trudging after the other. It'd be another long day. As she turned the corner, she could barely make out Yuri's sigh and response.

"I really don't know."

Another day, another hell.

◊

The initial shock and horror of the attack had waned, and a different despondence took its place. The chaos and crush of triaging had faded and subsided into a sea of whimpers and groans, and the clinic was a different beast than the sites she had been working before. Miriam tried to ignore the swell of noise as she stepped away from the room of makeshift gurneys.

She had stopped checking for her. It wasn't difficult, not when everyone was a generous blend of the earth's previous races and most humans' hair was on the spectrum of a certain brown. The clinic and its set-up supplemental space were for the injured—hurt, but living and breathing marines. Miriam would have to go around the corner and down two blocks to check the other area, but she wasn't brave enough. She had seen the traffic of large black bags, and she didn't want to see how many there actually were.

Miriam swallowed, but her mouth and throat were dry. Water. She needed water. The realization of thirst only made it that much worse. She searched, ambling by rooms and wards of patients and peers, a woman on a mission for something to satiate her maddening state—whether or not it was hydration she actually desired. By the time she spotted a box with the familiar symbol, Miriam found herself somewhere she didn't recognize, somewhere inside the clinic, off-limits to patients. There were no gurneys, no cries of pain, and no one else. A brief sanctuary.

Miriam crouched to retrieve a water packet and, in no rush to stand back up, she filled her mouth and parched throat. After several gulps, she held the liquid in her cheeks, letting it swish as she peered around the tranquil space. Lab equipment was pushed to the side, as were most of the room's original functions, like the gym she and other reinforcements slept in. Supplies from Station now filled the room, on top of and around aisles of metal tables.

So focused on the discovery of water, Miriam hadn't noticed

the space was not entirely quiet. The soft whoosh and blips of tubes and machines were clear now, and only now.

She almost choked when her breath caught, and she stabilized herself with the table leg. She hadn't seen it while standing, but now, at a lower angle, her eye caught something in the back of the room. It was just a strand, but she'd know that color anywhere. A light, golden blond.

Miriam set the water packet on the ground, her eyes holding their line of sight as if that color would disappear if she looked away. She maneuvered around the tables and boxes, her breath quickening as she approached.

It couldn't be.

Dried blood tangled in long strands of hair beneath a bloody dressing. Miriam stepped around, carefully avoiding the cords and devices. She surveyed the swollen and bruised face of the recon specialist who had joined Echo a couple weeks prior, the marine, the woman who had gone through hell and back. Those days were forever ago, like years compressed into one mission.

Sam had saved her life.

Miriam let out a shaky breath and her hands trembled as emotions rolled through her. She hovered her fingers over the woman's face, afraid that what she was seeing was only a figment of her imagination.

Was this real?

Sam was dead.

No.

Sam was alive. In front of her and real.

Miriam's fingers brushed along the woman's skin—warm, but not as warm as she would have liked. She followed the multiple tubes twisting around and under a draped coat—a makeshift blanket—and Miriam slowly peeled it back, unable to contain a soft whimper.

She had seen worse in the clinic, but the sight was still a

crushing blow. A bloodstained bandage wrapped around a stump just below the shoulder, the rest of the tattooed and scarred arm gone. Her eyes drew to the bloody material covering Sam's rib cage, the only dressing on her naked torso, and Miriam dropped her gaze. After everything they had been through, seeing Sam like this... It was disturbing how fragile the woman looked on top of that table.

Miriam froze as Sam's breathing caught and labored. The machine chirped faster, and she tried to remember her training. What did she need to do—or not do?

Behind her, a door slid open and a woman in scrubs rushed in. With barely any acknowledgment, the doctor took the coat from Miriam's hand and pulled it back, letting it hang on Sam's hip. She lifted the gauze, revealing a small gauge embedded deep into the skin between bruised ribs. With everything exposed, Miriam scanned over the colors and wounds punctuating Sam's side and torso. She swallowed again. Sam was alive, but in awful shape.

The doctor manipulated the gauge, and Sam's breathing stabilized. As the machine's strained chirps died down, its regular beats resumed, filling the space with its steady sound. The woman in scrubs sighed, then looked up past Miriam. "There's clean gauze in one of those," she said, jutting her chin to a stack of boxes.

Miriam scanned the different containers until she found what she was looking for. She opened a packet and handed a fresh cloth to the other woman, who draped it over the gauge. Miriam glanced again at the injuries before they were obscured, a grimace remaining as the coat-blanket covered Sam.

Across from her, the doctor relaxed and leaned back against a parallel table, shifting her weight off her feet. She threw her gloves into a nearby bin. "You're from Station?"

"Ye—" Miriam's voice was a hoarse whisper. She cleared her throat and willed moisture into her mouth. "Yes."

The doctor kneaded her temple, her eyes searching over the boxes, and Miriam knew what she wanted. "I just opened one over there." She pointed to the area she had ransacked; she would've gone and grabbed a packet for the woman, but her feet remained glued to the floor.

The doctor hummed and disappeared behind the table and containers. When she returned, she held several packets in her arms and offered one out. Miriam took it, and they stood in silence with Sam between them, taking slow sips.

"Thanks for the help. Station, all of you. It's been…"

"A lot," Miriam murmured. She couldn't take her eyes off Sam.

"An understatement." The woman huffed, reached out, and introduced herself.

Miriam looked up, a spell broken, and shook the outstretched hand, although she immediately forgot the woman's name. Was this person who she needed to thank for saving Sam?

"Tanner," she stammered back, then gestured at the small insignia on the doctor's scrubs: compressed shapes making up an animal's claw underneath the UMF letters. "You're with Ursus. Were you here when the bombs went off?"

A corner of the doctor's mouth pulled back.

Miriam nodded absently, returning her gaze to the bruising on Sam's face. "Sam—" She caught herself. "Valkyrie. She'll be okay?"

The doctor spared a smile and dipped her head. "I think she's through the worst of it. Collapsed lung and internal bleeding, but it's manageable. As well as the…other stuff. Wish we had more MedJets, but…" She took a deep inhale. "We'll recover. *She'll* recover. Sam's resilient."

Miriam's ears perked at the casual use of the first name, different from the Ursus custom for callsigns.

"You know her?"

Miriam nodded.

"I see." The doctor shut her eyes and took another deep breath. "I've known Sam since she was a kid running around this place. My husband used to carry her on his shoulders, and she'd laugh so much. This..." She placed a gentle hand on Sam's forehead, then lifted it with a sigh. "There was an announcement. They're saying it was the Altered?"

"Wunbies. Apostates," Miriam muttered. "This isn't their first attack. The South...not Station, I mean. Further south."

"Sam just got back. We were supposed to grab lunch before Ursus sent her out again." The doctor cleared her throat. "My husband said the Altered are attacking their own capital, said it's a coup. Have you heard more?"

Take back what was promised.

The doctor's question traversed through her. Finding Sam had let out a crash of unwinding tension, and Miriam struggled to remember what she had read or heard.

Someone shouted in the background, and the woman turned in its direction, a world away.

"I should get back." The doctor's attention returned to Miriam, then Sam. "The pressure builds up every half hour or so. I hear Station is bringing more MedPorts soon, but until then, it's a manual release. I'm here, and I know you're probably busy as well, but..."

Miriam waved. Now that she knew where Sam was, that Sam was alive... She wasn't going to mess this up. She'd be there for her.

The Ursus doctor finished her water, then pushed away from the table, scooping the rest of the packets into her arms. "She's always been strong, you know. She'll bounce back," she said. "It's nice to meet you, Tanner. Don't forget to take care of yourself, too." And then she was gone.

Miriam leaned back on the counter. She watched Sam's face and the rise and fall of her chest with each breath. The woman was resilient. Miriam knew it. She had seen and witnessed it.

Sam would be okay.

She kept repeating it to herself, each time a relief from the guilt and regret she had previously felt.

Sam was alive.

And she'd be okay.

A WING, CLIPPED

SAM DUG HER FINGERS IN, twisting the sheets in a silent scream. She wanted the fabric to tear, her nails to rip and claw through, but it didn't. The motion was frustratingly unsatisfactory.

Useless.

If only it had been a different limb. Why her dominant arm? Her gun hand?

She was a marine—she had been one almost her entire life —and now she was... One fucking useless, one-armed marine.

Disgusted, Sam shook the sheets away and stared at the one hand. Her fingernails were disorderly, a couple long and uncut, and the others broken.

Like her.

Nothing had been right since the attack. One of the most important parts of her, the part that made her good at what she did, was gone. What use was the Valkyrie if she couldn't bear a weapon? If she couldn't fight?

Fucking useless.

It was only made worse when UMF confiscated and locked away her carbine and gear. They said it was temporary, a precaution, but it only cemented the fact she was no longer an asset. Ursus's poster child was damaged. Ruined.

Her rifle had been with her on every mission since she joined SOG seven years earlier, and she missed it the most. She missed its presence, its routine, and its significance. The Apostates took her arm. UMF took her weapon. Life knew how to grind salt into an open wound.

Heal and recover, they said. How was she supposed to heal and recover from this? She became worthless the second she lost that arm. In mandatory consultations, MED talked at her, told her the emotions she felt were normal. With time, she'd adapt and move on. They looked at her as if she was depressed. Sad. She hated how they pitied her, and it took all her remaining strength to keep from screaming at them.

Sam wasn't depressed. She wasn't sad.

She was furious.

She hated her new, temporary quarters and its proximity to the outpost shooting range, dumped in the back of the compound with others who had lost their base homes. But they were still intact, still working. Their traffic and noise would seep through her cell like a constant reminder of an unattainable normalcy.

Sam was angry with her brother, Scott "Mute" Reckert, who constantly hovered around her when he was back on compound. She hated his worn uniform and the reminder he had renewed his contract with UMF, with SOG, despite everything she had gone through to accept his initial resignation before.

He had been out. Done.

Liar.

She was equally spiteful when his irritating presence was gone. Out on missions. Without her. It was supposed to be the other way. Now here he was, teamed up with another recon specialist. Not her.

Worthless.

She was irate with Echo, whose check-ins the first days were crushing and so full of pity. She was indignant mostly with Miriam, whose kindness was overbearing, whose presence was just a reminder of rejection and something she'd never amount to. Especially now. Sam hated herself for the flashes of hurt on Echo's faces when she lashed out, and then her fury would circulate again, an unending spiral.

Maybe she shouldn't have survived. Maybe the attack should've killed her. Just ended it. She had hissed it to her brother more than once, and the visible pain on his face had been enough to punish him, then restart another cycle of self-hatred.

MED encouraged her to talk, to vent, but no one wanted to hear her raw and unfiltered thoughts, so she barricaded herself in when she wasn't needed. Which was all the time. She was left with this broken version of herself, a constant reminder of what she once was and could never be again.

Sam stared at the ceiling. The metal panel was bare, naked of any finishing coats in its containerized form. Crumbs of barely eaten meals dug into her skin as she lay in her bed, dark thoughts swirling and sinking their talons into her mind, rendering her unable to concentrate on anything else. She didn't know what time it was and didn't care. She had boarded up the room's one window early on and it betrayed nothing. Her commcuff lay underneath the mess, but she didn't need it; the notifications had petered out, anyway.

Lightning speared through her arm, and Sam sat up, grabbing at...

Nothing.

Her hand touched flesh where the ghost of an arm ended. Gasping, her body curled forward as pain lashed through her. She wanted to cry out, but it subsided. The torment was gone as quickly as it had arrived, and the only evidence was a small crown of sweat forming on her forehead. Flesh, bones, and muscles no longer there still bared their teeth, their phantom anger at her.

She grabbed the nearest item—a dirty cup—and launched it across the room with all the force she could muster. It was a disappointing effort, and it felt wrong. Weak. And worse, it missed her target: the small display broadcasting the latest news on the Altered coup. The metal clanked unsatisfyingly against the door instead. The little things that were once so easy, so simple, were now a thousand times more difficult. She couldn't even throw a cup right.

A sharp knock rapped on her door.

Sam glowered, then felt for the console underneath the folds of her sheets. She jammed a finger into the screen, and the feed volume grew, blasting the room with the broadcaster's pitched voice.

"—reporting the latest updates from the new embassy in Station City. In an unexpected offensive surge, the Altered supremacists, also known as Apostates or Promised, took over another sector in their capital, which puts approximately twenty percent of the city now in their control. The Altered's main military body, the legionnaires..."

The knock came again, and her commcuff vibrated from somewhere within the chaos.

"...continue to push back with raids and sweeping defensive maneuvers. The Altered government is assured that new offensives will regain these areas, and the violence will end in the next month. Meanwhile, with the new arrival of delegations in Station—"

The banging on her door grew louder, as if someone was kicking it.

"—go live now to City Center, where the Royals are..."

The incessant pounding continued, and Sam's cuff buzzed. She relented, digging around for her new communications device before her fingers closed over its cool, light material, and the movement engaged its display. Setting the device on her thigh, she swept aside the incoming notification, but between the lack of familiar use and the unsecured position, it jostled and opened a window of messages instead. Sam's lip curled as she eyed the various channels she had ignored for weeks. Another bout of guilt and anger passed, spearing at her colleagues for their pity and their desire to help. Even as emotions smashed against her, she knew it was unfair and hated herself more. She gripped the device, wanting it to break, but it didn't. Frustrated, she thought to throw it across the room, but it buzzed once more, the display illuminating.

She winced at the message between her fingers.

> S. RECKERT: Open up. I know you're in there.
>
> S. RECKERT: I'm not leaving until you let me in.
> I can do this all day.

Her brother.

She believed his message. Scott *wouldn't* leave. It'd be much worse for her if she made him wait, ignored him longer. He had a way of reversing a situation, diverting her irritation until *she* was the one suffering. He was the only one left who continued to visit her; she had lashed out at everyone. Part of her didn't care if she lost her few friends and teammates, but another part also felt guilty she had already pushed them away. It wasn't their fault. But she was and wanted to be mad.

Sam inched herself out of the bed, but only after a wave of agitation surged at her first attempt, a reliance on a limb no longer there. She crossed the room and hammer-fisted the panel. With a hiss, the door opened, and a blond man filled its frame, a disposable container tucked under an armpit. Her brother's expression flattened, a frown along thin lips as his hands moved swiftly. HAVE YOU SHOWERED TODAY? OR IN THE LAST WEEK?

"Fuck off." She glared and turned back to her bed, kicking

aside partially filled containers. The network feed turned off and threw the space into an unsettling stillness.

He cleared his throat behind her, but she ignored him. Something hit the back of her head, and she whipped around, scowling as a crumpled piece of packaging bounced into a pile of clothes.

His gray-blue eyes gleamed. They shared the same blond hair, but their eyes revealed their slightly different gene pool. Half-siblings, eleven years apart. Which didn't matter, because Scott was a full, irritating big brother.

You haven't been eating, he signed. He wiped the counter and set down the thin box as she took a seat at the edge of her disheveled mattress. I brought your favorite.

His stare bored into her, and Sam didn't have the will to meet it. Her jaw tensed, ready to lunge, to bite. She had raised her voice at him after his return from his last rotation. He was too patient with her, too kind.

Have you seen the new construction? The station engineers are doing fast work, well, faster than I've ever seen. Guess it takes a terrorist attack to get the place rebuilt. Scott played with the edges of the box, then set it aside. It was meaningless chatter—he was avoiding any substantial talk of SOG's activities. He did it whenever he visited—if she let him in.

She stared at the muted feed, footage of destruction in the southern settlements and the ongoing recovery efforts. With no human assets in the Altered territories, the network didn't have many recordings of the actual fighting there. Everything was repeated clips from whatever scrubbed visuals the Royals passed along. Even without a media presence, Sam figured she had a good idea of what Arshangol looked like—similar to the destruction Echo had seen in the South, perhaps more urban and progressive in technology and architecture. Was that how

Ursus had looked? The attack on the outpost hadn't been a two-way fight, though. She only remembered the beginning—waking up to the first blasts, the alarms, and then the rush of panic that she and Scott had while moving people to safe havens.

"I think you should get out of here."

Heat blossomed along her neck and into her ears at Scott's hushed words. The snarl in the back of her throat rolled into her mouth.

URSUS, he signed vigorously. YOU SHOULD GET OUT OF URSUS.

They were familiar words from another time and another life. It confused her, stopping the venomous curse on her tongue, and something different shot through her. She was useless to UMF, to him. Sam knew she was ineffective, but to have her half-brother confirm it, that was something different altogether.

I TALKED WITH DOC AGAIN. SHE SAID THERE'S A GOOD RECOVERY PROGRAM IN STATION. MUCH BETTER THAN WHAT MED HAS YOU DOING HERE. THERE MIGHT BE OPTIONS.

Sam narrowed her eyes.

MED. Sam's declared enemy. Her third contract with UMF was finishing soon, and though she had received her renewal notification before the attack, with the loss of limb, she was on medical probation, an administrative purgatory where most washed out. Her clearance was pending and undetermined, but it wasn't a good sign. The military had no need for a one-armed, angry recon specialist, especially not now with the Altered conflict and the chaos it brought, even if the fighting would allegedly be over soon.

IT'S SOMETHING DIFFERENT, SOMETHING NEW. NEW CAN BE GOOD.

Her eye twitched. Sam didn't want something different or

something new. She wanted her arm. She wanted her rifle and SOG status. She wanted to be back to normal.

It's in Station City, Scott signed, his shoulders inching up.

Sam glanced up at her brother's gray-blue eyes, then knocked her mind for its betrayal. She had been trying to avoid any thoughts of the largest human city—thoughts of one person there in particular. The SOG medic she had met, worked with, and been interested in had made her want something more than the military. But now that she was sidelined... It was ironic. Now she was dead weight, practically out of UMF, and she hated it. Sam hated that she had kissed Miriam—she had thought there could've been something there, been inspired after the mission to make a move. Sam hated that she wasn't what Miriam wanted, and by some wicked extension, she wanted to hate the woman.

She couldn't, of course.

It wasn't Miriam's fault. She had been there at the clinic. She had been around as much as possible before Sam launched a pointed tirade at her, upset at her sympathy, her consolation. *You can stop pretending. I don't need your fucking pity. Go fuck someone else. You're good at that, aren't you?* Even if she considered going south, to Station City, it didn't matter. Miriam wouldn't want to talk to her after those lanced words. It was better Sam stayed away.

Asshole. Sam was such an asshole.

She crossed her arms. Arm. Singular. Her left hand grabbed at air and touched the stump. She grimaced as pain shot up her shoulder, and she awkwardly clutched her rib cage instead.

Scott sighed. They don't have what you need here.

"And *you* know what I need? What *do* I need, Scott?" She ripped into his name. It was childish and unfair, but everything was unfair.

I'm not fighting with you. It was his turn to fold his arms.

She wanted a fight, but the emotional surge dissolved as he stared at her. Scott looked haggard and exhausted, his hair dull and pressed down, the lines on his face more pronounced. The constant shifts and reconnaissance on the border were draining Ursus, even with reinforcements from other posts.

He wasn't supposed to be back in UMF. He was supposed to be done, working on his apartment garden or over the range back in Gould, the settlement they had grown up in, doing non-military things. Whatever that entailed. She was still pissed about that, too.

He had gone back on his decision to get out of the military. He had said he was done with it, with all the death. It was only recently that Sam had learned her brother had killed their father when she was young. It had been a defensive act, but it had ultimately thrown them both into UMF's hands. And after almost eighteen years, he was done.

Deep down, she understood why he'd renewed his contract, especially after the attack on Ursus. If she were in his shoes, she would've, too, in a heartbeat. Destroy the Apostates. Kill them all for what they did. But this was how it was. *She* was the one who had been blown up; *she* should've been the one with nightmares, but her issues were limited to phantom pains and a raging sense of worthlessness.

"Are you…" She stared at the litter on the floor and plunged her fingers into her thigh. "You don't need me. You're getting rid of me."

He stared at her incredulously.

"You should've let me die—"

"Sam." His voice splintered. His face contorted with hurt.

A tendril of defensive rage wrapped around her, and she recoiled, shooting up from the bed. "Fuck you. You're a fucking hypocrite." Blood rushed to her head, her mind and mouth flustering with conflicting thoughts, so many incomplete words that didn't fit together in any congruent manner.

"Sam," Scott repeated, his voice firm. His hands and fingers flew in the air. YOU CAN BE MAD AT ME ALL YOU WANT. I TOLD YOU I'M SORRY. I SHOULD'VE TOLD YOU BEFORE I MADE THAT DECISION, BUT IT'S DONE. AND YOU CAN'T PUSH ME AWAY. NOT LIKE YOU DID WITH THE OTHERS. WITH TAN.

Her fist raised in the air, quivering. Every day she replayed all her words, at least the ones she remembered. All her interactions with him, Echo, and the others sliced at her over and over. Horrible things had come out of her mouth to hurt people, to hurt Miriam. Sam wanted to push her away just as the woman had done before. She knew it wasn't the same—she had gone too far, and she hated herself for it.

"You're pushing me away. What if the coup succeeds? What if the Apostates come? I can—" She stopped. What if Scott's new partner failed him? Who was she kidding? She couldn't help.

"I'm not," Scott rasped as he kneaded his palms into his brows. "I'm not getting rid of you."

Sam raised a hand in protest, and her brother leaned over to grab her palm with a soft grip. When she didn't resist, he pulled back.

"I want you to get better," he said. His hands lifted. GOING TO THE CITY WILL HELP YOU GET BETTER.

"What if I can't?" Sam whispered. She stared at the fleshy scar on his right palm.

His scoff was loud and pronounced. YOU ARE THE STRONGEST PERSON I KNOW.

She gave him a skeptical look.

YOU CAN DO THIS. AND WHEN YOU'RE BACK, WE'LL DO IT TOGETHER. I PROMISE. He repeated in a whisper, "I promise."

Sam shrank back, but something fluttered within her. "What about you?"

He smiled, then fanned his hands. Don't worry about me. I'll be okay when you're okay. Better than okay.

Sam had nothing to say. She didn't know if she could be okay, much less better.

We'll still talk. Every day. If you call, I'll answer. You know this. You can't get rid of me.

A reticent harrumph escaped her throat, a strained gurgle.

Scott settled a warm hand on hers. "Sammy, go," he said. It was a request, a plea, an order. "I love you. Go." He sealed it with a slow, articulated gesture from his other hand.

Her eyes widened, then averted. She knew he loved her. *He* knew she loved him. But she could count on her one hand how many times they had actually said it out loud to each other.

She reached out but winced as she looked down, her lack of limb forgotten in the moment. Instead, she forced a weak smile —an odd grimace at best. That was it. Her concession, her decision. She would leave Ursus again, and this time, without him. She was still angry, more nervous and scared, but there was also a little sprout of something dangerous.

Hope.

3

____

RISING TENSIONS

MIRIAM USUALLY RELISHED the low thrum of the city in her apartment—the chatter from the street shops, the hum of vehicles, even the sanitation trucks as they rolled through their routines—but that same background noise didn't feel the same as it usually did. She had somehow overslept despite a restless sleep.

Outside the door, her cuff vibrated against her skin, but Miriam dismissed it with a shake of her wrist. She didn't feel like dealing with her mother, who probably wanted to chide her for not stopping by in the last weeks. What was it this time? Another photo spray or investor presentation where she pretended to be the happy, devoted child of a loving marriage? She was already not sleeping well; Miriam didn't need the extra frustration. She shoved it out of her mind as cool air hugged her, swirling with the smells of modern civilization.

Around the corner, a booming voice fragmented into her sluggish brain. "No alties in Station! No alties!" Two individuals stood on the corner of the street with voice amplifiers and raised displays hovering over their heads. "ALTERED OUT" blared at her in large neon letters. It was too early for this.

"We get it! Shut up!" someone shouted from another building. The sentiment echoed her thoughts, but the harsh delivery added to her irritation. Miriam kneaded her cheeks, already missing her bedroom.

Her annoyance faltered as a woman with short hair approached her on the sidewalk. She had a pretty face and a slim frame, and the corner of Miriam's mouth twitched upward. It promptly fell, and she kept from rolling her eyes at the realization of an outstretched tablet. As she passed, the woman followed.

"Are you interested in signing this petition? Their embassy is a farce! The Royals and alties can't be allowed here. We, as citizens, need to remind City Center they're allowing terrorists and criminals in our good home."

Ducking her head, Miriam maneuvered around the woman, a dismissive wave fluttered as she continued on her familiar commute. With the interruption behind her, she lost herself in her thoughts until she arrived at the wide street dividing the city from the military base. She watched the movement of pedestrians and vehicles, the daily life and grind in Station City unchanged, even with the attacks. *Resilient*, City Center politicians had said. Miriam thought the city's apathy or ignorance toward events was less resilience and more an insulation due to distance from the violence. The human capital seemed immune to most of it.

Miriam walked toward the high wall of UMF headquarters, where a series of sentries milled around the main gate, a brute show—possibly the only show in the city—of heightened security. It was just that though, a show, mostly for the military to feel better about itself. Two outposts had been attacked back-to-back, and it had done little to prevent or retaliate. Everyone had been antsy the first weeks, but with little to no action on the northern border since, the sentries looked aloof.

She eyed the latest fixtures and additions to the perimeter, the top of their towers peeking over the wall. The anti-aircraft weapons were gray, freshly painted to blend into the rest of the UMF compound after the city complained about their ugliness. Normally, Miriam would have laughed and agreed, but their presence gave her a reinforced sense of security. The wunbies didn't have the tech or means to fly to Station, and its location was too far for land travel. There was the ocean, but with how the city sat in the bay and UMF's reputation and experience at sea, it was unlikely.

As she neared, a young group of sentries straightened as they eyed the black SOG diamond tab on Miriam's collar. She raised her cuff to the pedestrian access panel, and one marine gave her a confident nod.

"Fuck, I'm jealous. Soggers are on missions killing alties while we're stuck here," one half-whispered behind her.

Miriam scoffed at how wrong he was. City Center had pressured UMF to pull the two Station SOG teams and other groups back from supporting Ursus, afraid of devoting too many resources elsewhere, especially with the uncertainty of Arshangol's fate. And in the meantime, with Center and Command playing things conservatively, Echo trained and ran tedious duty shifts along with the other SOG Razor and Spartan teams. The initial anticipation had been nerve-racking, but the days, weeks, then months rolled along, and the expected offensive on more human populations never came. It was as if the wunbies had a plan that made sense at one point, and then fell apart during their uprising. Nas, of course, had theories—some outright bizarre as time passed—but most of it went over Miriam's head. She was grateful nothing else happened, that even the network discussions of the attacks were petering out as other distractions and domestic issues became more enticing. She had enough reminders of the alties in her dreams.

Her mind preoccupied, Miriam moved through the compound. It was only when she looked up at the gray SOG building that she realized she had defaulted to her routine. This wasn't her intended destination. She checked her cuff and veered back toward the center of the base. She was already late.

By the time she made it to the main auditorium, the officers onstage were almost finished talking. The place was packed, the air stuffy and warm. Miriam squeezed through the crowd of uniforms and slipped to the side, using Fox as a monument, where he stood a head above everyone else, even slouched.

Yuri acknowledged her with a cocked eyebrow, and she passed a hushed greeting to the others. "Who calls one of these in the morning?" she muttered. Town halls. What a bane.

"Sadists," Nas whispered back. "They provided coffee at least."

"It's the same coffee from the DFAC," Kai said before Krill cut a harsh glance at them.

The officer continued his speech behind the podium. "We'll assist Station Center with the Royals and incoming Altered."

A sea of groans rippled through the crowded room.

"Isn't that SecTeam's job?" someone shouted out.

The crowd's reactions didn't faze the officer. "Between increased Children of Charon activity, new checkpoints, and riot blocks, District SecTeam has a lot on their hands. We must remember we're all on the same team here."

Murmurs followed like a chorus.

"Many of you are already at the docks. Our fleet will meet the incoming wave of ships in the next weeks, and shifts will be added to chutes and the relocation camp." The officer raised his voice over the scattered groans. "We appreciate your hard work and efforts. Maintain professionalism and let's get through this together."

"How long they gonna be in Station?"

"Why are they still coming here?" another voiced from the opposite side of the room.

The crowd echoed their concerns.

The officer raised his hands in placation. "The fighting in Arshangol is ongoing and—"

"It was supposed to be over."

"That's their problem. Not ours!"

"We're supposed to be killing them, not welcoming them into our homes!"

"—and we'll have more information from Center," the officer concluded.

"Fuckin' alties should stay and fight their own battles," muttered a company marine near Echo.

Miriam wouldn't voice it, but she understood the sentiment. Despite fighting against the wunbies, she struggled to differentiate the terrorists from the "regular" alties. What was regular about their longtime enemies, anyway? They had done nothing to her in particular, but the lived lessons from the generations before had taught them the genetically engineered race was to be feared and hated.

The speakers concluded with a repetition of UMF's priorities: the defense of Station City and the North, the rebuilding and taking back of the South, as well as determining which alties were responsible for the attacks. There was another point made for collaborative approaches with the Royals in the city, but Miriam was certain it was only intended to ensure the alties would expedite their departure from the human capital as soon as their infighting stopped. She also rolled her eyes at the mention of the South. If the human-supremacist terrorists survived the rolling sweep of wunbies there, they wouldn't want to work with UMF. Children of Charon and UMF didn't mix well.

The buzz of conversation increased as the officers dismissed the gathering. Miriam pulled closer to the wall, using Yuri and Fox as shields from the exodus of marines as the room emptied with fervorous mumbling and retorts.

"Can't trust any of them. Should lock them all up," grumbled a passing marine.

"Not even that. Why are we lettin' them in? Numbskull politicians," another person said as they bumped into Fox's frame. They peeked up, their features frozen, and after a mumbled apology, they hurried away. Her Echo teammate didn't seem to register the interaction at all.

"Command should've sent someone higher-ranking to address this," Yuri said. "It's not a good look."

At Miriam's side, Kai nodded. "Especially with this rowdy crowd. Most of these marines haven't even seen an alty in person."

"Well, they're going to meet a lot soon. They're lucky it's not the wunbies."

"For now," Nas injected.

"If they wanted to attack us, they had the last months to do it. Guess Arshangol wasn't as easy as they thought. I personally will be happy to never see one again," Yuri replied.

An icy shiver shot up Miriam's spine. She could still see those glowing night-eyes and hear the whistling firebombs and the Temunco marines' screams as they burned in napalm.

Krill sighed. "Everyone's just scared. We've had better town halls." He chucked his chin at Miriam. "Better late than never, huh? Another eventful night? Conquest conquered?"

Miriam scratched her forehead with a prominent middle finger, but she was happy for the change of subject.

The team lead huffed and gave her a thin grin. "I'll be back. Gonna talk with the other leads." He pattered off, weaving through the sparse remaining uniforms.

"Right. They usually have snacks in the back," Nas said as he craned his neck.

Kai flicked him in the shoulder. "That's all you can think about? Food?"

"I need my comfort. With more alties coming over, can't say I disagree with some comments here."

Kai crossed her arms. "You think it'd be better to turn them away? After everything that's happened?"

"Is that an option? Can we block them from coming here? Kick them out?"

"What happened to trying for peace?"

"What peace?" Nas scoffed. "We're not all diplomats like you."

"I'm not—that's not fair. It wasn't the Sovereign or Royals who did this. The wunbies…"

"I was there. I *know* it was the wunbies, but listen to everyone. Now we're housing them? For what, so Center can play tea party at the Royals' shiny new embassy? The wunbies were already attacking us, and now we're giving asylum to the other enemy. Alties can live almost anywhere, so why here? And okay, say we're improving diplomatic relations—aren't we creating more incentive for wunbies to come after us now?"

"That means they win over there. That's not going to happen."

Miriam sniffed. "Regardless, I don't think most will see it that way."

"Right. If these marines can't differentiate between the *good* and *bad* alties, imagine the rest of the city. My neighbors are leaving because of it," Yuri added.

Miriam turned to him. Having grown up in the same sector, her mind ran through a list of their mutuals. "Who? The Sandinos? Kims? Patels? Where to?" It was another reminder she hadn't been back to her parents' place, her childhood home, in a long time.

"Different family." Yuri shrugged. "And don't know. Further out?"

"Further out? They can't go south. It's too hot. And that's not counting the radiation zones. Maybe east?" Kai said.

Nas shook his head. "That's not smart. Station's still the safest place, *even* with the alties and Royals here. Especially now that we've learned our lessons from Temunco and Ursus."

Next to Miriam, the fifth member of the group was silent. His arms folded across his wide chest and his face remained in a deep scowl. Fox avoided her gaze and looked to the side, watching the rest of the room.

As Nas and Kai continued in an offshoot discussion, Yuri ducked his head toward Miriam. "Any word from you-know-who?"

She sighed and shook her head. "You?"

He shrugged. "The usual update now and then from Mute. Seems to be the same old, same nothing on the border."

She raised an eyebrow.

"He mentioned outpost leadership's considering relaxing their shifts, but we saw that coming. It wasn't sustainable, anyway. Rebuilding Ursus should've been their priority. The other op posts can't function long-term without that support. I heard the engineers are working miracles, but they're behind schedule on other parts. Typical."

It was good to hear Ursus was healing, but Miriam couldn't help but be disappointed with Yuri's response. She had hoped his friendship with the recon specialist would give her more information, but with everything happening, it seemed silly to push for updates on Sam.

Yuri frowned as if he read her mind. "Sorry, Tan. He doesn't really say much about his sister. He's chatty but quiet, you know?"

She didn't. She didn't know much about Sam's brother, only what little she had garnered from their mission in the South. Yuri patted her on the shoulder then turned to join Kai and Nas's conversation.

Miriam pressed her lips together. The last time she saw Sam, it hadn't gone well. It was understandable with the situation; the injured woman had said some scathing words, and after time and distance, Miriam knew the outbursts had been through anger and pain. It still stung, though. It hadn't been the words so much as the pure ire behind them. She had bowed out of the room, nothing else to say—not that anything would've gotten through to Sam anyway. Her attempt to say goodbye had failed, just like it had with the kiss and awkward farewell in the back hall of Duncan's.

Miriam's commcuff vibrated on her wrist. She knew it wasn't who she hoped it'd be—that private channel had been stagnant for some time. She flicked the message away. Another buzz came immediately after, and she ignored it.

"Look who the boss dragged in," Yuri said, shifting.

Miriam turned to watch Krill return with a dark-skinned man in tow. A dimpled grin plastered his profile.

"Jace!" Kai opened her arms, and the man received her embrace.

Yuri thumped their former Echo teammate on the back. "Warrant officer looks good on you."

"Thanks, Yuri. Hello, Echoes." His smile widened at the two youngest marines. "Baby Echoes."

Kai feigned offense. "That was a quick TDY."

"Right. Can an assignment be *that* temporary? You were out for what, a few days?" Nas jabbed.

Jace shook his head and chuckled. "Command diverted me. I'm back here to get some things sorted out."

"Pegleg's too good for us—off doing better things. BigInt treating you alright?" Nas said.

Jace sucked his teeth. "It's going as well as a Command job can go."

"Right. I noticed you've put on some weight."

"I'm going to ignore that, Nasiri." He motioned to the auditorium. "What a mess, eh?"

"Not the best, but what can you do? Speaking of which, what *have* you been up to? Any news?" Yuri asked.

"Nothing concrete or what you're hoping for. I'm a little bummed I couldn't go with y'all on that Temunco mission."

Miriam huffed. "I think you might've gotten the better deal." She glanced at the side of Fox's face, whose sullenness, once uncharacteristic, was now a permanent feature. "But who knows, maybe you would've figured this out before we did— prevented the whole thing."

Jace grimaced. "Hindsight's easy. I read the unabridged debrief. Y'all did what you could."

Had they? Had she? Miriam wasn't sure.

"Did you check the infrastructure and connections I mentioned? Any signs of sabotage?" Nas rubbed his neck. "They messed up the routes and bridges pretty good in the South."

"Command informed the other outposts and settlements to watch for it. BigInt's piecing together more stuff down south, but with what's happening in Arshangol, the Altered— Apostates really—don't seem to be focusing on us right now."

"No shit."

Jace shot a look at Nas. "I don't think anyone expected the fighting to last this long, but what do you think will happen when they *do* focus on us?"

Nas gave Kai a presumptuous side-eye. Apparently, Miriam had missed something in their previous discussion.

"But that won't happen," Krill said. "The events in the South were meant to derail the summit, right? Done. Summit derailed. And the attack on Ursus was what, a distraction for their coup?"

Kai chirped, "Derailed summit and all, it still backfired on the wunbies. We're working together now."

Nas gave her another look.

"Fine. Working slightly together. Nothing is perfect in the beginning. The latest news from Center was that the legionnaires gained back some of the city. Things are turning around."

Nas rolled his eyes. "Then why are alties fleeing and coming here?"

The group looked at Jace expectedly.

His mouth pinched. "I have my theories. They're not very optimistic. Let's just say I think we're wildly underestimating the Apostates."

"Are we going to have problems?" Miriam said, her forehead furrowing. She quickly added, "*More* problems?"

"Honestly? This is all uncharted. We know the Altered have a history of coups and uprisings, but I don't know. This is something different. The Apostates are more organized than any of us expected. And on all fronts. The South? Ursus? Are they connected? They have to be. We're too many steps behind. Command is keeping a strong face on, but between us? I think they're just as baffled." Jace sighed. "And that's not talking about our own issues at home. This is a recruitment harvest for the Children of Charon."

Miriam frowned. Echo didn't have a pleasant experience with the human-supremacist terrorist group, but if she had to choose, she'd rather deal with COC than wunbies. The Charonites were human, and she knew their limits, even if drugged up.

"I hear you're gearing up for another mission soon. So, that'll be a nice distraction."

"It's on the schedule," Krill replied.

Nas groaned. "It's been on the schedule for ages, but still no instructions. No mission. SOG leadership's been baiting us since they pulled us out early from Ursus, but look at what we've been doing since: training refreshers and security duty alongside the rest of UMF."

"We're bein' punished," Fox muttered.

His low voice startled Miriam. Their teammate didn't take part in conversations much anymore. Before, his salty commentary was always reliable.

"For what?" Miriam asked, but Fox had already looked away.

"For not respecting their order to leave Temunco? They knew we made the right choice after the wunbies attacked. They wouldn't punish us for that," Kai said, then turned back to Jace. "Are you returning to SOG?"

The team lead perked up. Miriam and Yuri had known Krill

since their basic training class, but the lead and Jace went further back.

"Sorry, probably not. Even if I weren't on this assignment, we're slammed trying to stay ahead of all these refugees coming in. Refugees, ha. Never thought those words would be used for Altered."

"You're as close to official as we can get. Do *you* know why they're coming here? Why not other places?" Nas asked.

Jace smirked. "Gotta work on your trade skills, brother. Butter me up before you ask the hard questions."

Nas grumbled and ignored him. "They have most of the continents, anyway. They can survive in the places we can't."

"The Royals—well, Center—reported the fighting hasn't been limited to Arshangol." Kai brushed her face. "I guess there were more wunbies than we all thought. The new embassy must've worked something out with Center."

"Station City offers some comforts," Miriam said. Station was probably medieval to them, but if their other options were radioactive zones or deserts, a city, no matter how outdated it was, would still have its solace. She had thought the South was quite primitive, but it had its own particular charm.

"Yeah, but they're *our* comforts," Nas whined.

"Be prepared to share," Miriam quipped. More like, be prepared for issues.

Someone called out across the auditorium and Jace turned and raised a hand. He shrugged back at the group. "Gotta get going, but it's really good to see y'all. We should catch up more, grab a meal like old times."

Yuri nodded and clasped Jace's hand. "Hell, why not? That's actually a good idea. We can reinstate team dinners, starting what —" He looked around the group. "Tomorrow night? Are you free?"

"At Tsutsumi's? Send me the time, and I'll make it happen." He squeezed Krill's shoulder, crinkled his eyes at the group, then jogged off with a toothy grin.

Krill rubbed the back of his head. "Speaking of next mission, we do have something."

The group straightened.

"No instructions yet, but it's hopeful."

The vagueness made Miriam nervous.

"We're receiving a shipment. I'm guessing it's related. I need volunteers to meet the courier in a few hours."

No one came forward.

"It could be new tech. Bravo and some of the Spartan teams were fitted out with new-gen visors."

Nas's eyes widened. "Me. I volunteer."

"Anyone else?"

Miriam sighed and raised a hand half-heartedly. "I need to pick up some new gels from the depot. It's on the way."

"Great. Hopefully we don't need it." Krill winced. "And about duty tomorrow... Command's asked us to pull a shift. Order and peace."

"Alty duty." Nas groaned again. "If Command *asked*, can we say no?"

No one responded, but the answer was obvious.

◊

Alone and waiting, Miriam leaned against the sentry post. The courier was late, and Nas had run off into one of the depots, probably to snoop at other shipments of tech and gear. A line of rabbit vehicles and urban prowlers filled with personnel and cargo rumbled out the perimeter gate. UMF Station was normally busy, but since the Altered relocation efforts, it had become an anthill with nonstop movement.

Loud conversation pulled her attention away from her cuff, and she peered up at three marines. Two had thin metal gadgets balanced between their lips. A nicosynth break.

"This isn't even our war. The fuckers are killing each other over there and it's good for us. I hope they all die." A young marine took a long drag.

"What are you on about, dickhead?" the oldest of the group retorted. "The lab rats declared war on us, too. Shitters stuffed us on both ends."

"That's what big guvvy says."

"What conspiracy are you listening to now, asswipe? It was on the network and reports."

"Yeah, but so what? Alties bomb yoomy to bits, and then we let them move in?"

"Who? The Royal Rats? Weren't them, I thought."

"Don't matter. I'm sure they wished they did it first. Alties are all the same. All think we're shit. You hear what they call us? Roaches."

"Fuck them. We ain't no roaches."

The third marine elbowed the other in the ribs and inclined his head in Miriam's direction. She redirected her gaze toward a line of workers moving large containers into a rhino van. Their chatter continued shortly after, more subdued this time.

She strained to listen further, but her commcuff pinged— their contact was a few minutes away. Miriam scanned the area for Nas, but he was nowhere in sight. Other than poking around, her teammate was probably also avoiding her; she had harped on him on the walk there. Although his leg had healed from its injury from the southern mission, Nas still carried a slight limp. She wasn't thrilled about his lackadaisical manner toward his treatment. After a hasty ping to Nas, she sighed and walked out the gate.

As she passed, the three marines' conversation diminished again and they took inhales of their stimulant. Two acknowledged her with a nod after a long stare at her diamond-tabbed collar. The usual military folk held a reverence for SOG, and these three first-contract marines were no exception. And though she was certain they didn't know who she was, rumors of Echo's time in the South had already circulated around the compound. Miriam thought it mildly amusing. Much of it was thanks to the prestigious Ursus siblings, their reputation already known, and their rare blond hair in a land of mixed races and brunettes only added to the story.

It surprised Miriam how much her thoughts returned to Sam. She had only worked with the woman a little more than a week, not a terribly long time. Perhaps it was the close quarters, the shared trauma and fear in discovering the wunbies, or fighting Charonites, but Miriam felt an affinity for her, even after their last interaction. She could've sent messages or called, but her hesitancy had become more permanent over time. She told herself she was giving Sam space to recover, but Miriam knew she was hiding behind the distance as well. Regardless, she missed Sam. She thought about those blue eyes flitting around, their acute penetrating focus, and the soft nervousness after…

A two-seater rabbit screeched to a halt some meters away, music thrashing from the open cab. The driver unclipped his belt and jabbed a finger at a handheld. Subsequently, Miriam's cuff vibrated. Instead of checking it, she approached the vehicle and its rhythmic clash.

The driver's head jerked up, and surprise gurgled from his throat. He swallowed it back. "Shitballs, lady. You scared me." He recovered and looked over her uniform. "You Miriam Tanner?"

"Yes."

"Cool. Cool cool cool. Where do you want all this?" The man jerked a finger behind him. The rabbit's compartment bed was filled to the brim with containers.

Miriam furrowed her brows. She hadn't known what to expect, but it hadn't been this bulk and quantity. A smaller box sat nestled on top of the otherwise uniform packages. That one she recognized, barely making out the familiar logo of the UMF-affiliated design labs. New tech. Nas was going to be thrilled. If he would only respond and show up.

"Give me a second." Miriam shot a glance back into the compound, past the open gates, but couldn't see their vehicle parked around the corner. She impatiently pinged her missing teammate again then offered a weak smile to the porter. "You know what? Let's unload here. I can walk it back."

While the courier hopped to the other side and began loosening cargo binds, Miriam watched the outer loop of Station City, the open space between the military compound's walls and the city's first hedge of buildings. She gazed absently at the usual ministrations of the largest human city on the planet. It was another mundane day, another day before Echo went back out to the boonies to play shepherd and police the relocation of alties, another unknown number of days before they headed off to another mission, vague as it was.

And then she spotted a glimpse of that color. That hair.
Sam.
It couldn't be—the hair was too short. Mute?

Miriam shaded her eyes and strained her neck to get a better view when her attention broke, turning back to the porter who had toppled one stack of boxes. By the time she whipped back around, the color was a passing patch, and then gone around the corner into the city.

Invigorated, Miriam yelled a quick comment to the courier and made chase.

4

———————

CONVERGENCE

"HOW WAS YOUR SESSION TODAY?"

"Fine," Sam lied between breaths. She urged her legs to accelerate, her heart pounding steadily.

Her earpiece trilled five blocks later, and a mirrored response came through. The program's selected speech for her brother didn't match him or his gravelly voice. It was too cheerful, and irritation edged as the humor in his one-word reply failed. It was followed by another message.

"You're not at the hospital anymore?"

She grimaced. She forgot she had allowed her brother to track her location. She considered disengaging the feature on her cuff—it wasn't like he'd be able to come to her aid if she was lost or in trouble. She could handle herself.

"Stop following me," she panted, and for the next stretch, he didn't respond. Sam refocused on her breathing as her muscles strained, weaving between other pedestrians. Inhale. Exhale. And repeat. This pain was good. This suffering, good.

Yet, as she pushed herself harder, a wave of melancholy washed over her. Farewells were difficult for Sam. The goodbye with her brother, whom she had spent twenty-three years practically glued to the side of, had felt near impossible—

especially since she didn't have a return trip scheduled. Scott assured her he would call as much as he could, and he was always a message away. It wasn't as if they hadn't been separated before; she had been acclimating to the reality of his UMF departure before the attack, but parting ways at the Ursus docks had been strange. Sam nearly changed her mind several times until the bay doors sealed, marking a final decision. No sooner than a step into the galley, her brother had already sent two messages.

The emotions and anxiety had slightly lifted when she stepped off the transport ship and eyed the colors and lofty structures of the city, so different from the military grays she had spent an entire life in. The awe she felt the first time she arrived in Station City, months before, rushed to welcome her again. Although this time, the feeling came alongside a fresh onslaught of insecurity. This time, she was truly by herself.

Either through her reputation or UMF's connections, something expedited Sam's entrance into a program at Station's largest medical center, and before she knew it, weeks had passed. She still wore her status uncomfortably—not fully marine, not fully civilian—somewhere in the purgatory between. Her new identity came with clothes that felt wrong, alien on her skin. Though they all remained dark and neutral, unlike the flashy colors of the city, they weren't her usual uniform. She also wasn't used to how crowded the place was. It was nothing like the suffocating narrow structures and population of the South, but it was also excessive in comparison to the vaster North. However, there was one advantage: anonymity. It was a relief to hide in a large city where no civilian knew who she was, especially in the medical sector. The blond hair was an issue, but it was nothing a simple covering couldn't fix.

Her earpiece trilled. "Weekend plans? Have you gone to the museum yet?"

She hadn't. She didn't have the time. Readapting her left

arm had become a full-time occupation. The anger she embraced back in Ursus dissipated with each passing day, expelled little by little with hours of exercise and therapeutic sessions. An unending energy twisting around itself, her rage now funneled into a fixation, a new mission. The phantom pains came and went, but pain was a boon. In Ursus, it was a reminder of everything she'd lost. In Station City, it propelled her forward.

Sam had always enjoyed routine, and it was no different with one arm. If anything, routine was more meaningful now. Her days were a segmented blur of exercise, therapy, and recovery sessions—anything that kept her out of her spartan studio apartment.

Routine was good. Reliable.

Except when it broke. And that day, it had been derailed by a frustrating consultation. Station's medical center team and staff were fantastic, but she avoided the counselor as much as she could. Sam didn't want to talk about herself. She was only in Station, in this program, to get better, to get an experimental prosthetic prototype, and return to Ursus, SOG, and UMF. It had taken some time, but Sam accepted her new situation. She thought it counterintuitive to discuss it endlessly; it only made her feel worse. And she had to admit, even if it felt slow, she *was* getting better. Her strength and balance were consistent, her motion felt good, and she was already retraining her hand and arm with whatever makeshift items in dry runs and internal visualization exercises. In her home-made drills, her accuracy wasn't as good as it was before, but it was at least developing in the right direction. So, the counselor's veiled threat to postpone her coming procedure had unleashed a fury inside her. She'd do whatever she needed, say whatever she needed, put on a mask, but the rage screamed inside. To burn it off, Sam ran. It was a significant stray from her regimented routine, but she needed the pain.

With the pavement underneath her feet, Sam let her

emotions disperse into each steady beat. She hated running, but there was a release in the motions. Pouring her contempt into each step was a way to distract from her bitterness at everything else.

"You should go. Maybe with others?"

Sam frowned. Another unsubtle attempt to have her reach out to Echo. Sam had explicitly told her brother not to tell Yuri or the others she was in the city. He didn't understand, but respected her wishes, at least. She was still embarrassed and ashamed of how she had treated the Station team back in Ursus. Specifically Miriam. Until she was intact and back in her uniform, rifle in hand, Sam didn't want to be seen.

"Another time," she said dismissively between short pants. Her eyes squinted into the contrast of light as the sky opened before her. Her pace slowed, having pushed more than she should've, and she realized where she was: the stitch between UMF's headquarters and the city's limits. The military's familiar grays and boxy structures loomed across the street, and she peered at the uniformed marines around the gates. Though UMF had taken her visor, they couldn't take her eye implant. It didn't work well without her gear, but it was enough to watch the activity on the other side.

She'd be back soon. *She'd be useful again.*

As her eyes locked onto a figure outside the compound walls, her heart froze. Sam could recognize the stature and braid. Miriam looked grand in her uniform pants and undone jacket, the SOG black T-shirt underneath. Sam had only met her a few months before, but the attraction had been instant. Even with the distance, she was drawn forward, and her brain betrayed her, briefly considering crossing the busy street to say hello. She shook her head and swiped at her hair sticking to her forehead. Her legs protested as she sprinted a quick burst around the corner before she did anything so stupid.

Another message recited in her ear, but Sam couldn't focus.

In the cooler shadows of the city's structures, Sam stopped

to catch her breath. The surprise had jolted her heart more than the run itself. She had graciously avoided Echo her entire time in Station City, and after weeks, she still didn't know what she would say to any of them, to Miriam, if she saw them. It was too late for apologies.

She shot a response to her brother, that she'd talk with him later, and checked the time on her wrist. Though it wasn't in her internalized schedule, Sam had a sudden need for a shower to wash away the unexpected emotional ambush. She started back into a light jog.

"Mute?"

Sam paused mid-step. She inhaled, braced herself, then turned.

Meters away, Miriam gripped her hips as she caught her breath. "Oh, sor—" The woman's eyes widened. "Sam."

"M—" Sam cleared her throat. "Tanner. Hey."

Miriam gave an uncertain smirk as she moved closer. "Oh, that's formal."

Sam's jaw clenched. The last time she saw the Echo medic, she hadn't been in a good place. And before that, the kiss. In the most random times, her mind would betray her, and she'd relive that memory where everything dropped away, where it was just warmth and comfort.

And rejection.

"Sorry." Sam steadied her breath and brushed her short hair back. Injecting false confidence into her voice, she added, "It's good to see you."

That was the truth. Even now, with the gulf of space between them, she still gravitated toward Miriam, the same feeling she had months before. Perhaps her mind was playing cruel tricks, but with the breeze, she could make out the soft scent of cinnamon through the smell of musty water and city street.

"You're here. In Station," the woman said, the start of a smile stuck on her face. "When did you get in?"

Underneath her forced composure, Sam panicked. "A few weeks, maybe a month…"

"A month," Miriam echoed. She blinked, then frowned. "Do any of the others know?"

"No, I didn't tell anyone. I mean, Scott knows I'm here." Her weight shifted from one leg to the other as the other woman waited for more. "Before. I said some things…"

Miriam waved absently. "It's okay."

Sam exhaled, and she was aware of the medic's examination of her. As pedestrians passed, she moved to the side, grateful for the momentary distraction from scrutiny.

The commcuff on Miriam's wrist buzzed, but the woman ignored it. "You look good."

Sam's jaw clenched again. She angled herself so her loose sleeve and the harness underneath were behind her. She wasn't prepared for this meeting at all; her training clothes were too little, too casual, and she was a mess, her perspiration increasing now that she had stopped.

"I mean it. The haircut is great," Miriam reassured.

Self-conscious, Sam ran her fingers through her shortened hair. One side had only recently grown out to hide the pinkish scar across her scalp. She wasn't quite used to the length, not after having it long her entire life, but it was a compromise after frustrations of managing it with one hand. She had sheared it off after arriving in Station City, another milestone in her new focus. The style was a practical convenience rather than a fashion statement.

"So, what are you doing here?"

"I'm in a recovery program." Sam gestured behind her, although she felt silly immediately after. The motion hadn't been in the right direction. She'd also made herself sound like an addict. Idiot.

But Miriam nodded. "Of course. And how's that going?"

"It's okay. I actually—"

Miriam's commcuff buzzed angrily.

"I'll be getting a new—"

The device vibrated again.

"Sorry." Miriam winced. "Shit. Dammit, Nas. I—shit. Hold that thought." The medic turned her head toward the compound, then twisted back. "Are you doing anything right now? I mean, are you free? I want to catch up. If you can wait fifteen, twenty minutes tops? I just have to finish some stuff and I'll be right back. We can grab coffee or something?"

Sam's heart skipped in a different panic. "Okay." The word was already out of her mouth before she remembered how she looked.

The woman grinned. "Great. My apartment's close by. You can wait there if you'd like."

Sam's throat closed, but she managed a curt nod.

"I'll shoot over the address and access. Your cuff works, right?"

For a second, Sam felt the barbed tone, but the medic gave her a quick wink.

"Help yourself to whatever. Make yourself at home."

The earpiece trilled in Sam's ear, whatever message Miriam sent, now delivered. She managed a nervous smile as they parted, then stared at her commcuff, at her next off-routine and unscheduled destination.

"Sam?" the medic called out behind her.

She turned.

"It's great to see you."

Something fluctuated in her stomach, and Sam swung between loving and hating it. That warmth, that hope... This woman. Why did she have such an effect on her?

◊

Miriam's apartment was a few blocks away in a colorful neighborhood filled with cafés and shops, and its buildings tiered and opened onto different levels of the city's vertical landscape. The surrounding streets and ambiance fit the medic's personality, no surprise to Sam. This sector was a sharp contrast from where she lived, its neat and uniform streets matching the broad hospital buildings and their many wings, almost like UMF, but sterile in a different manner. If not for her unscheduled run and meeting, Sam avoided these lively areas.

When she arrived in front of a bold red door, its paint chipping away at the parts where it slid and met the frame, Sam couldn't help but smirk. She considered remaining outside, waiting in the street, but curiosity overcame her. She held her commcuff to the console nearby, and the door slid open.

The pleasant scent of cinnamon met her before she crossed the threshold. Sam awkwardly stepped inside the spacious flat, pausing at the edge. Her fingers dragged along a faded loveseat, the worn fabric soft to the touch. She sat, then stood back up, too restless to stay still. Instead, she gave herself a small tour of the place. Sam glanced into the kitchen and stopped at the door to the bedroom. A glimpse of the bed inside was like the aftermath of a storm, its sheets and pillows in disarray. Sporadic decor hung around the space: tasteful, but with no particular pattern or relation between the items. This apartment was actually lived in, unlike her own.

As Sam paced, anxiety coursed through her, and she willed the minutes down. She tensed at movement near the bathroom and faced her reflection in a narrow mirror. Her hair was a mess —one side matted in uneven parts—her scars pink and visible, and her clothes hung loosely. Embarrassing. Then, her eyes drew to her asymmetry. The hanging sleeve barely covered a harnessed stump. The pressure straps helped with the pain, but it looked silly. Her brows furrowed.

Before a familiar emotion could boil over, the front door opened, and Sam's gaze pulled away. "Mir, I'm sorry about—"

It wasn't Miriam.

A stunning woman with red-dyed hair set a small bag on the counter, her large eyes raking over Sam. The woman's skin was dark and smooth, her makeup luscious and spectacular. Floral perfume wafted into Sam's nose.

She tensed. A phantom finger scratched against a nonexistent thumb.

"Hello," the woman purred.

Anger reared inside Sam's gut, but it gave way to a deflating insecurity. She replied with a soft, mirrored greeting.

"Tan's not here, I presume." The woman prowled past and disappeared into the bedroom, sliding the door completely open.

The flat, once spacious, was suddenly too small.

"Have you seen a green blouse? This morning was such a rush, I must've left it..." Sounds of rummaging and ruffled sheets floated out from the room.

Sam cleared her throat and shifted closer to the front door, an eye on the now fully exposed bed. "No."

The woman made a soft noise, paused, then smoothed the bed cover before sitting. She leaned back on outstretched arms in a bold, possessive manner and watched Sam in the exterior space. "Guess I'll have to try her again. It's one of my favorites..."

The stare was far too intense, too predatory for Sam's comfort, and any comprehensible small talk fled her mind. She made to cross her arms but grasped the air before fixing her left hand upon her ribs. This was one of Miriam's paramours. And she was far more beautiful, far more *intact* than Sam. A void opened inside her, and she bit her lip as her fingers rubbed over thin fabric and the scars underneath.

Sam never had a chance.

Friends, Miriam had said.

She cursed herself for the raised hope, that she still wanted something more. A heavy stone settled in her gut, and she couldn't bear another second in that apartment.

◊

Back outside, Sam swore under her breath. Her fingers tapped her palm and the commcuff display illuminated, waiting for the next query or command. She pictured the woman inside, then disengaged her device. Her shoulders sagged before she grudgingly lifted her chin and pushed into a jog. As her pace quickened, insecurity hardened into anger, and by the next intersection, those emotions flowed around and off her. She couldn't do anything about the insecurity, but she could funnel and steer the anger. She had months of unbridled rage, and that was easier to tame.

Blocks passed by as she fell into an unsustainable sprint, navigating and ignoring choice words from other pedestrians and drivers. Her muscles burned, one hurt replacing another. By the time she slowed, her heart hammered against her ribs, her lungs gasped for oxygen, and a sheen of sweat cascaded down her face and neck.

In this sector, the buildings had muted in color and trash littered the street more than before. Large grilles filled windows, and run-down, seedy-looking shops speckled the block. Lines of clothing hung from multiple apartments above. Station City was much bigger than any settlement she had been to, and she rarely ventured away from her routine areas. Now, Sam didn't know where she was. She drew her cuff and startled. Time had somehow flown by. She had also shot kilometers southeast, a distance from her flat.

As Sam brought her breathing back to normal, a wet, dark outline greeted her on a nearby wall. The ink was fresh, dripping in thin trails. The box lantern was a message, a sign of the Children of Charon. The human supremacists were rampant in the South and outlier settlements, but the mark felt odd in the human capital. As she stared at it longer, it reminded her of everything that was still happening despite her own intermission.

Around the corner, someone shouted. Sam peeked down a narrow back alley. Two men towered over a pair of small figures, children no older than twelve. One adult pulled on a child's skinny arm. Sam spared another glance at her cuff and considered turning away. Her schedule was already off-track, but her feet stuck, and she observed instead, willing her implant to attune. She missed her UMF visor, wishing for its enhanced capabilities to better gauge the situation, but she didn't need it to interpret the party's postures.

Bullies. No matter where or when, there were always bullies.

Without further thought, Sam inched forward. But despite her stealth, the children's heads whipped to the side, and she gulped. Horrifying yet beautiful golden eyes glowed in the partially shadowed alley. The dark-haired boy and girl glared hawkishly, fearless—as if her attempt to intervene was an interruption, not a rescue.

The man turned and stared at Sam, and then her loose sleeve. "Damn. Thought you were SecTeam." He tugged again on the boy's limb. With his other hand, the man loosened the apron hanging around his neck above his sizable gut.

"As if SecTeam would help," the bearded man next to him responded.

Sam monitored the young Altered, then observed the men as she approached. There were no visible signs of Charon marks. "What's going on?" she asked cautiously.

"Little rat bastards stole from my shop," Apron grumbled. He shook the boy's arm and swiped at the other child, who nimbly dodged away.

An unpleasant memory jarred loose, and Sam's stomach tensed.

"We did not," the girl reprimanded. She pulled a ripened fruit from a pocket and thrust it out. "You can have it back!"

"You're hurting the child," Sam said. They were lucky these Altered were young and prepubescent. She doubted the men had the same courage to take on Altered adults. Even *Sam* was wary of that.

"Ain't no child. Bloody monstrosities these are. Movin' in and ruinin' everythin' they touch."

The boy yanked back, but his wrist was stuck within Apron's grip. He whimpered.

"Let him go." Sam scowled. Something coursed through her body when the man didn't comply, and that *something* felt good. Her muscles edged toward an anticipative precipice, an opportunity to unleash accumulated emotions. "We can figure this out."

That was a partial lie. She didn't want to settle this civilly. This wasn't her fight, but she wanted it.

Beard rolled up his sleeves. "Fuckin' alty-lover. Move along, this ain't your business." He spat to the side.

Sam's skin prickled, and her lips cracked into a grin. "You a fuckin' Charonite? It'll make me feel better when I kick your teeth in." It was a childish jab, but the words felt good as they rolled out.

Both men's faces scrunched as they scanned her over.

Beard laughed. "You can't be serious."

Within seconds, Sam crossed the short distance, and all the coiled rage surged through her feet and hips, sharpened through her arm, her fist, and bludgeoned into the man's nose. He stumbled back, clutching his face with both hands, eyes wide over his fingers. The satisfaction in motion and impact after months of pent-up frustration overrode the pain in her knuckles.

However, her smugness was short-lived as the man drove her back, his arms swinging wide. Beard had no technique, but his fists had a meaty weight behind them. Sam sidestepped the barreling limbs, and her foot whipped forward to create distance. Even with one arm, her SOG training and muscle memory exceeded his wide motions. He stumbled back, then pushed forward. Beard swung a wild hook, but Sam redirected its motion and shoved his body away with the ball of her foot square along his hip.

Easy.

And then her side exploded in pain. Apron had joined the brawl.

Sam angled back and slammed her shoulder into the man's sternum with a crunch, but without a full limb, she lost control of the follow-through motion. Another hand swung toward her, and she stepped into it, the blow glancing across the back of her head. Sam thrust her crown into the man's face, and he cried out. Pain flooded her senses, but it felt good.

She twisted away, and then the air left her diaphragm with a grunt. She resisted the urge to double over as she tried to suck in oxygen. Hairy limbs clamped around her, pinning her, and she willed a useless, phantom arm to fight.

Sam knocked her head back, but Beard was smarter this time, keeping his vulnerable face at a distance. She stomped a foot into the man's instep, and his grip loosened. Dropping her weight, she pushed away, but his hold tightened higher on her torso. Dread nipped at her. The confidence she had seconds before was gone. Sam had taken on more than she could handle. She was fighting as if she was the same person she had been before.

She wasn't.

A blow crushed into her gut, and before her mind could register it, another hit glanced against the side of her head. Warmth flooded her ear, and her vision doubled, flares dancing between the outlines of everything.

Idiot. She had been naively ambitious.

But then the restraint around her slipped, and her knees buckled. It was a mark of pure will—or stupidity—she didn't fall to the ground. Sam swayed, and her arm shot out to steady herself, but of course, the memory of an arm couldn't hold any weight. She fell into the wall instead, her shoulder crushing into the hard surface.

The alley and its figures swam in front of her, and Sam shook her head, trying to knock her vision back into focus, but it only made the throb worse. Someone shouted and footsteps scuttled away—she wasn't sure who; she was preoccupied, desperately trying to gather her senses. And then despite the teetering nausea, she felt a presence behind her. Sam staggered around, bracing herself for whatever came next.

Only to face the chest of a tall, slim man. Dark pupils bore down, their surrounding irises a dark shade of red with amber flecks. Fear rose in her throat, past the previous pain, and she flinched back. She had met Altered before, fought alongside legionnaires, but she had never seen one with eyes like his. His cheekbones were high and sharp, skin smooth, and black hair swept back. Everything about him was cold yet alluring, if not for the implication of a genetically designed nature.

Sam's muscles tensed instinctually. Previous generations of conflict and violence between two races were suddenly right in front of her. Golden-eyed Altered children were one thing; red-eyed adults were another. Her fist raised in defense, but Sam knew she was in no shape for another fight. Her ear was ringing, and it throbbed something fierce. Shame mixed in with the fear and reemerging anger. She was nothing like she was before. Broken.

But no assault came. Just the apathetic and eerie stare.

Sam startled and stumbled to the side when a raven-haired woman stepped out from behind the tall man. Golden eyes flashed down at the children, a wordless admonishment, and the boy's head hung as he rubbed his arm, red from Apron's grip. The girl whined in a different language.

The woman hummed, then said in a song-like voice, "Xiaoling, other tongue."

The girl made a face, then jutted her chin out. "We did nothing wrong!"

"You shouldn't be out here. Where is your mother?"

"We wanted *shuǐguǒ*. You know there aren't any in the shops near us! And this isn't that far. They said we stole from them, but we didn't, and then they chased us and, and then..." The girl's eyes drew over to Sam, and the woman's and the boy's golden irises followed.

Sam recoiled under the undivided attention. Her eyes darted between the four and the alley exit.

"The *gǎzuà* helped us," the young boy said.

Sam didn't understand the word.

"Longwei," the woman snipped. Her eyes flashed a warning.

Not a good word, then.

The girl thrust out the round pink object. "This isn't even actual fruit!"

The woman gracefully lowered herself to meet the children at their eye level. "We talked about this. We're not in Arshangol. It's different here. You need *qián* to pay for things."

The girl scrunched her nose, and the boy sniffed.

"You were lucky this kind person stopped to help." She stood and elegantly swirled two fingers. The man stepped back, his red eyes never wavering from Sam since they arrived. "Thank you," the woman said. "For stepping in. Are you alright?"

Sam brushed her swollen knuckles against her cheek. Something wet streaked across the back of her hand, but she ignored it, her eyes shifting between the others. "The fruit. I can give you cred—"

The woman's mouth tugged to the side. "Thank you, but no. *We* will mend things with our new neighbors, won't we?" she said to the children.

New neighbors. That's what the Altered were now.

"I'm Kuan-Lin," the woman chimed. Then, she introduced the others: her niece and nephew, Xiaoling and Longwei, and the man—who Sam presumed to be a bodyguard in the way he held himself—was Dmitri. Kuan-Lin's manners were ever so diplomatic and careful, and Sam was wary. All her interactions with Altered had been bellicose, hesitant and guarded at the very minimum. She thought of the two legionnaires they had temporarily allied with in the South, but they were different. That situation had been different.

The Altered watched Sam expectantly, waiting for her name in the transaction. How was she supposed to introduce herself? In the recovery program, the staff and trainers called her Ryan per UMF Station surname culture. Her "Valkyrie" callsign felt too connected to the military and her reputation, and she wasn't worthy of it, not after that beating. In the end, Sam muttered her name. It was informal and civilian, but that was her new reality.

Kuan-Lin smiled kindly. "Thank you, Sam. The children— you know how they are—they're curious, not used to being cooped up. I'd love to thank you properly for your assistance." Her eyes pierced through Sam, and she paused, considering. "Do you know where the embassy is?"

Sam shook her head.

The woman swiftly pulled a small, palm-length rod out of her clothes, and a holoscreen expanded from its side. She hovered her thumb over it. "Let me see, you must be..."

With a graceful flick, Sam's earpiece—slightly ajar from her scuffle—trilled with a new message. An address recited in her ear, but Sam ignored it, dumbfounded. The fact that the Altered's tech connected so easily with hers was a drop in the ocean of scrambled thoughts.

An embassy. Gold irises. A haunting, red-eyed bodyguard.

These were Royals.

Sam's stomach contracted at the realization. And her proximity.

A notification chimed in her device again, and Sam thought the Altered's ears twitched and seemed to turn toward her— she wasn't sure. She had, after all, taken a blow to the head. A message from Miriam dictated, but Sam shook her wrist, reducing the connection to her earpiece.

"I have to go," Sam stammered.

"Come by anytime!" The Royal's voice followed after her as she backpedaled toward the main street.

Around the corner, Sam broke out in a run, retracing her way back to the medical sector and her sterile studio apartment. As her feet pounded a steady beat, the fear and strangeness were replaced with a renewed fervor. Despite her failure, violence had placated something inside her, or at least staved off the boiling point, like ice into hot water.

Fuel the fire.

She would be better.

5

EROSION

MIRIAM DRUMMED her fingers against her kit while the other hand tapped a sporadic beat on the grip of her holstered pistol. Her slung rifle provided additional comfort for what was about to arrive. It was at least loaded, unlike the duty company's, whose magazines were empty of ammunition, their frames merely a show of power. At best, the weapons could serve as blunt objects. UMF had either yielded to City Center's lack of confidence in the judgment of company marines or the lack of understanding on jurisdiction and authorities with Station civilians. Perhaps it was both. Either way, dry weapons couldn't fire and create a media shitshow.

The military was there to bolster SecTeam's numbers and help keep the peace—that much was obvious. But if it came down to it, were they there to protect the public from the alty refugees or the alties from the mob? Whatever the reason, the illusion worked. At least with the growing mass on the street, corralled by linked barriers. A couple dozen SecGuards mingled nearby, their donned protective equipment and heavy gear a premonition.

Miriam's commcuff buzzed.

S. RYAN: When?

She grinned. She was disappointed when Sam hadn't been at her apartment the previous day, but Miriam was in higher spirits now. The woman was, at least, responding to her messages.

M. TANNER: Tonight.

She quickly added another line of text below it. Sam still seemed skittish, and Miriam wanted to assuage her, coax her out.

M. TANNER: The food is amazing. I know it's late notice, but the team would love to see you.

Miriam glanced up. Krill, Nas, and Kai conversed nearby, and Yuri and Fox stood further away, their expressions conveying varying degrees of boredom. She hadn't told the others yet, but they wouldn't mind. Sam and her brother were honorary members of Echo, having bonded on their previous mission.

S. RYAN: Maybe. We'll see.

Miriam could work with "maybe."

"How did we pull this duty again?" Nas whined. He rubbed the back of his leg but stopped when Miriam eyed his motion. "Fox might be right. This has to be punishment."

Miriam narrowed her eyes as the SecGuards' shields glinted and caught in the angry sunlight. "Moan and groan all you want; it won't change the situation."

"It's not just us, either," Krill said. "UMF assigned a role for everyone."

"Well, good thing it's only a day this time. Doing this for

weeks would kill me," Nas muttered, tossing a sympathetic look at the company marines. "I'm glad we have an actual mission soon. *Supposedly*."

"How many are arriving in this wave?" Miriam asked.

"I don't know, but they sure keep on coming."

She stifled a shudder. "And how many do you think are here now?"

"Thousands," Kai chimed as she looked worriedly behind her shoulder. "Per the last sitrep from Center."

"Hell, can the city fit that many?"

Kai shuffled her feet. "Who knows, but the embassy and Center have come to some kind of agreement."

"Supposedly it's mostly the elite families and their scientists," Nas said. "BigInt's bogged down with all the verifications and background checks. Although it's pretty pathetic, considering we're relying on the Royals' word."

"I thought you'd be more excited about that. The intellectuals and tech."

Nas scoffed at Kai. "Not when they're invading our city and personal space. I know, I know. Not an invasion, but still. Oldtown isn't happy with their new neighbors. Did you hear about the last riot? At least this isn't too bad." He jerked a finger to the chanting mass.

"And they keep coming," Miriam muttered. "Can't be a good sign of what's happening over in Arshangol."

"Yeah, well, we're just the welcome and processing committee. At least we're not in the Alley."

"What?"

"That's what they're calling the main street separating Oldtown from the new alty sector."

Krill hushed them. "We have admirers."

A trio of young marines watched the SOG team from a few meters behind. They bore the same gray-and-orange circular patch designating one of the larger UMF companies, and sported peach fuzz haircuts of newly graduated, first-contract marines. One individual, who looked like he was recently out of university, inched closer to Fox. The diamond tab on Echo's uniforms enthralled them. The attention was also likely due in part from the rumors of Echo's role in the South. The team had certainly been the topic of conversation and conspiracy theories at their timely—or untimely—involvement in two destroyed human settlements and the defense of Temunco Outpost. Fox, being the largest, was the most recognizable.

The teenager found courage in Echo's indifference and sidled up, a nervous grin shining upward. "You're Razor-Echo, right? Fox?" he stuttered. "You're my hero, man. Did you really tear an alty apart?"

His doting bounced off the quiet mountain of a man. Miriam's eyebrow raised, and she regarded the young man with a polite smile.

"Would you like a strawberry drop?" An outstretched palm proffered what looked to be a small box of local sweets. "We had some extra and thought you might like some."

A vein twitched on Fox's temple, and his face darkened. His response was a low rumble—so soft Miriam strained to hear it. "Don't want your shit."

Miriam tensed, and the marine's expression suspended in confusion, his hand still out. Fox straightened to his full height, an ominous wall of muscle. Miriam and Kai raised their hands, but their warning was too late.

"Get the fuck away from me," he said louder between gritted teeth. He swatted out and a single sweet clattered on the pavement.

"Fox! Hell," Kai exclaimed.

The young marine recoiled and stumbled backward. He apologized profusely, although unsure of his offense, then retreated to rejoin his teammates.

"Whoa, big guy." Miriam's fingers splayed in a placating motion. She threw an apologetic gaze to the marines, but they had already hurried back to their larger group.

Fox huffed.

Miriam shared a look with Yuri, and Krill's lips pinched together, his thick brows furrowing, but the lead only shook his head. "Heads up," he said, chucking his chin toward the depot.

Two individuals dressed in white and blue emerged from the building with datapads in hand. Two legionnaires in white uniforms followed, their colossal size realized as they passed the first city administrators, who stepped out of their way. Behind the barricades, the crowd seemed to gasp and simmer collectively in horrified awe.

As the four passed, the hairs on Miriam's neck stood. Even without their armor and weapons, the legionnaires set off all of her internal alarms. Their separate green and blue eyes floated over Echo, the other marines, SecTeam, and the congregated crowd. Their faces betrayed no emotion, aloof and apathetic. At the tented station in the middle of the lot, they stopped and stood post while the other two settled themselves at the table.

"Emissaries from the embassy. See their lapels?" Kai whispered.

Miriam's visor scanned over the metallic pin on the breast of the two others: a sun-like shape with its top ray stretching up like a pointed dagger.

"And their eyes. Not the Royal gold. More silver…"

One legionnaire's ear twitched and seemed to point toward Echo, and Miriam swallowed. Unnatural.

In the near distance, an engine growled and a marked SecTeam prowler and a pair of wasp bikes turned the corner, leading a caravan of people-movers toward the transportation depot. The sight set off the crowd and the stench of hate grew like something rotten, mingling with the musty harbor air. Miriam grimaced as the shouted insults merged in an increasing roar. She froze. For a second, she could hear unearthly howls and feel the heat of napalm as it scorched against her face.

"Tan."

Miriam nodded at Yuri and hurried after her teammates who had moved toward the receiving lanes and station. Her heart pounded faster as they stopped meters away.

Several seconds passed before the first alty stepped out, and then others followed in a line. From a distance, they looked normal—paler, but almost impossible to differentiate from humans. Though they had probably spent days in transit, their hygiene and dress were immaculate. These alties held themselves in high regard. Almost *too* high of regard. She could sense the elitism in their posture. Even the children and adolescents held their chins out.

"There goes the neighborhood," Nas grumbled.

Kai held a glare, then softened. "You were right. These have to be Arshangol's intellectuals. Do you realize how significant this is? We're looking at the brains behind all their science and advancements here in Station City. The Royals must be prioritizing them."

"Prioritizing themselves, you mean. And of course I'm right." Nas's hand fluttered up. "And *their* science, Kai? Really? It's our science, too. It's not our fault they've sabotaged and kept us in the stone age. Plus, *their* science didn't really do much to prevent *their* civil war, did it?"

Krill hushed them both.

Miriam eyed the legionnaires and administrators. "Where are the Royals?"

"Probably already locked themselves in the bougie flats City Center gave them."

Kai harrumphed.

The first alties arrived at the station, their smaller frames a staunch contrast to the towering legionnaires. The emissaries' mouths opened and closed, their fingers moving in fast procession. Miriam strained to catch the exchange, but the shouts of the city residents drowned out the conversation.

Once processing was done, the alties moved in an orderly queue toward the depot. Miriam wasn't sure what happened inside, but she assumed the newcomers would receive supplies and provisions before they were shuttled to their new home.

She returned her attention to the sorting point where an alty woman passed. Her dark hair was pulled back in a sleek fashion and her eyes radiated a deep hue of orange, shattered by flecks of yellow, as if a permanent sun had caught her face at an angle. The alty's chin raised at Miriam and though she couldn't understand the muttered words, she understood their tone and the additional caustic look.

These people looked down on her. On all humans.

It was as if Miriam's anger materialized when an object connected sharply with the alty's head. The woman's black hair flung to the side and the thick smacking sound lingered in the air, followed by the clanging of metal on the ground. The alty clutched her face, a line of red seeping between her fingers.

Miriam almost smirked. Alties bled just like humans. Nothing superior in that. But her amusement was cut short. Beside her, the legionnaire turned, and her gut twisted.

"Echo!" Krill's hand sliced in the opposite direction.

A discordant roar erupted as the seething mob bashed against SecTeam shields. Contorted faces surged in a roiling mass, and time stuttered as something sailed through the air toward her.

A firebomb.

Miriam's heart rabbited in her chest and her hand clenched around the grip of her rifle.

In front of her, trash slapped and broke apart on the ground. She blinked. Not a firebomb. Miriam stared at the mess before her attention shot back to the barriers. A SecGuard slipped, and the mass sprung at the sudden opening. Her breath hitched at the snarling faces as glowing eyes barreled toward her.

She blinked again. Dark, but not glowing. Normal human eyes.

Krill's voice boomed out, and her teammates set into a practiced ballet. Most of the enraged civilians were stopped by the company in a heavy clash, but eight individuals dodged and broke through.

"Incoming! I got the one on the right," Yuri shouted. "Tan! Some help!"

With a flick of her hand, Miriam secured her rifle behind her. These were humans. Angry, but still human. Not alties or wunby terrorists. There was no justification for lethal use of force. Not yet, at least.

She squared her body as a curly-haired man charged forward. Her shouts deflected off his barreling momentum. She sidestepped, evaded his outstretched arms, and her hand clawed into a shoulder. His body swung like a scrawny pendulum, but he found his footing, then tried to twist away. Miriam kicked at the inside of his knee, and he staggered to the ground. Before he could get back up, she quickly stabbed her fingers into targeted muscles. He resisted, but a decisive spin of his wrist smothered the attempt quickly.

"Don't," she warned. Her fingers clamped down and his fight left with a whimper. "Stay down."

With his hands restrained, Miriam checked on the others. The charge and rush on the alties had been squashed almost immediately, never making it past Echo. Closest to her, Yuri attended to a stocky woman who screeched curse after curse, even with her cheek smashed into the ground. Nas held a younger man in an armlock, and his foot stomped atop another. Once her own civilian was subdued, Kai moved to assist.

Something shuffled behind Miriam, and she whipped around. The legionnaire stepped back into his position, his hollow eyes watching. Next to him, the emissaries and alties hadn't looked up, as if nothing had happened. Miriam peeked at the legionnaires again. If Echo and the others hadn't intervened, what would they have done? She shrugged away the shiver of possibilities. These civilians were lucky UMF had stepped in.

"Why do you have to be difficult?" Nas chirped, pushing his foot down. The man underneath it squeaked.

Kai placed restraints on the other detainee, but he jerked back. The young man hawked and spit a fat gob of saliva onto her cheek. "Whose fuckin' side you on? UMF should be fuckin' ashamed of you alty-lovers," he seethed through clenched teeth.

Before Kai could wipe her face, a shadow blurred by, and a giant fist slammed into the man's jaw. Miriam's eyes widened, a command at the tip of her tongue, but Fox had already backed away, sucking his teeth. Impervious to the lead and second's admonishments, their teammate turned on his heel and stormed toward the depot. A just-processed alty couple rocked back as he pushed past.

"Let me. I've got it," Miriam said, transferring her detained subject to a company marine who had jogged up. She called after Fox, his surname gritted out between clamped teeth. His protectiveness of Kai was understandable, but he had intervened with zero tact. Was he trying to get himself—Echo —in trouble? Fox's recent temperamental moods within the UMF compound were one matter, but this outburst had been flagrantly public. There were too many eyes on them, both alty and civilian.

"Fox!" She reached for his elbow.

At her touch, he wheeled around so suddenly she almost barreled into his chest, a familiar scent in her face.

"Shit. Are you drunk right now?" she hissed under her breath as she searched his eyes for dilation, his face for any flush.

"Relax, Tan."

"Relax? Seriously?" She glanced over her shoulder. Though they were out of earshot of the others, the alties could probably hear them. Her voice lowered again. "Level with me. Have you been drinking?"

He huffed.

"Fox."

"No."

Miriam leaned in and sniffed. The smell of alcohol wasn't there anymore. Had she imagined it? "When's the last time you did?"

Fox narrowed his eyes and pushed his face closer to hers—a challenge. "You policin' me? Nothin' in the regs about drinkin' in my own time, Tanner."

"You hit an unarmed—"

"That shitstain insulted Kai."

"That's not enough, you know that."

"Don't give a shit. You gonna rat on me?"

A muscle in Miriam's cheek twitched, and she glared up. *That* offended her. If he was under the influence, she'd figure out another way to go about it—discuss it with Krill, maybe. Fox's outburst here would hopefully go unnoticed and this situation could pass without major consequences, but if it happened again…

"Do we need to talk about this?"

Fox scoffed and started to turn.

"Hey, we're not done—"

The man stopped, and Miriam froze. Noise grew behind her, and she angled back. This time, the commotion didn't come from the marines or protesting crowd. A murmur spread through the Altered lines like a wave, and at the crest, an ugly shriek wailed out. Miriam's skin bristled and the haunting sound pierced through her as it died and another called out in its wake.

What now?

She hurried back with Fox in tow, her eyes searching alty faces. It was a strange and eerie sight; some had paled, their stares forlorn. Hands clutched their necks, faces, and their companions. Others cried out, both audible and not. When she rejoined her teammates, even the marines and apprehended rioters stilled to watch.

"Krill. What's happening?"

The team lead shook his head.

One legionnaire pushed into a column and took a small datapad from a petrified alty. Miriam couldn't make out the soldier's face as he read whatever was on the screen, but his broad shoulders tensed, then deflated.

"The network," Kai whispered. She repeated it louder. "Check the network."

"There's nothing up yet," Nas muttered, already a step ahead. "They're getting something live that we don't have access to. Is it another attack?"

No, this was something worse.

Miriam's instincts screamed as she gravitated toward the tented station, one foot in front of the other. Her body and brain conflicted, she cautiously observed the towering legionnaire, but he made no movement toward her. None of the alties acknowledged her presence as she stepped closer and peered at the datapad.

At the top of the screen, the characters were partially comprehensible to her, but she didn't need the words. The moving image was enough. A building—what must have once been a beautiful and ornate palace—burned, flames licking out and up. In the foreground, a naked body swung with a sign around its neck. Behind a once-powerful Sovereign, corpses swayed in the air in layering rows. Arshangol, the capital and seat of the Altered government, had fallen.

6

———

REUNION

Sam toweled her hair. From a sliver of the covered mirror, a blue eye stared back at her. She ignored the question. "How's the news affecting Ursus?"

Her cuff chimed, confirming the sent message. She surveyed her sparse studio, tossed the towel into the cramped bathroom, then picked at the hem of her shirt. She could easily change into more comfortable clothes and settle in for the night.

A call request filled her display. Sam sighed, then arranged herself—angling her body so the day-old scrapes and bruising didn't show—before she gestured, extending the holo out where Scott's face appeared with eyes narrowed.

"So? Is the outpost back on high alert? Are they sending units to the border?"

He said nothing, motioned nothing. If not for a slight movement in his hair, she could've sworn she was talking to a picture.

"You're really not going to tell me?" She huffed. If the network was correct, Arshangol was in Apostate control. The Altered's capital was landlocked and a distance from the border regions, but Sam was antsy. In the South, the Apostates had blazed through human settlements in a matter of days. The northern human territories were more technologically advanced in comparison, but it was still disconcerting and problematic, especially with Arshangol's deterioration within months.

"This is more important than a stupid team dinner."

Was Echo her team? They had been for a temporary mission, and yes, Sam had felt a closer affinity with them than the Ursus groups she and her brother normally worked with. Regardless, she wasn't truly a teammate. She wasn't even technically SOG at the moment.

Her brother's hands lifted into view. IF I TELL YOU, WILL YOU GO?

Sam wrinkled her nose.

PROMISE.

If that's what it took to get him to spill any information. "Sure. Fine. I promise." He couldn't see her full frame, but she had already dressed for the occasion in the nicest civilian clothes she owned. Which wasn't much. The outfit was plain and modest.

Scott studied her for a second longer before he shrugged. WE'RE WAITING. READY. YOU KNOW HOW IT IS. THE NORTH WON'T GIVE UP ANY LAND.

It was true. The North was stubborn. And most of the region was inhabited by UMF pensioners, marines who had completed their seven contracts, retired and richer with their earned acre of land. The pensioners weren't active anymore, but they had grit, and their muscles still held the memory of military training.

IT'S ALMOST DARK SEASON.

Sam's eye twitched. The days were getting shorter, and though she was used to a life of dark seasons, she didn't miss it. The next months would be full of long nights that brought out the worst in everyone. Humans and Altered.

"What's happening at the FOBs?"

Scott tilted his head, and Sam sneered internally. OpSec. He couldn't say anything to risk the security of Ursus's operations over this unencrypted channel. She knew the drill, but she didn't like it. She hated being on the outside, sidelined.

The latest news had come while she was at an occupational therapy session, and Sam was still trying to digest everything and what it'd mean for UMF and Ursus. How had Arshangol fallen so fast? How did the Apostates have the numbers? The strength? She hated not knowing, the lack of control. Everything was over her head. Since the attack on Ursus, there had been almost no other human confrontations with the Altered terrorists elsewhere. At least not anything reported on the network.

Sam's heart sank as Scott played with the chain around his neck. "You're assigned, aren't you?" From his expression, she already knew the answer. "FOB Domovoy? Who are you going up with? Titan-3?"

He shook his head and pointed a finger inward. Just him. Just the recon unit. His fingers flurried together as he tried to reassure her about the other units already at the forward operating base, but she looked away.

Fuck.

Scott's new partner, Ace, was competent, and he'd been at Ursus for two contracts, but he was a recent first-term addition to SOG. He wasn't her. How did they communicate? Sam knew Scott; she knew how he worked. And he knew how she worked. They were siblings and had been at each other's side in SOG for two contracts—seven years. What if something happened to him?

"Sam."

Her attention shifted back to his voice, to his holographic face and his moving hands. DON'T WORRY. IT'S LIKE ANY NORMAL DAY. NORMAL OPERATIONS.

Right. Normal. Altered terrorists who wanted the extinction of humans, who had never been organized before and were *suddenly* organized, had sprung up and overthrown a generations-old government that, although also awful, had mainly tolerated and ignored the human race. Normal. And if the Apostates continued their ambitions, Scott was going to be at the front lines.

"It's my fault."

Scott's face contorted in confusion.

"Your contract."

He squinted. I CHOSE THIS. THIS IS NOT YOUR FAULT.

Sam stared at her feet and crimped her toes on the cool floor. "But you're—"

"Sammy," Scott said.

She looked up. He rarely called her that, and he was the only one allowed to.

His hands moved swiftly. I CHOSE THIS.

"Because of me." Something in her jaw pulsed as they stared at each other through the display.

BECAUSE THIS IS BIGGER THAN ME. WITH EVERYTHING HAPPENING, HOW CAN I SIT THIS OUT? I'M CAPABLE.

Sam frowned. Her brother hadn't meant it that way, but the unintentional jab at her uselessness was painful.

AND WHEN YOU'RE BACK, WE'LL DO THIS TOGETHER. AFTER IT'S DONE, I CAN FINALLY SIT AT HOME, TRY MY HAND AT FARMING, AND DO NOTHING ELSE. OKAY? He offered a weak smile. SO, DINNER?

Sam scrunched her face. The team dinner was so trivial compared to the looming threat of Apostates. "Why are they doing this? It feels wrong."

I DOUBT THEY'RE CELEBRATING. ECHO PROBABLY NEEDS IT. FOR MORALE.

"Morale."

Scott's eyes cut through the holodisplay, and Sam flinched as though she had received a reprimand. WE ALL NEED SOMETHING GOOD RIGHT NOW.

She tensed. Selfish idiot. Everything was crumbling and on

the brink of collapse around them. Not just her. Sam mumbled an incoherent apology.

Go socialize.

"Is that an order? I'm not really in SOG or UMF," she quipped with a manicured smile. "And you're not the boss of me."

Scott's eyelids fluttered, and a hoarse voice pushed past his lips. "It'll be quick. You'll be back to annoy me like you always do." He added in sign, You promised.

"You didn't tell me anything of worth."

But I told you, didn't I?

Her lip curled.

Scott tapped his wrist. I'll know if you don't go.

Sam rolled her eyes. Part of her *did* want to go to the dinner. After a month away, she wanted that connection to UMF, even if it was only in proximity and association. She sorely missed being around other marines, around others who understood her lifestyle, her identity, but part of her was afraid. Her last encounter with Miriam was one thing, especially after Sam's subsequent escape from her apartment with only a thin excuse for cover. It was another thing, a tremendous step, to reunite with five other marines who had also seen her at her worst.

Scott stared expectantly, and she begrudgingly returned his gaze. After a long second, she caved. "I don't get it. You're so far away. I don't know how you can still be this irritating."

Scott smirked. You miss me.

She snorted.

◊

If she passed by on a regular day, Sam wouldn't have given the restaurant a second thought. Its facade was small and underwhelming, decorated by a sign missing a few light nodes and stained with age and weather. Her footsteps padded softly as she paced across the street at an angle, ensuring she wasn't visible through the window. She checked her commcuff again. She was late. Uncharacteristically so. And only made later by her hesitation now.

Her stomach growled in betrayal and she tugged her hood, then adjusted the extra fabric on her right sleeve once more. To think she used to run with little to no qualms into much worse situations. Firefights, Apostate attacks, human terrorists? Sam could do all that. But a team dinner? This was her undoing.

Fuck it.

She propelled herself toward the eatery, entering before she could dither more. Well past the usual dinnertime, the establishment had few customers, but the abundance of tables and seating hinted at its popularity. Echo's noise caught her attention before she could spot them. Among the chatter, Yuri's hearty laugh bounced across the warm space. The six—no, seven—marines were in a mix of UMF and civilian wear, lounging at a long table in the back.

Panic boiled in her stomach, and she gritted her teeth. This was a mistake. Sam took a step back, reconsidering. But a petite hostess spotted her from the kitchen cutout, already moving forward, a greeting on her tongue.

It was cut short.

"Holy shit. Is that—"

A chair scraped harshly against the floor. The table hushed, and everyone's gaze turned toward the entrance. Toward her.

Sam froze. Her face warmed, and she steadied herself with a deep breath. Her eyes found Miriam—a lopsided smirk etched across her face—and Sam raised her hand to the group. There was no turning away now. Before she could figure out her next step, a sudden blur knocked her off balance. Arms squeezed around her, and Sam failed at holding back an embarrassing squeak. Her hand, stuck in an awkward position, patted Kai's hip.

"You're actually here? Is this real?" The engineer specialist pulled back and studied her intently.

Sam chuckled sheepishly and nodded before Kai guided her to the table, where the rest of the group welcomed her with hugs and affectionate thumps on her back. Her former teammates bombarded her with questions, their voices overlapping in a jumbled symphony that left her struggling to respond with anything more than nods and smiles.

"The golden locks, gone!"

"You look great, Valky," Yuri said. "Don't listen to Nas. I love what you've done with your hair."

Sam's chest tightened with a mix of panic and annoyance, overwhelmed by the focused attention.

"What are you doing here?" Kai asked. "How long have you been in town?"

"Alright, alright," Miriam's voice cut through the chaos. "Give the poor woman some space."

And then Sam could breathe, as if the air had opened. She turned at a gentle touch to the small of her back, and Miriam mouthed a greeting with a smile in her light brown eyes. A comforting warmth unfurled within Sam's gut.

"No one's going to introduce me?"

An unknown individual hovered at the edge of Echo's reunion. His complexion, slightly darker than Nas's, complemented his smooth features. Heavy brows framed a pair of curious dark eyes as they fixed on her.

Krill cleared his throat. "It's damn good to see you, Valk. This is Jace."

"Iniko Jace. I'm a 'once-Echo,'" he announced with a grin. "And I know who you are. I've read the reports extensively. You and your brother did great work in Ursus. Sam Ryan, callsign Valkyrie."

Sam forced a nod, feeling awkward about the praise. She never quite learned how to take a compliment, and frankly, didn't think she ever would.

"Alright, intel-guy. Stop showing off." Krill clapped him on the shoulder. "This guy's too good for us, sitting at the top."

Jace shrugged him off and laughed. "The top. Right. More like MED yoinked me and, well, y'all know the rest."

Sam's curiosity piqued. "MED pulled you out of SOG?"

With a slight grimace, he cracked his knuckles and shook his leg. "Well, no—"

Nas leaned in. "Does it matter? He's BigInt now. Took a temporary assignment during his probation period, and the asshole did such a good job, they stole him from us."

"Too smart for us loonies," Fox grumbled as he sat and pitched his drink back.

"Smart? Ha! Smarter than the team? Perhaps." He grinned at the others then shifted to the gruff marine. "Than you, Fox? Definitely. Save some alcohol for us and the city, yeah buddy?"

Fox dismissed him with an inebriated chuckle.

With her initial alarm and doubt diminished, Sam found a seat, and the rest of the group followed suit: Jace and Nas next to her, Fox, Miriam, and Yuri on the other side, with Kai and Krill in the center. She glanced at Miriam again, whose brows unfurrowed when she caught Sam's eye. As a cup and plate were set in front of her, Sam muttered a thanks, still overwhelmed by the social flurry.

"When did you get in?" Krill said.

"You should've told us! We would've met you," Kai added.

Sam flushed, and her arm instinctively crossed over her chest. She fidgeted with the fabric over her shoulder. The last thing she wanted was for Echo to find out she had been in the city and avoided them all for an entire month. "I, well..."

"You're here for one of the programs?"

Relief flooded Sam as she stole another look at Miriam and nodded.

"Of course. Which one?" Krill asked.

"Station General."

Miriam blinked and frowned.

"Hey! Tan's parents run that one. It's the best in the city. Hell, anywhere." Yuri tutted and Sam caught his stern glare at

Miriam before he turned back. "How is it? Are they taking good care of you?"

Sam nodded again. She had known Miriam had gone to higher university and came from a wealthier class, but the news of her family's connection to the hospital was a surprise. That entire time, she was a degree of separation away from Miriam. She took a sip of the drink in front of her, but her tongue recoiled, and Sam stifled a cough. The alcohol was very strong. The last time she had drank, things hadn't gone well. She set the cup down, nudging it and the memory of Miriam's rejection away.

"So? How's recovery going?"

"Shit, Krill, you make it sound like she's an addict," Miriam cut in.

The lead's mouth drooped.

Hiding another cough with her hand, Sam adjusted her position so her right shoulder angled behind her. "The program's fine. It's mostly retraining with mobility exercises."

Jace nodded. "And a prosthetic? I assume they'll fit you with one."

"The procedure's next week."

Across the table, Miriam straightened. Sam intently poked at the food on her plate.

"Do you know what model?" Jace asked. "I've seen a couple before, but those marines were in LOGS and Administration."

Sam winced. She didn't want to hear that. "The hospital, UMF, and some tech lab signed off on a prototype."

Nas's eyes widened. "Which lab? Advanced Biotics? Baihu? No, they don't do prosthetics. GenTech? Verte—"

"Sorry, I don't really know." Sam didn't follow the latest technologies like Nas did.

His disappointment was short-lived. "How long's the procedure?"

"A day?"

"That's lengthy. With all the latest improvements, at least.

Nerve synchronization takes a while, but not that long." His voice dropped as he muttered to himself. "Stabilization? Spinal sync? You must be getting something with better reactivity and function, especially for…" Nas gestured at her right side. Kai threw her napkin at him, but he waved her away. He then knocked himself on his forehead as if it had all become clear. To him, at least. "Of course. The last reports had something in the works. Maybe that's it? I can't believe UMF would approve something like that, though, but I guess you're you. Makes sense for a field test. Not my area of expertise, but they'll connect nerves, muscles, even bone structure."

"Nas, breathe," Miriam said, her eyes apologetic.

Sam shrugged. She always seemed to be an experiment for UMF. They allowed her to be raised on an outpost, then made her their poster child. Sometimes, successful experiments had perks.

Kai winced. "Sounds painful."

Sam's head bobbed. It probably would be, but if pain meant she'd have utility, it was worth the cost.

"And then you'll return to SOG? Well, after MED and whatever clearance gauntlet they'll run you through, of course."

Sam's face fell, but she forced it back up. "That's the plan."

"Will Mute be here? To accompany you?"

"No."

Miriam leaned in. "You're doing this by yourself?"

"What?" Kai exclaimed. "No, that won't do. We'll be there."

Krill raised his hand. "About that." He hesitated. "I'm sorry, Valk. We can't."

"What do you mean? Of course we'll be there."

Miriam frowned, but then she leaned back into her chair, folding her arms. "The mission came through. We have the green light?"

Krill nodded. "Heading out in two days. Just got the news before this, and I was going to mention it, well, now, I guess."

Sam swallowed back disappointment and jealousy while Nas hooted and Fox raised his cup high before tipping it back.

Miriam returned a soft gaze to Sam. "I can have someone swing by the hospital for you."

"No, that's okay. I'll be fine." She didn't want anyone to witness her weakness.

Kai sighed. "Well, that's equally disappointing and exciting, I guess. Sorry, Valk. Unless you'd be able to push it until we're back?"

Sam shook her head, trying to mask her horror at postponing her opportunity for normalcy.

"We'll see you when we get back then." The engineer perked up. "And after, you'll join Echo? After everything, of course."

Join Echo? Sam hadn't thought about that at all. She fidgeted in her chair, itching to conceal her right stump, but she tucked her hand underneath her thigh instead.

"One step at a time," Miriam said, either a warning or reassurance—Sam couldn't tell.

"Either way, you'll do great. Is there anything we can do to help?"

"Yeah," Yuri said. "Where do you plan on working out? Can we help with training? I can't imagine General has the best gym, or at least what you're used to. Come over to ours." He waved away Sam's look of doubt. "It's SOG's. You're still one of us."

She mumbled gratitude. While the hospital facilities were impressive, she had been training with their civilian resources for military-specific movements and applications. An SOG gym would have what she needed to get back to SOG standards. But it also meant she'd have to show her face, and frankly, that was terrifying as well.

"If you end up wanting to stay here, if you want to transfer, I'll put in the request. We'd love to have you and your brother here with us full-time," said Krill.

"You can replace Nas," Fox grumbled. He grunted shortly after—an elbow nudged into his side.

Thankfully, the conversation turned elsewhere. It gave her time to savor the delicious aroma and taste of the food in front of her. In between bites, Sam discreetly studied the Echo marines, captivated by their camaraderie. She tried to gather the hazy details of their upcoming mission—not much, they were being guarded or they simply didn't know—and observed as their bodies and tongues relaxed the more they imbibed. Her eyes lingered on the growing stack of cups surrounding Fox, while Miriam and Yuri exchanged occasional glances.

"—wish you all a great victory day! Our fates—"

Heads whipped toward Nas, who palmed his commcuff. He mumbled an apology. "Just wanted to see if there were any updates."

"You thought the network would have information before BigInt?" Yuri gestured a finger at Jace.

With a shrug, the former Echo teammate responded, "You'd be surprised. We don't have enough information coming out of Altered territories. Less now."

"Did we ever? Have information, I mean." Yuri said. "What happened? A few days ago, the Royals were confident. They had the numbers, the support, Legion."

"Even with the new embassy?" Kai added. "City Center said—"

Jace laughed. "I'm not sure politicians know what 'cooperation' means. The lip service that's happening at their levels isn't trickling into actionable anything."

"Seems about right. It's not like we're scrambling to give them our information either." Yuri scratched his head with the end of his utensil.

Nas scoffed. "Yeah. Beyond our city and resources, what more can we give them?"

"The situation's getting worse. More riots and protesters

every day. Foxtrot said another one broke out downtown. Is that close to where you're staying, Valk?"

Sam looked up from her plate at Echo's second, aware he was trying to bring her back into the conversation. "I'm closer to the medical sector."

A hush fell over the table, possibly anticipating further discussion—something about her apartment, routine, or her. Sam's leg bounced as she racked her brain, searching for anything more to contribute. "I actually ran into some Altered the other day. I think it might've been a Roy—"

"You met a Royal?" Kai's jaw dropped.

Sam shrunk back as the table stared at her with an unnerving intensity. Anger sharpened in the back of her throat. Why did she have to say anything? She swallowed it back and nodded. "She invited me to the embassy."

Jace leaned closer. "And? You're taking that offer, right?"

"I wasn't planning to..." It hadn't crossed Sam's mind. She had the impression the Royal's offer was only a polite courtesy. "Lip service" as the BigInt marine said. Even if she had been interested, it wasn't part of her schedule. Or her priorities.

"But you should. This is big. The only official line to the Royals is through City Center, but UMF doesn't have a seat in their meetings, if there *are* any meetings. You happened upon an organic channel and a tremendous opportunity. You have to take up that invite! Imagine the good it can do for UMF. Your brother's up North, right? What if they have info that could help Ursus?"

That grabbed Sam's attention. She could be useful, especially while she waited for her broken body to be fixed. But doubt tugged at her mind. She had fundamental training in intelligence collection and sensitive site exploitation, but how effectively could she actually apply it?

"If you're uncertain about it, don't worry. I can hold your hand through it, hell, have you introduce me—"

Miriam cleared her throat. "Jace, I don't know. These aren't just *any* alties. It could be dangerous. It *is* dangerous. She should focus on her procedure and recovery next week."

Sam gulped as Miriam's statement reminded her of the red-eyed bodyguard. Was the cost worth the benefit?

"Dangerous?" Jace swooped his utensil in the air. "We're in Station City."

Miriam sighed. "That's not the statement you think it is anymore."

The man turned back to Sam. "Take up the Royal's offer and see how it goes. It's just talking, and if you're not comfortable, that's that, but I doubt that you're ever uncomfortable; you've gone against much worse."

She would've scoffed at the inaccuracy of that statement, but his flattering confidence made her consider. It *was* a chance for Sam to do something. "Maybe. I'll think about it."

"Please. And let me know." Jace beamed.

"Lucky. I'd love to see what they brought over."

Yuri tossed a wad of bread at Nas. "I thought you were excited about this next mission."

"I was excited for the new tech, not another vague mission," Nas said. "Do we know what we're doing? Or is the boss holding out on us?"

Krill crossed his arms. "I'm not holding out on any of you. And if I were, we're not talking about it here."

Nas nudged Kai before he stood. "That means he doesn't know what we're doing."

Kai sighed, and turned back to Sam. "I wish you were coming with us."

"But it might be better that you aren't. With my luck, it'll be lame," Nas said over his shoulder as he moved to the serving counter.

If she could, Sam would take any mission, lame or not, but she held her tongue. Instead, she followed Miriam's sightline to the slight limp in Nas's left leg. The medic stood and followed him to assist, and Sam returned to the ongoing conversation at the table.

"Tan, I'm fine!" Nas returned, a tray of drinks in hand, with Miriam on his heels.

"I swear…" she grumbled.

Nas placed the tray down and dropped into his seat. "It's *fine*. I'm walking and doing everything fine. Okay, it acts up now and then; it's not my fault the first sessions didn't take. You'd think with MedTech these days…"

Miriam's hands threw into the air. "You're supposed to continue the sessions. Maybe if you actually took your recovery seriously. Like her!" She gestured across the table. "You're making my job difficult, Nas."

He groaned. "We're not at work, *Tan*."

"Fine. As a friend, then."

Jace grabbed a drink. "Tan's right, you know. Please don't make it an intel thing. We'll never hear the end of it."

Nas shot an exaggerated glare. "I already never hear the end of it."

"Do it." The marines turned to Sam. Her own voice was a surprise. She cleared her throat, a crumb of anger stuck there. "You can at least fix it."

Nas's eyes swept to her right shoulder, then dropped.

"You don't want to become like me," Jace jested as he rapped his left shin against the table. It gave a metallic thwack. A prosthetic.

Fox snorted and slurred, "That'd be an improvement."

The air returned, and nervous chuckles scattered. Sam bit the inside of her lip until she tasted the tang of copper. She hadn't meant to bring down the mood. As the table reignited in separate conversations, she excused herself and slipped out of the restaurant. A squatting cook on a smoke break paid her no mind, and the cloying scent mixed with the city's fumes in the cool air. Over the past months, she had intentionally and unintentionally isolated herself, aside from the necessary interactions with program staff. She was glad she'd joined the dinner; she'd actually missed Echo more than she'd expected, but the dive back into socializing was overwhelming.

With the momentary breather, Sam sorted the maelstrom in her head, pulling each string of thought out of a tangled pile. She mulled over the Royal's invitation and the idea of training at the SOG gym. Massaging her shoulder, Sam gazed at the space above where the city's light pollution erased all traces of stars and satellites. Thoughts of Ursus flooded her mind, remembering the vastness and the glittering sky in the observation posts far away. The night would shimmer with a mesmerizing array of universes and lost opportunities beyond. A wave of homesickness hit her, stirring up a whirlwind of emotions. She missed Scott.

"Hey."

Sam startled and spun to see Miriam approach. The thought of their previous meetings flitted through her mind, but she recomposed herself. Somehow, this woman always managed to sneak up on her, physically and mentally.

"Sorry."

Sam shook her head.

"The team's thrilled you're here." Miriam chuckled. "But they can be a bit much."

A faint smile played on Sam's lips as she shifted her stump behind her. Was the medic happy she was there? Sam still didn't have a good apology or explanation for why she hadn't messaged or told anyone about her presence in Station City. Or why she had left the apartment before Miriam returned. She hoped Miriam wouldn't ask.

"You've been avoiding me."

Sam jerked her head. "No, I—" She huffed when she noticed Miriam's smirk. Her phantom finger scratched at a phantom thumb. She had made a move on Miriam before...before everything, and the woman had rejected her. Miriam just wanted to be friends. "I've been—I haven't..." Sam fumbled with her words before realizing she didn't know how to finish the sentence.

Miriam waited, then nodded. "It's okay. I'm just glad you're here. I missed you."

"You missed me?"

"Yes."

A sharp jolt shot up her arm, and she grimaced, clutching her shoulder. The pain, as quickly as it had come, passed. Embarrassment and shame consumed her, and she turned away. She felt Miriam's touch graze her back, but Sam instinctively shrugged it off, a gesture she immediately regretted.

"Phantom pains?"

Sam nodded and took a step away; Miriam was too close.

"What do they have you on? I can get you meds if—"

"No." Sam shook her head curtly and faced the woman. "But thank you."

"Okay." Miriam hummed with hesitation. "How are you? Otherwise?"

A vehicle drove by, its occupants howling in song and laughter.

"We never grabbed that coffee. You weren't..." The woman trailed off.

After Miriam had messaged the other day, Sam had left a flimsy excuse. The medic had provided no mention of the other woman in her apartment, and Sam didn't want to be the one to bring it up. And how was she otherwise? What could she respond to that? That every day was a struggle? That Sam knew she was making progress, but it was frustrating and slow, and she felt no closer to rejoining SOG? She couldn't.

A soft breeze brushed the tiny hairs on her neck, and Sam flinched.

Miriam apologized and lowered her hand. Her brows knitted together. "I thought I saw this from across the table. Where did you get these scrapes from?"

"It's nothing. Just a stupid scuffle."

"Alties? Charonites?"

Sam shook her head.

Miriam sighed. "You get a break from UMF, from all of this, and you're still getting into scuffles. Why am I not surprised?" She leaned into the wall and smirked again.

They lapsed into silence, their attention captured by the traffic passing by. The city never seemed to sleep, and despite a month spent there, Sam was still adjusting to the hustle and crowd. She still felt like a stranger, a visitor, alone in a sea of people.

"I'm sorry. About before. Your apartment, I mean. And the other stuff, too."

"No, I'm sorry. I didn't know Ana was going to do that. She, well, I..." Miriam stopped. "It doesn't matter. I'd still like to catch up. How long are you here?"

Ana. So Miriam knew. Sam let the words roll a few times in her mind before she remembered the woman was waiting for a response. "Hopefully not long. I just want to get back to normal, get back to how things were. Scott said I should take however long I need, but I need to be back. And yes, we can catch up," she added.

Miriam observed her for a moment before she spoke. "Well, let me know how I can help."

Sam gave a weak smile. *Friends*, she reminded herself. The woman wanted to just be friends.

7

MISSION

KAI'S EYES BULGED. "We're going *where*?"

That explained the new equipment. Miriam squinted at the open boxes in the corner of their team room.

"There's nothing there! That's in the radiation zone."

"Technically, it's on the *border* of the radiation zone." Nas winced as he propped his feet up on the table.

"Same difference."

He balanced a semi-translucent cylinder on his palm. "I thought we were going to join the rest of Razor. Head back south with Bravo and Charlie, or Ursus with the others. The latest reports from recon say there's Legion movement across the strait. Which we all know means the wunbies are expanding east."

"Already?"

"It still needs to be substantiated, but something's going to pop off in the coming months, and what are we doing anyway? A week near a rad-zone in the middle of nowhere. Even if whatever this is is relevant, a week's a bit long for my comfort."

"Worried 'bout your sperm count?" Fox grunted. "As if anyone would want kids with you."

Kai shook her head. "He's worried about his beautiful skin and hair."

"No, assholes," Nas quipped. "I'm worried about my DNA."

Miriam shared an amused look with Yuri at the front of the table. As per usual, their pre-departure brief had barely started and it was already derailing. She didn't mind this time—it was easier to find amusement in her teammates' banter than to focus on the thought of another strange mission. It was an odd feeling. She hadn't been conflicted with missions before, and as much as she wanted to get out of the city, away from the alties, and stay busy, something was holding her back. Maybe she was too exhausted to process anything properly.

"So what exactly are we doing? We haven't trained for maneuvers in this environment and there's nothing out there."

Krill folded his arms and glared at Nas. "If you ever let me finish a damn sentence, I could tell you. You know that, right?" He sighed and pinched the bridge of his nose. "It's not our usual tempo, but we're delivering this to some location along the coast." He pointed at a small, airtight package sitting on top of the table.

Nas groaned. "Right. We're a delivery service now. And if that's *actually* the mission, what a fantastic use of SOG. Elite units, my ass. There's nothing even out there."

The lead ignored him. "Coordinates show it's not too far north, so we're taking the cruiser. And before you ask, instructions have been minimal." He flipped around a strange tablet—an old-generation device with a narrow display. Two lines of smaller text stared back at the team. "This is literally everything I've received. I promise I'm not holding anything back."

"Command fuckin' us over again," Fox muttered.

Miriam kept her mouth shut but silently agreed. It was a simple mission on the surface, but they all knew it could be something else. What happened to the days where their objectives were direct and straightforward? Were those days gone with the new threat, the new generation of wunbies?

"Why do we get this cryptic shit when the other teams are getting some?"

Miriam turned. "Getting some? Really, Nas? Are you a recruit?"

"We're SOG. What's the point of this diamond tab when we've been downgraded to security guards running errands? What is it, anyway?" He poked a finger toward the parcel. "Better be the key to the weapon of all weapons, or the origin of life. Something good, at least."

"I thought you'd be more excited. Between the location and cautioned discretion, you like this cryptic stuff." Krill's hand waved, and he turned to the team second. "Anything else I'm missing?"

Yuri shook his head. "Don't expect to have any comms once we get within the zone. Receiving *and* transmitting."

"Right. With that, I recommend everyone get squared away before we head out. Hopefully we learn more as we go. Stay flexible."

Fox scoffed as he stood and made for the door. Miriam watched after him, then caught Kai's eye.

"Maybe he was right," the engineer whispered. "We *are* being punished."

◊

From the back door of the SOG building, it was easy to spot the brightness of blond hair in contrast to the surrounding equipment of the outdoor gym. Miriam dipped her head at a Spartan-8 marine as she passed, weaving between the machines. The place was emptier than usual with most of the teams deployed.

In the next row, Miriam stopped and leaned on a weight

rack. She watched Sam and smiled at the tuft of hair sticking out on the back of the woman's head. A line of perspiration bled through the spine of her shirt and a dark harness outlined it. The asymmetry was still strange, and Miriam reminded herself not to let her eyes hover too long. Although Sam's body seemed to ripple now, a live-wire network of muscles, Miriam had seen the cracks in confidence and the frailty in their brief encounters. Even if Sam tried to mask it.

Regardless, watching her repetitions now, Miriam was impressed. Of course, she was biased. She had been impressed ever since the woman saved her life in the South, at those cliffs. Sam was strong. And determined. Miriam had never met someone so intense.

"Fox mentioned you were here," she said, after Sam placed her weight down. "I'm glad you took up Yuri's offer."

Blond hair bobbed as the woman stiffened.

Miriam raised her hand apologetically. "Shit. Sorry, I did it again." She wasn't trying to sneak up on the woman; Miriam had been quiet since she was little, careful not to alert her parents in their separate bedrooms when she snuck out.

Sam adjusted her sleeve and turned around. "I forgot how much I missed this. Echo's heading out soon?"

"In a bit. We just finished the brief. Checks, LOGS, you know how it goes."

Sam's cheek twitched.

"But anyway, this was good timing," Miriam continued. "I was going to message. We'll be radio silent for a week or so, until we're back, of course."

She was glad Sam was there so she didn't have to hunt her down. The woman's responses were more reliable now, but there was a reluctance and stiffness in her words. And was it good timing? Miriam had just found Sam, only to leave the city before they could reconnect. The entire month they'd been there, a few sectors apart and nothing. She pushed the pang of hurt away.

"Ursus?"

"No. We're going, well…" Miriam wanted to tell her about the delivered rad-suits, the strange mission, but she couldn't, not with the indicated discretion.

Sam exhaled. "It's fine, I get it. Need to know only."

Miriam bit the inside of her cheek. "Is there anything you need before we leave? Before your procedure?"

"No," the woman replied shortly. She pulled at her shirt collar and dabbed the sweat beading on her neck in the brief silence, then added in a softer tone, "But thank you. Just feeling left out."

"You're almost there. You'll be back in no time." Miriam wanted to place a reassuring hand on Sam's shoulder, but the couple meters between them seemed to stretch and expand. "I'm sorry I'll miss it. I want to be there. For you."

Sam's lips pressed together, then broke apart. "It's okay. It'll be pretty uneventful. Jace already offered—"

"Jace?" A pit grew in Miriam's gut.

"It's not the same, but he's been through it, too. He has his prosthetic, and we're going to chat about the Royals, the embassy…"

Sam and her former teammate had only met the previous day. Miriam hadn't realized they were already talking. The pit in her gut snaked its tendrils out, and she tried to keep a composed face. Discussing tradecraft and work-related topics was one thing, but offering to be with Sam at a significant procedure? That toed the line of something else.

"I think this is something I'd like to do by myself, though," Sam said.

Miriam exhaled. "Can I arrange something with the hospital? I might know one or two people…" She held back from rolling her eyes. Growing up around the medical center could count for something other than a lonely childhood and the daunting pressure of future expectations.

"It's really okay. The program has me covered. And I live close to the center. It's not a big deal."

"Are you sure?" Miriam's eyebrow arched. "I tried looking up what I could, and I don't know about the tech, but that op sounds…" She didn't finish her sentence, worried that she was now making things worse.

Sam nodded. "I appreciate it, but I'll be okay. They said recovery should be fast. If not…" She inhaled. Her blue eyes flashed to the space where her right arm had once been. "It can't be worse than this."

"Well, I hope everything goes alright. Please keep me updated? I won't see anything for a while, but please do. I'll worry if I don't get anything from you." Sam gave her a look, and Miriam winked. "Friends worry. Let me worry for you."

◊

Jellyfishing boats shrunk to little specks, and the city's structures merged as the UMF scout cruiser pulled further out to sea. When it was all but a line with the horizon, Miriam turned away from the small port window and joined Fox on the other side of the bay. He sat on the locker bench, limply holding his light machine gun across his thighs. He made no acknowledgment to her, his eyes unfocused, staring into the middle distance.

A memory of Sam checking her carbine on the same bench skipped through Miriam's mind. She shrugged it away and found work in checking her kit. Her hand patted various pockets and packs where medication, jabbers, gel bandages, trauma shears, tourniquets, and other items sat. Everything was there. Or at least everything she thought they'd need for an unknown mission. Her fingers found the pocket of anti-radiation jabbers and traced over their narrow frames all in a line. She had packed several more, just in case. As she closed her bag, she eyed the vial of enzyme nanocapsules in a stashed compartment. Instant enzymes to break down alcohol intoxication. She glanced over at Fox again. Just in case.

Although done with her checks, Miriam pretended to busy herself in front of the locker as she subtly tried to smell the air around her teammate. Nothing. At least no alcohol. That was a relief and one less thing to worry about.

Fox tapped the cover of his LMG shut. "You're good at some things, Tan, but leave the snoopin' to Nas."

"What?" The word exited Miriam's mouth too innocently, too quickly.

"I haven't broken any rules. You can stop tryna sniff me out. Search my locker, team police." Fox heaved his gun up and carried it to the weapons rack. "What's goin' on with you and blondie?"

Caught off guard, Miriam grimaced as the second "what" fluttered out. "Nothing. What do you mean?"

Fox grunted. "Somethin' happened. Few months ago, both of you were about to blow up in a sex ball and now you're both tiptoein' 'round each other."

Her face scrunched in disgust. "Sex ball? You've been so quiet lately I've forgotten how great you are with words."

"Did you two fuck?"

"Fox." Her voice was low and cutting. A warning.

"Or did you fuck up?"

Her glare stabbed into his back.

"Jus' do somethin' already." He turned; his hazel eyes burned back at her with a sudden seriousness. "Don't got as much time as you think."

Confusion replaced her annoyance. Her words failed as Fox lumbered toward the stairs and the ship's inner workings. Now by herself in the cargo bay, Miriam sat on the bench and stared at the cylindrical capsule inside her locker. She wasn't tiptoeing around Sam. At least she didn't think she was. They had that awkward moment after Sam kissed her, and their conversations had been slightly off since, but they were fine. They were talking, and when the mission was over and Miriam was back, they'd catch up. They'd hang out. Like friends did. Anything beyond one-night stands, arrangements, or friendships was a disaster in waiting. Sam understood that, too.

She plucked the capsule up, opening and unfurling the dark orange contents from within. She shook it until the suit and its sleeves rolled out into its full shape. The thin material rustled, and Miriam examined it for the third time. If she had a choice, she wasn't sure what she preferred: the very tangible, drugged-up alty supremacists or the invisible poison of radiation. Miriam attempted to scrub the thought of both from her mind as she rolled the suit and tucked it back into its container.

"You good?"

Miriam nudged her locker shut. Yuri's boots clanged against the stairs before he came to a stop, leaning on the set of lockers behind her, two mugs of the cruiser pilot's coffee in hand.

She took one. "Yeah."

"Thought it was strange you weren't up by now. Your favorite chair awaits."

Her eyes rolled.

"I saw you with Valk back at base. Guess she's missed UMF. It's still odd though, isn't it? Seeing her like that."

Miriam tilted her head, neither a nod nor a definite answer.

"What were you two chatting about?"

Miriam looked up at the catwalk. It was only the two of them in the bay; the others were probably scattered throughout the rest of the ship. "Her? Or Fox?"

"Your pick, I guess."

She sighed. "I don't really know."

Yuri hummed, unconvinced. "You knew she was in Station. Before the dinner, I mean. I'm guessing you invited her."

Miriam didn't deny it. "I found out a little before. It doesn't matter."

"You tell me about your snacks, your escapades, and the dumbest stuff, Tan." Yuri frowned.

She shrugged. "It slipped my mind. Sorry, I'm tired," she added. As if that were an excuse for everything. But wasn't it true? She lifted the coffee to her lips and hid behind the motion.

Yuri watched her, but when she didn't continue, he acquiesced. "You two alright?"

Her eyes snapped up. "Why? What do you mean?"

"You seem different around her."

"Not you, too," she mumbled.

His eyebrow raised, and they both sipped on their coffee. Rich and aromatic. The pilot brewed magic.

"Fox. He's not getting better."

"No," Yuri replied. "Watching a settlement burn—two, actually—was hard on all of us. For him, losing Jun must've been the tipping point."

Miriam tapped the cup to her bottom lip. "At what point do we intervene?"

"Is MED concerned?"

"*I'm* concerned. As a friend and teammate. MED's too conservative. They'd pull him. I'm not saying I agree with them, but yes, I am concerned, Yuri. He's not himself."

He sighed and looked up at the high ceiling. "Or maybe he *is*, and we don't like it."

"That's dark of you."

Unusually dark for her normally chipper best friend.

His face held its seriousness before it cracked into a sad smile. "Krill's tracking, but Fox's new pastime hasn't impacted the team or mission—" He held up a hand before Miriam could respond. "If we intervene, if MED gets involved, what's the cost? What if Command pulls him? He's better off with us. We're his team, his family." Yuri sighed. "We're all coping in different ways. He just needs a bit more time and love."

Miriam inhaled, then let the breath out slowly. "How are you? Are you sleeping okay?"

"Eh. I've had better days, and I've had worse. Can't complain when I have my health and my friends around me." Yuri rapped his knuckles on the locker's thin metal. "You?"

"Yeah," she lied. Her nightmares and lack of rest weren't as important in the scheme of things. It'd only worry him.

"You've been different."

Miriam exaggerated a groan. "What does that mean?"

Yuri's stare intensified and his lips cracked open, a response at the tip of his tongue, but after a long second, they closed without a sound. He shook his head. "Hey, you were the one who diverted the conversation from *the* Valkyrie. I've known you forever. You're avoiding the subject." He winked then watched her for a bit longer with a toothy smile, but she didn't fold. "Not a bad different. You seem lighter. May I even say 'happier'?"

"Happier." She scoffed. What did that mean? "I'm not happy about a no-details mission to a radiation zone."

"Technically, the edge of a rad-zone," Yuri said in his best Nas impression.

Miriam chuckled, but it faltered quickly. She wasn't thrilled about the alties in Station City, the protesters and riots, or that wunbies had become such a threat and humans were just waiting for the next big event to happen. They were all constant reminders that the world was falling apart.

Yuri shrugged. "It is what it is, Tan. We follow—"

"Orders, I know. Such a good marine."

◊

Her oxygen tasted off, but Miriam couldn't tell if it was due to its purity or something in the suit's filters. There was no hint of the brackish ocean air—which was reassuring, considering the getup's purpose. The mounted node on the back of her hood whirred in her ears despite the ship's noise and waves lapping at the open platform. She waited as Kai and Yuri lowered the RHIB into the water below.

This was where Echo would split off from the UMF scout cruiser. Miriam had no idea where they were or why, only that they were somewhere between Station City and Ursus Outpost in a vast stretch of no-man's-land. When the ship anchored, she wasn't sure they were in the right place—no structures in sight, only the barren cliffed shore ahead. Miriam hoped there wouldn't be more trekking involved beyond. Especially not in these suits. She wasn't fond of cliffs.

In the small boat, ocean spray misted her hood. She twisted her body as best she could to watch the ship accelerate and disappear—their connection and link to Station City gone with it. Miriam hadn't asked how the crew would know when to pick the team up, but Krill hadn't seemed concerned, so she pushed it out of her mind. The old device in the lead's possession had to be their ticket home; it was their only medium of receiving instructions. They had their new visors, but those were on a closed communication system between the team. The lack of contingency was morbidly hilarious. If they lost that device, or if the team was separated, what would happen?

Yuri pointed at something as they neared the coast, and Fox redirected the boat without a word. There was something eerie about the situation, and this place bordering death seemed to demand silence. Echo respectfully obliged.

Some seconds later, Miriam's eyes widened. The RHIB turned into a beautiful hidden bay where the waves were noticeably calmer. The color of its water reminded Miriam of Sam, a blue so intriguing and vivid. Past it, a thin strip of beach led straight up to barren, vertical rock and a small concrete pier peeked out as a wave dipped. The tide was low enough to see it, but it was out of place leading into nothing.

Fox brought the boat as close to it as possible, and Miriam

gripped her rifle as Krill shakily stepped onto the water-covered platform. The team lead tested the surface with a pump of his legs. When nothing happened, he grabbed the watercraft's mooring lines and assisted in its stabilization. Nas was next out and pushed further toward the cliff, his rifle up and scanning. Miriam followed. Their strides were slow at first, careful of the slick surface, but they picked up their pace when they found traction under their boots. Ahead, Nas stopped, his weapon and body taut.

The wall face had a deep cave, hidden by the natural placement of a ridge. It was only visible from their specific position and angle. Not only would someone have had to be dumb enough to venture this close to the radiation zone, but they'd also have to know about this hidden bay, come at this specific time when the tide was low to find the hidden pier, and been crazy enough to walk along it to what seemed like a barren wall of rock. The amount of secrecy was baffling. What was this mission? This location? And why were they being sent here?

Krill motioned at Yuri, Kai, and Fox, who had dragged the small boat onto the platform behind them. His whisper floated in Miriam's ear. "Push in."

Moving around the wall into a hidden mouth, Echo was swallowed by darkness. A bead of sweat dripped down Miriam's back, despite the cool, temperature-controlled suit. Her visor adjusted and scanned for movement and outlines.

"Torches," Krill directed.

Red light illuminated and swept the space around them. There was no noise, other than the soft splashes of their feet in the water and the muted dragging of the RHIB. Miriam's rifle light traced along the lines of the walls and ceiling. She swallowed. They were too straight and too perfectly curved to be natural.

"Two o'clock," Yuri whispered.

Four lights merged on an inclined ramp that branched into a dry and level nook.

"Copy. Move up."

Miriam pushed forward with Yuri and Nas, grateful to have dry ground under her. She cast her light in a slow and constant sweep while Fox and Kai secured the boat. Other than the mysterious man-made bay, there was nothing else in the cavern.

Krill pulled his device from his rig and its dim light glowed next to Miriam. She resisted glancing over at him, just in case something popped out of the nothingness.

"Weapons down," he said. "We don't need them."

Miriam and the others slowly dropped their rifles, and they switched to other handheld lights. It was a confusing relief. No hostiles? Alties? Not even Children of Charon. Miriam glanced back at the lead, who observed the device. His eyes moved side to side as he read whatever incoming messages. He slid past Nas, moving up.

"Tan."

She followed and directed her light at a looming wall—the end of the cavern. Krill walked to the corner, then took meticulously large strides before he stopped. About five meters in, he tucked his rifle behind him and swept a gloved hand back and forth, searching. When he found what he was looking for, he placed the device back into his rig.

"Hold the light there. Nas, give me a hand."

Together, the two tugged on a latch that had popped out from a previously seamless wall. It didn't budge. Krill peeked at the device, then brushed a hand over the wall surface, this time a meter away in the opposite direction. Miriam moved closer to assist with her light in speechless curiosity. As she neared, a panel sprung open revealing a series of manual switches. There were no displays nor anything fancy and modern, just like the device. Nas murmured and Miriam heard the soft rustling of the others' suits as they shifted in perplexion. After a series of random flicks, the lead motioned to Nas who braced and pulled at the latch again. This time it gave and slowly swung out.

Miriam shined her torch into the next space, but the threshold doused any light, allowing no visibility within.

Nas peeked around the thick slab. "What is this place?" His usual enthusiasm and chatter had muffled.

"We sure about no weapons, boss?" Yuri said behind them.

"Everyone on me." Krill moved into the center of the frame, red light glowing around him. His hood rose then dropped with his exhale. And then he walked in.

Miriam fell in behind Nas, a new trepidation taking shape. The last time she had gone into a dimly lit tunnel, it was underground and had ended in the belly of a terrorist den. When she and her teammates resurfaced, they had been ambushed. What was the point of making mistakes if they never learned their lessons? Biting back against every survival instinct, Miriam followed into the closed void, her visor and torch only showing an empty corridor ahead, meters at a time. Krill's device emitted its own glow as it brought them further in.

"This isn't creepy at all." Kai peeked around Fox's large frame.

When all six of Echo were inside, a soft hiss of hydraulics engaged behind them. Flashlights swung as the wall closed, sealing them in an unknown tomb. Miriam clamped her teeth and swallowed. Soft, muttered expletives filled the open comm.

"Nope. Not horrifyingly creepy at all."

"Keep moving," Krill ordered, but Miriam could hear the uncertainty in his voice.

Echo moved forward in silence. There was *only* forward. Miriam could make out the faint sounds of clicks, as if something was engaging and shifting, but when she scanned with her visor and light, it was only a solid wall.

In front of her, Nas checked an old-generation radiation gauge. Their commcuffs had lost signal in the couple hours before they anchored. When the scout cruiser dropped them off, Echo still had a rough idea of their location, but now, it was hard to say. She didn't know how long they had been walking, how far or in what direction they were moving. Miriam swallowed back the fear of being interred, entombed inside this strange place.

"What kind of mission is this again?" whispered Kai.

"Follow the tunnel wherever it goes kind of mission," Miriam muttered.

Time and space were confusing when there was nothing but darkness and the rustling and steps of others. It could've been minutes or hours. After a series of nonsensical turns and wherever the path opened, the team came to a stop in a widened space: a small room with no doors. A dead end.

Nas wandered to one of the side walls and touched it. "I've been trying to figure out what this place is made of. Alty tech? Construction at this scale—and secret, no less—is..." He trailed off.

"Now what?" Kai whispered.

Krill consulted his device, but the display had gone dim. Previously a messenger of cryptic instructions, it was now of no use. The lead switched to his light, and paced the room, trying to catch any seam, panel, or out-of-place marker. There was none. Krill turned. "I'm not sure."

"Uh, guys?" Kai's voice trembled. "What happened to the hall?"

Miriam's red light bounced off a wall, then around to three more smooth surfaces. There were no openings, no evidence they had come from a corridor, just their collective memories. Her heart pumped in tune with Fox's muttered expletives. They were trapped.

Something sounded around them, but Miriam couldn't place the origin. She felt the slightest movement underneath her feet, but it almost felt like she was imagining it. It was an uncanny feeling, like she was moving while standing still.

"Hell, are we—are we going down?" Kai squeaked.

Cold shivered down her spine. She wasn't imagining it, then. Miriam couldn't tell if it was up, down, right, left, or diagonal. Her sense of orientation was blasted by the suit, the darkness, and the labyrinth. Her body shifted slightly again, and she cursed under her breath as she braced herself for whatever would happen next.

And then she was blinded as white light flooded the room.

8

INTENTIONAL RELATIONS

SAM'S FIST tensed until it shook, mirroring how her stomach felt as it contorted. She blinked hard, took a deep breath, and counted slowly in her head. One one thousand. Two one thousand... At the height of those long four seconds, she held the air in, forcing her insides and thoughts to calm, then counted the exhale out. Four. Three. Two. One.

She could do this. What else was she going to do? Sit in her empty studio until her operation? Her program had dwindled in anticipation of the event, and she could only run the city and lift at the gym so much. *Rest and prepare*, they advised, but resting meant unwanted thoughts.

She could do this. Jace had briefed her as best he could, refreshing on training that felt both outdated and not appropriate for the task, the "opportunity she had been given" per the intelligence warrant officer. She could do this. Sam had taken on worse before.

Fuck.

One one thousand.

Everything before was based on her physical skills and her training.

Two one thousand.

This was something she didn't normally do. This was all contingent on her social skills.

Three one thousand.

Give her a rifle, put her in a bar fight, or throw her into a den of drugged-up Charonites. *That* was her forte. Even with slim chances of surviving, she'd rather face off with Altered legionnaires or Apostates. But charming people? A Royal, no less? That was better suited for others. Not her. She was an SOG reconnaissance specialist.

Four one thousand.

Fuck.

Sam swiveled to the empty street around her and adjusted the cap over her hair. The sector was full of government and business structures, immaculate via their clean-lined architecture. The recently established Altered embassy was only a few blocks away, but it felt like kilometers, sitting in its own gash. Speckles of paint had survived the recent pressure wash on the facade of the building, and crude messages were scrawled out along the walls of neighboring structures with hurried outlines of a familiar lamp mark.

Her fingers splayed until the little bones and joints cracked. She curled them in and raised her hand to knock on the metal door just as it opened abruptly. Red eyes stared down at her, and Sam took an automatic step back, her fist up and ready.

"Dima."

Even with the soft but firm voice from behind, he stood there like an unbudging guardian. His eyes bored into Sam's, and she forced herself to hold the extended contact like a challenge. She knew hostility. She could work with that.

"Let her in, please."

The Altered's sightline rolled above Sam's head, and his ears and nostrils seemed to twitch as he took in the street behind her. When he was satisfied, he stepped to the side, revealing a small, clean space. She hadn't known what she was expecting; this was the service entrance, in the back of the building. Out of view. The Royal didn't want to be seen with a one-armed human. Sam felt the heat of shame rise in her neck, but she shoved the thought away. She reminded herself this was unofficial. On both sides.

Drawing in an inhale, Sam pulled courage and confidence from the city air. She took her cover off, gave her hair a quick shake, and stepped past the threshold.

"Good morning, Sam. You're early." The Royal stood regally in a dark green dress that flowed around her. The outfit seemed too lavish and gaudy for a simple workday, but what did Sam know about politicians? Or Altered Royals? She preferred function over form, but who needed function in fashion when one had specifically-designed genes and a red-eyed bodyguard?

Sam surveyed the room, wishing she had her visor to scan for any threats. Her optical implant didn't seem to work within the building, and with just her naked eye, she saw there was nothing.

Kuan-Lin dipped a hand toward another door that led further in. With another look behind her, Sam considered her options. She could leave and nothing would have changed. UMF didn't have direct intelligence from the Altered, but the military was resourceful. They could find another route somehow. *Or* she could try to develop something now by walking further into this unknown Altered fortress where they could easily hold her, kill her, or chop her up inside. No one would come to her aid. She regretted not telling her brother that she had gone for it before her hesitation won out. Miriam and Echo had already gone silent on comms. Jace knew, but this was an unofficial visit. Off the books meant no permission. No support.

But Sam could be useful. The intel she might get here could help UMF. And though she had her procedure soon, it'd be a couple more weeks of recovery. She was tired of sitting on the sidelines.

"Come," the Royal said. "We can talk in my office."

Fuck it. She could do this.

As they walked through the next door and into a wide corridor, Sam took everything in. The walls were lined with beautiful art she had never seen before, colorful figures and abstract shapes that made her head swim. The place was much nicer than anywhere she had been before, and it was significantly more beautiful than the exterior with its deteriorated street.

"Welcome to our embassy. Our administrators tried to decorate this place like our palace back home. I think it's a tad overboard, but my family and others find comfort in familiarity." Kuan-Lin gave her a smile. "I'm glad you reached out. I wasn't sure you would. We haven't had many visitors."

Sam made a small noise of acknowledgment, but she was surprised. Surely, she couldn't be the first human to step foot in the embassy. Weren't Station's politicians working with the Royals? Maybe they knew something she didn't. She gripped her cap in her fist as she followed the Royal past a set of lifts and up a flight of stairs. Too late now.

Kuan-Lin continued in amicable conversation, describing various pieces of art and history, but Sam only nodded out of politeness. She feigned interest in a canvas of what she could only call chaotic drippings as she tried to remember their route and looked for exits or means of escape. On the third-floor, they turned down another hall garnished with paintings and artifacts until the Royal paused outside a frosted glass wall and stretched a hand toward an open door.

Sam cautiously stepped into the room. It was a long office, with a low tuxedo sofa, matching armchairs, and a minimalistic desk centered on the far end. There were no windows, but some kind of screen illuminated against the back wall with slow-moving images of a forest. Green plants in a medley of bases and containers decorated the space in a pleasing manner. Sam peered back at the two Altered, a flash of fear returning as she grasped for direction, unsure of the right protocol. She should've asked Jace more questions on courtesies before she came. Sam was no diplomat.

"I promise the chairs are more comfortable than they look. We sourced them from a nearby shop. Well-made. This city has a lot of talent." The Royal beckoned Sam to the sofa. "Please, sit. Would you like something to drink?"

Sam shook her head but took a seat. Her thumbnail scratched along the edge of her hat as she spared another glance at the tall guardian who posted himself outside the office, the back of his dark hair visible over the middle portion of frosted glass.

The woman walked over to a small bar and pressed a long finger onto the top of a box-shaped contraption. "I've been enjoying much of the cuisine here, but I can't seem to shake the craving for our tea. Thankfully, we were able to bring some over. I'll have to add that onto our discussion list—sharing some of our seeds and bushes. I'm sure we can figure out the right environment for it here." As the machine whirred, the woman turned and studied Sam. "I apologize. This must be a lot for you. You're nervous."

Sam inhaled, then murmured an affirmative. There was no point in lying. "Do all Royals have their own personal bodyguards?"

Kuan-Lin's eyebrow arched in amusement. "You mean Dmitri?" She shot an endearing look at the man through the translucent partition. "Dima's harmless." She quirked a smile at Sam's doubtful look.

A Royal with a sense of humor. Another first.

"He supports a handful of us, but he tends to worry a bit more about me." She tilted her chin. "Don't you, Dima?"

The man didn't respond, but Sam knew he was listening from the way his ear seemed to quiver under his black hair.

Kuan-Lin chuckled. "He takes his duty seriously, but perhaps it's his nature. He *was* designed that way. I often tell him to stand next to me, not *behind* me, but we fall into our defaults." She turned back to the machine and when she refaced Sam, two small ceramic cups were in her hands. The Royal's smile widened. "Please don't be nervous. You are safe here."

Sam gave her hat one more squeeze before she received the warm cup. A fresh grass-like smell wafted up as she brought it closer. She'd had tea before, but this smelled both sweet and bitter at the same time. Sam resisted shifting under the woman's gaze as the space fell silent. While the Royal seemed to be quite comfortable, Sam racked her brain, trying to form words and sentences that didn't sound completely idiotic. She was comfortable behind the sights of her rifle, not this pseudo-diplomatic and social role. Reminding herself it was just another mission, she recounted her objective and craft basics. Build rapport. Draw out information. And the best way to build that was through a shared experience.

"How are..." She set the cup aside and tried to recall the Altered boy and girl's names. "...the children?"

Fuck, she was terrible with small talk.

"It's kind of you to ask. Xiaoling and Longwei are sequestered away for now. They're not used to being confined, but with all the transition, it *is* necessary. Thank you again, for stepping in."

Transition. Such polite speak for the fall of their capital, executions, aggressions, and mobs.

"It was nothing. It's not safe around here right now," Sam murmured, working at a wrinkle in her pants. She palmed the fabric, trying to press it smooth.

The Royal tilted her head. "For whom?"

Sam looked up to curious golden eyes and swallowed. "For everyone."

"Will you face repercussions for being here?"

"Will *you*? I came through the back."

The Royal winced. "That wasn't my intention. I thought you'd feel more comf—"

Sam snorted and wiggled her right shoulder. "Don't worry. I'm invisible."

It wasn't entirely true. Inconsequential, maybe. Eyes tended to draw to her, to her brokenness, but then they'd shoot away, as if they were embarrassed and ashamed. And it had been surprisingly easy to fall under the radar in a big city, even with her unique hair color. No one cared about a broken person, a *broken weapon*.

Strangely, she didn't feel conscious of her asymmetry with the Royal. The Altered already considered humans inferior. How much further could she drop? In this situation, her pathetic stature could be advantageous. It was a conflicting feeling.

"I see you."

Sam inhaled sharply and she angled her shoulder away.

"You have a lot of fight in you, I can tell." Kuan-Lin leaned her elbow into the armrest and pulled a finger to her temple. Gold eyes dipped to Sam's right. "Am I correct to assume this was recent? You carry it like it's a weight."

Sam didn't miss the irony of the statement, but she said nothing.

"Was it them?"

Her jaw clenched.

Kuan-Lin made a sound in the back of her throat. "Of course. Which garrison?"

"Ursus, our outpost in the North."

"I see. Such unnecessary loss. The Apostates must've thought your forces would come to our aid." She huffed. "I think they overestimated our efforts with this city, with your politicians. Even with what happened at your southern border."

"I was there, when everything…happened." Sam's leg stuttered, but she pushed her palm into her thigh, forcing it to still.

"You're angry."

Until that moment, she hadn't been. Between the city,

recovery, Miriam, and now the Royal, she hadn't realized the constant rage had lessened. Distractions.

"I'm angry, as well."

The woman's relaxed posture said otherwise.

"Underneath, I am. I'm *Huángzú*. Royal." Kuan-Lin sighed and straightened. "Image and saving face is everything. Don't let our reserved behavior fool you. I am furious about my home, my people. It's all such an unnecessary loss. Did the Sovereign deserve that execution? Did my uncles, aunts, friends, anyone who didn't agree, did they deserve what the Apostates did to them? They cut them down, mutilated their bodies, and strung them up in the streets. So much hate, so much death. All for what?"

Sam averted her eyes to the moving forest behind the desk. Her anger was selfish. She knew it—it was cyclical *because* she knew it—but in its isolation, she hadn't thought about the Altered and what Arshangol's fall meant to them. Until now.

"This was all preventable. Or perhaps that's hindsight and idealism talking."

Shared experiences. This was her window.

"Why did they do it?"

She held back from asking more. Why did they attack the South, Ursus, Arshangol? Sam wanted all the answers. Not only for herself. She wanted something useful to bring back to UMF.

"Depends on who you ask." With Sam's baffled look, Kuan-Lin quickly added, "You can't make everyone happy. We make enemies no matter what we do. Perhaps it was when we removed the previous Sovereign; he had gone unchecked for all those years. I was younger, but I remember parts. Between his new army, the tactics, the expansions, exterminations, everything, it was barbaric. It still is. After all, you and your kind are who we came from, even if it was generations ago. We should've known. So many of them hated us for trying to find a better solution, a peace, but we all have different definitions of peace, don't we? Or illusions, at least. Perhaps I *was* too much of a dreamer thinking we could come together. We're not that different." The Royal sighed and leaned her face into her fingers. "We—I thought we could stop it all here. History will only keep repeating. That summit would've been a way out, a step forward."

Sam straightened and her eyes grew. "The summit was your idea."

The Royal took another slow sip before she spoke. "Not entirely."

Behind the humility, Sam knew it to be true. "You've been in Station City since."

Kuan-Lin puffed air. "Who knew being the thorn in the family's side would also protect me from the horrors back home."

"And you're the reason the others are here?"

She offered a weak smile. "If it backfires, yes. If it's a success..." She dipped her head and chuckled sadly before looking back up, her face returning with a pleasant expression. "What do you call something that is neither a success nor a failure? Is that just life?"

Sam brought the small cup to her lips, but then remembered where she was, and placed the untouched tea on the side table again. "You're not what I thought for a Royal."

"Am I not bloodthirsty enough? I was curious to know what your schools teach about us, but I guess our encounter the other day was enough." Kuan-Lin made a bemused sound behind her tongue but coupled it with a reassuring glimmer from her eyes. "The family is different; we all have different opinions. It's the same for our people, especially the Apostates and their factions. Perhaps we failed them as their leaders, didn't listen enough or heed more caution. Looking back, there were so many warnings."

"You're an idealist," Sam blurted.

Kuan-Lin laughed. "I was hopeful, does that make me an

idealist?" She shook her head. "Stupidly hopeful, but peace has to be possible. It has to be an option. Are *you* not hopeful?"

Sam didn't think so. She was a marine, or at least, she was before. The idea of peace sounded nice, but she had faced more reasons cementing the fact it was just a fantasy, an illusion, like the Royal had said before.

"That day, you helped the children. Did you know who they were before you stepped in? Did it matter? How many others walked by before you came along?"

"I'm not good," Sam mumbled.

"I didn't say you were."

Sam bit down. She hadn't expected that.

"But what is the definition of 'good'? I thought I was good, but the Apostates think I'm destroying everything we are. The majority of my hometown turned to them or let them through. They think I'm a villain. I call what they want a genocide. They call it necessary, a means to an end." She scoffed. "And here, I'm not good either. To this city, your kind, I'm an oppressor, a liar. Perhaps my family doesn't so much see me as good or bad, but they think I'm too liberal, possibly an imbecile. And maybe I am. It's all subjective." She laughed. "But that's beside my point. You *stopped*. For whatever reason you had. You don't think peace is attainable?"

Sam's thoughts turned to Matam, to New Zapala, the Charonites, the sentiment and the violence. There was too much of a generational divide. Hatred ran deep. But for the first time in months, she remembered the glimpse of a joined future in the chaos. A surreal hybrid child, born of human and Altered. Had that little girl survived the massacres in the South? Did the Royals know about her? The current atmosphere would never embrace a hybrid. It was too extreme, too radical. How long had it taken history to overcome racism, sexism, and more? And had they actually progressed past that? It had taken a giant catalyst, the creation of the Altered, and the threat against their own survival to unite humankind.

"It doesn't matter what I think. I'm no politician. Isn't that what you and City Center are working on?"

Kuan-Lin took a deep breath then let it out. "Yes, but I'm making more progress with you."

It was Sam's turn to scoff. "I have no power. A nobody. Invisible, remember?"

"So many of us thought the Apostates were nobodies, and perhaps they were invisible because of our own ego and projection. We thought they were insignificant; their numbers and ideas were split, but look at them now. People with no power, suddenly, *have* power." Kuan-Lin gestured a finger between herself and Sam. "We aren't so different. I may have a slightly divergent construct, but you were designed to survive dire conditions as well. You survived."

Kuan-Lin studied her as she brought the cup to her lips. "I think you've taken a hit. We all have. And perhaps, after we get past our anger, we might find there are more overlapping interests than we think. This may be the idealist in me, but there is a foundation somewhere; we just have to find it. Even if that means we level the ground to build it."

◊

Sam's head was unsettled and swirling when she left. She stood outside, letting the adrenaline, tension, and anxiety crash against her. It had only been a meeting, but it had felt oddly similar to a sparring session—one that she hadn't been equipped for. After one last glimpse of the embassy, she checked her commcuff and started at a brisk pace toward UMF.

As the usual lunch hour ceased, the streets bustled with activity, and though she was never one for crowds, she was grateful to follow along its current, mostly undetected. Sam slipped into a quaint café—a location sent previously through a private channel. With a quick nod of greeting to the barista, she strode toward a booth where a new but familiar face waited.

Jace set down the nicosynth device he had been twirling between his fingers and met her with a couple of clunky steps. Now that Sam was aware of his prosthetic, she could recognize his gait.

"How'd it go?"

She scooted onto the bench and tapped her fingers. "Better than expected."

The intelligence warrant officer sat across from her. "You're alive. It went very well."

Sam's forehead wrinkled. "You thought they'd kill me?"

"No, not really." He laughed and stretched an arm over the booth. "Sorry, bad joke."

Her eyes narrowed, but only briefly.

"You were there for a while. I, uh, did start to worry a little. Might've had to call the cavalry." His face broke out in a dimpled grin.

She rolled her eyes.

"So, what did you do?"

Sam tested the coffee, but it was too hot. She intentionally paused, a lazy attempt to punish the man for his own teasing, but it was short-lived as she shifted under his sharp gaze. He, like the Royal, seemed to be perfectly comfortable with silence.

"We just talked. Well, she did most of the talking."

"Anything about the Apostates? Their plans? Movements?"

Sam winced. "We didn't really—it was more philosophical." She paused. Their first meeting had been laying a foundation like the Royal said. "I don't know. I'm not sure I got you anything useful."

Jace reached across the table and patted her hand. "You're too hard on yourself. How many people have gotten a one-on-one with a Royal? Now, tell me everything."

For the next minutes, she regurgitated as much of the discussion that she could remember. He asked questions, and Sam felt silly rehashing how little control she had in the conversation, but the man was enthralled, nodding his head and taking quick notes on his cuff. When she was done, Jace sat back, one arm folded, and the other hand stroking his chin. His lips pinched downward in a frown as if he were in deep thought.

Or disappointment.

Sam fidgeted with her empty cup, tilting it on one of its sides. "I know it wasn't much. This isn't... I'm not great at this."

His face contorted as he shook his head. "I disagree. We can work with this. I can start a reporting chain when I get back to base." He laughed at Sam's expression. "This is the hard part, and I'm impressed. It seems like she likes you. A lot. But who can blame her?"

The compliment hit Sam with a delayed satisfaction, manifesting in a warmth from the back of her neck. She doubted his words; the meeting with the Royal had been amicable, and Kuan-Lin was far more forthcoming than she had expected. Jace was giving Sam too much credit. She hid a conflicted smile behind her cup.

"You have a knack for this." His hand slid across the tabletop closer to Sam again. "I know you have your procedure soon, but with everything that's happened, have you considered something other than SOG?"

Sam stiffened. "No."

The door opened and Jace's attention diverted to a customer's arrival in the otherwise empty café. It was well-timed. Sam's face fell as a grip of doubt twisted inside her. Was he suggesting she wouldn't be good enough to get back into SOG?

"You should think about it," he said, his gaze still on the front of the shop. "When can you meet the Royal again?"

"What exact information are you looking for?"

He sighed. "You've heard SOG has been sending out teams?"

Sam nodded. She hadn't been told directly, but from what

she'd gathered at the team dinner, the lack of SOG marines around the gym, and her brother's vague mentions, she knew something was happening. She wasn't as connected as she was used to, and it was frustrating.

"We're looking for the Altered responsible."

It was Sam's turn to lean in. "Ursus?" she whispered.

"Ursus, Arshangol, the South, it's all connected, we know that much. But why specifically in the order that everything's been happening? We know it's the Apostates, wunbies, Promised, whatever you want to call them, but it's strange. They weren't organized like this before. There're supposedly multiple sects, so who brought them all together? The big question is who's behind all of it?"

Sam nodded her head. "Cut the head off..."

"And the body falls. But we have to figure out who's the brain first."

"So?"

"We have some ideas, but you know how it goes. We need confirmations, and confirmations on those confirmations. You see why this is so big, you talking with a Royal."

She nodded again. The pressure was heavy. It was a paradoxical feeling as it simultaneously gripped and propelled her. She could still be integral to UMF on this side of operations, gather and cultivate intelligence that helped identify their targets, but what she wanted was to be out in the field, behind her rifle sights. No one had outright said it, but the procedure and the prosthetic weren't a guarantee—it was experimental after all. Sam kicked the invasive thought away.

Jace studied her, his brown eyes softening with an endearing glimmer. "You're doing great."

She lowered her gaze to the empty cups between them.

"You are," he reassured. "Sorry, I've been so caught up with this whole situation and meeting you—I mean, you're the Valkyrie, I've been reading and following the reports, your old reports, and well. What I mean to say is...you're fascinating."

Sam grimaced. She placed her hand on her neck but then moved to massage her shoulder underneath its harness instead, trying to divert away the warmth flushing into her face.

"Oh," Jace said. "Are you—is it still painful?"

She started to shake her head, but changed it to a nod, a strange wobble.

"Yeah, the phantom pains are awful. Mine went away with the new leg." He tapped the table surface, a finger down to his prosthetic underneath. Jace then cleared his throat and watched her intensely. "I know you said you were fine before, but I'd like to offer my services again—if you'd like someone to help, to wait for you at the hospital, it'd be my pleasure."

Sam's mouth pulled to the side in a lopsided acknowledgment at Jace's dimpled smile. It caught her off guard and let a thought slip through. When was the last time she had fooled around, let off steam? Her throat caught, suddenly dry. "That's kind of you, but I think I'll be okay. This is...this is something I'd like to do on my own." She gave him a smile, less awkward this time. "But thank you."

It wasn't that she wanted to be alone. She didn't. As much as she wanted the company of her brother, Miriam, or Echo, the timing wasn't right. They physically weren't there. Part of her wanted to entertain the idea of Jace accompanying her, but she also wanted to do this on her own. If the procedure didn't work, Sam couldn't bear the thought of witnesses.

9

A SECRET FACILITY

"PLACE THE CUBE ON THE GROUND."

A voice reverberated through the thin material of Miriam's suit and into her bones. It came from nowhere and everywhere all at once. As her eyes adjusted to the brightness, she made out a door in front of her, its outline and presence only known by its darkening color. She quickly counted her team—all six of them were there. All dazed by the flood of lights, but they were there.

Cube? What cube? Miriam watched as Krill motioned to Yuri and remembered they were there to deliver something. The second retrieved the package from a small compartment and set it down.

"TAKE OFF THE SUITS."

"Is it safe?" Kai asked.

"TAKE OFF YOUR SUITS AND LEAVE YOUR WEAPONS AND BELONGINGS."

Miriam blinked, still trying to locate the source of the voice, but there was no one there, no speakers or intercoms. Other than the gray door, the walls were smooth and bright, devoid of anything. The lights seemed to come from the ceiling and walls themselves.

The lead found his outfit's external catch and cautiously pulled at his hood. His shoulders lifted as he inhaled then lowered. Satisfied, he turned and nodded. "Do it," Krill instructed softly.

Miriam and the others followed suit. When she felt the cold air on her skin, she waited for an additional second, trying to process any burning or change in sensation. Nothing.

"Where are we?" Yuri whispered next to her. "Are we still outside the radiation zone?"

With a shrug, Miriam peeled the rest of her outfit off. "Your guess is as good as mine." She set to work on unbuckling her pack and light armor—uncomfortable, especially knowing they were being watched, but not knowing from where or how. With the lack of her kit and its leftover imprint of perspiration, Miriam shivered. She set her gear on top of the discarded suit.

"PROCEED INDIVIDUALLY THROUGH THE DOOR."

"Just leave them here?" Fox asked, his face in a twist.

"Do we have any other choice?" Miriam muttered. No one liked the vulnerability, but they were now hostage to whoever had brought them here. There was no way out, no way back.

"I'll go first." Krill squared himself in front.

Yuri stepped forward. "Lead's never first in the stack. I got it, boss."

The door noiselessly split down the middle and opened.

"ONE AT A TIME," the voice reminded.

Yuri stepped through before Miriam could say anything.

"Hell," Kai whispered. "What is this place? I've never seen anything like it."

For once, Nas was quiet, his own dark brows furrowed.

It seemed like an eternity before the door opened again. This time, Miriam peered into the next room with the others, if it could be considered that.

Empty, and no Yuri.

The next space looked to be just as sterile as the one they were in, but about the size of a small supply closet. Krill glanced back with a semi-reassuring smile and stepped through. Then the door closed, and they waited, their numbers dwindling.

It was Nas next, then Kai. With two remaining, the door opened, and Miriam gave Fox a curt nod. He returned the gesture with his own: a raised middle finger and a head tilt. "See you on the other side," he mumbled.

She half-smirked, half-grimaced as the door closed behind her.

"MOVE FORWARD."

She did, now only an arm's reach from the front wall. Mid-step, it split open into a short, empty corridor, its walls as white as the previous ones. The partition shut behind her, and her eyes were drawn to a new color: a green line along the floor. Before the voice could instruct her, Miriam followed it. Something in the walls shifted, and she froze as a jointed, mechanical arm with what looked like a giant flat paddle extended out of the surface. She flinched as it approached her, but it stayed within a hand's distance, outlining and scanning her head and body. As it drew down toward her legs and feet, Miriam tried to study the technology, but it was already folding away.

Preoccupied, she didn't notice until it was too late. Something pricked against her deltoid through her uniform shirt, and she startled with muttered curses. Whatever it was had already retreated, merging back into the wall. She rubbed her arm, the surprise worse than the itch of pain itself. The green line illuminated again, but she ignored it, swiveling her head, just in case something else popped out.

"MOVE FORWARD."

Miriam glared up at the ceiling, or wherever the voice was coming from, but she relented. With a few steps, a partition formed behind her, cutting her off from the previous section. She looked back, unsure, and then faced forward as a wide circle, like a halo, dropped from the ceiling.

"STAY STILL."

Miriam stubbornly brought her chin level. The ring lowered over her crown, and then her ears. A green light bathed her before it climbed back up. She blinked, focusing on any changes in her eyesight or feeling. She didn't enjoy the lack of understanding or control. Scanning and screening, she assumed as much, but for what? Or was it doing something else?

She walked through another open door before the voice could echo in her ears. Even as she joined the five others in a wide, spotless foyer, she felt trapped.

"You survived," Yuri said with an uncertain grin.

"Sure," she replied as she looked around. The floors and walls were a pristine glossy white and two benches were in the middle, but no one sat. On both sides of the space, double doors closed them in. It reminded Miriam of the hospital back in Station City. Two interconnected triangles were engraved into the wall in front of them. She didn't recognize the symbol.

Yuri squeezed her shoulder. "Secure much?"

"What now?" she whispered back.

He shrugged. He gestured to Nas, who was muttering to himself, his fingers dancing in the air as if he were drawing invisible formulas. "Wonderkid is in his own world over there. And I guess we're waiting until all of us get through."

It didn't take long. Fox's choice words cracked through as he emerged in the space, his hazel eyes sharper than before. He threw an obscene gesture behind him. "Fuckin' pricks," he grumbled.

Miriam ignored him. With Echo all together, her attention turned to their youngest teammate. If anyone would know what was going on, it'd be Nas. Miriam called his name, and he startled.

"Eye check, temperature, and some kind of sensory input. Something auditory?" The corners of his mouth curved up. "I counted eight, no, nine."

Her forehead wrinkled. She knew they were being screened

through some high-tech security measures, but wherever, whoever was here, didn't want anyone getting in. A *specific* anyone.

"Perspiration or skin test, and then the blood draw, or was that something else? Interesting."

"Close."

The team turned to the unfamiliar voice at one of the side doors. A thin, irritated-looking man wearing a long white lab coat stepped into the room. "An infusion of our chemical cocktail."

Miriam's throat closed.

"What?" Kai blurted. "You can't do that."

"What was in the injection?" Miriam said with a dry gulp.

"Nothing that will affect you permanently."

"Why?" Nas asked.

"It's a new test to make sure you are who you say you are."

"Who else would we be?" Kai said, angering.

"One can disguise themselves, but one can't change what's within." The man stared at them, unamused. "UMF's marines, I presume. Of course, if you weren't, you wouldn't be here."

Krill stepped forward. "Yes. Where—"

A bony finger raised up. "You have a lot of questions, but we can revisit this another time. Your gear will be sorted and delivered to your rooms, and your weapons will stay locked up for now. We've already kept the station chief waiting. Let's try to be a bit quicker." He turned stiffly, already walking through the automatic doors, no intention of waiting for the team to follow. The command was explicit.

Past the double doors, the corridor opened into a vast atrium with curved walls in an almost perfect circle. As Miriam edged toward the left half wall, she gaped up and down. It wasn't an atrium; rather, what looked like an enormous silo. She counted at least five floors below. Each floor was uniform, with windows of labs and different facilities connected by two staircases mirrored across from each other. The levels themselves were separated by what looked like three passageways, splitting the circular floors equally apart like a spoked wheel.

When had this place been built? It had to be before the world wars given its location, but then what about the gamut of new technology she'd never seen before? Her head spun as the flood of unanswered questions piled up. What kind of mission was this, and what did it have to do with the Altered? Was it relevant at all?

She heard a squeak and looked up. Another individual in a wrinkled lab coat froze at the corner. His eyes widened at the six marines, then more fearfully toward their thin guide. "Doctor Cato."

Already passing at an unbroken pace, their guide threw his voice over his shoulder. "Doctor Paksima?"

"Lab Four," the other stammered, before he hurried back from where he'd come.

Doctor Cato's long strides prevented Miriam and the others from focusing too long on any one point of the strange facility. They followed—Nas's limp growing in the hurry—down the stairs to the next level and into the second hallway before their guide came to an abrupt stop outside a thick door. The number beside the access panel indicated they were at the correct destination. Echo followed him into a contained vestibule, and once they crammed in, three beeps sounded. The interior door slid open.

Three individuals dressed in similar long white coats were spread out at stations across a pristine laboratory. Only one looked up to acknowledge the visitors before returning to their work, a clutter of vials and machines around them. Miriam and Yuri poised their hands behind Nas, ready to stop his curiosity from inching forward. Everything about the space screamed, don't touch, don't bother the scientists in their super-secret lab.

"Zoha," Doctor Cato called out.

The one scientist who had looked up before flitted his eyes between a petite woman at the other bench and the group. The woman's dark hair was cut in an unflattering bob and her spectacles were too large for her face.

"Doctor Zoha Paksima."

Without looking away from her terminal, the woman tutted and fluttered her fingers. When she was satisfied with whatever was on the display in front of her, she turned to the other scientist next to her. "Excellent. Start on the next sample and note the protein's effects," she instructed, patting the air behind the individual. Her brown eyes, magnified by her glasses, shot over to the entrance. "Ah, Quillien."

The woman looked to be in her sixties, but she moved with spritely little steps. Stopping a comfortable distance away, Paksima slipped her glasses off and raised her chin, hungrily taking each of the marines in. "Finally. It's revolting how long it's taken to work this out with your organization. The military is so restrained in its approaches. So antiquated."

"Ma'am." Krill stepped forward and extended a hand. If he was as overwhelmed and befuddled as Miriam, he hid it well. "Vallen Krill, team lead of SOG Razor-Echo."

The doctor drew back, her fingers curling as she pulled her hands in. "Yes. Lovely."

The lead closed his hand and let it drop.

"Manners," the doctor said, seemingly to herself. She looked up, her eyes big. "We haven't had guests in a long while. It's nice to meet you, Vallen and comrades. I am Dr. Zoha Paksima, station chief of Axiom RF-4."

Miriam didn't understand what any of that meant. She looked to Nas, who seemed to be on the verge of wetting himself with excitement.

"Thank you." Krill made a show of looking around the lab. "I apologize, but I'm not sure what all of this is, Doctor. Where exactly are we?"

"Oh?" She raised a brow at Cato. "You haven't told them?"

He looked down his nose at her. "I figured you'd want to."

"Quillien, you know me too well." A grin etched into one side of her face. "Location-wise, you have the basic gist of coordinates, but I believe your real questions are who, what, and why. Axiom is an independent research organization under Vertex." She lobbed a finger at Nas when his expression shifted. "You know of Vertex? Impressive."

With the acknowledgment, Nas shifted weight onto his good leg and his words stumbled out. "Well, not that much, but I know the name. There was a merger, but it wasn't covered by the network, which is strange considering tech and pharma—"

"You're a sharp one. How enthralling." Paksima tutted and eyed Nas and his posture before she returned her gaze to Krill. "This research facility is one of several sites where we study and test various…disciplines."

Axiom? Vertex? Miriam had never heard of them. And one of several sites? There were more of these hidden facilities? Where?

"Why all the caution?" Krill asked.

Caution was a nicer word for secrecy, games, and gimmicks.

"Certain things don't germinate well in uncontrolled environments." Paksima waved a finger upward. "We must test before we *contest*."

Krill waited for her shrill laugh to cease, shifting from one leg to the other. "Thank you, but I'm afraid we still don't know why we're here."

"Don't be afraid." The station chief beamed. "The reason's quite simple—"

Cato cleared his throat. "Should we take this conversation back to your office?"

Paksima made a face and swirled her fingers. "I always forget I have one, but Doctor Cato is right—let's relocate to a quieter space. What would I do without this magnificent man?" She gestured toward the door behind them. "After you."

A while later, Echo and the station chief settled in a luxurious office around a long table. It was sparsely decorated —a show that Paksima, indeed, spent little time in the dedicated space. Cato tapped a console on the main desk and muttered commands under his breath. Within a minute, a soft sound whirred in the wall, and he lifted a panel to retrieve a tray full of tall water glasses and a small plate covered by an equally small cloche. He brought it over to the table, then retreated to a square-shaped armchair, away from the others.

Echo watched as Paksima took the plate and daintily pulled the cover off. Three sugar-coated gelatin sweets sat in the middle. Miriam balked. Was this what had been in the airtight package they had brought from Station all the way to wherever they were now?

Krill eyed the colorful shapes and cleared his throat. "Doctor...ma'am. You were saying before, about the reason we've been sent here."

"Ah, yes. Thank you for bringing this along. It's the only thing I miss from outside." She popped a sweet into her mouth and sucked on it, oblivious to the marines stewing in a spectrum of restrained reactions. When she was done, she popped her lips and sighed. "It's actually quite simple. We'd like your help with our...security research."

Miriam's brows furrowed. Beyond the insult of the delivery, it wasn't an abnormal ask. SOG units had been called out before to help consult SecTeam and organizations, but there was no security force here, at least none that she had seen. Plus, the facility didn't need more security. The shroud of secrecy, the access controls, the location, all of it was a formidable system of its own. Echo surely wasn't a team of technological experts, barring Nas as an enthusiast and Kai's role as an engineer.

"This is quite the location," Krill said. "The radiation zone is already a strong countermeasure—"

"For us. Not so much for others."

Altered. But why would scientists be concerned? The location was a stretch of dead land between human-settled territories.

"This is only one of our sites," Paksima continued. "We try to stay on top of the latest encounters to update all facilities, regardless of our locations."

"You're concerned about the wunbies—the Apostates, I mean," Krill corrected, the plain slang seemed too casual and inappropriate for their hosts.

"The Apostates, the Promised, the Corrupted, whatever names they call themselves now. I always find monikers preposterous. They're all neogens. It's fascinating how they multiply so rampantly unchecked. Are they still fighting?" She scoffed. "I'm not versed in the silliness over there. Quillien enjoys it more than all of us, but I find it distracting from what matters."

The man didn't bother to look up, now busy with a thin tablet.

Silliness over there? How isolated were these scientists from the real world? Did they know Arshangol had fallen, that surviving Royals and alties were now taking refuge in Station City, that the wunbies had attacked? What did they know outside and above these thick, reinforced walls?

"We can review your security posture and physical—"

"We're behind meters of concrete and steel. Our physical security is adequate."

"Ma'am?" Krill's eyes squinted. "What other security research did you have in mind?"

"*Our* security."

Miriam adjusted herself in her seat and watched the station chief. "You're talking about the human race."

The doctor's eyes latched onto her. "Yes. Humans are outdated. Our bodies don't adapt as well; we don't move as fast, see, hear, smell as fast. The world and neogens evolved past us, so how do we equalize ourselves? How do we get the advantage? Nature won't do it for us, so we must do it ourselves."

So why was Echo there? They weren't scientists.

"We're marines," Krill said.

"Yes," Paksima replied with a grin. "It was actually Quillien's idea to bring you in. UMF and City Center updates are so humdrum, so tedious, but he passed me your report. Very fascinating updates in the field."

"Report?"

"From your time in the South." She made it sound like they had been there on vacation. "Did you not encounter NG-C5s and K7s?" She brushed her fingers across the smooth table surface. "I believe your terms were 'legionnaires' and what I figure are one of the later K strains of neogens." We specifically requested your team to better understand what you discovered, although I see you are missing—" Paksima bobbed her finger, counting. "Two individuals."

"We're happy to discuss more about the Apostates and their tactics, ma'am. Valkyrie and Mute were on loan to us at the time, and we weren't given any instructions to include them on this mission. But everything we did, it's all in the report. We could've clarified what you wanted in Station or via the network," Krill said.

Paksima waved a hand. "We prefer to do things in person around here. Containment, you understand. It eliminates spread."

Miriam narrowed her eyes as she waited for the rest of the sentence or at least some clarification. She didn't get any.

"I know you've come a long way, but I assure you this is a priority for our survival. These next couple days, a small team will thoroughly interview each one of you. Barring a re-creation of the events that led you here, we'd like to form an accurate picture. It is of the utmost importance."

"Everything we know is in that report."

"Regardless, you're here now."

It was a semi-polite way to say they were stuck until the scientists were satisfied.

"Vallen, you and your team have the most experience with these newly affected neogens. What's in your heads, even if you don't think it's important, could be the smallest detail that makes or breaks our future, our species' *security*. When we're done here, we've worked out a priority request with your organization. They may not fully understand, but rest assured, we are all working toward the same interests."

"Ma'am? A request?"

She sighed, either disappointed or frustrated that she wasn't being understood. "Let's get through these interviews and we'll discuss more. I've been assured that you and your team are quite decent."

High praise. Miriam would've rolled her eyes, but she gripped her hands instead.

"Enjoy your stay. There's a gym somewhere around here, I believe you marines like those. And you." She flicked a finger in Nas's direction. "Stop by our infirmary. I think we might have something for that leg of yours, something the best hospitals in Station don't have yet."

Though Nas perked up, Miriam had reservations about an unknown band of scientists trying out a remedy on her teammate. Her eyebrow twitched and she motioned forward to protest, but Paksima waved her hand again.

"It's almost through the certification process, don't worry. I use it—just the tiniest bit. Does wonders for my back pain. Wonder drugs, these things. Knowledge hoarded is a travesty."

As if to prove a point, the woman sprung out of her seat, then paused. "Oh, and I don't want to insult your intelligence, but I do have to remind you that everything said or seen here does not leave this facility." An ominous threat hung at the end of her sentence.

◊

That night, Miriam couldn't quite shake the day and her thoughts away. She lay in the small bed in tight quarters across from a softly snoring Kai, staring up into the darkness. No matter which way she turned, rest eluded her. She could feel the weariness in her muscles, aching from tension and uncertainty. She lifted her wrist, but without her cuff, the default action was of no use.

Sam. She hoped the woman was okay. The prosthetic procedure was soon, and though Sam said she'd be fine, Miriam wondered how much of that confidence was a facade. She had witnessed the woman discover buried trauma and break down, but she had also been terrified and impressed with how easily Sam had compartmentalized those emotions.

If only her mind could do the same, maybe Miriam could get some rest. She knew her cycle of no sleep and crashing wasn't healthy. There had been some relief realizing this mission had zero combat, but she was on edge about reiterating her experiences in the South. She had pushed aside the tablet with Echo's report; she didn't need to refresh her memory. It was still fresh in her head, fresh in her dreams.

Frustration reared up within her. This was the safest place from the Altered and wunbies. Her nightmares were moot here. So why couldn't she sleep? She sat up and rubbed the space between her eyes. Maybe taking a few laps around the level would help.

Maneuvering out of the small room into the hallway, Miriam squinted into the bright lights. They were the same as they had been when Echo first arrived—it could've been the middle of the night or noon. The underground facility made it easy to lose track of time.

"Can't sleep?"

Miriam's hand fluttered to her chest. Fox leaned on the inner half wall as he gazed out into the empty center and its levels below.

"You, too?" She joined him, planting her forearms on the cool banister.

"They got an entire village here, but no bar, not even a liquor cabinet. Bunch of prudes."

Her eyebrow arched.

"Relax. Didn't explore like Nosy Nas explores. I haven't fucked up the mission, yet."

She was sure there were highly combustible ingredients tucked away that could be concocted for dangerously strong cocktails, but Miriam didn't offer the comment. Instead she hugged herself, rubbing her arms. Her thin T-shirt was no armor against the cool, recycled air. "I didn't say anything."

"Didn't need to."

A circulation system somewhere switched.

"We have some days ahead of us. Are you going to be okay?"

He leveled a stony stare at her. "You don't have to worry about me. Unless these secret scientists have a superdrug that goes down like moonshine."

"I don't think that's—"

"Was a joke."

Miriam looked away so her expression wouldn't betray her. They stood in silence, watching the stillness of the silo, listening to the hum of faraway generators and the distant footsteps of some scientist working into the night. She let a few sentences roll around in her head, trying to determine if it was the appropriate time to talk about Fox's increasing activity, his coping mechanism, as Yuri called it. She considered cracking an ill-tempered comment, that feasibly, there was something the scientists had, something to take that was strong enough to make the nightmares go away, to fix everything. Was this the opportune time to patch the emotional and mental damage he had sustained in the South? She gamed out her options, but in the end, the timing was wrong.

"It's all fucked, 'innit."

Miriam let his comment hang.

"UMF is sendin' teams out to defend, to figure out who's responsible, but not us. No, we've been held for whatever wimpshit mission this is, and meanwhile, the South's fucked and no one in Station cares 'bout what's goin' on."

"You don't believe the spiel about *our* security?" Miriam said.

Fox didn't answer, and for a second, she wondered if the sarcasm hadn't been blatant enough.

"Station's insulated from what's happening. People's interests only go as far as the city limits. You've seen it. They're more upset that the alties have moved in."

Hell, the scientists in this research facility didn't seem to care what was happening beyond their walls. How long had they all been interred here? They all seemed detached from the same humanity they were supposedly trying to save.

"If any of those coward Royals are the ones responsible, I'll wring their necks myself, but they're jus' a fuckin' distraction right now." His knuckles whitened around the banister. "It's been months, Tan. Those wunby fuckers are out there. And we let them burn those towns down, we let them get away with it. *We* should be the ones huntin' every one of those bastards. Not the other teams."

What could Miriam say? She didn't disagree with him, but she was also glad she didn't have to face the wunbies again so soon.

Fox's voice strained. "They fucked us on both ends and we're doin' nothin'. Months, Tan. Months. Now they have a city, the numbers, whatever tech the Royals left, and they're gonna attack us again—I know it. I know you know it, too, but what are we doin'? Babysittin' alties at home and gettin' interrogated like fuckin' lab rats in some under-fuckin'-ground hole, runnin' errands for scientists with their fuckin' heads in the ground. What are we even doing here?"

Miriam grimaced as he pushed away from the half wall and

his shoulders heaved up and down. She chewed on the inside of her lip, wondering if he was going to vent more or if he was waiting for a response in agreement. Regardless, this wasn't something she could fix. Miriam could mend broken bones, cuts, and scrapes, but this was a different raw and open wound.

Fox kicked his boot into the wall. "I need a fuckin' drink."

10

A NEW WING

ALCOHOL WAS NEVER HER PREFERENCE—EVEN if her brother hadn't steered her away from it growing up, she wasn't keen on the taste. But sitting in the hospital, Sam found herself wishing for a potent cocktail to distract her dancing nerves. She couldn't, of course. No drinking or eating before the procedure. As she watched the seconds drag, intoxication felt like a worthy risk. Waiting was the worst part.

She could hear the network feed in the adjoining room. Some broadcaster droned on about the latest speculations in Arshangol and the Apostates' new government, but she tried to tune it out. It only made her more restless, a reminder that the world had continued on without her. But she was getting back. She wouldn't miss out on anything else once this procedure was done. It wouldn't fail; she had no contingencies for failure. She'd get back to SOG, back to her brother.

Her cuff vibrated on the stand next to her—another message of encouragement from Scott. Part of Sam was upset he wasn't there, but it was no one's fault. She couldn't rub it in either, as his disappointment was already tangible. She was fine. It was an experimental procedure, but the hospital and tech company had assured UMF it wasn't any risk to her life. But they hadn't mentioned the estimated failure rate or the possibility that the connections wouldn't sync.

It wouldn't fail, she reminded herself. The benefit was well worth the cost.

She glanced again at her cuff. Sam knew Echo was away on mission, and Miriam herself had told her they wouldn't be able to communicate, but she had held on to some silly string of hope that maybe, maybe there would be an exception or break.

There wasn't.

Part of her wished she had taken Jace up on his offer. After a couple days of discussing craft and UMF, she didn't really know the man, but he was a growing friend who had given her a breath of relevance. She'd said she wanted to do this on her own. And here she was, on her own.

"Sam Ryan?"

A nurse peeked into the room, and Sam straightened. Her mind, once a flurry of anxiety and anticipation, now stilled under the masked indifference from a stranger's presence.

"Ready?"

Sam swallowed.

◊

As the drugs faded, pulling Sam from unconsciousness, the doctors' and technicians' words blurred into nonsense. She thanked them repeatedly in a slurred drawl, more reflex than understanding.

Something vibrated on the small table to her right, but any movement she tried to make was a monumental feat. Irritation spiked through the heavy throb of pain. Who thought it'd be smart to put her commcuff on the side she couldn't reach? She made a weak effort to lift her unaffected arm, but whatever the hospital had done and for however long, Sam's whole body felt beaten. Every tendon and ligament was sore, as if she had clenched and contracted them for hours.

Was this all worth it? To have her life again?

In her daze, a thought burst into her mind. It was an arm, right? Not something alien or odd they wanted to experiment with? Sam's eyes drew to the dark box that encased the area up to her shoulder. Something was written on it—a brand or a laboratory name—but she couldn't read it from her angle. The mysterious concealment only added to a growing itch she couldn't scratch.

The hours crawled by as she waited, stared, slept, and did nothing. Even when she felt less pained, she resisted the temptation to prod the box, to peek inside to see her recent addition, her new replacement. Sam wasn't sure if it was the fog from the pumped medication or her fear holding her back. It could be anything inside. Success. Failure. Disappointment.

When her consciousness was less muddled and a nurse assisted with her cuff, Sam continued to ignore the burning ache in her shoulders and neck. She busied herself with the network and answering Scott's check-ins. If this didn't work, she'd be forced to accept her reality. Would UMF take on the liability of a one-armed once-wonder? Would she be forced to answer Miriam's question from months before—who did she want to be?

A marine.

Sam wanted to be a marine. More so now, with the Apostates in power and Scott back in UMF. She couldn't miss out; she didn't want to.

When the white-coated doctors and staff returned in a large group, Sam managed a few breaths and a meek croak before careful fingers maneuvered her shoulder and manipulated the case apart. As she gazed at the apparatus, awe briefly overtook her horror. It looked like art, not a limb—sleek, alien, and impossibly integrated with her flesh. It was minimally grooved and bare, its matte gunmetal color dark with her pale-in-comparison skin. As much as Sam hated that she had gotten used to her scarred and disfigured stump, she wasn't prepared for the sight of skeletal, alloy-like material joining her flesh—slivers of healing pink skin spreading past the bandages—as if the prosthetic had swallowed and welded into her body.

Her stomach clenched and pushed against her spine. Her emotions were unclear to her, a mix of horror, awe, excitement, anger, disappointment, and regret. She felt asymmetrical before. What was she now? She was technically balanced, but the asymmetry was still there, now a split world of flesh and tech.

What had she expected? A newly grown arm, the same as before?

This was her new arm.

The surgeon, or scientist—she couldn't tell one occupation from the other—pulled a thin tool from a pocket and prodded each joint of the new fingers, wrist, and elbow. With each point of contact, Sam felt an odd sensation. It wasn't a true sense of touch, but rather what felt like a delayed tickle, like a limb that had fallen asleep. Each test of slight movements and the following questions and answers seemed to elicit professional excitement, but by the end, Sam was drained. The procedure, nervous enthusiasm, and crowd had taken their toll.

After another day's worth of specialty therapists and her promises to continue on a precise recovery schedule, a burgeoning emotion replaced the anticipation and fear. Despite the instructed caution in maintenance, cleaning, weight and pressure limits, Sam was back on the path to functionality and overall utility.

As she stood outside her complex and watched the hospital transport disappear beyond the block, she let the cool city breeze wrap around her. She dodged a passing bystander and adjusted her jacket over the alloy limb. The motion sent a sore throb along its seams, but she smiled. Invisible, but in a different way. A better way.

Was it worth it?

Sam allowed herself to ignore the doctors' instructions this one time and curled her metal digits into a loose fist. The strain of the motion held, and at the growing pressure along her newly welded nerves, she let her fingers unfurl, her grin growing.

It was worth it.

◊

LET'S SEE IT. Scott's hands mirrored his impatience and excitement. His gray-blue eyes lit up, but she wasn't blind to the pronounced dark rings under them—especially in the cuff's illumination.

Sam backed away from the display to bring her upper body into frame. With careful effort and her left hand supporting, she raised the arm and splayed out her new fingers. "What do you think?"

"Wow," her brother rasped.

Wincing, she lowered her prosthetic. *Small motions*, the specialists had said. She was recovering and adapting fast, but pushing the newly fused tissue and nerves would only set her back.

The ache lingered in the days after the procedure, sharp pangs until it lulled into a throb with her frequent injections, but there was something about feeling pain again, and not the invisible phantom sort. Just like the soreness she felt in training, the ache now meant she was on the mend.

CAREFUL, Scott signed.

"I know."

BABY STEPS. EASE INTO IT.

"I know," Sam emphasized. She had been experimenting with her movements from her therapy sessions. It was the longest she had spent constrained within her apartment, and she pushed past her aftercare instructions several times, yearning to do more, and faster. Her body was restless, and after a month's routine of training and time away from her flat, impatience was tapping its foot.

Okay. How does it feel?

"Weird. I don't know how to explain it. It feels like I'm dragging my hand through water, but at least I can..." She trailed off. She could *feel*. "I can't wait to show you in person. The therapists are happy with everything so far, and I think I can get them to sign off on my progress, get the clearance process started with MED."

Her brother just smiled and nodded.

"What." Sam clamped her lips shut. She knew she was talking a lot. "What?"

Scott shook his head. Are you happy?

Happy wasn't the right word. But so far, she *was* satisfied. Sam looked at her partial reflection in the half-covered mirror. The prosthetic felt odd, not entirely hers, but in the last days, she hadn't felt any phantom pains. Her asymmetrical feeling was lessening, and her back and neck muscles had eased up. Human biology was strange, especially as she witnessed her own thoughts and movements adopting the grafted technology as their own. Her motions were clumsy and rigid, but who was she to complain? Sam had a right arm. A hand.

She gingerly flexed the fingers again. "I still have some work to do, but yes. So far." She stepped away from her device and tried to pick her jacket up from her bed. After a day's worth of sessions, her muscles—wires, whatever—were too sore. Sam grabbed the clothing with her other hand and popped back into frame.

You're heading out? I thought you were done for the day.

Sam nodded. "Yeah. And...no."

He gave her a look.

"I'm not pushing anything." This time, she rolled her eyes. Maybe it was good her brother wasn't around in person. His coddling and hovering would've been intolerable. Her mouth twitched as the thought touched a sensitive memory. He had done the same when she was recovering from the Ursus attack, but Scott was holding back. Her voice softened. "That Royal, my new contact—I told you about her—she reached out, and I'm not doing anything else..."

"You should be resting."

Scott's voice startled her, and she paused before responding. "We're just talking. I feel good. It's sore and I know I have a way to go, but I'm taking care of it. I feel good. I just want to get back..."

To Ursus? Sam thought of Echo and Miriam, even if the medic only wanted to be friends. Okay, maybe she wasn't as interested in getting back to the outpost. She had just started enjoying her time in the city, but she wanted to be back with her brother. She had, after all, been twenty-three years with him.

"I want to get back to work."

To normal.

To him.

STUBBORN. He smirked but conceded. CAN'T WAIT TO SEE YOU.

Sam's tongue poked out of her mouth as she concentrated on her hands. CAN'T...WAIT...TO... Pain fringed at the motion, and she gave up signing with a wince. She had a difficult path to go with her recovery and exercises, but she had hands now.

Hands. Plural.

Sam grinned at her brother through the display. "Can't wait to be back."

◊

Though she had only visited the Altered embassy once, her feet navigated the streets as if drawn by instinct. This area was less trafficked, the business day already well over. With no crowds and her new arm concealed in her right sleeve, Sam was content in her thoughts. The alloy still felt foreign, but it carried something better than the void of a lost identity. She pulled the pinky of her new hand along the rough walls and boarded windows, still in awe of the strange, delayed sensation.

She paused at the shift in texture, her fingers lingering on an unexpected coolness. Sam slowly bent her elbow, bringing her prosthetic hand closer for examination. Red color contrasted against her dark finger. Sam looked back. She had mindlessly drawn a line through the start of a fresh Charon lamp. Two canisters of paint sat abandoned on the sidewalk below.

Something clamored from the intersection, and her head swiveled. A shiny flash skittered past her on the pavement, and her eyes followed its reverse path to the corner where three individuals had stumbled into view, curses floating around them. Another figure, outrageously tall, stepped forward.

Sam's heart skipped when red eyes blazed toward her. The Royal's bodyguard. Dmitri.

"Motherfucker! I think it broke my hand!" A clean-shaven man gripped his arm and raised it to another male, whose bare arms were covered in tattoos. His hand was a swelling skin pouch, odd angles protruding from it. Definitely broken. "Mitchell! The fucker broke my hand!"

Mitchell paid Pouch Hand no mind, his bared teeth whipping between the Altered and Sam. The other next to him, Mohawk, brandished a knife expertly, but Dmitri seemed unconcerned as he continued to watch Sam, his eyes lingering over her right sleeve and her new limb. Her breath grew short under his impassive stare, but her gut clenched at the trio's stupidity. The Altered's thin frame was deceiving, but they should've known better from his unnatural irises. Were they not aware of his complete lack of concern toward them—the danger in his apathy?

"Go home, fuckin' lab rat!" Mohawk spat.

Mitchell pulled a baton from his pocket and cast it forward.

Pouch Hand stepped forward, despite his face of pain. "Get 'im!"

Sam took a step closer, unsure of what to do. She knew the Altered bodyguard could handle himself, but the sight of two weapons versus none was alarming. She wasn't sure whose side she was on, even if it was only to save the youngsters from their own ignorance.

"Hey! Look at me when I'm talking to you, freak!" Mohawk darted forward.

Sam's hand shot up, but any warning—to one side or the other—was already too late.

Horror turned into fascination in the millisecond of motion. If she had blinked, she would've missed it. The knife, once in Mohawk's hand, was now in the Altered's. In the following second, Mitchell lunged forward, his baton thrust like a needle at Dmitri's midsection, but his momentum slammed to a stop.

Three pairs of eyes widened along with Sam's. Mohawk stood there dumbfounded as Mitchell tugged at his end, trying to free the weapon from the Altered's grip. A single tendon in Dmitri's forearm flexed as the metal bent in his fist. He let go, and the youngster stumbled back, a crooked scrap in his trembling hand. Dmitri lifted Mohawk's knife up and with his other thumb snapped the blade off.

"What the fuck?" Mohawk stammered as he tripped over his feet.

Dmitri tossed the handle with effortless disdain, leaving Mohawk scrambling to catch it. Terrified silence hovered until it was broken by Pouch Hand's squeaks and subsequent pattering footsteps away.

"Freaks!" Mitchell called out over his shoulder as he scurried off, Mohawk along with him.

The plural use was obvious, and an edge of anger sharpened in Sam's chest. She had done nothing to them.

"Hello, Sam." Kuan-Lin stepped into view, her clothes regal in comparison with the street's shutters and graffiti. "We meet again."

Sam watched Dmitri as she drifted closer, his nonchalant stance and posture the same as before. His ear twitched before it settled a second later. She knew he was monitoring her, despite the lack of overt regard.

"Were you coming by to see us?" The Royal's fingers fussed with the front of her jacket. In between motions, Sam noticed a slash along its fabric. "Did you message? I'm sorry if I missed it, I was a bit preoccupied."

"What happened?"

"Oh, a silly mistake. You've caught me in my hypocrisy, telling the children they shouldn't roam too far, and here I am." She made one last effort to smooth her jacket then sighed softly. "Thank you, Dima. I apologize for the inconvenience."

Had the Royal walked around the area by herself? Sam shook her head as she looked over the Altered woman. The cut fabric seemed like the only blemish. If she had encountered those three by herself, had she tried to appeal to them? Or were the Royals equipped with hidden strengths as well? She wasn't certain with the way Kuan-Lin held herself, but she didn't want to make an underestimation.

"Are you hurt?"

"No, no." The Royal threw a dismissive wave in her direction. Sam caught the sight of blood on her palm before it dropped. Kuan-Lin lightened. "Ah, your arm! How lovely. I presume everything went well. How does it feel?"

"Should we go back to the embassy?" Sam ignored the Royal's question with an eye on the surrounding street. The diplomatic facility was a couple blocks away and red paint peeked out from the shadows. "This isn't the best place to have a conversation."

"I was actually headed back to housing."

"Alone?"

"Not anymore," Kuan-Lin chimed. "You'll join?" She turned to her bodyguard before Sam could answer. "Dima, you can return to the embassy. I'm sorry I pulled you away. The others are probably wondering where you ran off to. I'll let them know it was entirely my fault."

Sam's eyes met Dmitri's. His red eyes betrayed nothing, whereas she was sure he could read all her skepticism and doubts. Her motions were limited, and her new limb was only days old. She wasn't sure if she could defend *herself* at this point, and she was definitely unable to protect someone else, a textbook enemy on top of that. Maybe she should've stayed in her flat and called it a day.

"I don't know if that's a good idea—"

"Nonsense. You're a marine, aren't you? You'll notice trouble before it happens and get us out. From what I've researched, you're quite a good one. You have quite a reputation."

Sam blushed at the compliment, but then her brows narrowed. How did she know? Perhaps through Station's politicians and their connections to UMF? With her brief interactions with the Royal, she wouldn't be surprised at Kuan-Lin's ability to charm.

"We both need the air." The Royal started a confident stride before she halted and turned around. "Unless—are you able to? With your recovery? Forgive me, I forget sometimes about your —our different limitations."

Sam scoffed. It felt like a challenge. "How far is it? We can take a people-mover back. I'm not sure when the next one is, but it'll be better than..." She trailed off.

Than getting shanked.

"I prefer walking. It won't take long, not with good company." She gestured with her head. "Dima, go back. I'll see you later. Thank you. I'm in excellent hands."

Sam reluctantly fell into a matching stride with the Royal. Unsurprisingly, the bodyguard disregarded Kuan-Lin's dismissal, and he hung a few meters back like a long shadow. It made her uneasy, but it was mixed with reassurance and relief.

"So, the procedure went well? You're happy with the results?"

Sam nodded. "For now." She'd be happy when she was back in uniform with her carbine in hand.

As if she read her mind, Kuan-Lin responded, "I admire that about you, your sense of duty. Why do you do it?"

The question stumped Sam. She opened her mouth but closed it when she realized she didn't have a suitable answer. UMF's canned mission statement had been at the tip of her tongue. Protect and secure humankind's ideals and interests. That response would be brushed aside by the sharp Royal. Sam wasn't in the military for altruistic reasons—they were a bonus, sure, but she had been in since she was young and until she met Echo, she hadn't considered anything else. Her current answer felt silly as well: she did it because that's what she was good at. And she enjoyed being good at things. She liked the feeling of being needed, wanted. Belonging.

In the end, Sam said nothing, and Kuan-Lin didn't seem to mind as she led the conversation in a different direction. Before Sam knew it, they arrived at a substantial fence wrapping around what looked like a couple blocks of high-rise apartments. How many Altered were in the city?

"Do you think it's more for our safety or for yours?"

Sam studied the thin and simple fence. She doubted it would actually keep anyone in or out, but something visible, something tangible provided assurances to the surrounding sector. Sympathy twinged in her throat, which felt strange. Sam was educated with the knowledge that Altered were supposed to be evil and oppressive—she had seen a lot, but before everything with the Apostates, UMF operations were mostly against humans who were arguably just as terrible.

"Am I allowed to be here?" Sam asked, ignoring the Royal's question.

"Why wouldn't you? This is your city, isn't it?"

Not really. Sam wasn't from Station, but she felt the question was more pointed at it being a *human* city. The question felt like a test, and she also chose not to answer it.

"Come in for tea. You too, Dima, unless you're heading back?"

The man remained a distance away with no expression or response. The gate opened, and a patch of white color presented itself. Sam flinched, but it was only an unarmored legionnaire, a small knife sheathed at his side. This Altered soldier stood about the same height as Dmitri but was full of muscle along every inch of his body. He bowed his head to the Royal, and then his dark green and bright blue eyes shot to Sam with a curious glare. They dropped as they passed, in deference to the Royal—or was it the bodyguard?

Sam followed Kuan-Lin through a courtyard of curving sculptures and a small playground. She could tell this had once been an area of poverty but was thriving now with its new tenants. In fact, the gated district was much cleaner than its surrounding perimeter streets. Sam's head turned with the realization she had unintentionally followed the Royal into a place no other humans went. It was a credit to Kuan-Lin for how at ease she had put her. Panic flickered in Sam's mind, and she cursed under her breath. She hadn't told anyone of her whereabouts. Her brother knew, but he thought she was at the embassy.

As they maneuvered further between the buildings, Sam tried to reassure herself. When they entered one structure indistinguishable from the others, her mind remained a hurricane, unable to take in everything as the anxiety multiplied. They exited the lift and walked down an unassuming hall, and her shoulder throbbed at her prosthetic fingers' anxious movements.

A door at the end opened and a familiar boy stood inside the frame. He muttered something in another language, then rolled his eyes at the face Kuan-Lin must have given him. "You're late, Auntie."

"Longwei, you remember Sam."

"I remember. The ga—" The boy cut off as he spotted Sam's prosthetic. "She grew back an arm."

"Manners." Kuan-Lin rapped her fingers on the top of the boy's head. "Make some tea, please."

Sam paused at the threshold as the boy pivoted and followed his aunt in. She glimpsed the stony Dmitri behind her, waiting for her next move. With a deep breath, she stepped into the living quarters. The space was as pleasant as Kuan-Lin's embassy office. However, there were nuances that made the flat more *human*, a line of leafy plants to the side and a tapestry of bold colors.

"Dima, I'm alright. Thank you for accompanying us. You can go back to the others. We're safe here."

The Altered man stood in the middle of the doorframe, his expression flat. His red eyes followed Sam a second longer before he turned and exited without a word.

Sam sighed, relieved, although that feeling dropped as the door shut and she remembered where she was. She swallowed back the thought before it could fully manifest, and gave her prosthetic fingers a small flick, a reminder of confidence. Information. Intelligence. She was on a mission. She was good at missions.

"Please, make yourself at home. Would you like something to eat?" the Royal's voice lilted from the other room.

Sam shook her head then squeezed an eye shut. Even with heightened senses, Altered couldn't see through walls—she was pretty sure, at least. "No," she replied. She added a soft thank-you to match the politeness. Unsure of what to do, Sam wandered toward their voices and turned into a kitchen. She took in the wide space, homier than the previous room.

"How was school?" Kuan-Lin said as she quickly doted over a small vertical garden of sprouting plants hanging above the sink.

The boy stood on his toes to manipulate a familiar box-like contraption. He finished whatever he was doing, then pulled himself into a tall chair at the kitchen counter, sticking out his tongue.

"School?" Sam blurted. "They're in school here?"

Kuan-Lin shot a smile over her shoulder as she moved to wash her hands. Pale red mixed into the short burst of water. From what Sam could see, a clean cut lined along her palm, although it looked like it was already closing. "Of course. Education must endure, even in times of war." She quickly added, "It's a privilege we can have here. Plus, it keeps the young busy and out of trouble."

Sam's eyebrow arched, and she glanced again at the Royal's hands as they dried.

Kuan-Lin chuckled. "I have a lot to learn as well." She retrieved two cups from the device and placed one in front of Sam, before handing the boy the other. "Tell our guest what you're learning, Longwei."

"Biochemistry." His eyelids fluttered. "But I don't see the point. It's silly. I should learn history or economics. That's what the scientists are there for. *Ah-pah* said we're meant to rule."

The Royal's smile tightened, but she hid it by turning back to the tea machine. "What else did my brother say?"

Longwei recited as he swirled the liquid in his cup, "We are the supreme and rightful rulers of everything and everyone."

Sam looked into her own drink before she reached out for it —left hand first, then her prosthetic, and back to her left hand. Now didn't seem the time to attempt holding something delicate with hot contents. She watched the others drink first before she let the liquid touch the tip of her tongue. Bitter, as expected, but there was a sweetness at the end. It was fine, but she preferred coffee. She set it down and rubbed her prosthetic, trying to find comfort in motion.

Kuan-Lin sighed. "All under heaven."

"All under heaven," the boy repeated with a shrug. "*Ah-goo*, but if that's so, and the rebels have taken over..." He quieted, his eyes dropping as if he were too shy, or scared, to continue.

"Go ahead."

He leaned forward and whispered, "If we're better, how come we're here now? We're the rightful rulers and we're stronger, but we're losing. Does that mean we've lost our right to rule?"

"What do you think?" Kuan-Lin prodded.

The boy shrugged again and placed his tea to the side. "I don't know, but *Ma*...she said this was temporary. We'll be back home soon and capture the *pai-lang* and everyone involved, but she hasn't talked much since Arshangol, and Ah-pah..." He drifted off and pressed his chin into the counter. "Ma said it's a deep shame we're living amongst..." He peeped at Sam and then away. "Roaches."

Sam's stomach twisted.

"But is that what *you* think?"

His mouth pinched to the side.

"Do you think Sam is a roach?" She kept a soft gaze on her nephew. "She didn't have to, but she helped you and your sister."

The boy pondered, rolling his chin in a small circle on the smooth surface. "Don't tell Ma, okay?"

"Whatever you say here is safe with me."

With another reassuring nod from Kuan-Lin, Longwei whispered, "I don't think we're that different."

A shiver ran over Sam's skin, and then her commcuff buzzed against her wrist. She shook the notification away and apologized in a murmur.

Kuan-Lin tapped the side of Longwei's cup. "You're an

intelligent boy." She gave him a warm smile. "Go ahead. You can play with my tablet in the bedroom."

His eyes brightened, and he clamored off the chair, disappearing around the corner.

With him gone, the Royal patted the counter. "Come." She took Longwei's vacated seat as Sam hesitantly moved forward and sat in the next chair.

In her nervousness, Sam realized she had forgotten the cup of tea and reached out to handle it. Dark fingers fumbled, and she winced. Hot liquid splashed onto the counter surface, and for a fleeting second, she expected the delicate container to break. Sam's neck flushed, and she jumped up.

At her side, the Royal barely flinched. Her voice was calm as she gracefully stood and returned to the tea machine. "Don't worry. This is nothing to stress about." While it worked, she wiped at the mess with a delicate swoop.

Sam sat, her ears growing hot from the mix of embarrassment and frustration.

"You can't be too hard on yourself."

Kuan-Lin produced another cup, and she held it out in front of her. When Sam shook her head, the Royal offered an encouraging nod. "Try again."

The warmth in Kuan-Lin's voice stoked an ember of Sam's frustration and a spear of anger formed, aimed at the woman, but Sam reached out slowly, her prosthetic palm up. The cup of tea set down and Sam supported the delicate item with her left hand, cradling it toward her.

"It's okay to use both, to have support."

If Sam hadn't been so focused on redeeming herself, that rage would've sharpened and found Kuan-Lin's words patronizing, despite their lack of hostility or condescension. The Royal returned to her seat and watched Sam meticulously place the cup back on the counter before she held out her palm with the pale, already healing cut. "May I?"

Sam shook off her jacket and grimaced as she placed her

arm on the surface. The motion hurt with the day's strain already settling in. Kuan-Lin shifted and studied the prosthetic with hovering fingers. Shortly, Sam's cuff vibrated again on her left wrist. She dismissed the call.

Without looking up, the Royal hummed. "You can answer, if you'd like. UMF? Or someone else? A romantic interest?"

Sam's jaw pulsed. She would've welcomed positive news from the military. And Miriam, anything from her.

"Just my brother."

"You have a brother here?"

Sam paused. The Royal knew enough that she had a good reputation. Anything she found would've informed her of Scott as well—they had been working together for years. Kuan-Lin was either bluffing before or she was feigning a lack of knowledge now. It was a reminder that Sam was trying to work with someone she didn't know or trust. She wasn't the only one with an ulterior motive.

"No. He's up north."

"Do you miss him?"

She did, but what did this have to do with anything?

"Yes," Sam replied.

Silence descended as Kuan-Lin poked along the panels and seams of her alloy arm. Sam stared at the vertical garden. It reminded her of Scott's in his apartment back home.

"Your bodyguard actually reminds me of him," Sam said, trying to fill the space.

"Dima? In what way?"

"He's quiet. Although if you get to know Scott, he isn't, not really."

Kuan-Lin quirked her mouth amusedly. "The quiet ones usually have the most to say; they just need the right medium." She then hummed again in acknowledgment. "I'd love to know more."

Sam hid a nervous swallow. She hadn't meant to divulge that.

The Royal waited, but with no response, she patted the prosthetic. "I've never been one for the sciences—not my strength, I think—but this looks like solid work. The connections seem well-fused, very similar to the tech I've seen on our side of the world. Are you satisfied?"

Grateful for the change of subject, Sam pulled her arm back to her side and made a fist underneath the counter. She wasn't an expert in the field, but she figured her prosthetic and the excitement around it was due to something reverse-engineered from Altered technology. She didn't care about that; she was just the willing experiment, and so far she had no complaints.

"I think so."

"Then everything is good." The woman took a long inhale and sighed.

Another lengthy pause sat between them. Sam brought the cup of tea back to her lips and fished for some segue or opening to lead into what Jace wanted. Information. Who was responsible? What was happening across the ocean?

"What would you like to know?"

Sam paused mid-sip. Had she said it out loud? Or was she that obvious?

"Aside from whatever your unit wants, of course. It's why you came in the first place, it's why you're here now, isn't it?"

Denial caught in Sam's throat, and she glanced at the exit.

"Don't worry. I don't have the constitution for murder. Longwei, on the other hand..." Kuan-Lin held an even gaze before her eyes crinkled and she laughed. Sam watched, frozen, while the Royal wiped a tear from her eye. "Ah, sorry. Poor attempt at a joke. It wasn't appropriate, but it feels good to laugh. There hasn't been a lot to laugh about." Kuan-Lin offered an encouraging smile, but Sam was skeptical.

"You've known this entire time."

The smile grew wider.

"Why?"

"Why not? What do we have to lose? We've already lost so

much." The Royal sat her chin in the palm of her hand. "Call it personalized diplomacy. And if we're being honest with each other, I needed a friend."

Sam scrunched her forehead. Friend. The word had a bitter taste to it, but it wasn't the time to dissect that. Plus, she didn't want to be friends with a Royal. This was work. This was a mission, but she'd play along if it meant getting out of there alive and getting what UMF wanted.

"If you tell me more about yourself, your brother, and life over here, I'll tell you what I can, I promise. You don't know what a relief this is, talking normally outside of politician rings and bureaucratic nonsense." Kuan-Lin smiled again. "Go on. Ask me what you want."

With a hesitant stare, Sam was deliberate in her next words. "The Apostates. They're responsible."

"Yes."

"Who?"

To Sam's surprise, Kuan-Lin didn't hesitate. "The man you've seen on your network is Beric Rahul, but he's only a mouthpiece. We believe the one who brought the factions together, organizing the coup—everything—is a man by the name Kartik Finlay. His followers call him General even though he never held that rank in the People's Army."

It was a bomb of information. Sam swallowed with the realization that the door had fully opened, and repeated the names in her head, committing them to memory. "Legion?"

The Royal shook her head. "The People's Army. Disbanded since we detained the last Sovereign, of course. Created by him to *supplement* Legion. A force of non-designs and mixes. If only they knew what he actually thought of them... Perhaps they never would have served, become the fanatics and radicals they are now."

"And where *are* they now?"

Kuan-Lin gave her an amused look, and Sam's hand

tightened. She wanted everything she could get, and at this juncture, the rapport-building had been tossed to the side.

"It pains me to say most of them are advancing east, expanding faster than we imagined. We underestimated them and their eagerness to destroy the land, and to be truthful, we underestimated our own willingness to burn and ruin crops to try to stop them. Decades of growth and regrowth gone. Just like that." She sighed at Sam's confused expression. "If you can't feed your soldiers, they cannot fight, but it's a balance. If you starve them, what will they do in desperation?"

Sam sat, trying to process the flood of information. "Does City Center know all of this?"

Kuan-Lin shook her head again.

"Why me?" Sam's eyebrows pinched together. The Royal had given her this so freely.

Kuan-Lin laughed. "I don't know. You caught me at the right time." She ran her hand across her jaw as if she had just realized what she had released in her frustration. "We actually met with your politicians earlier. Both sides—yours and ours—continue to be as tight-lipped and empty-worded as you would expect." She huffed. "And I'm a backbencher; I have no seat at the table with the others here now. Customs and traditions before everything, of course, even if it's to our detriment."

"Will this get you in trouble?" The words escaped Sam's mouth. When did she start caring? Sam was getting what she wanted.

Kuan-Lin took another sip. "What will they do? Exile me? We're all in exile now."

With her other hand, the Royal made an elaborate gesture in the air. She stared into her cup as a holodisplay projected over the counter next to them, a feed in a different language. Sam's stomach turned as the picture changed to naked bodies, maimed and cut open—some castrated—swinging on rows of constructed gallows. She couldn't tell who they were, but there was one bloody face that held resemblance to the Royal next to her. Sam looked away to confirm the corpse's son, Kuan-Lin's nephew, was not in the room.

"If we don't start talking and working together, it'll be too late. It's already too late for my brother, my friends, and my family." Kuan-Lin's eyes unfocused as she waved her hand in the air, and the feed dispersed. "If we don't do something, anything, regret will haunt all of us."

11

ADHESION

"I DIDN'T KNOW I could be simultaneously intrigued *and* bored with a mission like this," Kai said as she swung her legs over the edge of the bed. "We're in one of the biggest secrets of the human world, with a crazy amount of whatever science on every floor, and here we are, *stuck and blindfolded.*"

They were essentially prisoners—*guests* confined to certain levels, their movements restricted by invasive surveillance.

"It's been a day since our last interview, and I can only stare at the wall for so long. I don't know how the people here do it."

Miriam bounced a ball she had found in an unused game room against the concrete wall. She shuddered at the memory of hooked-up wires and nodes as each interrogation progressed. She'd relived what had happened in the South, her encounter with the Altered farmers, their fight with the Apostate scouts, and their stand in Temunco Outpost against the horde. She cringed at their grilling questions on how many bullets she estimated each Altered had taken before they were subdued, how much she estimated they bled, how long they continued to fight while burning in napalm.

It had been one day, and Miriam was growing restless like the others, but she was also grateful for the lack of news from the scientists. It meant no more questions, no more reliving the nightmares raging behind her closed eyes.

"They're done with us, right?"

Miriam shrugged then added a quick nod to her teammate. She and Kai had been separately pulled to discuss the hybrid Altered-human child they had seen in Matam's matriarch den. Miriam had little to say on it though, with everything else that had been happening. The scientists were visibly frustrated with her answers, but Miriam was certain they wouldn't have been satisfied with anything barring the actual DNA, blood, or living tissue samples they apparently should've taken while they were in the middle of an invasion and slaughter.

"What a waste of our time," Kai grumbled.

"I don't think they care. We're just military grunts to them."

"They don't seem to care about what's happening in the real world. They were so clinical, so...divorced from it all. How can people live like this?"

Miriam scoffed. "At least we're being released soon."

She had theorized—semi-jokingly—they were being observed and held in case the scientists wanted to experiment on them. Yuri's theory was that the Axiom scientists were lonely, and Echo's presence was a novelty, a reminder that there was another world outside the thick silo walls. Both ideas were awful, and Miriam wanted to be back home where her nightmares weren't prodded with nowhere to escape. At least in the city, she had distractions.

"Do you think Center sanctioned all of this? UMF? The Royals probably don't know about this—I doubt we'd want them to know... I still have so many questions, and it's killing me with how little they're telling us. Maybe Axiom will invite us back. Do you think they'd let us into the labs or at least tell us what they're doing here when we're done?"

Miriam gave Kai an acknowledging but noncommittal shrug. With how the week had progressed, she doubted they'd have any satisfying follow-up from Axiom, UMF, or the city's politicians.

A sharp knock rapped on their door, and Miriam and Kai sat up as it opened. Yuri stood in the frame and gestured his head. "Come on. Boss wants a team chat."

Kai untangled herself and scurried after their second. Miriam tossed the ball one more time before she followed them both to the cafeteria nearby. Echo had the space to themselves, but they convened at a small round table in the corner.

"No Doctor Cato?" Kai asked.

Miriam rolled her eyes. Though it was Cato's idea to bring Echo to the facility, the scientist was not subtle in his indifference.

Krill shook his head, crossed his arms, and leaned back in his metal chair. "Doctor Cato passes along Axiom's gratitude for our cooperation."

Miriam doubted the scientists had actually said anything to that effect. They had rarely seen Cato nor Paksima after their initial meeting.

"We're heading out. No debrief when we get back."

"Awesome," Nas blurted. "Wait, no. What?"

Every UMF mission had a debrief, whether immediately after or within the following weeks, depending on priorities. It was unsettling and concerning to not have one.

"Debrief or not, remember what we were told. Discretion. We'll rejoin the SOG rotation, but Axiom's request will be added as a priority."

Miriam shared a look with Yuri, then turned back to Krill. He was dodging a significant chunk of information. "And what exactly is this *request*?"

The lead rubbed the bridge of his nose, and Miriam braced herself. Whatever he was going to say, she knew she wasn't going to like it.

"Snatch and grab."

"Okay...and UMF knows about this?" Kai asked, her dark brows furrowing.

"Someone in Command does. UMF wouldn't have sent us here if not."

Miriam's chest constricted. She wasn't concerned with the chain of command. "What do you mean snatch and grab?"

Krill rubbed his arms nervously. "We've done a couple before."

Yuri caught on as well. "Boss, who are we grabbing?"

Part of Miriam already knew the answer. She had a feeling but was holding out hope that it wasn't true. Not until the team lead confirmed it.

But it was Nas who stiffened then jumped out of his chair. "They want us to pick up an alty?"

Miriam's insides churned faster, and cold shivers rushed along her spine in violent jolts. She closed her eyes. "They want us to pick up a *stimmed* alty."

Axiom, Vertex, or whoever these scientists were working for, was focused not on the alties themselves, but the drug that made them significantly faster and stronger, the stims that created almost unstoppable monsters with no fear of death.

Yuri's stare hardened. "Boss?"

Krill nodded once.

Miriam's stomach lurched as the others descended into a mix of whistles and muttered expletives. More excited than the others, Nas hopped on both feet and shook Kai's shoulder.

"Sit down," Miriam snapped, and then her tone softened. "Don't mess up your leg."

Her teammate gave her a simmering look. "It's fine. Whatever Axiom is, their stuff is good. Look." He did an arrogant jig and Miriam grumbled.

"But what are they going to do with a stimmed alty?" Kai asked.

"Does it matter?" Nas said. "We have our next objective."

Krill cleared his throat and glared until everyone hushed. "I don't know. I'm not thrilled about it either, but Echo delivers. *We* deliver."

Miriam clenched her fists, wishing she had brought the ball along, something to squeeze. The last time they had been assigned an ambiguous mission, it had opened a box of chaos and disaster. Nothing good would come from this.

◊

With nary a farewell from Doctors Paksima or Cato, Echo left the facility via a separate access point. Their gear, weapons, and radioactive suits met them in an exit chamber as a heavy door swung shut behind them. After a series of dark twists and turns, they were back in the cavern, the small RHIB where they had left it. No one was surprised at the waiting scout cruiser, coordinates sent mysteriously through higher channels.

In the first hours, Echo was quiet. The isolation had rendered each one tired in their own ways, sitting in their brooding silence. Even Nas, who had been bouncing off the walls, had folded into himself alongside the others. Reliving their experience to scientists—their decisions, reminders of death—had been sobering in itself, gnawing at their edges, leaving them frayed and haunted by unspoken thoughts. The added knowledge of their next objective had already lost its excitement as the weight and risk of it settled.

Despite everything, everyone's spirits rose as they reunited with their devices, and once more when they regained full connection to the network. A week's worth of messages and updates flooded in. The strife in Arshangol had lost its front-page status, buried behind tensions in the city and the increase in crime and vandalism. She ignored the cold business messages from her parents and short-worded pings from one-night stands she couldn't remember. But with a certain private channel, Miriam couldn't hide a chuckle. Though she was disappointed at the quantity, the block of messages brought a warmth that soothed the week's planted anxiety.

> S. RYAN: Hi. Good luck and be safe. Sorry if I missed you. I think you might've gone off-grid already.

> S. RYAN: I'm attempting contact and on my way to the embassy. Do you think this is a bad idea?

> S. RYAN: Ha. I think it might be a bad idea, but what else can I do?

> S. RYAN: Hope I don't die.

> S. RYAN: Didn't die. That's good.

> S. RYAN: I'm in pre-op. Your hospital is nice. I saw a kiosk with your parents' picture. If Yuri hadn't mentioned it, I wouldn't have known you were related. They look lovely together, but your mother looks like she'd scold me all the time.

> S. RYAN: It feels pretty silly sending these messages knowing you're not able to respond.

> S. RYAN: Hii m oyt sirhurti o moss ipo

> S. RYAN: That's not embarrassing. The prosthetic is good. I'm still at the hospital. It's taking me a long time to do this with the new arm, but I'm trying to get better with my fingers.

> S. RYAN: Joints. Fingers. All the mechanics.

> S. RYAN: I think you and the others are getting back today. I'll check with Jace and meet you.

> S. RYAN: Welcome back, I think. Or whenever you get a signal.

By the time they passed the base's administrative buildings

and the shuttle crossed the compound, Miriam had reread the messages multiple times with a wide grin. In the time she knew Sam, the blonde wasn't entirely reserved like her brother, but she lived in her head a lot. Miriam made a note to message Sam more, amused at the woman's awkwardness but increased verbosity. She enjoyed peeling back Sam's layers and cracking open her otherwise tough exterior. There was an untapped softness and vulnerability underneath that drew her in.

And outside the SOG building, Sam's presence was a pleasant surprise. She stood there in dark civilian clothes with her left arm cradling her right, and the return of confidence was obvious by the way she held herself. Miriam was unnerved by the tug in her chest as the others descended on the woman. Nas fussed over the new prosthetic, picking it up and trying to manipulate it, followed by Yuri and Kai flicking him for his lack of gentleness. Even Krill and Fox hovered, their own excitement cutting through whatever had been on their minds before. Miriam followed the flush of color as it spread up Sam's neck, jawline, cheekbones, and up to those nervous blue eyes.

She shook aside a warm, but uncomfortable feeling. "Nas, give the woman her arm back. Didn't you say you have to get home and check in with your family?"

"Sure, sure," he groaned. "Valk, walk me through whatever you remember later. And schematics. If they gave you any, I'd love to see them."

Sam shot Miriam a look of gratitude as Kai and Nas sandwiched her, guiding her inside to their team room.

As the rest of the team followed, Yuri's elbow dug into Miriam's ribs and he whispered in her ear, "Shouldn't *you* check in with your family?"

She glared at him, but didn't answer. She wouldn't put it past either of her parents to message her best friend to get to her.

Inside, Echo put their items away with a renewed fervor. Most of the team was still sore about the anticlimactic lack of actual *mission,* but the return to the city had brought life back to them.

Nas, having shoved all his gear into his locker, brightened. "We're all still hitting up Duncan's, right? I'd like to get my lips on a cold blender bender."

"Ew, why did you have to say it like that?" Kai threw her crumpled suit.

He swatted it away and laughed. "And Tan can get her lips on someone!" He puckered his mouth.

Miriam's eyes flung daggers, then flitted to Sam, whose own had dropped to the floor. "Kai, smack him for me."

Skin slapped against skin and a yelp followed.

Miriam peeked at Fox. It was actually a line their teammate would have normally said, but the man was already heading for the door. She stepped in front of him. "If we're going to hang out, let's get out of here. How about somewhere in the city?" With Fox's inevitable bender after a week of going dry, it'd be better away from UMF.

"Oh, I've been meaning to try Buzz Hallow since it opened," Kai said.

"Fox?"

The man sidestepped Miriam but grunted a response, which she took as an affirmative, and then he was out the door.

"Valk, you're coming. And that's not a question," Kai whooped.

"I was actually going to meet—" Sam recoiled at the engineer's pointed finger. "Okay."

"You all have fun." Krill shut his locker and clapped his hands. "But please, be smart. Watch what you say, and don't make terrible choices." He glared around the room, a reminder to keep their mouths shut about their strange mission and instructions.

"You're not joining?" Kai whined.

The team lead was probably off on a date with a certain cruiser pilot. Miriam threw a wink. "Dress nice for Elly, boss."

He responded with a heavy eye roll and exited behind Kai and Nas. Sam made to follow, but Miriam threw up a quick hand.

"Wait up?"

Sam shifted her weight and nodded.

Yuri stood still before he looked between the two women and closed his locker. Miriam ignored the curious lift of his brow as he passed. "See you later, Valk. The arm looks fantastic. I'm sure your brother can't wait to have you back."

Sam grinned then stared down at the ground as she waited for Miriam to finish up, her shoe making small movements along the floor.

"Yuri's right. It looks great." Miriam surveyed the prosthetic as she exited the building with Sam and made their way toward the compound gates. "Everything went well? Are you on medications? I'm sorry I missed it—the procedure."

Sam's foot scuffed against the ground mid-step. "Yeah, and it's okay, they took care of me."

"Still. I would've liked to be there. For you." Miriam glanced over at the woman but her gaze was elsewhere. "How's your mobility?"

"Getting better each day." Sam raised the prosthetic and wiggled her fingers.

"Good, I'm glad. Make sure you get plenty of rest. Listen to your body."

The woman shot her a look, and Miriam shrugged.

"I'm sure you've already updated MED, too?"

Sam tensed. "I started the process."

"Well, MED's a bane. You'll have to exercise a shit ton more patience with them. Trust me, I know." Miriam laughed. "But this is movement—*good* movement. You'll be back on missions soon."

As they neared the gate, Sam's pace slowed, and Miriam turned. "You're heading to Buzz, right? I can send you the location if you're not familiar with it…" She paused, studying the woman's expression. "You know you're one of us. With everything that's happened, you're part of this team forever."

Sam stopped and rubbed her hand through her short hair. "No, yeah. I'll be there. I just—I told Jace I'd meet with him after I saw you guys."

"Jace? Wh—" Miriam composed herself. "Is everything okay?"

"No, I mean, yes, everything's fine. He's been helping me with the Royal—"

Miriam's brows furrowed. "Did he push you to do it?"

"I—"

"By yourself? It's—"

"Mir." Sam's eyes hardened. "I know you think—" She exhaled. "I can handle myself."

"No, of course you can. I'm sorry, I didn't mean it like that. It's just—" Miriam cut off. Shit. Why was she so thrown off?

Blue eyes shifted to something behind her and before she could turn, footsteps bounded toward them. Miriam's jaw clamped down as Sam disappeared into someone's embrace.

"Holy fuck, Ryan. You are absolutely brilliant."

Sam pulled herself out of the man's hold and let out a sheepish chuckle.

"Hey, Jace." Miriam bit the inside of her lip, her chest tight.

"Tan! Hi! Sorry, I was so tunnel visioned." He squeezed Sam's left shoulder. "How was the mission? Did it go well? Everyone intact?"

"It was fine." Miriam slanted her eyes. "What's going on?"

His grin grew. "Valkyrie created a bridge for us. It's huge."

"I really didn't do much." Sam's cheeks flushed.

"Stop being modest. You're a natural at this. I've been telling you every day, and I really wish you'd accept it."

Miriam's jaw set again. Sam and Jace had been talking every day? Echo had been gone less than a week. What happened while she was underground? How were they this close when they had just met?

"We're going to the base café. Do you want to join?"

Miriam gandered down at her clothes. They were clean-ish, but they felt dirtied with every painful interview and revived memory. She wanted a shower. She wanted sleep. Miriam shook her head. "I should pop by the apartment, change before Buzz."

Sam shifted. "I'll catch up with you later?"

Miriam caught her gaze and forced a muscle in her cheek to pull up. "Yeah. See you in a bit."

And with a deepening frown, she watched as Sam and Jace headed in the other direction, back toward the center of the compound. What happened while she was gone, and why did she hate it?

◊

Buzz Hallow's air circulation system stretched past its capacity as heat congregated and perspiration mixed on the dance floor. The latest trendy beat thumped in Miriam's chest and ears, a languid melody weaving itself between. No one would've figured a war was happening on the opposite side of the world or that the city was combusting with anti-alty rhetoric. She regretted suggesting a bar in the city, or really, letting Kai decide which one. She normally would've been fine with the crowd, but now, she secretly wished for something less busy.

Miriam shot a look across the bar, her finger drawing jagged lines in the condensation on her cup. She frowned as Jace's hand slid forward and touched Sam's. The woman didn't seem to notice, too busy smiling and laughing at Nas, Jace, or something they said.

"You know, I never really thought about it until now, but they'd make a cute couple. Do you think they're dating?"

Miriam's head snapped to the side. If her eyes had points, they would have pierced bone.

But Kai didn't notice. "A lot can happen in a week, I guess. I mean, hell, remember my first mission with you guys? It just took a few days, and it was love. Team love."

"Sure," Miriam mumbled. Her eyes narrowed as Sam laughed again. Jace was fun, but he wasn't *that* funny. She eyed the drink in Sam's hand, then returned to the woman's face. *Had* the two already been together? Her gut knotted at the thought.

Kai balanced a few cups between her hands and shouted over the bellowing bass, "You'll grab the rest?"

Miriam nodded.

The music dropped into a flowing melody, its volume low enough to hear her teammate's sigh and parting words. "Oh young, sweet love." And then Kai was off, the drinks held protectively from the rolling wave of patrons.

Miriam flicked at a crumb as she waited for the rest of the order. *Love.* Whatever was going on between Sam and Jace wasn't love. Young, sweet lust maybe. Infatuation. She welcomed the cool burn of alcohol down her throat. It warmed in her core but did nothing to ease the knot in her gut. What did Kai know about love, anyway? What did any of them?

"Need some help?" Yuri slid into the space next to her.

The barkeep placed two more drinks down as Miriam finished hers in another large gulp. She shook her head. "Kai already took some back. Just waiting on one more." She turned to watch Sam reach for her cup, her prosthetic overshooting. Jace nimbly caught the wobbling container before it tipped.

"Yeah! I can't tell if the city's forgotten the world's gone to shit or if they're *trying* to forget," he shouted over the thrum.

Miriam would love to forget. Especially what she was watching now.

"Seems like Jace has a crush."

Scowling, Miriam grabbed at one of the fresh drinks. "No shit. He's practically hanging off her. Wasn't he supposed to be on an assignment?"

Yuri thumbed the edge of the counter. "Tan, are you…" He raised an eyebrow.

"Don't you dare." She stabbed a finger at him. "It's not that at all. She's vulnerable right now. She doesn't need—"

"What? Someone to look after her? Someone to make her feel good? Safe?" He laughed. "Look at her, she's enjoying herself. You and I saw her—what, months ago, after everything—and she was in bad shape. Really bad shape. She deserves this." Yuri gave her a look, a particular glint in his eyes. "It's pretty surprising though. Jacey-boy has more game than I thought. It's a good thing her brother isn't here. I wonder if he'd approve."

She brushed him off.

"I'm kidding. What happened between you two? I thought you were getting along?"

They both watched as Sam left the table and disappeared into the crowd. Jace followed shortly.

Barely restraining herself, Miriam turned back to Yuri. "We are getting along. We're friends."

"*We're* friends."

"Yeah. And I don't…" She waited for the music to drop to a manageable level. "You know. With friends."

"Sure, but you have me and I'm enough; you don't need more friends. Live a little! Isn't that what you tell all the ladies?" Yuri grinned as he dodged her open hand. And then he swiped up the drinks, winked over his shoulder, and joined the others before she could retort.

Miriam glowered as she downed the second drink. A quick raised hand procured another, and she muttered curses into the cup as the alcohol kissed her lip. She was off. That was all. What she needed was her usual game, her usual fun and relief. She peeled her eyes away from where she had last seen Sam and pushed both her and Jace out of her mind.

It was disappointing. Even with the number of bodies in the room, none of the options were enticing. Miriam drifted her fingers over her commcuff and opened a private channel. Ana was an exception. She was there when she needed a distraction or something quick. The woman was always willing, and she didn't loiter. Ana knew their arrangement.

Her fingers hovered over the unsent message when her eye caught something bright. Underneath an updo of bold, platinum-dyed hair, the woman bore pouty lips and her dress hung off a curvy frame—an interesting choice, almost desperate for attention. Miriam bit her lip. She could work with this; she'd worked with less. A mutter of gratitude bubbled into her drink before she knocked it back. This was the better choice. She'd never seen the person before, and she wouldn't have to think of her the next day.

Miriam's eyes followed swaying hips as they weaved to the other side of the room. She wasn't the only one. A young man pushed away from a table, slicked his hair back, and pursued the woman, two drinks in his hands. He reminded Miriam of Jace following Sam. Where had those two gone off to? Did Sam like him? Sure, her former teammate and the blonde had a couple similarities bringing them together, but was there something more?

She shook her head, trying to knock the thoughts away. She and Sam were friends. They had kissed, but Miriam wanted nothing beyond that. Maybe she should've slept with Sam that night—maybe it could've saved the woman from the attack, and maybe she could still do it, satiate whatever she was feeling now.

But a sliver of her wanted something else.

But nothing beyond friendship lasted.

Miriam sighed. She knew herself. She'd get bored. And she certainly didn't want to be tied down. Worse, she didn't want to disappoint or hurt Sam, because Sam was something else. Sam had saved her life, and they had grown close in a way that she never had with others. They had fought by each other's side, and Miriam had been there as the woman broke emotionally and pieced herself back together. It was a vulnerability entrusted to her, and she hated that she *hadn't* been there when the woman had broken physically and come back.

Miriam shook her head, sharper this time. She was off. She looked up to find that platinum color, but her mark was gone, receded into the surging body of inebriation. Miriam gritted her teeth, then sent the message through the private channel.

What she really wanted was sleep, but since she knew that wasn't going to happen, she went for the next best thing. A release.

◊

It was a near-perfect arrangement. Purely physical. No emotions involved.

Ana pulled her close, their skin flush together, and Miriam adjusted her balance as fingers trailed from her waist and up her rib cage. Her body conformed, its motions automatic as it yearned for something to do, but despite the distraction in front of her, Miriam's mind strayed.

She had slipped away while Sam, Jace, and the others were lost in the thrashing crowd. Sam. Was she with Jace now? Still at the bar, or worse? Had they moved beyond?

Miriam raised her arms as her top eased off. Lips brushed her jawline before finding hers, a breath of alcohol tumbling with her own.

Sam. Their kiss in Duncan's had been something else. Was that also why Miriam had suggested a different location before? Was she avoiding the memory of that moment? Something heavy clawed within her.

"Tan."

Miriam blinked.

"What's wrong?"

Miriam forced herself to focus on the woman in front of her.

Ana studied her with a mix of curiosity and irritation. Dark eyes.

Not blue. Not Sam.

"Nothing. Sorry."

The woman brushed a strand of hair out of Miriam's face and raised an eyebrow. Miriam shook her head and before her thoughts could reform, she pressed back in. Ana smiled into her lips, and they shuffled toward the bed, Miriam's hand already working the clasp on the woman's pants. She needed a release. Something was pent-up, and this was the best way, the healthiest way she knew how. A bit of fun never hurt anyone. The two fell into her sheets, and somehow, Miriam was underneath with teeth nipping at her chin, then down her neck and chest.

She stared at the ceiling.

Did she want Sam?

No. Miriam didn't fuck her friends.

But she had said the same to herself last time. And then she had almost lost Sam. Had thought she was dead. But Sam wasn't dead; she was here in Station City, and she wasn't like the others. Or was she? Was Sam like Ana? Ana wasn't exactly Miriam's friend, more of an acquaintance really. Someone she knew from the hospital—someone who understood the arrangement. Emotions weren't involved.

Sam was a friend.

But not if she messed things up.

"Tan. What's going on?"

Miriam crushed her eyes shut. She didn't know.

Ana lifted herself off her, and Miriam's skin cried with the sudden absence of warmth. She pressed her palms into her eyelids. "I'm sorry." She winced. "It's me, I'm off. I haven't been sleeping well…and I don't know."

"Oh." Ana brushed a hand along Miriam's cheek, a motion so tender it only made her feel worse.

Miriam sat up. "I don't think I can do this right now."

Or any night.

Her breath caught. The thought scared her.

"That's…okay. We can just… Do you want me to stay? I can."

Miriam shook her head.

Sam wasn't an arrangement nor a fleeting one-night stand. She wasn't just a friend. Sam was something else, and Miriam couldn't ignore that anymore. Miriam had already pushed her away once. If Sam moved on with Jace, with someone else, *anyone* else, and Miriam had to watch her do that… The thought hung, a suffocating presence.

It was a fearful thing, the awareness of one's own conviction, even if it meant diving headfirst into the scary unknown and taking the risk. Everything would feel empty and meaningless until she did, because the true reason remained the same underneath it all: Ana, the girl with the platinum hair, all of them…

None of them were her.

None of them were Sam.

12

PURSUIT

SAM DRANK IN THE AIR. It was refreshing in her throat and on her skin after the warmth and mugginess inside. Despite the reinforced concrete, the deep bass thumped in her chest like an additional heartbeat. As expected in this lively sector, the main street was busy with patrons milling around bars and restaurants. She stared after a couple, their hands locked together as they laughed at whatever trivial topic.

She was glad to be included in Echo's libations; Sam had forgotten how much she enjoyed their easygoing company, regardless of the tight-lipped solemnity from their recent mission. But she could only tolerate the loud noises and crowd so much, especially with her energy still draining from her recovery. Sam missed the quiet nights of Ursus and the controlled routine of the surrounding settlements. There were perks to her brief city life, but she had certainly taken the open land and sleepy towns for granted.

Something fluttered against her leg, and she shook away a plastic flier. As it caught in a passing vehicle's wind stream, it flipped enough for her to glimpse the bold print of the first three letters in the top two lines: "ALT" and "OUT." With the city's growing rhetoric, it wasn't hard to decipher.

A melody sandwiched by bass and drums wailed before the door closed and it muffled, captured inside its cage again. A young group passed by, the smell of alcohol and sweat a cloud behind them as they moved on. Someone sighed behind her and Sam turned to watch Jace lean into the wall. He took a long drag on his nicosynth device before offering it to her.

She declined.

"It's weird, isn't it? How the city, how people continue to live like normal, as if nothing happened," he said, before taking another inhale. "Attack? Five seconds of coverage. Another attack? Five more seconds and back to the weather and local sports. The Altered government crumbles and terrorists control an entire city? Nothing."

Sam rubbed her prosthetic and she joined Jace along the side of the building. He watched her curiously, waiting for her to add something, but she didn't.

"They're sending me out."

Sam's forehead wrinkled. He hadn't mentioned it before at the UMF compound or inside with the others. "Where? Ursus? When?"

"No. Down south."

Her face contorted further.

"We still have a lot of work to do there. The Apostates that retreated, the other settled Altered... They could try to take more ground with whatever reinforcements they're getting—however they're getting there. UMF is talking with COC—"

"Charonites?" Sam recoiled. Her mind struggled against the alcohol in her system, like she wanted to sprint, but her feet were stuck in a bog. Why was UMF talking with human supremacists?

Jace squeezed an eye shut and his mouth quirked to the side. Sam was sober enough to understand the man had said more than he wanted. His lips were either loosened with intoxication or he had forgotten that Sam wasn't technically in SOG nor privy to the information. Her throat constricted. Even after her work with the Royal and her progress with her arm, she was still on the outside, still in purgatory.

"When are you shipping out?" she managed.

"Tomorrow."

Sam frowned.

"I know."

She looked away.

"I'll have someone reach out. Keep that connection with the Royal; you're on a gold mine here. And shit, we're going to need whatever you can get in the days to come."

Sam was only half-listening.

"Valk."

He leaned forward and she pulled her chin back, her eyes widening. Jace flinched in response but recomposed himself quickly. She wanted to apologize, but the surprise of it had locked up her vocal cords.

It was Jace who finally spoke in a whisper. "Sorry."

Sam shook her head. Her first "no" was too soft, so she popped her lips into her mouth and tried again. "No, don't be." She wasn't certain why she had pulled away. Part of her yelled in frustration that Jace was a perfectly nice person, and she did like him, but something was holding her back. "I think your news threw me off." It was true. She had just started to know the intelligence warrant officer; he had helped her find focus.

And now he was leaving.

She considered bridging the gap between them and trying for whatever Jace had intended again.

"If they knew what's coming..." He shifted his weight off his prosthetic.

Sam straightened. "Did something else come through?"

He sighed. "You know parts of it already. Your contact, your Royal, she mentioned Apostates are pushing east, right? She mentioned scorched earth campaigns, or at least the willingness for them." He pushed off the wall. "Your brother hasn't said anything about the border?"

A grain of fear trickled through her. She squinted, then glanced down at her commcuff. What did that mean? Was Scott okay?

"Keep working your contact."

"You can't do that." Sam stepped closer to Jace, and she ignored the mixed signals her body sent. "Give me something."

His eyes dropped to Sam's lips, and the tangy scent of alcohol mingled between them. "It hasn't been confirmed." He lowered his voice and Sam leaned closer. "But there've been reports of increased activity outside of Ursus's AOR."

Her cheek twitched. "How close?'

"Scouts along the coast and the Altered town across the strait."

"Nakuan?"

Jace didn't answer.

Sam exhaled. The sweet aftertaste of whatever drink Kai had given her danced on her tongue. "Who? The Apostates? Are they moving on us?"

Sam was so close she could see the muscle in his jaw feather.

"I don't know. The legionnaires—they're stuck between us and them, their supply chain... If they haven't been compromised..." He stopped himself. "It hasn't been confirmed, but with everything, it makes sense. Your Royal—if you can..."

A pause bloated over them. What made sense?

"Until we can get another credible source, we're in the dark." He pulled back and rubbed a palm into his forehead. "Sorry, I didn't mean to put a damper on the night with... Well, and now this."

Sam shook her head. "No. Thank you." She paused and repeated it, more genuine. She packed those two words with everything else unsaid. *Thank you. You helped me. You made me useful, gave me some purpose back.*

He gave her a lopsided smile and another silence wedged

itself in between them, unbroken by the thrash of music as the door opened and closed again.

"I wish I wasn't leaving so soon," he said, his gaze never straying. "I wish I met you earlier."

Sam swallowed.

He pulled her into a firm embrace she wasn't ready for, but she let herself relax for a second in his arms. It reminded her of how her brother had held and squeezed her before they separated months before.

"You'll stay in touch?"

She muttered an agreement into his shoulder before she initiated a small tug away. The man lingered as if he wanted to say or do something else, but Sam gave him a thin smile and nodded. Perhaps if they had more time, something more could have happened between them.

◊

ARE YOU OKAY?

Sam waved dismissively. "What's happening over there?"

The frame jostled as her brother adjusted his device on the other end, and for a second, her eyes hurt trying to make sense of his orientation. She squinted, straining to decipher the chaotic movement. When the picture stabilized, Scott's face appeared, dimly lit, his head resting on a rucksack. The device was clipped or suspended somehow, freeing his hands to sign.

He rubbed an eye sleepily. IT'S LATE. YOU'RE STILL UP?

Sam's slight intoxication muted the feeling of guilt for waking him. "It's fine. Are you at Ursus? Wait, no, you're close to the border. Domovoy, right?"

He stared at her vacantly, his eyes more gray than blue.

"What's going on over there? Across the water. The town, you know the one, with the harbor, the ports, the Legion garrison... Nakuan. Has there been fighting? Any attacks?"

He blinked, and his forehead wrinkled.

"You're not fucking with me, right? You really don't know? Don't give me this OpSec shit for just one second, okay. If something's—"

Scott held up a hand, and he mouthed her name. She stilled as his hands motioned. WHAT ARE YOU TALKING ABOUT? ARE YOU OKAY?

Her face flushed and her heart pumped, emphasized by the aftermath of whatever she'd imbibed at the club. But Scott seemed genuine. He didn't know.

Unless he was lying.

He wasn't lying. After their last spat, they had promised they'd tell each other everything—barring her purgatory non-SOG status and mission sensitive information, of course. So what did Jace and BigInt know? And why didn't her brother, who *was* at the border, not know?

Her brain flooded with multiple strands of possibilities and scenarios. Jace had told her to get confirmation from Kuan-Lin. She reached for her commcuff and then remembered Scott was still connected, watching her worriedly. "Charonites. Are the Charonites out there?"

His eyebrows pinched together.

"He said something about UMF working with Charonites. But he also said he's going to the South. Unless... How many SOG teams are in our AOR right now? Do you know?"

"Sam."

Her eyes snapped up.

"What are you talking about?" he continued, a scratch of a whisper across the commcuff connection. If she didn't know him, didn't watch his lips move, she wouldn't have understood it without turning the volume up.

Sam shook her head. "Someone I know here, he—" She stopped, trying to find the right way to say it. "Something might, could be happening soon, Scott. Please be safe."

I ALWAYS AM.

"Yeah, well, be careful." She reached for her commcuff. Her

prosthetic's motions were clumsy, or maybe it was her own inebriation, and the cuff was knocked off the counter to the ground. When she retrieved the device, her brother gave her a thin smile.

ARE YOU DRUNK?

"What? No. I mean, I had a little—"

ARE YOU ALLOWED TO? WITH THE PROCEDURE, WITH THE MEDS?

"I didn't have that much." Sam glared at her brother. Neither of them was a big drinker, but she had imbibed a bit more than usual this time. And to answer his question, no, probably not, but she felt fine. A little slow, as if everything blurred together, but she was fine. Her hands fluttered up. "That's not the point. Don't be a pain."

To her annoyance, he cracked a grin. YOU CALLED ME.

She let out a sound of frustration.

YOU'RE WORRIED ABOUT ME, he teased.

Before, yes. But no, at that moment, she was annoyed with him. An anger that had been suppressed in the past week sharpened for a split second, but she clenched her prosthetic hand and its ache soothed her. The feeling retreated. "You're the fucking worst."

His grin widened. CAN I GO BACK TO SLEEP NOW?

Sam was about to press her middle finger forward, but something buzzed loudly in her apartment, and she startled. In her entire time in the studio, she had never heard it before, and its newness was more surprising than its volume. Her head whisked around trying to locate the source, but when she realized it was a notification for someone at the door, she relaxed, but only a little. No one had ever come to her apartment.

She ignored her brother's waving hands in the display, and she listened for whatever, whoever was in the corridor. It could be a person at the wrong address. It was late, after all, and no one knew she lived there. Not even Echo. The buzz came again, and she searched for her studio's mobile console, but it was somehow lost in that tiny, spartan space. Instead, her eyes tried to bore through the door. Had a Charonite near the embassy followed her home? Dmitri? Her countersurveillance skills *were* a tad rusty with her leave of absence. Thoughts and questions sloshed together.

"Sam?" Her brother's voice came from her forgotten cuff. "What's going on?"

She reached for her device, her attention on the door. "Sorry I woke you. I'll call you back later." Before he could say anything, she ended the connection.

Sam rose and hesitantly crossed the small distance to the entrance, and activated the viewfinder. And then her mind emptied, sober from whatever occupying intoxication. She paused, ignoring the vibrations of her commcuff on the counter behind her, then smoothed her day-wrinkled shirt and fussed with a small stain from someone's spilled drink. She combed a hand through her short hair before she palmed the door console.

Miriam Tanner stood outside.

The last time Sam saw her was at the bar, before she disappeared, before Sam had gone out for air and talked with Jace. Now, here Miriam was, in a different outfit, more casual, with her brown hair swept around her shoulders, out of the usual braid. Sam's heart danced against her ribs and her stomach tightened as those light brown eyes swallowed her.

"Hey."

That one word sent a shiver through her skin. Sam managed a soft, mirrored response while the woman's eyes skimmed around the small studio as if searching for something. When Miriam was satisfied, her eyes locked back with Sam's.

"May I come in?"

Sam pressed down the regurgitating questions and stammered out a response. They stood there for a second longer before she realized she was blocking the doorway and stepped to the side. Miriam entered with a grace Sam would never have, but stopped short, in close proximity to her. Sam's mind went blank, and the rush of her heartbeat flooded her ears and warmed the base of her neck.

"Hospital contacts," Miriam said, to both Sam's confusion and relief. "That's how I got your address."

Sam only nodded and watched the medic carefully, taking a step back, as if distance could mask the heat rising throughout her.

"It's a breach of information, but I figured it'd be okay. Shit, I hope that's okay."

It took another second for Sam to realize what Miriam was talking about. Was she nervous? Sam had never known the woman to be. In that instance, with the brief lapse of sobriety, she wished she hadn't drank the amount she had. Was the alcohol affecting her mind? She shook her head slowly as if this were some hallucination or dream, but Miriam was there, so close the scent of cinnamon and something else floated around her.

Miriam's eyes hung on her and Sam's breath snagged as the woman carefully stepped forward. The last time they had been this close, Sam had kissed Miriam.

And been rejected.

Sam took a step back.

Into the wall.

She tried for an inhale.

One one thousand.

Miriam just wanted to be friends. Miriam didn't want someone who was broken. Sam was nothing like the women Miriam flirted with, like the beautiful red-haired woman who had been at her apartment...

Two one thousand.

But Miriam was also there. In front of her.

Too close to her.

Three one—

Fuck.

A hand gently caressed her cheek, followed by a whisper. "Is this okay?"

Sam leaned into Miriam's warm fingers. How one touch could undo her. How one touch could simultaneously stir up all the emotions, but still them in a juxtaposition. Her eyes widened as Miriam leaned closer and their breath danced together.

Was this really happening?

Their lips met, searching softly, then pressing together more intensely, a taste of sweetness lingering on her tongue. Sam could stay in this moment forever. No thoughts, just warmth and the satisfaction where everything just *fit*. In a hunger she had known was there but had tried for months to stifle, her hands pulled the woman closer as their bodies pressed together into the solid wall behind them.

What had changed?

Her prosthetic?

Sam stiffened, hesitancy spreading amidst her desire. Miriam broke away first and Sam's chest ached in protest. In betrayal. Her hand dropped from its place on Miriam's hip and hovered, held by a thin string of doubt. Now, with the separation, even in close distance, confusion and fear seeped in.

Why now?

Did Miriam mean to kiss her?

What had changed?

Of course, she wanted Miriam still. Her thoughts churned and resurfaced, as if waking from a dream. Miriam had pushed *her* away. *She* was the one who wanted to be friends. And that was before the attack. *After* the attack, Sam wasn't whole. With the prosthetic, she was better, but the uncertainty she'd never recover or *be* the same was rampant. She wasn't like the woman she had seen in Miriam's apartment. Ana. Beautiful.

Whole.

She'd never be.

"Sam?" Miriam's darkened eyes searched hers. Worried.

Sam's mouth opened, closed, then opened again. She knew her glances at Miriam's lips were a betrayal and temptation in themselves. How many times had she thought about that night and their first kiss? What would've happened if Miriam hadn't stopped it, rejected her? A one-night stand? Or something more? Her heart had soared at the hope of something more, but it was short-lived. Sam had seen the woman's flirtations and the potential paramours she had pursued. Her gut plummeted at the idea of just being another notch on Miriam's belt.

"I don't think I can do this," Sam whispered.

Hurt flickered in Miriam's eyes before they dropped to the side. Sam's body cried out as the distance between them grew.

"I thought I could, a one-time thing—"

Miriam froze. "Oh. I thought—" Her breath hitched.

Sam wanted to recoil and curl in the woman's intense gaze.

"Is that what—" Miriam stopped herself, then inhaled. "I don't think I want that."

Confused, Sam blinked several times.

"I want you."

Sam's lungs and diaphragm caught in suspense. She wasn't sure if she had heard correctly.

"Sam, I want you," Miriam repeated, slower and penetrating.

And with that, everything she had been holding in for the last months—and what felt like her entire life—came tumbling out in a tangled mess of desire.

PART 2

DERMIS

13

—————

THE ALLEY

SOMETHING DRIPPED down the back of Sam's neck, soaking into her jacket collar. Her arm lifted automatically to the base of her skull, but she froze with a hovering hand when a putrid stench tugged at her nose.

"You've got to be fucking kidding." Her upper lip curled as she whipped around to the blockade of protesters and searched for the culprit. "Who the fuck—"

"Valkyrie."

She sneered again. In her entire career with UMF, she'd never had to deal with piss as a weapon. There were other bodily fluids, but urine? Never. In that minute, her irritation and disappointment were pure and concentrated. Humans were disgusting.

"Valkyrie."

Sam glared menacingly at the crowd for a second longer before she turned. Goyer, a marine who looked to be in his late teens, offered her a small rag. She reached out to take it, but her motion paused as she stared at her gloved right hand. After a couple of months, her prosthetic's motions were almost smooth and automatic, but now and then, the feeling of it threw her off. Though the glove hampered some of its sensations, its masking effect created more normalcy and less noticeability.

"It's clean, I swear," the marine stammered.

With a muttered thanks, Sam took the cloth and patted her head dry. It was good that her hair was still relatively short. The effort did little for the lingering smell; she'd have to wait until after the company's shift to shower. With her temporary duty assignment, she had access to the barracks on the compound, but because of her experience, it wasn't a requirement to stay there. As Sam was uninterested in reliving the boot life all over again, it was a relief. The last months spent in a company of first-contracts had already been humiliating enough. If she had been forced to rack with the recently graduated marines and relive that daily tedium... No, thanks.

Sam wiped at her collar one last time and offered the cloth back to Goyer. His nose twitched, and she understood. She tossed the sullied rag to the side, adding to the line of trash from the previous day's protest. And the one before that.

Biting back rage, Sam glared beyond the barriers in the "Alley," the fenced area drawing a boundary around the main access point to the Altered Sector and Oldtown. After shifts of what the Station marines called "alty duty," Sam had grown to tolerate the ebb and flow of objectors, the counterprotests, and other riffraff in between. Didn't these people have better things to do? Their demonstrations and presence weren't pushing the Altered away. Where else were they supposed to go? Their city and territories were overrun with terrorists. But maybe she was biased from her conversations with Kuan-Lin. She didn't understand or care for the politics between the Altered and the city, but Sam understood the threat of radicals, Apostates and Charonites alike.

Having visited the Royal in the Altered housing sector several times now, she was familiar with the area, at least enough to know the location of several discreet side entrances. The Alley was more for show, a designated corralling area for the recurrent dissenters and the fear-mongering media with their mobile broadcast hubs. Their cameras loved to sweep along the four legionnaires standing post inside the sector's internal gate. They were only armed with sheathed knives, but their white uniforms, build, and height were daunting enough. Sam hadn't seen them, but she was certain Altered weapons *were* within reach, tucked away in the small post. Only as a last resort, though. SecTeam and UMF weren't there for the Altered. Their presence was meant to keep Station civilians from getting into trouble and hurting themselves.

"Do you think Dense Ned is in a better mood today?" Goyer asked, his fingers tapping against an empty rifle.

Sam made an indifferent noise and crossed her arms around her own issued rifle—a prop with no actual bullets. The weapon was far more alien than her prosthetic—too long, too heavy compared to her carbine sitting in some armory locker in Ursus.

Company Lead Densaned, a tart asshole who liked the sound of his own voice and harbored grudges like no other. Normally, Sam gave little regard to marines like him, but when there was nothing exciting to look forward to in her new day-to-day, it was difficult. She reminded herself it was only temporary.

But she had said the same thing a month ago.

And the month before that.

She scowled. Four more days until the next expected update from MED on her clearance and return to SOG.

Something caught in her peripheral vision—a capped head behind two rows of people popped up, then dropped back down. Goyer continued whatever small talk he'd begun and Sam only half-listened while she inspected the suspicious individual. Her eyes tracked a few others with the same dark knit cap as they weaved through the crowd toward the main gate. Then, she glimpsed the familiar box-shaped tattoo, the Children of Charon's lantern.

She hushed the marine next to her. "Come with me."

His mouth puckered, mid-word, and his eyes widened. To his credit, Goyer obeyed and hurried into step behind her, no questions asked. Sam kept her primary suspect and his bobbing dark cap in the corner of her eye as they hastened along the lane toward the gate.

One of the other paired marines from their company squad stepped forward and blocked Sam with an outstretched hand. "Hey, get back to your post. We're not rotating yet."

Another young do-gooder. "Keep your eyes on the line," Sam muttered as she easily stepped around her. Goyer stammered something incomprehensible, something possibly apologetic, but he followed.

"Get back here," the marine hissed. "I don't want to get yelled at again—"

Loud shouting cut the reprimand off as a scuffle broke out at the gates. Sam's attention drew away for a second to take it in, and then immediately peeked back to track her capped man, who had reversed direction. A distraction? For what?

Her thoughts were broken by bashing noises as the mob kicked at sections of the fence. Sam started in a jog. "Call for backup, now," she ordered over her shoulder, before she stuttered her pace to stomp a boot into the nearby barricade, dissuading sets of fingers from rocking it.

Goyer shouted a string of expletives before he fumbled for his comm device, an older-generation model strapped to his upper chest plate.

Sam waved at the two SecGuards, but their focus was locked on the fence swinging wildly back and forth and the mob behind it, threatening to spill over. The senior SecGuard, Buzzcut, yelled and pumped his hands at the perpetrators, but the commotion drowned any words of placation. Sam swung her rifle forward knowing it was an empty bluff with no rounds; she didn't bother brandishing it the proper way.

Sam gestured at the two marines they had passed. They had already started moving, although hesitant and stiff. Between her, Goyer, the two SecGuards, and the others, it'd be six against a flood of protesters and what she knew were Charonites.

The senior SecGuard's voice was shrill. "Stop! Back up! Stop!"

Sam shouted out friendly identifiers as she and Goyer joined behind them. It was standard practice, more necessary now as she didn't want to startle the youngest one, Ponytail. The SecGuard's knuckles were white around her holstered weapon. Sam didn't need her to panic, turn, and shoot her or the incoming marines. Unlike the military, SecTeam *had* rounds in their weapons.

Buzzcut dipped his head at Sam, as if experience recognized experience. His hand unclenched over his radio and moved to his baton. His eyes darted between Sam, her held rifle, and the creaking fence, one hinge already separated. A curse wedged between a silent motion of his mouth, and then his hand moved to unholster his sidearm.

"Don't shoot! That's what they want!" Buzzcut shouted, although his own brandished weapon betrayed his words.

Sam shook her head. These SecGuards were already planning for the line to break, waiting for the danger to come to them. Another joint on the fence broke and the sliver between the sections widened.

Goyer's elbow bumped into hers. "Valkyrie?"

"Follow my lead," she answered. She raised her voice louder for the others. "Don't fucking shoot me!" But she wasn't sure if they could hear her over the chaos. She lifted the butt of her rifle and slammed it along sections of the fence where fingers and bodies pressed through and against it. At first, it felt so minute, like punching at a large wave, but then Goyer and the

SecGuards joined, kicking and knocking back individuals on the other side.

Their combined motion startled the first row of offenders, but Sam could see their faces contort, teeth gnashing worse as they realized that their action had set off an unanticipated reaction. Were they expecting SecTeam and UMF to allow them through? Not if Sam could help it. She jabbed at an individual's collarbone as he tried to push through the growing gap. He recoiled but was replaced by a different body. Goyer and another marine shoved their weight into the barricades, trying to keep the hole from warping further. Fingers clawed at them through the mesh, but then the weight shifted.

Sam stood back as heavy boots padded around her and military grays reinforced the effort, their added bodies and strategic blows turning the balance. Their backup arrived faster than expected, and the threat—the crack in the dam—had knitted up just like that. SecTeam and UMF uniforms were already marching forward, the crowd dispersing wildly in response. With the current vulnerability addressed, Sam looked for the black knit caps.

"What exactly was your plan here?" she murmured. What *was* the Charonite plan? She briefly considered a scenario where they broke through the barriers. Even if the mob had made it past the fences, past SecTeam and UMF, there was the other wall and gate with legionnaires behind it. Had they wanted to disrupt the area and make a scene? Force SecTeam to shoot? Incite violence?

"Get those fucking recorders out of here!"

Sam turned to the shrill voice of the company lead, who was waving at the mobile broadcasters as they scurried over. In her motion, his eyes latched on and he strode right for her.

"What the fuck, Ryan?" Densaned growled, his breath hot. A vein branched above his temple. "You left your fucking post."

Sam could smell his lunch—spiced jellyfish and coffee, a

terrible combination—as it blew into her face. Her upper lip twitched, but she forced her composure to even and held her ground. "Children of Charon, sir. They were about to break through," she answered flatly.

"And you had to be the hero."

A flippant retort threatened to slip from her tongue, but Sam bit back. Was it her fault she had noticed and swiftly addressed the problem?

A burly SecTeam sergeant saved her from a strangled response. "Push the line back, will you?" he said to another SecGuard on the other side of the fence. His tired stare swept over the broken fence and the marines. "We can take it from here."

Densaned whipped around, his mouth twisted and ugly. "Can you? Can you really? Because it feels like we're doing your fucking job." The lead was always in a mood, but today, he was in a particularly foul one. No one was exempt from his dissatisfaction. He pinched his thumb and pointer together and didn't let the sergeant respond. "I'll get my engineers over here." He looked over at Sam, and she could swear his eyes glimmered. "Actually, Ryan will coordinate it. Fix your shit."

Anger spurred in Sam's chest.

He gave her a scowl as he left. "Follow hygiene regs, hero. You smell like piss."

Her hands clenched into fists.

When the company lead was out of earshot, Goyer stepped to Sam's side. "Wow. Dense Ned *really* doesn't like you."

"No shit," Sam said between gritted teeth. She took a deep breath, then counted it out slowly.

Four more days of this shit probation.

Four more days until MED approved her return to Ursus and SOG.

Four fucking days.

◊

"That's one thing I don't miss."

Scott made a rude gesture in her commcuff display. His wet hair was plastered to his forehead, and the static of rain in the background was audible every time a gust blew the flap open behind him.

Sam chuckled sympathetically, grateful for her brother's call after another shit shift, another day in her holding pattern over. "Also, I thought your rotation was done. You've been there for weeks now. Is Titan-3 there, as well?"

He shook his head and shrugged. EVERYONE'S RUNNING DOUBLES.

Her brother was never one to complain, even in the rainy and dark seasons. Sam knew Scott missed his apartment. She hadn't cared for the extra humidity of his small indoor garden at the time, but she missed it now.

"Don't worry," he said hoarsely. His hands and fingers spun together. WE'RE HEADING BACK IN A WEEK. ONE MORE OP. BUT IN THE MEANTIME, I'M LIVING THROUGH YOU.

Sam scoffed. "You might want someone else to live vicariously through."

CONSIDER IT A TEACHING OPPORTUNITY.

Sam rolled her eyes. "You come here and teach these boots. I'll gladly switch places with you."

EVEN WITH THE RAIN?

"Even with the rain."

A grin cracked across his face, and she couldn't help but smile with him. HOW ARE THINGS WITH THE ROYAL?

"Ongoing." She shrugged. "I said it before, but I think you'd like her a lot."

TRYING TO SET ME UP ON A DATE? THAT'S SCANDALOUS.

"Fuck you. You know that's not what I meant."

He smirked. ANY OTHER UPDATES?

That brought a scowl to her face. "No. Next one's scheduled

in four days." Anxiety spiked and she scrambled to find something else to talk about. "Have you heard from the other teams?"

Scott tilted his head. EVERYONE'S BUSY.

Except for Sam. She frowned.

WHAT ARE YOU DOING NOW? STILL ON BASE?

"How do you—" Sam remembered her brother knew her location. It was unfair, considering she didn't know his, but she waved it off. "I'm waiting for Mir...iam."

Her brother raised an eyebrow.

"What?"

He shrugged.

Sam's eyes narrowed. "What?"

IT'S JUST NICE.

"Why do you have to get so weird about this every time?"

He didn't motion, a mischievous grin on his face. Sam's false annoyance petered out, and she fought against a mirrored smile. After all, it was her first relationship in a long time, the longest she'd ever had, but as a sister, she couldn't give him the satisfaction.

"Hi, Scott."

Sam's stomach fluttered as she watched Miriam approach, her jacket thrown over her shoulder. Everything fell away. Her anxiety, her worry, her anger with the company lead, everything. It was as if the sun unfurled itself and swallowed her whole—made her full of brightness. Of clarity.

"We might see you soon if you're still up there," Miriam said, loud enough for the commcuff to pick up her voice. She sniffed at the air and her eyes floated around as if trying to locate something.

Her brother waved from the display, and Sam recomposed herself.

YES, I CAN'T WAIT TO HEAR HOW MY SISTER LANDED SOMEONE SO OUT OF HER LEAGUE.

Dick.

She raised her prosthetic, a middle finger to the display. She then relayed to Miriam, "He says he can't wait." A bit of jealousy came through in her words. She should've been back in SOG by now. "I'll talk to you later. Tell the others I said hello." Sam didn't wait for her brother's response and ended the connection.

Miriam pulled at her braid. "You didn't have to do that. I didn't mean to cut you short."

Sam shifted her weight, a gravitation toward the woman. "It's fine. We talk all the time, anyway. How'd the brief go?"

"As usual. The mission should be quick—a lot of travel time just for a few hours on the ground. I guess I should call it early tonight." The medic rubbed her eyes with her index finger and thumb. She lowered her hand and leaned toward her. After all this time, Sam's heart still leaped at any affection and attention from the woman, but then Miriam's nose wrinkled, and she recoiled. "Oh hell, it's coming from you."

Sam's shoulders fell.

"Why do you smell like a camp lavatory?"

Fuck. Sam hovered a hand over the back of her head and turned her nose into a shoulder, sniffing hard. She had washed her head in the barracks sink, but the scent from before must have saturated into her shirt. She shuddered at the thought that she had gotten used to the smell over the last hours, but something else came over her, and with a grin, Sam opened her arms toward Miriam.

"No. Absolutely not." Miriam wagged a finger at her and darted out of reach. "Why haven't you showered? Changed?"

"You messaged me to wait!"

The woman held her hand over her nose. "If I had known you smelled like this... Who was it? Stationers? Did they literally pee on you?" She clicked her tongue as they moved together for the compound gate. "I don't miss alty duty at all."

Sam normally would have bristled at the reminder she was running with first-contracts in the Alley, but there was no ill will in Miriam's comment. It wouldn't have mattered, anyway. Her mood had lightened considerably.

14

CONTUSION

THE NIGHT STORMED with impacts and the whistling of turrets. Flames licked at her skin, the heat a counter to the cold running through her blood. The gate cracked open and dark shadows charged through, their weapons glinting in the air.

Her finger tensed, and a stream of rounds loosed into the incoming wave. One fell, then two. Three. Each body should have slowed them, but nothing did. They surged forward like rapids over jagged rocks.

A shadow leaped into the air, latching and ripping aside kit and armor, one on top of the other. Screams and gunfire washed together in mayhem. Her rounds found their mark, pounding, slashing, penetrating, but did nothing. It raised its head, bright teeth below a green glow.

She willed her body to move, her gun to fire, but she couldn't. She watched, horrified, as its face elongated, its shoulders and limbs longer. And then it lunged, its claws aimed directly for her heart.

Miriam's eyes shot open. The smoke and carbon lingered in her nose as she stared at the familiar speck on her bedroom ceiling. She dug her fingers into the sheets around her and willed her racing heart to settle. It was just a nightmare. She was in Station. In her apartment.

A stupid nightmare.

The dreams had lessened in the past couple months, her sleep schedule mostly restored when she was back in the city, except for the night before missions. It had to be the anticipation and her nerves.

She grounded herself in the morning light peeking from the crack where her window hadn't completely shut, a reminder that life was oddly normal in the city, its distance and distractions an insulation of sorts, despite what was happening elsewhere. Repetitions of a slowed effort had raised calluses in Station's mind. Frankly, in UMF's, too.

Across the room, the clock flared numbers that showed she had woken up minutes before her set alarm. Fists rubbed into her eyes, more a habit than anything. She was fully awake. The nightmare had made sure of that. Miriam pulled herself upright at the edge of the bed and disabled the pending notification on her cuff. She ignored the reminder that she needed to stop by the base clinic to replenish items before she met with Echo at the secured dock in a couple hours. The team would stop by Ursus, but only briefly, before they routed out to the forward operating base further northwest. Even if they had enough time at the outpost, Miriam didn't want to take from them if she could help it. Their supply wasn't precarious yet, but with the disruptions in the past month, items were becoming more scarce.

A soft groan came from behind and Miriam turned with a deep stretch. In the dim light, she gazed at the shape next to her, tracing the curve of the sheet up to a face buried into a pillow, soft blond hair like a nest around it. Though the woman was in her early twenties, she wore her time in UMF and SOG in her face and body, but in slumber, Sam's skin was smooth and unburdened. She looked her age—younger—with no creases or lines, almost free from the worry and world around them.

An eyelid opened, a glimpse of blue underneath. "Too early," Sam mumbled. Her eye squeezed shut.

Miriam hummed and rose to dress. With her pants on, she peeked back at Sam, who had fallen asleep once more. Her morning routine continued, and Miriam returned to the bedroom after some time, tossing her uniform shirt and jacket onto her side of the bed. She engaged the window setting, its panel changing gradually to allow the full sunrise into the apartment.

Sam groaned again and Miriam poked her ribs, a protesting mutter in response. The woman turned onto her back and drew an eye open. It wandered up Miriam's bare navel and ended in a squint as their gaze connected.

Miriam cocked a brow. "Morning. What happened to the always punctual marine?"

"Apostates blasted her arm off, and then she wasn't a marine." Sam squeezed her eye shut again. "At least not a full one, anyway."

The comment was said lightly, but bitterness laced within the words. Miriam would have to tread carefully—the woman put too much value in her military role, but could she be blamed? Starting UMF indoctrination at a young age, being a military experiment, would do that to a person.

"Still a marine. Just one with a fancy arm waiting for her next orders."

The prosthetic shot out and grabbed her wrist and for a split second, Miriam's skin and bones protested at the rough pressure as it pulled her forward and down. An unintentional squeak escaped her lips, but she didn't resist, relaxing into a long kiss.

As she pulled away, Sam protested, but Miriam silenced her with another peck. "You're dragging your feet. Ride it out for a few more days, and don't get on your lead's bad side."

Sam shot her a look.

"*More* on his bad side."

The woman groaned and turned her face into the pillow, and Miriam took the opportunity to rub her wrist. Sam had surpassed the hospital's recovery and therapy sessions; her prosthetic's speed and coordination were phenomenal, a testament of hard work, technology, or a mix of both.

"When are you leaving?"

"A couple hours," Miriam responded. "And you have drills in less." She threw the pillow at Sam, whose right arm stopped it easily. Miriam righted herself and grabbed her top, deftly weaving her arms through. "Your reflexes are faster."

As the woman sat up, sheets pooling around her, concern flicked across her face. Sam pulled her knees toward her and stretched the prosthetic over them.

"Don't worry," Miriam said. "MED's conservative; they're notorious for taking their time."

Though it was what Sam needed to hear, it wasn't entirely true. Miriam swallowed back her doubt and traced one of the fading scars along the seams of the woman's prosthetic and skin. The issue with experimental prototypes was that they were experimental prototypes. They had no history. Miriam knew the medical board was hesitant about something. If it wasn't the hardware, then it was the person it was attached to. Maybe MED realized that UMF was wrong in allowing a five-year-old girl to grow up on a military compound, enlisting her at the ripe age of twelve years. But maybe this was all her own projections.

"Sure." Sam shifted. "Are the others really okay with me joining…?"

"Krill has the request ready. And of course, yes. If that's what you want."

"I…don't know what to do. Ursus is home. Well, Scott's there, and he's only there because of me—"

"It's okay, you have time to figure it out. Talk to your brother. It's whatever you think is best."

The bed sheet bunched in an alloy fist, and Sam's forehead

wrinkled. "I hate being stuck here. I wish I was going with you."

"I know. Three more days until the next update, right? It'll go fast, we'll be back in no time, and then we can all celebrate." Miriam leaned toward Sam. The woman smelled like fresh linen. She combed her hand through tufts of blond hair and ran a finger along a scar on the side of her head. "This one's almost gone. Make sure you keep up with that new ointment when I'm away, okay? If you need more, I can have someone drop it off from the hospital—"

Sam stilled her hand and unfolded her legs.

"Sorry. I know." Miriam shook her head. "Trying to fix things again."

The woman gave her a weak smile. "I know how you can make it up to me."

Before Miriam could respond, Sam pulled her gently back into bed and she fell clumsily forward in a sprawl.

"Sam." She sighed. "You're going to be late."

The woman didn't answer, fingers already finding the edges of her shirt.

Miriam could spare fifteen minutes.

◊

> A. CHO: Haven't heard from you in a while. I passed your place the other day and wanted to say hi. I imagine you've probably been busy with work. Message if you need a break.

Miriam deleted the private message. Knowing Ana, she would've come up to her Station flat and tried to get in. Access *had* been part of their arrangement, but that deal had ceased when Sam started staying at hers—the studio in the medical sector had an inconvenient commute to UMF. And Miriam didn't mind. She wasn't there half of the time, every other week away or something else related to the damn Axiom mission.

Regardless, Miriam had hoped the rescinded access and silence would've put Ana off. It had for some time, but with the third correspondence in a week, Miriam questioned her tactic. If this ignored message didn't do it, she'd have to figure out what to say to Ana the next time she saw her. *If* she saw her. Between missions, administrative time, and Sam, Miriam was doing a decent job of avoiding her usual waterholes.

What would she say if she ran into Ana or another arrangement? *I'm in another one right now. I'm with someone else?* Different scenarios and conversations popped into her head, and Miriam winced. She didn't have to think about this right now, especially not with a mission in a few hours.

Her commcuff buzzed again, and she glanced at her wrist. She quickly dismissed the notification and took another sip from her mug before placing it aside on a shelf. The coffee warmed her from the inside, guarding her from the cold against her skin.

Outside, darkness stared back at her, no lights beyond the glow of the garage as it melted into shadows on a pocked and muddy road. Clouds dimmed the crescent moonlight, the remnants of a passed storm with another on its tail. *Good conditions*, the report had said. Which meant terrible conditions for the normal human. No one in their right mind would be actively out in the northern once-tundra while the storm raged.

She turned into the portable bay, a temporary structure open enough to squeeze in a couple mechanic stations, two large prowlers, and a squad of SOG marines. From the cage down to the suspension and thick wheels, the prowlers were bigger, more menacing than any she had seen in Station. She didn't question the necessity. Ursus Outpost was the second largest UMF presence for a reason; the northern border was large and neighbored the Altered continent—much closer to the threat than the South had been.

"You're not going to answer? Brutal, dismissing Valk like that," Yuri teased from his seat in the second prowler.

Before Miriam could respond, Nas popped out from the first vehicle, a half-eaten sandwich in one hand. He snapped his other wrist forward and made a whipping sound out of the side of his mouth. Her eyebrows rose, and she gave him a long look, a pseudo-warning. His hands instinctually splayed out and Yuri grinned, avoiding her subsequent stare.

"Wasn't her, shitstains," Miriam shot back, her voice dry and edged. It was too late; Sam was probably asleep with the rest of the city.

"Wait, what?" Kai's forehead scrunched as she looked up. "Valk?"

Nas palmed his cheek. "Seriously, Kai?"

"What? I don't understand."

"How are you so bad at this? Tan and Valkyrie."

Their teammate's face slackened, then hardened as the information registered. Her body straightened like an electric current had run through it and Miriam was surprised she didn't drop the tool in her hands.

"What! When did this happen?"

Yuri suppressed a laugh. "Might want to step back, Tan. I can't tell if she's mad or happy."

"So oblivious." Nas shook his head.

To be fair, Miriam thought she and Sam had kept their arrangement quite private back in Station. They took care to avoid any public displays of affection, especially around Echo and UMF.

"I don't—I'm not—" Kai smacked her lips and jutted her chin forward. "I'm finding this out now?" She harrumphed. "Well, I love Valk, and I think that's very sweet. Is it—are you two…" Her eyes widened as she silently mouthed, *together together?*

Nas snickered. Yuri, at least, had the decency to hold back.

Miriam took a deep breath and rolled her eyes again. "Hell, are we back in academy?"

"I'm just...surprised? I never thought you were one for...commitment."

"We're just—" Miriam said, flustered. She scratched at her skin, suddenly itchy, as if something were crawling underneath it. She looked around for the team lead, for a distraction, but there was none. "We're enjoying each other's company."

Why were they talking about this? She glared at Yuri, then Nas, who gave her a sassed eyebrow back.

"Alright, alright. They're both consenting adults." Yuri barely stifled another chuckle. He silently mouthed to her, *I'm happy for you.*

Miriam tried to shrug it off, but the uncomfortable feeling remained. She thrust a middle finger toward him and her mouth opened in silent response. *Fuck you.*

Kai tapped the tool on her clavicle. "Well, the boys can tease all they want, but I think it's brave that we continue to find the positive things. Just because everything else is falling apart doesn't mean we stop living."

Nas tossed the sandwich at one of the bins next to Miriam. "Tell that to my taste buds. This situation has really been affecting the quality of food. Or the cooks are somehow worse out in the borderlands."

"Seriously? That's really all you think about? Food?"

"Don't forget tech and super-secret facilities," Yuri said. He popped out of his seat as their team lead walked into the bay. "Hey, boss. We still on?"

Krill nodded as he joined the group. "Just got off the long-range. Command and BigInt confirm the report's good, and recon should be getting into position soon. We'll give it another hour or so."

"Alright, round three. We're ready to go," the second said. "We'll bag one this time. It'll be nice when this is over and we can stick around, help these guys at the front."

"We're already well past the front," grumbled Miriam.

She stared out into the darkness again. This was their third attempt at Axiom's hush-hush objective, and it had pushed Echo to the northern coast: a newly conflicted territory northwest of Ursus Outpost and its forward operating base, FOB Domovoy. It wasn't like the North wasn't prepared, but the borders were more permeable than ever, even with a Legion garrison stationed across the narrow waterway between the human territory and the expanding wunby offensive. According to UMF, it remained strong with loyal legionnaires, and the Royals prioritized its supply and position. Sam herself had expressed confidence from her time at the outpost; they had never had major issues before. But despite the legionnaires, the northern territory was so vast that wunby scouts could navigate the distance over the thin body of water and poke into the small towns and settlements nearby. It wasn't the first time alties had set foot in the North—Ursus SOG marines dealt with lone-wolf attacks regularly—but this time, the strikes were coordinated and deliberate, with whole towns evacuating or going dark.

"Technically, we secured one the first time," Nas said with a finger up, "but no, Axiom really wants a drugged-up *specimen*. Is it our fault that alty didn't have any stims?"

Kai frowned. "I still don't—"

"We already went over this," Nas whined. "The only good wunby is a dead wunby."

"No. You're right. That alty was a wunby, but we found out *afterwards*. Whoever gave us that intel lucked out. *We* lucked out. What if the Royals or the others find out we snatched farmers from the South?"

Nas scoffed. "They're all complicit down there, Kai. Do I need to jog your memory? Remember Matam?"

"Alright, kids, settle down," Yuri said.

"Regardless, stimmed alties aren't showing up in the South anymore. You heard it from Jace. And now, BigInt's saying it's fifty-fifty that the scouts in the North are or aren't on them. Gotta love factionalized wunbies…"

"Like the Charonites," Kai said. "Decentralized."

Miriam tapped her fingers on her kit. Since everything went south, UMF's central intelligence arm was behind. They knew little when it came to the wunbies, other than their overarching mission to eliminate humans.

"Well, Axiom doesn't like dead specimens either."

Kai shuddered. "Who knew they'd do that to themselves…"

Echo's last attempt had failed despite their successful capture of a stimmed alty terrorist. As the team medic, Miriam had done what she could, but there was only so much she *could* do when the prisoner had chewed off its own tongue. She knew wunbies were zealous, but she hadn't expected self-destruction like that.

"This isn't a clean space. Mind what you say," reminded Krill.

"We're the only ones awake at this hour and we're practically at the edge of the world," Nas said.

"Still." Krill rubbed his head. "Remember, minimal gear. Drop everything else. I want us in and out. If we do this right, we'll be five minutes tops. They won't know we're there."

Miriam patted her pockets another time to make sure everything was in place. She nudged her small sling at her side. Echo had prepared for minimal gear, but Miriam felt strange leaving behind her complete pack. This mission necessitated stealth and speed. She reminded herself the others would have their individual first-aid kits.

In. And out.

"Five minutes. That's what you said last time." Nas ripped a chocolate bar with his teeth.

Miriam examined her sidearm and rifle. Minimal gear also meant a limited amount of rounds against an enemy that seemed to absorb them like sponges.

"Well, the same goes for now. Let's make this the last time."

"And then we'll be plus one jacked-up wunby and back home in time for breakfast."

Miriam squinted an eye at Nas. "Do you feel the need to say something clever every time?"

He grinned. "It's my nature."

"It wasn't even clever. Childish, maybe." Kai pointed her tool at the team lead. "What's different about this one?"

Krill sighed. "I have a good feeling."

Miriam eyed him. As oblivious as Kai was to certain things, she was right to ask her question. The lead's confidence was different, stronger than the last two attempts. "What's changed?"

The corner of his mouth quirked. "The initial report."

She and the others stared at their lead, their expressions skeptical.

"Found out who it came from." Krill picked up his rifle from where he had left it. "How much do you trust Ursus's golden scout?"

For a second, Miriam thought of Sam, but Krill meant Scott, Sam's brother. There weren't any other blond-haired recon specialists they knew from the outpost—in operational status, of course.

"Mute will be on location?" Kai asked.

"Don't count on crossing paths, but who knows. As for the report, he was there with us in the South. He saw what we saw. If anyone's going to recognize stimmed-up wunbies, it'll be him." Krill straightened. "Let's just get this done and done *right*. We're sure these modifications are good?"

Kai reached over and flicked at the second prowler's center console. The expected start-up growl of its engine was surprisingly absent, its sustained thrum noticeably muffled. The others shared Miriam's impressed look.

"Right. Hang tight until we get the final green light." Krill looked around. "Where's Fox?"

"Antisocial's probably in the canteen, napping off a hangover," Nas replied curtly.

"He went to pick up the sacks, boss," Yuri said with a sharp glare, a warning to their young teammate. "He'll be back in a minute."

Krill waved his hand. "Copy. Hit the head, run your comms, do your weapons and visor checks—again, if you've already done so—but stay close, stay ready."

15

RELEVANCE

FOOTSTEPS SCUFFED upon the pavement and Sam winced. The marine could learn a few lessons from Miriam and her silent approaches.

"What are you doing?" Goyer stammered. "Where are we going?"

"Relax." Sam stopped beside a food stall and squinted her eyes past the racks of steaming trays. Across the street, three capped figures, each a different height, slipped silently into an alley, their movements fluid and deliberate and their faces obscured by shadows. She willed her implant to see further, but it was never meant for use without its complementing device, and her visor was locked up in Ursus alongside her carbine and kit.

Next to her, cups and silverware clacked and clattered. Sam glared at the nervous marine who placed his palms over the shelf, an apology written on his face.

She muttered an expletive under her breath and refocused on the individuals who huddled around a small dumpster. "You can head back to the Alley." She never told the marine to join her—he had followed her on his own.

"What if Dense—"

She hushed him. Fuck Densaned. Though the company lead didn't want to hear about the Charonites, Sam knew what she had seen the previous day. Something was happening along the Alley, and if her previous experience with the Children of Charon was relevant, they were up to nothing good.

Suddenly, two of the three figures walked briskly back toward them, their heads swiveling as they took to the intersection. Sam tucked herself behind the stall and pulled Goyer back before he tried to pop his neck out.

When the two disappeared around the corner, Sam peeked toward the alley they had exited. "We have a few minutes left, Goyer. Stay here or go back, do whatever you want. I'll be back before our break ends," she said over her shoulder. And then she strode out toward the narrow street entrance where the last one, a short and stout rectangle of a person, remained crouched, their back to Sam as they fiddled with something inside the dumpster. Behind her, Goyer muttered curses repeatedly under his breath.

Sam would've sighed, but frankly, she liked the company—she had long worked as a pair with her brother, and with the thousands of kilometers and MED clearance currently between them, well, she liked having company. Even if it was a first-contract marine.

She stopped at the corner and motioned Goyer forward with a discreet gesture. He padded over, a small nudge as he bumped into her. She glanced back at the sweat beading his forehead and tried not to roll her eyes. At least his rifle didn't have live ammunition. She couldn't get caught in friendly fire if he didn't have rounds in the first place. Regardless, it was better if she did this herself.

"If you're not going back, you might as well be of use. Stay here. Watch my six."

Goyer nodded, relief in his eyes. "Okay. What's the signal?"

"What?"

"The signal. You know, in case someone comes up. Or something."

Fucking hell. She missed working with her brother. Competent. Experienced.

"Make something up. I'm just gonna talk to them."

Before he could delay further, she was off, crossing the street and careful to make as little noise as possible as she entered the alley and snuck up to the unsuspecting Charonite. In that narrow space, the air hung heavier, thick with the stench of rotting food and stale urine, but she ignored it even as her stomach churned in both excitement and disgust. As she closed the distance, Sam let her boots crunch against the pavement.

The individual startled and shot up, shoulder-length brown hair fluttering as she spun around to face Sam. Her eyes widened and before any fight-or-flight response registered, Sam's dark fingers closed around a meaty wrist.

"Hold up."

The young woman twisted and struggled but stopped with a yelp when Sam added more pressure to her grip.

"Wunt doin' nothin' wrong!"

"Sure. Then what *are* you doing, Charonite?"

"Not—not a Cha—"

Sam twisted the woman's wrist around. The inked lines were bold black, a little red around the edges. It was recently done. Fresh. A new Children of Charon recruit. It wasn't a clean lamp, but it bore enough similarity. "What are you doing?" Sam repeated. She pulled the woman out of the way and tapped the dumpster with the tip of her boot.

"Lem'me go!" The Charonite swung her other fist, but Sam caught it with a free hand and forced it down. These new city recruits were weak. They were nothing like the deranged junkies she had encountered in Matam. They didn't even compare to the ones she came across in Ursus's area of operations. These Station Charonites weren't abusing stims. At least, not yet.

"Why are you and your friends hanging around the Alley?" she asked, aloof. Even if the three hadn't been behind the incident the previous day, they were still lurking around the fences. The black caps had been discreet, but not enough for a seasoned recon specialist who could identify basic surveillance craft. Emphasis on basic. They hadn't attempted to hide their recognizable branding with long sleeves or their matching headwear.

"Nunya business, fuckin' grunt. You dunt have—have..."

She was looking for the word "jurisdiction" or "authority," but Sam only blinked. When it came to Children of Charon and domestic terrorism, UMF did have both jurisdiction and authority. It was a thin line within the city limits, but SecTeam was already understaffed with the Altered population, and Sam had enough justification. She sighed, then forced the woman's wrists together, securing both with her prosthetic. With her other hand, she reached for a ziplet on her belt.

"I'm taking you back," she said. Maybe SecTeam or someone from Intel could get the young Charonite to confess to whatever plans they had around the Altered Sector, or better, where and how they were being recruited.

Sam felt the pressure in the seams of her shoulder as the woman pushed forward. Black color blurred toward her, and instinctually, Sam pulled her head back and shot her arm out at the same time, both the Charonite's wrists in her grip. She heard the sickening crack first, and then the delayed crunch as her prosthetic registered the sensation.

Fuck.

She let go and stared incredulously at the woman as she fell back and howled, both wrists held up at odd angles. A line of spittle dribbled past her lower lip and down her chin with each whimper.

"Caw. Ca-caw!"

Goyer stared meekly down the alley with his teeth gritted together in a nervous grimace, his shoulders up to his ears. Densaned and the company second stepped into view, the former's hands set firmly on his hips.

Shit.

"The fuck are you doing, Ryan?" he shouted, storming down the passage until he came to a stop next to her and the Charonite. "The fuck *did* you do? You pulling SOG shit and beating up civilians? What the fuck!" He gaped at the displayed broken wrists. "Goyer, get over here."

The marine scurried over to join Sam and the regiment lead.

Sam sneered. "She's with the COC. Three of them were surveilling the Alley—"

"How do you know she's COC?"

She pointed a finger at her own forearm. "Tattoo."

The lead didn't bother to look. "And what? You wanted to be the hero and chase them down on your own? Classic poster child syndrome. Always looking for some kind of spotlight, aren't you?" He squinted down at the woman and a thin smirk tugged at his lips.

A sliver of doubt feathered in.

Densaned's face hardened. "MED was right to hold you—you need to get your eyes checked. You assaulted an innocent, Ryan."

Sam's anger barely had time to boil. "They—" Sam regulated her tone. "They were watching—"

"Then why didn't you report it?"

"I did, I was—"

"So why didn't it come to me?"

Her jaw tensed and she stifled any visual betrayal of the fury searing through her. This was a battle Sam was going to lose. It wasn't worth it to explain.

Densaned stared at her, waiting for the challenge, but he didn't get any. "Alright, fucking hero. What did this civilian do to warrant excessive use of force?"

"Sir?" Goyer squeaked. "They *were* being pretty suspicious."

Densaned spun and glared. "Did I ask you, marine?"

Goyer's eyes dropped.

"Is that right? They were being pretty suspicious?" He ignored the crying Charonite on the ground and gestured at the street. "Well?" The lead waited, his eyes flitting between the two. Sam said and did nothing, her anger seething beneath her skin, but Goyer stared at the dumpster.

"Oh? Was it something in the trash?" He glared at them both. Densaned pointed at the container. "Then get your fucking confirmation!"

Goyer wiped at the sweat along his hairline and neck, stepped forward, and peered into the dumpster. His eyes darted around before they came up, a quick glance at Sam, before he addressed the officer. "I don't know, sir."

Sam's shoulders sagged and she held back a disappointed sigh.

"What the fuck do you mean, you don't know? Didn't you say they were being pretty suspicious?"

Goyer's eyes dropped again.

The lead whipped back to Sam. "Hero, what does he mean *I don't know?*"

It was less of a question and more of an exercise in humiliation and mockery. She pushed herself forward and looked into the bin, avoiding the oily liquid staining the pavement below. Her stomach turned and she winced at the hot soup of putrefaction.

Trash. Stained fabric, soggy containers, and food scraps in a macabre sheen of grease.

Just a dumpster.

Big fuck.

"Well?"

Sam swallowed back any attitude before she spoke. The nauseating blend of smells and discomfort coated the back of her throat. "I was wrong."

He sneered at her. "You're so desperate to be relevant, you're creating enemies that aren't there."

Her teeth threatened to crack.

"We don't do hero shit here, Ryan. This ain't fucking SOG, and we aren't your cool-operator speed. Call a fucking ambo and get back to your position. No, actually, you know what? You're dismissed. Go home. Consider this your last shift. I don't need you creating any additional paperwork for us. If this comes back on me..." He strode away, and muttered loudly, "I'm glad your time's up soon. You're a fucking bad influence on my boys."

Sam's hands clenched. It hadn't been there in the beginning, but doubt flooded her mind now. She felt the delayed rub of her prosthetic finger against her prosthetic thumb. On a regular hand, it would've broken the skin, but it *wasn't* a regular hand. She wished the Charonite's bones hadn't been that fragile; she wished she could have broken someone else's.

◊

In her return to the UMF base, Sam's anger with the company lead simmered. She was even relieved when she locked away the issued rifle and other gear. They were never hers, anyway. Temporary.

As she left the compound, something lifted in her chest. Densaned had given her a gift by letting her out early. None of this really mattered. In a few days she'd be back to active SOG status. She'd get her diamond tabs back and then her biggest decision would be whether to return to Ursus and her brother or remain in the city with Miriam and Echo. She liked the openness of the northern territories, but her brother also seemed open to transferring with her. It didn't matter much at the present, with most SOG teams spending more time in the

North. Regardless of her decision, she'd have the best of both options. Sam knew she shouldn't have been excited about it, not with the ongoing situation at the front and border, not with the black-capped Charonites, but she was used to conflict. There was always something going on.

When Sam returned to Miriam's apartment, she stood inside the entrance and stared at the space. She never tired of the welcoming cinnamon scent, but the flat was too empty, too still, and she missed Miriam.

Her commcuff raised and Sam deliberated on sending a message. Miriam would see through her words and know something had happened, and Sam was embarrassed to share the mundane squabbles of her probation life. Instead, she inputted a new message.

> S. RYAN: Any new updates on Beric or Kartik?

She doubted it—UMF networks hadn't mentioned the Apostate leaders in a long time—but she still sent the question off. She tried another line.

> S. RYAN: I don't know if you're around
> Temunco, but anything you can tell me about
> the Charonites? Their movement? It seems
> like there are more recruits here in the city.

Messages with Jace had gone stagnant in the last month, and Sam wasn't sure what the intelligence marine was doing in the South. She wasn't privy to that kind of information, but it was a shot in the dark.

Sam scrolled through the rest of her channels. All of them had gone quiet. Scott was working. Miriam and Echo were working. Everyone was either on mission or engaged in something mission-related. With that realization, a restlessness surged through her and her body ached for something to do.

She was never good at sitting still, and now, with her release from tedium and assholish leadership, she knew she could find work and relevance. Sam hurried into the bedroom to fish out a change of clothes. She could be busy, too.

16

ANOMALY

THE RIDE OUT passed uneventfully with faraway hills, wind, and darkness providing cover. Miriam scanned the flat topography of the North where waist-high, overgrown brush stretched endlessly under limited daylight. However, she remained alert, her visor scanning for any movement. By the time the vehicles came to a stop in a predetermined nook of a small hill, Miriam's limbs were stiff and cold. The northern temperatures weren't particularly low, but between the pending storm, its winds, and a long period in an open cab, she forced blood and warmth back into her legs, stretching her muscles as she stepped out of the prowler. Echo didn't have time to loiter. In and out. This is what they had been training for, and she was determined to complete the mission and move on.

The six marines left the prowlers behind and quickly ascended the hill in a spread-out formation. Their figures hunched in a balance of speed and concealment in the surrounding growth. Though the gusts of wind assaulted her at the zenith, she was grateful. So far, the reporting was correct. These were optimal conditions for a shit mission like this. Downwind of a coming storm. She hated it, but the elements were another veil of security, no matter how thin it felt.

Her visor scanned out as far as it could, but anything past the small coastal village below was shrouded in darkness. She could make out a large sign, its carved letters giving a name to a spot where pensioners' and backcountry folk could restock their wares and wet their lips. The town's spaced-out box structures and long, narrow streets were devoid of lights, a whole suburb gone to sleep. Abandoned. Or the illusion of abandonment. If the report was correct, a small detachment of wunbies had recently taken up residence—a comfortable prize for the offensive strike and push they had achieved days prior.

She felt eyes on her as her legs pumped down the hill. Echo was in the open, vulnerable as they moved toward the nearest two-story structure near the bottom of the hill. Miriam cast aside the thought, putting her trust in the fact that somewhere, shrouded in the environment, Sam's expert marksman of a brother was watching with his reticle aimed at whatever situation they had charged into.

Twenty meters from the shop's exterior, Miriam and the others slowed, reclaiming their breath as they rescanned their sectors for any movement, but there was nothing. It was late. Even alties slept.

The team filed into two columns and stealthily maneuvered toward the nearest door, what looked to be the back of the building. Shielded from the wind, Miriam searched its facade. A small window on the second floor exhibited the slight glow of a light source within.

Fox tested the door panel, but it was locked. Like they had rehearsed a hundred times, Kai slid in front of the large marine and made quick work. Delicate fingers stretched and pasted a thin strip of putty-like material along key seams. Within seconds, dull orange lines glowed, followed by a muffled series of pops. Yuri gripped the door's surface and slid it open. Like flowing water, Fox, Kai, and Krill moved in with Yuri, Miriam, and Nas immediately following. They cleared the bottom floor

—an open room split by aisles of shelves—and Fox and Yuri took point, training their barrels up at the only stairwell in the back. And with silent footsteps, Fox, Yuri, Miriam, and Krill ascended, Nas and Kai holding their taken and cleared space.

Miriam's heart thumped in her rib cage, a second round of adrenaline flooding her bloodstream. A small hallway led to three doors—the closest and furthest open. Fox poked his rifle in the first then moved along, holding his sights on the second one with Yuri behind him. Miriam stepped out to the side, her own weapon held on the remaining open door beyond.

In the corner of her eye, Fox nodded, and he and the two others barged into the second room. Still in the hallway, Miriam held her breath, waiting for something to lunge out of the darkness, out of the open door toward her, but nothing. Sounds of struggle burst out from within the breached space and something metallic skittered across the floor.

She glanced inside. Fox's body was sprawled on top of someone, his limbs locked with theirs. On the ground next to him, Yuri wrestled with the same figure's head. Krill stood half in the doorway, his eyes and barrel fixed on the opposite corner. A medium-sized weapon—only identifiable as such with its trigger and handle—lay flat in the doorway next to the team lead's foot.

Fox and Yuri eased up, revealing a slim female restrained by a muzzle lock around her mouth and face. She thrashed as the two quickly bound her bony wrists and feet, and Miriam could make out a pale and raised triangle with a circle at its top point on the bare neck. The wunby's eyes flashed out, full of rage and greenish glint in the dimly lit room. Shifting his rifle around, Fox angled himself so he could cover both the bound woman and whatever Krill's attention had been on. Yuri quickly disappeared into the opposite corner.

With firepower and coverage reinstated, Krill nodded back at Miriam. Together, they moved to clear the remaining open room. She had already expected it when nothing happened after the flurry of activity, but it was still a consolation when they confirmed there were no threats inside.

Next to her, Krill exhaled and clicked his visor twice as they returned to the occupied bedroom. Another alty with a dark, scabbed-over brand on his neck lay on his belly in the corner, his face, wrists, and ankles shackled in the same manner. Miriam frowned. He was a teenager, no older than eighteen, and unlike his partner's, his eyes were wide in terror. Miriam wondered if this was his first interaction with humans.

She flicked the thought away. The report was right. They had two manageable scouts in an ideal location in almost perfect weather conditions. So far, it was a perfect snatch job. All they needed were the alty stims—whether in their blood or in its untaken form. Echo had taken seminars on the trending drugs in the city and human settlements. Inhalants, capsules, jabbers, they knew about human stims, but no one had confirmation of alty ones.

Miriam studied the two bound captives on the ground, her eyes darting between the brands on their necks. This was what Echo had seen and reported in their southern mission with Sam and Scott, and it was a good sign. In their first attempt at this task, the farmer hadn't been branded. The second captive had, but that mission failed the instant the wunby killed himself in the process.

Inside, Yuri had already turned the room over. He moved from the young Apostate to the other, sweeping gloved hands over their writhing bodies. Miriam held her breath as the second paused then perked up. He handed a small bracelet-like device to her, and she scanned the metallic object over, unable to make out any screens or buttons. If not for the sharp contrast of style to the wunby, Miriam would've assumed it was simply a fashion accessory. She placed it inside a faraday pocket inside her sling.

Yuri clicked his tongue and held out something else to Miriam: a small box. As the second finished his search, Miriam held her breath and opened the thin container. She exhaled, tilting its contents forward to the other two. Four small, white squares with an almost-translucent paper texture sat apart in their own depression alongside two injection devices. They were thinner but weren't much different from the medical jabbers in her sling.

Krill reached out, a bare finger over the squares, but Miriam sucked air through her teeth and pulled the box back. She made a short movement of her head, a silent warning. Don't touch. Their training had barely mentioned it—the method had stopped in practice—but Miriam made an assumption. She had heard of membrane-permeable "stickers" before, but she couldn't remember whether it was in high university or around the medical center. She closed the box carefully and dipped her head at Krill. After two failed attempts, this third mission finally yielded results.

Miriam tucked the goods into her sling and took out a small pocket of jabbers. She scanned each wunby and adjusted the contents of each syringe. Fox shifted to the side and Yuri held the woman down as Miriam pressed the jabber into soft skin. Smug satisfaction radiated off her as she injected concentrated knockout serum into the center of the triangle-and-circle brand. It was a small justice and retaliation for every nightmare she'd had since Temunco.

Once finished, Yuri and Miriam stepped back and the woman fought with her restraints, her eyes glowing a multitude of hate and rage. But within seconds, eyelids drooped, and the thrashing faded. The wunby slumped to the ground. She wasn't of large stature, and with muscles now relaxed, the alty looked almost harmless. If Miriam hadn't witnessed two Echo marines wrestling her down, she wouldn't have believed the strength of the scrawny woman. Was she already on stims? What would she have been like if she had gotten more in her system?

She moved on to the younger alty. His eyes grew, and he struggled against his bindings but to no avail. He joined the other in unconsciousness soon after.

Miriam turned at the sound of a meaty smack. Krill stood over the other wunby, his open hand over the woman's cheek. He then dug his knuckles into the woman's sternum and rubbed it roughly up and down. Nothing. She was out cold, the knockout cocktail working well. Now it just had to hold their two captives in the same state, at least until they were back on an airship to Ursus.

The four made quick work of fitting the two into expandable sacks, the thin but sturdy material cinched tightly around the bodies. They had brought two mobile litters and it felt like overkill—Fox could've easily carried both—but no one wanted to take any chances. Echo had gotten this far, and success was only accomplished when one or both specimens were in Axiom's custody. They just had to get out, back to FOB Domovoy, then off to Ursus Outpost. Fox and Yuri modified the litters into pack form and after triple-securing their new cargo, they each heaved one wunby onto their backs. Krill took the lead with Miriam at the rear as they headed back downstairs.

Reunited with the rest of Echo, Miriam watched Nas's eyebrows lift at the two lumpy sacks. She bobbed her head in response as he fell in line behind her. Just like in their dry runs before, he'd be their tail for any potential issues. Miriam needed to be ready to administer additional doses to their packaged captives.

The lead spun his finger around at the ground-level shop and threw up a hand. Nas gave a thumbs up. He pulled a sleek-looking hand terminal out of his own light pack and then placed it carefully back in its faraday pocket. The shop and house weren't reported to have much, but from the quick survey of moved furniture and items on shelves, Echo's intelligence specialist had exploited the site for sensitive items. Whatever device he had found in the store and house was deemed worthy enough to be stashed there. From what little she saw, it wasn't any kind of human tech she had seen before. Although curious, Miriam knew it wasn't the time to inquire. If Nas thought it was good enough, she trusted him. His nose had a way of sniffing out crucial details.

Krill returned his own thumbs up, then made a fist and opened his fingers explosively, his cheeks puffing. Kai nodded. She gestured quickly around the floor space. In the darkness, Miriam couldn't make out the explosive pucks and devices, but while the four of them had worked upstairs, the engineer had rigged the place. It was a contingency, but also a little surprise for the rest of the detachment when they woke or alerted to their missing scouts. If it took out a few wunbies, it'd only help UMF's overall effort.

Satisfied, the lead nudged his head toward the door. It was time to go, before the other wunbies woke up or figured out something was wrong.

Echo slipped out the way they'd come and began the ascent back up the hill. Their return was slower, but stealth was a priority. With their new cargo, they wouldn't be able to outrun alties. Especially if the detachment was fitted with similar stim kits.

Loose pebbles clattered past her, and Miriam's breath seized —a jolt of fear coursing through her body. Even with the gusts of wind, the noise felt unproportionally loud as they seemed to miss every patch of moss, clacking against the hard rock down the slope. Echo paused in a synchronized reaction.

They held their breath, collectively waiting and listening for any movement, any sign that the sleeping genetically engineered beings had heard them. They waited for a long three seconds, and there was nothing but a lurking dark stillness swallowed by cold gusts.

Krill threw a stiff hand forward. Continue.

The team set off once more, quicker this time with a reinvigorated adrenaline. Miriam watched Yuri's feet, her surroundings, the lumpy sack in front of her, and then her surroundings again. The hair on the back of her neck rose as a bad feeling swam into her bloodstream.

She bumped into the bagged wunby and felt Nas nudge into her as their entire ensemble stalled. Miriam peeked around Yuri, and her throat constricted.

A dark outline of a lone figure straightened to its full height near the top of the hill. Its head and shoulders were obvious, especially as they heaved up and down. Its translucent eyelids shuttered to the side and two glows of dulled green stared down at them.

Miriam lifted her rifle and heard Nas's safety disengage, but it was too late. With her visor, she could see the shadow's mouth elongate, and the start of a guttural roar rolled up its throat. Her body tensed and an icy cold gripped every muscle and tendon.

A muffled shot cracked out and the Altered froze, its noise trapped inside its mouth. Miriam stared at the shadow uncertainly, but then it crumpled to the ground. Rocks and pebbles scattered as the body slid a short way down before catching on a patch of brush.

They were made. There was no way a detachment of wunbies wouldn't have heard a gunshot, even as suppressed as it was.

"Move!" hissed Krill. Whatever stealth they had attempted was gone. The priority was now speed and exit.

Miriam's feet picked up as they reached the crest of the hill. Her thighs burned from the burst, but she pushed through. They just had to reach the down slope on the other side and then their vehicles at the bottom.

"Two o'clock!" Fox said between heavy breaths.

Miriam's eyes snapped forward. Two individuals ran down the hill almost parallel to Echo about a hundred meters away, their trajectory pushing toward the marines. She squinted, forcing her visor to focus as she bounced down the decline at the risk of rolling her ankles.

The two bogeys had firearms in hand, but they weren't up or trained on Echo. As they converged closer, they weren't like the strange weapon they had stripped from their two captives.

"Don't shoot," Miriam gasped. "Friendlies."

"Blue blue blue!"

She didn't recognize the voice, but relief flashed through her body. In the dark, she could barely make out the man's features as he and the other joined Echo in their sprint, but she could make out his UMF kit and rifle.

"Overwatch," Nas breathed behind her. "We don't have space for you."

"No worries! We have our own ride," the marine said in a thick accent as the now eight of them slowed at the nook in the hill where their prowlers were parked. Kai, Nas, Fox, and Yuri pushed ahead to start the vehicles and offload their precious cargo. "We'll see ya back at Ursus! This was our last run." And then the two were sprinting off to wherever their transportation had been hidden.

The second marine turned back as Miriam jumped into the prowler. A tuft of light hair stuck out from under his headgear. Mute. Scott. Sam's brother. She didn't have time to process or verbalize it to the rest of Echo. This wasn't the time for a reunion.

The boom of an explosion ripped through the gusts of wind, and Miriam turned toward the hill. She only saw silhouettes of flying debris and the subsequent orange muted glow. She continued to watch until it dipped behind darkness like a sunset as Echo sped along with their prizes.

By the time they had dropped to a sustainable speed, Miriam's muscles still hadn't relaxed. She'd find no relief until they were back to FOB Domovoy, perhaps not even until they were safely behind the walls of Ursus Outpost. Despite the distance they made, Miriam's hand never wavered from its protective hold around her bag and the most precious cargo within. She didn't understand why this mission was a priority, but she understood they were close to being done. Until they were assigned to their next objective, Miriam wouldn't have to face her nightmares in the real world again.

17

ACCLIMATION

YOU'RE SO *desperate to be relevant, you're creating enemies that aren't there.*

The company lead's words reverberated in her thoughts as she neared the Alley for the second time in the same day. She adjusted her cap over her hair and made sure to avoid the areas closest to the fences. Her company was changing out shifts and she didn't want to be seen or recognized.

Sam clenched her left fist, willing it to stop trembling. She could remember the delayed sensation of the Charonite's wrists breaking, the easy snap. She told herself she wasn't upset—she knew the woman was a terrorist—but she didn't like that she hadn't known her own tipping point, the balance between enough and too much. She hated that Densaned's words were holding her hostage, that her doubt was growing. Maybe she *had* fabricated a situation because she was desperate to find an enemy or something to do.

And right now, Sam was irked that the tremors in her hand wouldn't stop. She tucked the wrapped package she had picked up at the market under an armpit and held up both hands. Her left shook with little motions while her prosthetic was like a statue, still and poised.

It was a betrayal.

"Evening."

Underneath the white light of the side gate, eyes stared down through crossbars. And then they were gone, a glint of green as they moved into the shadows. The pedestrian door opened, and Sam walked through.

"Artem," she said in greeting. "Is she in?"

The legionnaire folded his arms. Sam wasn't sure how old he was or if aging differed with the Altered, but he looked to be the same age as her—the youngest legionnaire she'd seen, at least. "Yes. Did I scare you?"

Sam looked around the small access area. Only one white legionnaire kit was hung next to the sentry post, a short baton-like rod next to it. The other spots were empty. "Not this time."

He stared flatly back at her.

"Don't be disappointed. I'm with someone who's somehow quieter than you." She squeezed the packet in her hand and turned back to him, his pale face stretched long in the glow of the single post light. "Is it just you tonight?"

Artem frowned. "You have not been here in a while."

"I was here yesterday."

"Here. Not out there."

"Yeah, well." She kicked her toe to the ground. "Been busy." It was a half-truth. When Echo wasn't away from Station, Sam had been trying to spend as much time as possible outside of her shifts with Miriam. Plus, she hadn't planned on being in clearance purgatory this long. "I told you before, that group out there...they don't know I visit. I can't just waltz over and say hi."

"Waltz?"

Sam shrugged.

"You said your seniors know."

"They're not the same."

The legionnaire mirrored her shrug awkwardly, as if he was learning the motion from her.

"Are you having a sparring session soon?" Sam had observed the legionnaires' last one after making friendlier acquaintances with Artem, but after her confrontation with Densaned, she had emotions she wanted to physically vent out. She wasn't fully confident in her strength and coordination, but her frustration was at an all-time high and it'd be enough to go head-to-head with a legionnaire in a friendly match.

"Not anytime soon, no."

Sam looked around. "Where are the usuals?" she asked. "I didn't see the others at their posts."

"Been busy."

Sam scoffed and waited a beat longer, but the young legionnaire only shrugged. "Fine. Keep your secrets." She thought to tell him about the Charonites, but with what happened earlier, doubt overruled her. "Keep your head on a swivel, yeah? Plenty of prying eyes about." She walked a few steps and then turned back. "See you later, legionnaire."

"Not if I see you first, marine."

Sam snorted and shook her head as she headed toward Kuan-Lin's cluster of buildings. She remembered something else and backpedaled. "Artem, were you able to check on the two I mentioned before?"

His semi-translucent eyelid blinked sideways.

That was disappointing. As she made her way to the Royal's flat, she thought about Hadeon and Varya, the two legionnaires who they had run into in the South. They would probably have found another stronghold to defend and fight back the Apostates. Hopefully, they were alive somewhere.

Upon her arrival to Kuan-Lin's apartment, the door was already open, and she poked her head inside.

"In the kitchen."

Sam followed the voice into the next room. The Royal had an apron on, her back to the entrance as she prepared food at the counter. Something boiled on the cooker, its fragrance hitting Sam both in the nose and stomach.

"You haven't been around in a while," Kuan-Lin said without looking up from the cutting board. She added in a whisper, "Xiaoling and Longwei missed you."

An offended voice piped up from around the corner. "No, I didn't!"

"Right back atcha," Sam muttered.

"I heard that, cyborg!"

Cyborg. That was new. At least the boy wasn't calling her a roach anymore.

"It's been...busy. A lot of shifts." Sam set her package on the counter behind the Royal and took a seat at the table.

Kuan-Lin turned, and her nose twitched. "I smell...what is that?" She touched the packet and smiled. "Is this coriander? For us?"

Sam nodded.

"Oh, perfect. Are you staying for dinner?"

A growl from Sam's stomach answered what words did not. She had been so irritated and conflicted from her shift, she hadn't thought about the timing. It hadn't been her intention to show up in the middle of the Royal's surprisingly late meal. "Only if you'll have me. I didn't mean to crash."

"You're a friend; you're always welcome here." Kuan-Lin returned to her station and dumped whatever she had been working on into a pot. She then glanced over her shoulder. "What happened? You seem troubled."

"No," Sam responded—too quickly. "Just work. Something stupid. It doesn't matter."

Kuan-Lin wiped her hands together and retrieved a cup from the tea contraption. The Royal set it down in front of Sam. "You're not picking fights again, are you? Trying to save children who don't listen?"

From the next room, the little voice piped up. "I heard that."

Kuan-Lin chuckled.

Sam took a small sip of the tea. "Not this time, but

something's going on around the Alley. The Children of Charon are up to something. There're too many new recruits…"

The Royal gave a weak smile, her gold eyes flat.

"What's going on with Legion? It's light around the perimeter. If the Charonites *are* up to something…"

The Royal hummed and delicately unwrapped the package Sam had brought. She retrieved a sprig of a green herb, its stem and leaves bright against her skin. "Let me enjoy this." She brought it to her nose, inhaled, then sighed. "You don't know how much you miss something until it's gone. I never cared much for our palace in Arshangol, but *tiān*, I loved that garden."

Her brother would've loved to see it, but Sam didn't say it out loud.

"It's such a disgrace, a shame what they did… I took it for granted. Oh, even the food." The Royal sighed again. "So much taken for granted." Her golden eyes caressed the herb once more before she placed it back on the counter. She took a large breath then exhaled slowly. "Thank you. For this. And yes, the legionnaires are working out a new schedule. As for the city, our people know of the advisories and limited movements. Curfew is in effect." Kuan-Lin took a graceful sip of her own tea. "Are you still having complications with your lead?"

"Temporary lead."

The Royal's eyebrow lifted. "Hm?"

"Never mind." Sam pushed down the irritation that came with any mention of Densaned. She was done with him, anyway. "He's an ego."

"He doesn't like that you talk with me."

Sam snorted. "He doesn't—he shouldn't know. The higher-ups in UMF know I talk with you, well, someone here."

Kuan-Lin chuckled and ran her finger along the side of her cup. "Sanctioned. As long as I continue to provide information."

Semi-sanctioned, but Sam didn't correct her. "That's not what I meant."

The woman laughed. "It's quite alright."

But the Royal wasn't wrong. Kuan-Lin's flippant comment jarred something loose. "Remind me why—what are you getting out of this?" Sam asked.

"Does it have to be quid pro quo?"

Sam tilted her head.

"I'm learning about you, your culture, your aspirations. I get a lot from our friendship."

Friendship. Was this friendship? Sam had seen it as a mission, but something had changed in the past months.

"Like I've said before, this is good. We talk freely. It's definitely more effective than the discussions we're trying to have with your government. The bureaucracy and passive-aggressive diplomacy, it's all such a headache." Her voice dropped to a whisper. "Your presence, our *friendship*, is also an example for our next generation. Isn't that right, Longwei?"

A small groan emitted from the other room.

Kuan-Lin fluttered her eyes, pleased with herself. "Why are you asking this again? What's going on?"

"Nothing. I—is there anything you want to know more about? That I can talk about, of course," she quickly added.

"This isn't transactional, Sam. Don't overthink it."

"Still."

Kuan-Lin chuckled, then considered. "Fine. Tell me again about the hybrid child in your southern mission."

That surprised Sam. She had almost forgotten about the half-human, half-Altered girl they had seen in Matam. Had she mentioned it before? Perhaps in passing, when she had tried to fill awkward silences in previous conversations. "I don't know much more about her."

"But she exists."

"A farmers' family." Sam nodded, her voice tight. An orphaned hybrid child with parents killed by the Apostates.

Regardless, she didn't know the science behind it. She couldn't comprehend the genetics, egg fertilization, or whatever.

"How old?"

Sam shook her head. She wasn't good at profiling children's ages. The Royal children, Xiaoling and Longwei, could've been anywhere from ages three to sixteen; she didn't factor in or consider the difference of Altered development. "A child. Young."

She really didn't know much more. The settlement of Matam had been invaded and razed shortly after that meeting. She knew Echo had gone to the South at least one more time since, and Jace was somewhere there with other SOG teams, but Sam had been kept in the dark. There was no word on what happened, no updates. "I don't know if she's still alive—if they escaped."

Kuan-Lin took another sip of tea, her gaze unfocused. In the silence, Sam fidgeted with her own cup, careful of her prosthetic's grip. She was about to ask for updates to the Altered's search for the Apostate leaders when a device on the other counter blipped, then blipped again. The Royal excused herself to check whatever notifications she had received. Kuan-Lin's body stiffened, and Sam straightened in response, the air shifting inside the spacious room.

"Is everything okay?"

The Royal paced, swiping her finger across the display.

"Kuan-Lin."

Golden eyes flashed and Sam recoiled. In that split second, every muscle in her body tensed, her instincts snapping in. The Royal had never looked at her like that before, had never shown any predatory behavior, and it was a sharp reminder of the danger she had gotten comfortable with, someone who, despite her pleasant demeanor, could probably destroy her in seconds.

But nothing came. The woman continued to engage her device, her fingers dancing about, and her lips barely opening as she whispered instructions on the other side of the room.

Sam stood. With the fleeting fear gone, she was now impatient. If Kuan-Lin had received new information that would affect UMF, Ursus, her brother, Miriam, or Echo, she wanted it.

The Royal returned to the counter and her hands splayed out, head slumped between her shoulders. "I need to get back to the embassy."

Sam wasn't certain if she was talking to herself.

Kuan-Lin walked to the kitchen window and engaged her device once more, whispering into it. It was spoken in the Altered's regional dialect, but Sam understood who it was addressed to. She had called Dmitri. Probably for an escort. The Royal then inhaled, straightened, and visibly regained her composure. When she looked back up, the Altered woman wore the face of her regal personality, although Sam knew the smile was forced.

"Apologies. I'm afraid I have to cut this short. Can we chat more another time?" She turned her head to the side, her voice even. "Longwei, I'm stepping out. Dinner is here. It should be ready in a few minutes."

"Kuan-Lin."

"You're welcome to stay longer. Help yourself, you know where the bowls are."

"What's going on?"

The woman stopped in her movement and stared back with a restrained sadness. For a moment, Sam felt she had asked too much, pried too far. She had gotten so used to being provided information freely that it felt alien demanding it now.

"You're going back to the embassy? It's late. I can walk with you."

"No." The Royal considered Sam for a moment. When she finally spoke, her face set back in its diplomatic composure. "Nakuan."

Sam's eyebrows pinched together. The Altered trade town

across the strait? The Legion garrison nearby? "What about it?" she pressed. "What does that mean?"

The Royal shook her head, and then gold eyes locked onto Sam's. "We lost."

The door opened, and she was gone.

Sam's jaw clenched.

We lost.

What did that mean? Did the Apostates attack Nakuan? If the Altered didn't have the town or the garrison, that left the entire northern border open for the Apostates. If they lost, there was nothing standing between humans and a flood of enemies.

◊

"We have marines out there. Whole settlements, farmers, a shit ton of people. You won't tell them?"

On the other side of the desk, Riley Shadid, an intelligence warrant officer, placed one hand over the other. "You're supposed to be in uniform when you're on base, Ryan."

Sam glanced down at her civilian clothes and rolled her eyes. Was he really going to lecture her on her attire when she was giving him important information?

He sighed. "We'll send what you relayed along for confirmation. When it's *verified*, we'll relay it to the appropriate parties."

At her sides, Sam's fists tensed. She remembered why she hadn't gone to see Kuan-Lin more often in the free time she had. She missed Jace and his ways of management and encouragement. Shadid, his referral, was not as interested in her assistance.

"Really. You're going to sit there and recite to me the canned response. This is coming direct from the top. She's a Royal."

"You're saying that your contact told you an entire Legion garrison is lost."

"Yes," Sam said. "No. She didn't say that exactly. She said they lost Nakuan."

Shadid's eyebrow twitched.

"It's the town—" Sam cut off. The warrant officer had probably never left Station or headquarters. He didn't know Ursus and their AOR like she did. "It's across the border. The legionnaire garrison is nearby. Just like UMF is to Station City. If the Altered lost Nakuan, they've essentially lost the garrison. Do you understand? We have to alert Command or Ursus, at least. They'll know what that means."

The man lifted his chin. "Ryan, I know this isn't your specialty or skill code, and you've been away for some time, but I'm telling you again. This isn't how it works. It may not be as sexy as SOG's run-and-gun instant results, but over here, we have checks for a reason. If we acted off every single thing coming in…" He gestured at her chair. "Can you please sit? You're making a scene."

Sam bit her lip, stifling a retort that would probably get her kicked out of the office. She forced herself to settle back into her seat and lowered her voice. "They need to know."

Her brother needed to know.

"I might sit behind this desk, but I'm not rusty from the field. I can tell you're thinking about circumventing, telling your friends in Ursus. Let's put a stop to that right now. Aren't you trying to get your status back?"

Sam's eyes sharpened.

"Don't do anything to mess it up. Trust the process."

She tried to keep from scoffing.

He sighed. "I believe you, I do. Your info has been adequate —I have you and Jace to thank for making me look good—but you know the drill. We have processes for a reason. It's been like this forever." Shadid sighed again at her unfiltered expression. "Let the system work. If your info is correct—"

"It's correct." Sam was confident. She held on to Kuan-Lin's expression, her initial reaction, and her composed mask after.

"—we'll get it out," he continued. "There's still time. Ursus isn't exactly twiddling their thumbs and lounging around. They'll check with the forward operating bases and whatever recon units and sensors they have. I know it's difficult for you, but chill."

Sam narrowed her eyes, but Shadid seemed unaffected.

"In the meantime, try to stop harassing the civvies. Keep things to scrapes and bruises. Broken bones are a bit difficult to sweep under the carpet."

Her cheek twitched. How did he know about her confrontation with the Charonite? A mix between a grumble and an unamused grunt caught in the back of her throat. Marines. Gossip and rumors were the currency of boredom and pertinence in the military.

Shadid stared indifferently back at her. "RUMINT," he confirmed. "You'll never escape it. Listen, I personally don't give two shits. Do whatever you want, but remember which side you're on. Jace and Ursus may idolize you—I think you're alright, too, but want my lowly opinion?"

She didn't. Not really.

He turned his attention back to his terminal, a sign their interaction was ending. "Don't go native on us now. Remember who you are, and remember that your contact, all the alties, are using you, just like we're using them. Don't let them fool you. Just because we have a mutual enemy, it doesn't mean we're friends."

18

INFLAMMATION

"BOSS WANTS US TO SIT TIGHT."

"We've been sittin' tight since we got those two. For more than a day now. We're jus' waitin' for confirmation. One drink won't hurt." The man trotted away from their temporary quarters.

Miriam gave the second a look. Fox wasn't wrong. The military was good at several things, but it didn't exactly have top marks with its administrative speed, especially when their own leadership didn't understand why a Station SOG team had captured Apostate scouts. However, Axiom had pull and some kind of closed communication. Beyond the initial and procedural UMF interrogations, there were clear instructions from "up top" to not touch or interact further with their captives. For Echo, the second they transferred and locked up the two wunbies in Ursus, their mission was done. They had gotten what Axiom wanted, but the team had to hold in place until someone else confirmed they *had* completed their objective. Beyond that, it was up to the scientists to arrange and deconflict their pickup and logistics.

"I hate to agree with the guy, but it'll take some time to crack that terminal and whatever device we found." Nas stood.

Miriam hopped up from her bunk and backpedaled toward the door. "We're back in civilization, Yuri. I think we deserve a little something after all of that." She lifted her eyebrow. Plus, she wanted to keep an eye on their teammate.

Yuri tutted. "Right." His stern glare did little to cut their intentions. "Fine. One drink, and then straight back," he called out, but Miriam and the others were already out the door.

When they caught up to Fox, he weaved through the compound like a tracker with a fresh scent. Along their walk, Miriam took in the outpost and its reconstruction. Aside from scaffolding here and there, there were few signs that the outpost had been under attack months before. Scorch marks had been painted over and buildings repaired. The temporary containers remained as housing and office space for the units sent up from Station and other UMF outposts.

She wasn't surprised when they arrived at the freshly rebuilt bar and saw it was just as much of a dive as Duncan's back in UMF Station. Inside, Miriam gave nods of acknowledgment to the few familiar faces from SOG.

And within minutes, the four had ordered a round of drinks and settled in. Miriam checked her cuff, but there were no additional messages. Sam was finishing her shift, and she had sent a quick message that she would be at the Royal's after. Miriam brushed aside a pang of insecurity. Should she be concerned? It was only the woman's continued effort for information gathering. And though Sam never said it, it seemed to be a friendship. Of course, that was still a foreign and strange concept. Miriam wouldn't say it out loud as such, but Sam's interactions with the alties were bordering on recklessness.

"Look who decided to join us," Kai chirped.

Miriam looked up as Yuri sidled onto the bench across from her. He gave them a shrug. "I told Krill where to find us. Plus, we're allowed to celebrate a little."

"Is Mute back in Ursus yet?" Kai asked hopefully. "I sent him a message."

"I sent him one too, but even if he was, I'm not sure he'd join us here, anyway." Yuri shook his head. "I should've known it was him."

"Part of me knew. Hell, I thought we were goners when that alty showed up. How far away was that shot? And with that storm? Saved us a lot of trouble." Kai tipped her cup back.

Fox's hand dropped to the table with a thud. "Mission's done," he grunted before taking another gulp. "When we see the blondie next, we can buy him a fuck ton of rounds."

Miriam's eyebrow lifted. She wasn't sure if it was a positive thing, but alcohol always seemed to bring their large teammate out of his quietness, a noticeable divergence from his previous demeanor.

Nas played with his cup. "It took us long enough. Now for the real deal."

"What exactly *is* the real deal?" Kai asked, rolling her eyes. Before Nas could respond, she quickly added, "I'm sure everything we're doing is for the bigger picture. It has to be, right?"

"I don't know. The other Razors are running recon and intel, and a couple Spartans are retaking the South, right? I heard Titans are spread out on their own ops. Hell, companies have been taking turns at the FOBs and keeping the wunbies at bay. I just want to get back into the real fight." He stood. "Regardless, one drink isn't enough for all this. I'm getting another one. Anyone else?"

They all looked at Yuri, waiting for him to protest, but he didn't. Fox threw up a finger and Miriam shook her head. As Kai and Nas excused themselves, Miriam downed her own alcohol and it burned her throat. In the relative silence, she let herself reflect on the mission now that they were a day and some distance away. She hadn't expected to freeze the way she did with the lone Altered on that hill. Maybe a couple drinks would help her sleep, soothe the next set of anticipated nightmares at least until she was back home. She slept better around Sam.

"Wow. Is that my old partner in crime?"

The three remaining marines turned to the sharp voice.

"Holy fuck! Tan? And Greggo?"

Yuri jumped away from the bench and crashed into a crushing embrace with someone in a Station-gray uniform. Miriam slid away from her seat. She knew that voice from a lifetime before.

The brunette woman laughed when she separated from Yuri, then flicked at his collar and SOG tab. Greenish-brown eyes twinkled. "That diamond looks great on you. Strong as ever, *da?*"

"Talya?" Miriam hadn't seen the woman since their university days. "What are you doing here?"

"It's been a long fucking time." The woman pulled her into a strong hug and Miriam laughed, patting her on the back. Thoughts of nightmares ejected from her mind as nostalgia filled their place.

"Nat…"

"And Tan!" the woman finished.

Yuri rolled his eyes. "The two terrors. Reunited here, of all places."

Still seated behind them, Fox cleared his throat, and the three turned. She rolled her eyes as his eyes scanned over her old friend. Perhaps alcohol reverting the man back to his usual self wasn't the best thing.

"Benjamin Fox, meet Natalya Nguyen. Talya, meet Fox." Miriam glanced over her shoulder to locate Kai and Nas, who were at the counter in an impassioned conversation with the bartender. "We have two more over there as well."

"Ah, you're a soghead, too," Talya said to Fox, her voice lowering into a flirtatious husk.

"The best one of this lot," Fox replied.

Miriam stifled another eye roll and waved her hand. "So? What are you doing here? I haven't seen you in how many years now? Just after uni? Are you with Ursus?" She pulled at the woman's sleeve. "And when did you join up?"

Talya playfully brushed her off and sat next to Fox. "It's been ages. We have so much to catch up on, but no, not with Ursus. I'm still in Station, but my company's up here—additional defenses and such, filling in holes while the outpost shifts people out to the forward bases. Personally? I'm ready to go home. I don't know how people do it here. I'm sick of the long nights. We don't have enough tech for this kind of darkness." She snatched Fox's drink, tasted it, then blew out a puff of air. Talya threw a wink at Fox. "*Very* strong. My kind of guy..."

"How long have you been here?" Miriam asked.

"A month, but we're rotating soon. Let another company deal with the grind. And you? Worst time to come, the locals say. Between the storms and darkness..." Talya patted Fox's hand, and he looked on, amused. "I thrive at night, but this is too much. The people here are a different breed, but if I recall..." She shifted her attention to Miriam. "You thrive at night, too. Have you met the locals yet?"

"Oh, I like you," Fox said.

"Tan's definitely met *one* local." Yuri laughed into his cup, and Miriam shot an unconvincing glare at both men.

Talya leaned into Fox. "See, Yuri and I've known Tan since uni. She's always had a penchant for...people."

Fox snorted. "Oh, I know."

Miriam shifted, her fingers rubbing into her temples.

"Speaking of... I have an eye on some potentials at your seven. I may have already claimed one or two, but it's not the first or second time our circles have overlapped." Talya smirked.

A peek behind revealed a small group of women in a fit of laughter. Miriam's eyes connected with one whose light brown hair let down around her shoulders and the woman's lips turned up in a curious smirk. She *was* quite attractive. The corner of Miriam's mouth pulled into a mirrored grin, but she turned away, shaking her head.

Talya's eyes narrowed, and she gripped Fox's arm. "Don't tell me she's switched sides."

Miriam scoffed, then shot another glare at Yuri, who leaned back and crossed his arms with a wide grin. He was enjoying himself. They all were. At her expense.

"No?" Talya's head cocked to the side, and she stuck out her tongue. "Don't be a snob."

"Tan's a reformed woman," Yuri said.

"What does *that* mean…"

He only grinned back. Talya looked between the three while Miriam's head dropped into her hand and she squeezed her eyes shut. She was glad for the distraction and the post-mission celebration, but this wasn't what she had in mind. Individually, the teasing was one thing. But this? Her friends and teammates didn't appreciate her tolerance enough.

When she reopened her eyes, Talya's face dropped, and the woman recoiled back overdramatically. "No." She pushed back into the table and studied Miriam, who braced herself.

Fox smirked. "She got a girlfr—"

Miriam shot a look. "Don't—"

"Fine. A really, really good friend."

"Hell."

"No," Talya repeated, her hands slapping the table surface. "He's serious? What happened to *the* Tanner? *The* Tan?"

Miriam sloshed the remainder of her drink in a circle.

"We're unbound, unfettered! Free for life!"

The inside of Miriam's lip crushed between her teeth.

"*Pizda.* You're boring now? What a shame," Talya teased. "But tell me more…"

Miriam downed the last of the liquid in one swallow. She craned her neck and pretended to look for Nas and Kai. "I'm going to find the babies. And I need another drink." She left the table before they could stop her.

On her way to the counter, she passed her teammates who were returning with multiple cocktails in hand. Miriam shook her head at an offered cup and waved the two on. She found refuge at the bar and set her order, watching the others join the conversation, the boys lapping up whatever new story her old friend had brought up. Fox howled with laughter and Miriam startled only at the reminiscence of a different time, at how something so frequent before was now rare. At least *he* was having a good time.

Her commcuff vibrated. A spike of excitement turned into disappointment at another UMF daily summary update. She perked up as someone joined her.

"So this is where you all are," Krill said. "What happened to waiting for confirmation?"

The question seemed rhetorical, so Miriam didn't answer. She slid her new drink to the team lead.

"You know, one of these days, all of you will actually listen to me… And thanks, but no thanks. Tonight's a beer night." He returned the cup back to her, waving at the barkeep. Krill pointed at the tap, then at the table where Echo was seated. "Guess I'll give everyone the news later. We have tomorrow off, anyway."

"It's what they wanted?"

The lead shrugged. "I don't know, they don't really tell us anything. I barely received a thumbs up, but I think we're good." He dropped a hand on Miriam's shoulder. "You doing alright?"

She nodded.

"Good." He gave her a hearty squeeze and then started toward the others.

"Wait, Krill."

The lead stopped.

"Have you talked to..." She gestured a thumb into her chest, in Fox's direction.

Krill deflated. They both turned discreetly to see their teammate with a grin plastered on his face. They hadn't seen that in a while. "I think it can wait, right? We finally snagged a win. I can't exactly tell him to stop drinking when we're all at a bar, *drinking*."

Miriam shrugged and raised her cup to her lips. "You're the boss."

"Yeah, well, sometimes I regret taking on this position." He walked back toward the others and dipped his head as he passed Talya, who took his place. The woman bumped her shoulder amicably into Miriam's, then turned to watch Echo's lead from behind. "Is he on your team as well? You have good-looking teammates, Tan. Very...pleasant."

Miriam made a sound of disgust. "He's taken."

"Boo. Boring." Talya hoisted herself into a stool. "And so are you...apparently."

Miriam took a giant swig from her drink. The alcohol wasn't strong enough for this kind of conversation.

"So. Girlfriend?"

She kept from squirming. Miriam and Sam weren't like that. The label was too restraining. It was too...set. "I—we're not—" She stopped from embarrassing herself any further. "We're enjoying ourselves."

"Oh?" Talya placed her chin in a cupped hand. "So this is another one of your arrangements? That's different, then." She puffed out air. "You scared me. The way the others talked about it, I thought you had joined the land of the dead."

Miriam's cheek twitched and her muscles constricted. She hadn't known what to say, but Sam wasn't an arrangement. At least not like Ana or the others before her. The last couple months were different, and Miriam hadn't needed to determine anything. Things were good. Easy. Refreshing. Sam was refreshing.

Talya grinned. "The Tan I knew wasn't boring, and I don't believe for a second that you are now." Her fingers twirled and she popped out of her seat. "Let's get back to your pretty team. You can be my wingwoman. Like old times!"

Miriam choked on her drink and let the motion turn into an uneasy chuckle. She let a disapproving smirk crawl onto her face, secretly grateful for the change of topic. With another long sip, she forced the knot in her throat down. It sat in her chest now, but it already felt smaller.

◊

She clenched her rifle grip as a stream of bullets penetrated the monster to no effect. She tried to create more space, but she stumbled. Green eyes jumped out and she scrambled away. Though her feet were heavy and slow, she ran, weaving through flaming bodies and barriers. And then she was in a dark room, the rifle in her hand gone, the sounds of battle gone. She wasn't in Temunco anymore.

A dim orange light emitted from around the corner, and she turned into a stairwell. One foot, one step, until she was at the top staring at a familiar hallway of three closed doors. She pushed the first door open. A wriggling figure lay shackled on the ground, its back to her. There was something familiar about it, something that made her want to look. She reached down, touched a shoulder, and fell in surprise as it turned.

Her own face stared back, mouth bound and eyes screaming.

Bright light pierced Miriam's eyelids. Someone had opened the barrack shutters, and she groaned and pulled herself up. It was morning. Considering the later sunrise in the region, it wasn't unreasonably early. Plus, it wasn't as if she had been sleeping peacefully. The alcohol had helped the first couple hours, but she had been in and out of nightmares since.

Across from her, Kai sat up and her palms dug into her eye sockets. "Why?"

"Get up." Nas nudged Miriam's cot as he passed. "Krill. Yuri."

The lead and second sleepily stirred, and Miriam glanced to her other side. The bed was empty. "Where's Fox?" she asked.

"Who knows?" Nas made a noise of discontentment. "I have news."

"Wunbies?" Krill asked, more alert. He grabbed his cuff.

"No. I mean, yes, but not the way you're thinking. We're not under attack. Sorry. Look, I was hungry, and I ran into one of the Intel guys at breakfast."

Kai groaned and fell back into her blanket. "Nas, I'd like to actually enjoy these last hours before we're stuck on an airship."

"This is relevant, trust me. Krill, did anyone yesterday mention anything more about the wunbies we picked up?"

The lead shook his head and set his device down, annoyance creeping into his face. "The usual interro from outpost Intel, but nothing I know of. The two were bagged and tagged for our underground friends."

"If you know something, tell us. Just get to the point," Kai said in irritation.

"They found stuff on the devices." Nas looked around the group, excited, but they didn't respond.

Yuri squinted his eyes. "I thought you said it'd take some time."

"Nas," the lead warned.

"These weren't nobody scouts. Well, one of them might have been, but I don't know. Luck? I don't believe in coincidences, but that terminal, the bracelet-thing, they found applications with updates to—"

"What does that mean?" Kai asked.

The intelligence specialist's hands danced in the air. "They're measuring the soil. Something! At least it looks that way with all the files and mappings, but that's not all—"

"Soil?"

Nas's fingers clawed at the air. "Yes! Land! But no! We're getting away from the main point. Intel intercepted something else."

"Nas, breathe." Miriam rubbed a knuckle into her eye again and sat up.

"Kartik!"

The room stilled at Nas's outburst.

"The guys said they were able to pull a couple marked files before the devices shut off on their own. BigInt is confirming it as we speak, but they think they're plans, schedules of Kartik's movements." Nas looked around the room and blinked. He was waiting for the team to come to the same conclusion as him, but Miriam was drawing a blank. She was too tired for this.

"I don't get it. What does this have to do with soil?" Kai asked.

"The files and maps? They're all about the North. *Our* North. They're areas the wunby scouts are pushing, and if Kartik, if he's moving behind them... Guess who's up next, guess who's free for the next mission?"

Kai groaned. "What? Are you saying Kartik is coming over? That's a big jump."

"It's not, not really."

"How? There's a whole Legion garrison sitting between the North and the rest of the wunbies. They're not just going to let Kartik through."

"They're letting scouts through. It's a big border," Nas rebutted.

"Could the wunbies be feeding us false information? You said they shut the devices off. They know we grabbed their scouts; maybe they know we took their equipment as well."

Miriam rubbed her fingers along the edge of her cot and irritation grew, spurred on by her lack of sleep. She was about to shush her two teammates with a flippant remark—had Nas really woken them all up to discuss theories? But she startled when Krill shot up, his attention on his commcuff. The others turned to him as he paced the room, his fingers swiping along his display.

"Boss?" Yuri asked.

The lead had gotten to the end of the small barracks when he turned back and looked up, his face contorted. "Something's happening across the border."

Miriam's brows pinched together.

"What do you mean?" Yuri pressed. "Nakuan?"

"I don't know, but Ursus is reporting the latest sensor readings are off. There's smoke, fires across the strait."

Miriam bit her lip, now more awake, her irritation receding into something else. Echo had been close to the bordering waterway a day or so before. When had this happened?

The lead continued, "Ursus is sending out advisories and units to start evacuations from the settlements around FOB Domovoy."

"Did we trigger something?" Miriam asked.

Krill shook his head. "No... I don't know. I don't think so."

"Can we request to stay and assist?" Kai asked.

"I can reach out, see if—"

Nas jumped up, cutting the lead off. "Holy shit!"

The others snapped to him, his bright eyes and wide grin contrasting the update and grim faces around him.

"Nasiri," Yuri warned.

Their teammate sputtered apologetically. "No, it's not good, I know. Shit—I know, sorry, yes, that's bad, but come on, you all know it was a matter of *when*, not *if* before the wunbies pushed in." He shrank under Yuri and the others' glares. "Do you know what this means? This just adds to what I'm saying. The scouts, the information, Nakuan? Kartik is coming over."

"Nas," the second growled.

But the team lead shifted. If he hadn't been taking the intelligence specialist seriously before, he now considered something differently.

Miriam squeezed her eyes shut. "Why—"

"Don't encourage him," Yuri said.

But she did something she wouldn't normally have done—perhaps it was Krill's own change of posture or Miriam's desire to have Nas get whatever theory or conspiracy he wanted out so he'd be more manageable. "Let's say you're right. Why would the most wanted wunby take that risk?"

Nas shrugged but nodded. "He's a leader. Wunby of the wunbies. Lead from the front."

"Legion…UMF wouldn't let that happen," Kai said.

"It's definitely a potential, though. Maybe this asshole wants to show his face to his troops, be some public propaganda piece, who knows, but he's responsible for the deaths of hundreds, thousands of us, and he's only going to kill more. If this is legitimate, this fucker is saving us the trouble of figuring out how to kill him on the other side. Especially if the Apostates have already pushed into Nakuan. We can't fight over there, but we can take him out here. It's our home turf."

"But if he's dumb enough to cross over, the North is enormous. He could be anywhere, and he definitely won't be alone."

Yuri spoke up, his glare on Nas already softening. He watched the team lead, who had returned to his commcuff. "Not if we concede strategically…"

"We're not that desperate," Kai groaned.

The second shrugged. "Kartik *is* a priority objective, but this is all speculation, just theories. Krill just received the updates. UMF will probably keep us here to help with evacuations, right? We're already here."

The group turned to Krill, who looked up and took a long breath. Miriam glanced at Nas, a smug grin already creasing his face.

19

ASSEMBLY

SAM TAPPED her foot repeatedly against the table. After a long minute, she stood, paced the team room, then sat back down. Her hands kneaded into her thighs, but the motion was short-lived as her prosthetic fingers dug in harder, more painful than she intended. It was odd to be in Echo's team room without them, especially without her black SOG tab. Her access and presence had only been allowed via a direct invitation received a few hours prior.

She wasn't sure why now or what the temporary access meant. The slim chance that Echo knew something about her clearance bled through and she fought the thought back. Miriam hadn't said much, only mentioning the team was returning from the North. Had something bad happened? Had UMF passed on her information about Nakuan? Was her brother okay? The questions and possibilities whirled in her mind. The team should have landed in the airfield an hour ago, and the shuttle from the hangar was roughly another half hour. She had so many questions. None of which were being adequately answered.

For the fifth time in the last ten minutes, Sam consulted her cuff. Her brother's last response had been shorter than usual.

He was fine, she reminded herself. If not, he wouldn't be answering. Maybe he was pulled into another double shift or something else. And Miriam's lack of messaging was also understandable, though still frustrating. The team was tired with the travel and mission. Sam missed knowing things.

Her ears perked as they caught the softest of movements outside of the sliding door. Sam stood, then sat, afraid it looked too desperate. Thoughts and emotions collided and dispersed as the door slid open. Nas, Fox, and Krill filed in first, their smiles and words of greeting releasing the first bit of tension in Sam's shoulders. There was something else in their eyes as they watched her, but nothing that boded bad news. Sam assumed their mission had gone well. She didn't think further on it as Yuri and Kai followed in quick succession.

"Hi, Valk. Missed us?" Kai chirped, flashing a wide grin before she glanced backward.

The last Echo member walked in, and Sam stood. She couldn't help but smile. Something fluttered in her stomach, and she reminded herself that it was too much—the others were in the room and watching—as she held back from pulling the woman into an embrace. Miriam winked and returned a smirk as she read Sam's intention and restraint. Regardless, her heart soared, and she moved toward the medic's locker.

Until something moved in the corner of her vision and Sam swiveled to the open door. There was no attempt to swallow her gasp. That blond hair was a mess and rough stubble lined his jaw and chin, but it was her brother. Scott.

Sam hardly registered Echo's laughs as her body stuttered in shock. Before she knew it, her feet had swept her across the room, and she barreled freely into her brother's open arms. They had an audience, but she didn't care as she squeezed him back, as hard as she could. His sharp inhale hissed into her ear, and Sam pulled back without letting him go. She looked up at his face, concerned. Was he hurt?

Gray-blue eyes gazed back, a smile enveloped within. The

past months of numerous calls through a holodisplay did no justice to the amount of life and expression in his face. Sam looked him over. He had kept a secret from her before, was he hiding an injury now? Was that why he was here? Was it something that the Ursus clinic couldn't handle? The onslaught of questions poured out as she took him in.

"I warned you. She doesn't know her own strength sometimes."

Miriam's words registered. Her brother was fine.

She squeezed Scott again, softer this time and more aware of her grip. His cheek rested on her forehead and then the shock and suddenness of it all overwhelmed her. She fought the building pressure behind her eyes and tucked her face further into his collar. He didn't smell the same—like his apartment— as she remembered. Faint hints of sweat and rain reminded her he had probably spent the last months away from his comforts. Amidst the sea of emotions, she grieved that loss for him as well.

"Miss me?" Scott whispered coarsely in her ear.

She blinked, laughed, then shoved him away. "What are you doing here?"

"Hitchhiked," Yuri called out. "He missed you too much."

Sam's cheeks warmed, now fully aware of Echo's observation. "You didn't tell me," she said with flashed looks between her brother and Miriam.

Scott signed at the same time Miriam responded, "Surprise."

She narrowed her eyes. She hated surprises, but this one, she'd allow.

Her brother touched her shoulder and circled around her slowly, examining her prosthetic. LOOKS BETTER IN PERSON, ROBOT SISTER.

Dick. She raised an alloy finger, alone in the middle.

Yuri chuckled to the side. He jabbed at Miriam. "Looks like you've rubbed off on the Valkyrie."

Nas locked his weapon into the rack and tittered. "From all the rub—"

Miriam's eyes flashed a horrible sharpness, cutting him off. "You're not going to finish that sentence, Baby Echo. Not if you value your life."

While the others laughed and the marine raised a hand in defense, a terrifying thought invaded Sam's mind. Her attention returned to her brother. "Does Ursus know you're here?"

The room broke out in another chorus of chuckles.

"Mute's gone AWOL," Kai joked.

Krill added with a smile, "Long story short, Ursus loaned him out. There might've been something about some reunion of a notorious duo or some deserved rest and relaxation."

Scott shrugged and then nodded as if it wasn't a big deal. He swung his large pack around and moved over to the locker Yuri had already opened for him.

"How long?" Sam pressed as she followed him, but then she held her breath. With her brother in front of her now she regretted asking. Maybe she didn't want to know the answer. She didn't want to be separated from him again.

Scott gave another shrug.

Asshole.

"But with the Apost—" She paused. She wasn't sure what had been disseminated out. "What about the border? They don't need you there?"

Scott's lips pressed together in a thin line as his fingers spun. URSUS IS STARTING EVACUATIONS.

So they knew, but it only puzzled her more. If UMF was evacuating towns and people, that meant more marines were needed to defend against and challenge the coming Apostate offensive. But Echo was here, with her brother, in the complete opposite direction. No one was critically injured from what she could see—that'd be the main reason to come back to Station

City. So why were they back so soon with the recent developments? She searched Echo's faces as they unpacked.

"I don't—" Sam started. Unless UMF wanted them here for something else. The city? Was something happening here? "What's going on?"

Nas's eyes darted around as no one responded. "Come on, we can say this right?"

Her eyes narrowed.

But before anyone could answer, he blurted out with a grin, "Dry runs!"

UMF had something planned for SOG. Razor-Echo specifically. And her brother.

"What about Ace?"

Scott's eyebrow raised and he shot her a dubious look. He was right. Sam cared little about his partner for the past months. Her replacement. *Temporary* replacement. Scott took his long rifle out of its case and locked it into the team's weapon rack. When he turned back, he signed, HOW MANY DAYS NOW?

Days? A newfound energy surged through her. In two days or less, she'd know if MED reinstated her SOG status. And her brother was with Echo, sans his temporary partner...

Sam's eyes flitted around the room. "Seriously?"

Yuri chuckled and threw a long bag to Scott, who cradled it in his arms for a second before stretching it forward.

Sam took it, its weight familiar. Something caught in the back of her throat, and she tore into it. Her fingers found the hard material and she pulled out her carbine, speechless. She hadn't seen it in months, not since the attack on Ursus. Like her brother's presence, Sam hadn't known how much she had missed her rifle, the extension of herself, until it was back in her hands. Its coolness permeated into her left palm and caused a dull sensation in her right. She curled alloy fingers around its sections, testing the pressure and weight, then turned the weapon around in her hands. She let the grip press into her left hand and then back to the right.

Sam gazed fondly at its parts, its scratches and nicks present from the last mission, and rubbed her thumb along the edges. Another heaviness pressed against the back of her eyes, and she blinked her feelings back.

"You're getting emotional about a gun," Miriam teased as she sidled up next to her. "A gun."

It was more than that, of course. This carbine had been with her since she joined SOG, since she became the other half of their sibling recon duo. It was an extension of herself, an extension of her arm. Her fingers wrapped around the barrel. She had a new one now, and she'd work to find that synchronization again. It was all another step toward normal.

◊

IT'S STRANGE. BEING AWAY FROM IT.

Sam had run the gamut of emotions in the past hour, and the rush of guilt only added to her exhilarated but tired self. Unlike her insulation from actual conflict, Scott had been at the border and front lines since the attack on the outpost. His temporary assignment to Station and Echo was probably his first relief from it all. The guilt cascaded as she remembered he had only renewed because of what happened to her, because of the Apostates.

Scott nudged her, breaking her thoughts. BUT GOOD STRANGE. THIS IS NICE.

She smiled at him then looked around the empty team room. The others had thoughtfully given them space and time to digest the change. "Where are they having you stay?"

Scott shrugged. WHEREVER UMF PUTS ME.

Sam made a face. "Not the barracks, hopefully." The perk of being SOG and multiple contracts into service usually meant nicer quarters. *Usually.* "You should take my studio. If you want. It's further from base, but I figure you might like that."

He shook his head. I DON'T—

Her hands patted his. "It's really okay. It's perfect, actually. You're not putting me out."

WHERE ARE— He paused then gave her a sly look. YOU MOVED IN? THAT WAS FAST.

Sam rolled her eyes but couldn't help but smile. "No. It's just been easier, convenient with the company's shifts. Plus, Echo's been on missions, and Miriam hasn't been around too often, so it's not like she's there all the time." She shut her mouth. She was rambling. "But whatever. Do you want it or not?"

Scott snorted, smirked, then nodded. Of course he'd rather be off compound.

With that decided, the siblings headed out. As they exited the base, Scott's eyes drew up at the clusters of city buildings and Sam smiled.

DID YOU EVER CHECK OUT THE MUSEUM I TOLD YOU ABOUT?

"Didn't feel right, going without you."

She watched his eyes widen and narrow at the people-movers, pedestrians, and otherwise busy city. His pace quickened and slowed following various leads and curiosities. They were born and raised in the North, and urban life was still bizarre. Whereas she found it initially overwhelming, he seemed to take it in with a bubbly excitement. Of course, she had also been distracted with loneliness, anger, insecurity, all of it, when she first arrived.

They could've taken a people-mover back to her studio, but her brother wanted the long and detouring route. Sam didn't protest, but she was an awful guide considering she had stuck mainly to her routine and had spent little time exploring the city. When he perked up and asked to see the Altered Sector, however, Sam's confidence jumped. It was one thing to go there on alty duty with her company, but it was another with his curiosity. She also wanted to show him the area where she frequented for her under-the-radar tasking. She was still useful and wanted that burst of pride that only he could give her.

Not eager to see Densaned or anyone she'd recognize, Sam took a different route that brought them within a block of the Alley. She also kept an eye out for the black-capped Charonites, but there was no sign of them. Sam made to cross the intersection to the side gate she normally took, the one where she had befriended the young legionnaire, Artem, but she stopped when she realized Scott had fallen behind. Her brother gazed down the street toward the Alley's barricades and fencing. From their position, the shouting and crowd was muffled.

"A little different from home, isn't it?"

An interval passed before he answered with his hands. IT'S PRETTY BAD HERE.

She scoffed. "The city thinks they've been invaded by Royals and scientists, a sleeper occupation." Sam snorted. "What's that compared to Apostates in the North? Station's lucky with this pick of Altered."

Scott frowned. WE'RE ALL FACING THE SAME DIRECTION UP THERE.

"What does that mean?"

Another voice joined the fold. "Less politics. It's more black and white when two sides have one concern to unite on."

Sam swiveled to the figures walking toward them. As they grew closer, gold eyes peered out from under a silken hood. The tall Dmitri lingered at an angle behind wearing dark eyewear. Sam stifled a cough at the Altered's lackluster attempt at disguise and then watched their surroundings, but only a lone pedestrian passed by on the other side of the street.

"Kuan-Lin." Sam added a nod to the bodyguard—who ignored it—before she craned her neck looking for any watching UMF, SecTeam, or others. "Are you coming back from the embassy?"

"I needed to stretch my legs. I thought I heard you and we came to see," the Royal sang out.

Scott's eyebrow twitched. Sam had been reasonably distracted with her brother, but both of them were recon specialists. Neither had noticed anyone following them. Even with the less-trafficked area, sound didn't travel too far—especially a one-sided verbal conversation. How close—or far—had the Royal been to hear them?

Although Kuan-Lin's attention was on Sam, one eye seemed to take Scott in. She glanced over his blond hair. "Dima and I are heading back to the flat. Are you here to see us?"

Sam shook her head. "I was actually showing him around."

The Royal turned fully to Scott and outstretched a hand. "You must be Sam's brother. I'm Kuan-Lin. She talks a lot about you."

Her brother raised a furtive eyebrow, then took the Royal's hand carefully. A subtle bemusement flashed across Kuan-Lin's face. With Scott next to her, Sam realized no other human had witnessed her interactions with the Altered. As a second party, she saw how effortless the Royal was with human customs. In all the time she'd been engaging with her, Sam hadn't noticed.

Scott bowed his head. Then to Sam's surprise, he responded verbally. "Thank you. For your kindness to my sister." Their hands separated.

The Royal nodded with a hint of a smile, a twinkle in her eyes as if she were making a point. "Of course, but you're mistaken. It's the other way around," she said with a light chuckle. "Would you two like to come over for some tea? Dima's going to have a fit if we loiter any longer."

The bodyguard's face was as still as a stone, his stiffness and lack of movement unnatural. She gave her brother a slight shrug and he nodded back at her, then Kuan-Lin.

It was enough for the Royal as she led the way back to her

building. Scott was unsubtle about his amazement as he took everything in. Watching her brother, she saw the uncertainty, the awe, and the curiosity that she had hurried through in her time with the Altered. Seeing it on someone else's face was a reminder that what she had accomplished and what she was doing was not entirely normal. However, he seemed to lack the fear that she had felt early on. Or he, at least, hid it better.

HOW MANY COME HERE? Scott signed, his eyes sweeping around the landscape and sculptures.

She wasn't sure if he meant how many Altered there were in this renovated sector or something else. Her hand raised, but Kuan-Lin spoke first.

"Not many. Your sister may be one of the first to enter here freely."

Scott gently squeezed Sam's arm, and a warmth spread from his contact through her body. When they followed the Royal into her flat, he ruffled her hair behind the Altered's back, and she swatted him away before stepping across the threshold. Once upon a time, she had been terrified. With her brother now, she radiated a new confidence.

"Scott, they won't miss your presence up north?" The Royal asked innocently, as if downplaying or pretending they hadn't just lost Nakuan and the Altered's last eastern hold against the Apostates.

He shrugged then added quietly. "No, ma'am."

Sam glanced at him, her own brows lifting to her hairline. His verbosity was rare. It was a reminder that they had lived separate lives in the past months, the only time in her twenty-three years that they had been apart for this long. Though nothing had changed between them, they *had* changed. Even if only slightly.

Kuan-Lin patted the counter, silently instructing the siblings to take a seat. She pressed a delicate finger into her tea machine. "Are you on rest leave?"

Sam kept her face blank as her brother nodded in response.

It was a lie, but it was innocent enough and easier to explain. He had come back with Echo, and they were preparing for something big. Big enough for UMF to pull the SOG team back while Apostates were surely planning to invade the North. And she'd be part of it.

"It must be wonderful to be back together. Especially good timing for good news. Any word on your medical clearance?"

Sam tapped her prosthetic fingers. "Anytime now, I guess."

"And when you're cleared, the two of you will return to your outpost? I'll miss our talks."

Scott cleared his throat. "She'll miss it too," he said with a slight rasp.

Kuan-Lin smiled at him, then lifted her hands, her fingers and palms already in motion. WE CAN TALK LIKE THIS IF YOU'D LIKE.

Sam's eyes widened then slitted.

The Royal mouthed *Dima* back at her, a head gesture toward the other room where the bodyguard was probably standing and listening.

"But it's a different...sign," Sam stammered. "How did you know?"

"Different, yes." She switched back to her hands and fluid motions. BUT I LISTEN. I WATCH. I LEARN.

Sam racked her brain, wondering how often she spoke of Scott unintentionally. She had thought she had done a good job at rapport-building and gathering information from the Altered, and she frowned at the thought that the Royal gleaned more information from her than she was aware of.

Her shock was cut short as her cuff buzzed. She ignored it at first, but with nothing else to add to the ongoing silent conversation between her brother and the Royal, she discreetly checked. It was probably Miriam, and Sam wanted to let her know why she was taking so long—an unexpected detour.

Her heart rate picked up.

Finally.

She opened the attachment and for a long second, Sam forgot to breathe.

"Everything alright?" Kuan-Lin said.

Her stomach caved in and something dark clawed at the edges of a sudden emptiness.

"Fine," Sam managed. "Excuse me." She stood abruptly and made for the door, but then turned around.

Her brother stood, and both he and Kuan-Lin watched her carefully, studying her face then hands.

At that moment, Sam hoped she wasn't trembling. It was taking everything to maintain her composure.

WHAT'S GOING ON? Scott signed. The lines on his forehead condensed. He started forward, but she shook her head.

"No. Stay. I just need a second."

He hovered there, half out from under the counter, and studied her. I'LL COME WITH YOU.

Sam shook her head as shock started to roll into something worse, an old friend, an old enemy of emotion. Shame ripped through her with the familiar rage roaring behind it. She needed to be out, away. She didn't want any witnesses, not even her brother, who, suddenly without a holodisplay between them, seemed too close.

He splayed out his hands, palms toward her, although the question remained in his eyes. OKAY. TAKE YOUR TIME.

Sam blinked, her gaze beyond the others, trying not to focus on their concerned expressions. "Actually, do you think you can find your way back? I can send you the location. I'll meet you at the studio later."

"Don't worry about that, Sam. Take care of whatever you need. He'll be fine with me."

In the corner of her eye, blond hair tilted hesitantly.

"Okay." Sam's feet shifted underneath her. "Thanks for... I'll talk with you later."

Before she could make more of a fool of herself, she was out of the residence, into the hallway, then the lift. Away. She struggled to catch her breath, counting them in, counting them back out.

One one thousand.

Two—

She focused on everything she had learned in recovery. She tried to find something to ground herself.

Two one thousand.

Three one—

Fuck.

Fuck.

MED CLASS 7—FURTHER OBSERVATION NEEDED

20

GESTATION

ABOVE HER RIFLE SIGHT, Miriam's eyes scanned her sector. Her heartbeat was stable and her breath controlled. Shadows and shapes pulsed in her visor display, each flickering outline demanding her focus. She kept her balance as someone's kit bumped into her side, a chain effect from Kai's reunion with the waiting stack. A second later, the engineer's whisper came through Miriam's visor loud and clear.

"Ready."

Krill's head bobbed in her peripheral vision. The command followed shortly. "Execute."

Air pressed against her exposed face as the gate seams popped subduedly in succession. Across the access point, a burly marine with a bandana yanked the door back, wide enough to allow Echo to flow into the small courtyard beyond. Miriam followed Yuri's frame, her eyes shifting in her sector as the team came to a halt at the outside wall of one of the two-story buildings. Lateral to them on the opposite side of the courtyard, Titan-4 mirrored them, holding to enter the other structure. She knew that as they burst in, the Ursus SOG team was mirroring the same maneuver.

Both floors of the small structure were cleared quickly, and

Echo flowed back to the stiff air outside. Their main objective was a larger four-story building that stood like a behemoth in the middle of the compound. In her peripheral, Miriam watched the eight marines of Titan-4 dash along the internal wall until they reached the side of the structure. They quickly filtered like one body into the secondary door.

Once the last one was in, Krill motioned, and the team split in half. Miriam followed Nas and Yuri as they took cover behind another container. Supported by a short barricade, she settled into a crouched position, her rifle fixed on the main gate with the general entrance of their target building out of focus to her left. Miriam caught motion within the compound across from them. Not Titan-4, but the third SOG team settling into their own cover positions as well.

No one was coming in. No one was getting out.

Muffled bangs sounded from within the main building, followed by a barricade of staccato pops. A beat of quiet, and then additional straggling pops came, growing in sound as doors opened. Miriam set her jaw but didn't look back, her eyes waiting, scanning her sector: the motionless main gate. Rounds exploded behind and across from her as the other half of Echo and Titan-6 downed whatever enemies had entered their designated areas. And then the air settled and drew silent. She could hear the collective breathing of her teammates around her.

"ENDEX, ENDEX."

The end-exercise order repeated and reverberated through speakers.

"LIGHTS COMING ON."

Miriam relaxed her grip and squinted instinctually as white light lit up a vast depot warehouse. She drew herself upright out of her crouch, her knees cracking audibly.

Nas rolled off his stomach and shook his head. "I rate this iteration a low two. I didn't fire my weapon once." He grabbed Yuri's offered hand and rose to his feet.

"Well, I did, and of course, with my luck, it jammed." Kai fiddled with her rifle. "You'd think with all the tech we've got, someone would've improved on simunition."

In the background, engines of military aircraft whirred. The SOG marines were close to the wasteland, on the furthest outskirts of the city where UMF's airfield was the only buffer between the city line and dead desert. The area wasn't radioactive, but with the lack of water and the swinging temperatures no matter the season, it might as well have been. Nothing good survived out there.

Miriam winced. That was what she thought about radiation zones, but they had seen the Axiom underground facility with their own eyes. The Altered could conceivably tolerate the radiation and wastelands, but if offered comforts, why would anyone choose to suffer?

The two other SOG teams convened with Echo as individuals wearing bright safety sashes moved toward them simultaneously. Conversation rippled before a uniformed man with a tablet stepped forward. The group hushed.

"Good. Little things to clean up..."

Miriam's attention waned as the training advisor ran through the main motions of Titan-4. She blinked and forced her focus back as he finished up with Titan-6 and turned last to Echo.

"I know it's muscle memory, but remember, silence is golden. No talking, no whispers." The man lifted his chin to the entire group as his voice increased in volume. "That's for everyone. I know this is tedious as hell, but this is why we're practicing. Visors are our last resort; we make as little sound as possible. The same goes for your gear and boots. If you haven't switched out any squeaky shit or made modifications, do it now."

He pointed at an auditory device another advisor was carrying. "Remember, these Altered may not be purebreds, but their hearing is fucking uncanny. Especially if they're 'roided up. We have the North's winter squalls, but don't depend on them. Stealth, stealth, stealth. That's the name of the game, people."

The bandana-wearing marine from Titan-4 hugged his rifle across his chest. "*Merde*. You want stealth, then why are we breaching with Hush Detcord? We're supposed to have the key to this gate."

"*Supposed to* doesn't mean shit in the field." The advisor sighed impatiently. They'd gone over this before. "You, of all people, know this. We're covering everything we can think of."

"*Sûr*. Jus' wish to get this done with," the marine responded as he shifted his weapon over his shoulder.

"Your wish is being granted."

Miriam turned with the others to a black-uniformed woman behind them. Her name tag read *Shaw*, and the clothes underneath looked as if they had been pressed, no wrinkle in sight. A Command officer, but surprisingly, without the usual trophy case of medallions and tabs. Miriam doubted it was a lack of honors, but rather a show of indifference—one could call it humility. Regardless, the officer's presence was unusual. In the past days, only the SOG teams, the advisors, and a smattering of SOG-B support had frequented the isolated training site, and in discrete transportation. No one from Command, though. Everyone had been conscious of keeping attention away from increased presence in the area.

Nas gripped Kai's kit. He whispered loud enough for Echo around him, "Shit. This is it."

Miriam held her breath, shifting with the others as they waited for the officer to continue.

Shaw nodded. "Mission brief tomorrow at the SOG TOC." She took a step back.

The others watched her expectantly, but the officer was done with her message. Miriam frowned. Two sentences? That was it? Maybe she had also watched their training. Shaw turned on her heel and walked away with one of the lead advisors.

The three teams were still as they watched them depart. Seconds later, the large group exploded in a fury of whispers and conversation.

A lean marine from Titan-6 looked up from their cuff and hollered out. "Just in time for the big storm, no issue with Hush Detcord now."

The two teams of Ursus SOG marines hooted and laughed, their own northern joke internalized. Miriam found the head of blond hair, and Scott gave her a thin smile and shrug.

"Take a breather. Hit the head," their primary trainer shouted out over the noise. "We start back up, original positions in thirty. Stealth, people! Stealth! Team leads and seconds to me for a quick rundown."

The group broke up, scattering in different directions with a new energy, as Krill, Yuri, and the others huddled with the advisors. Miriam followed the rest of Echo as they retreated to their claimed corner of the spacious depot, where its usual shelves and items had been either disassembled or shoved to the side for their exercise. She caught a draft of the outside air as she passed one of the wide doors.

Kai set down her rifle. "Don't get me wrong. I'm thrilled, but you know, we used to cancel missions with bad weather."

"And now we're singing halle-fucking-lujah for it," Fox muttered.

"We'll have to pack all our wetgear for at least some semblance of dryness."

"I don't think Fox knows how to be dry." Nas laughed.

"Nas," Kai warned.

But Fox had already turned and threw a finger into their teammate's chest. "Fuck off." He dumped his rifle and walked away.

Nas rubbed his sternum and glared at Fox's back. "Asshole."

"I think you deserved that one," Miriam mumbled.

Everyone's patience had been thinning in the past weeks.

The training had increased but had already become repetitive, and they had all been antsy about the hourly updates from the northern front. She wasn't thrilled about the conditions of the mission either, but SOG knew the storm would be an optimal way to get close to Apostates without being detected.

She relaxed on top of a sturdy-looking pallet next to Scott, who had set his long rifle aside and lain down. Her cuff buzzed, and she immediately dismissed and deleted the message.

"Did you bring any extra bars?" Nas rummaged through Kai's pack.

She swatted his hand. "Just the vanilla ones."

He gagged. "Worst flavor. Let's go raid the pilot's lounge. I'm pretty sure it's a couple hangars down."

Kai rolled her eyes but conceded. They were halfway to the exit when the engineer turned back. "Want me to get anything for you? Mute?"

Miriam shook her head and Sam's brother waved a hand. The others left as Yuri rejoined them.

"Any more updates?" Miriam asked.

The team second set down his weapon and kit. "We'll do a few more. Rinse and repeat, but they're going to call it an early night. It'll be good to have some time for ourselves before..." He squeezed Miriam's shoulder. "Scott, you and Ace feeling good?"

The recon specialist gave an affirmative gesture and sat up. Frankly, Miriam hadn't made an effort to get to know his partner, Ace. The marine hadn't been thrilled to be pulled last minute from Ursus during evacuation efforts, especially after being told he wasn't needed, but that had all changed with Sam's unexpected clearance update.

Miriam sighed. Sam was back in the apartment and as much as she sympathized with the woman, she didn't want to deal with her mood when she just wanted to rest. Especially since the nightmares were back. She didn't understand why now, after a good few months. Full nights of sleep were hit or miss, but she was hoping the exhaustion from training would have her lights out.

For a moment, she watched Yuri and Scott sign. She hoped they weren't talking about her, but why would they be? She reminded herself to start classes whenever she had free time—if there was any in the future—it'd be something Sam would appreciate.

"Just saying, we should hang out more. Haven't seen you around the past week, I miss our chats." He tipped his head as the recon specialist lay back down. "You too, Tan. Who am I? The friend everyone bails on now?"

Miriam rolled her eyes at him.

"Alright. I'm going to hit the head before we start up again, I've been keeping this in too long. Hold down the fort, will ya?" Yuri said, hustling away.

Miriam sat in silence with Scott. At first, it was relaxing, not having to speak, but as the minutes stretched by, she shifted uncomfortably. She knew Sam had told her brother about them. Hell, he knew his sister was staying with her in the apartment. And now, she found the quiet too much, an air pregnant with pressure and expectation. She wasn't hungry, but maybe she should've gone off with Nas and Kai when she could've.

"So, last night before the big event. Any plans? Dinner with Sam? Yuri? Or a night in?" Miriam said. She added jokingly, "Or out to the clubs? Meeting a ladyfriend? Or whatever friend."

Internally, she groaned. She was much smoother when talking with women—hell, even just normal friends and people. This was the first time she was alone with Scott, and he just had to be Sam's protective older brother. Miriam consciously leaned her hands back on the pallet to exude a confidence she didn't actually feel.

Scott peeked an eye open at her, a slight lift in the corner of his mouth. She was teasing about the clubs and romance, but the lilt in his face said something else. She grasped onto it—a piqued curiosity.

"Oh. There *is* a friend. Who is it?"

Both of his gray-blue eyes opened, flashing surprise, but he corrected himself quickly.

She chuckled. "I'm impressed. You've been here how long?"

He crossed his arms.

"Does Sam know?"

He stared at her, then shook his head.

Miriam's eyes widened, and her curiosity grew. "I'm a vault," she reassured. "Just because I'm—" She stopped. After months with Sam, she still froze and never knew how to categorize or describe her arrangement with the woman, Scott's sister. "This can be our little secret."

He sighed, but she had already wiggled her way in. This was stuff she was good at, *could* talk about.

"He? She? Them?" she prodded.

He raised two fingers.

Miriam smirked. A woman. She could definitely talk women.

"Do we know her?" Miriam kept from groaning the second she said it. It was a wasted question, and she knew their conversation was already pushing at the limits of the man's comfort. Sam didn't hang out with many people outside of Echo, and Miriam doubted Scott knew any of her previous one-night stands or arrangements. Before she was...

Boring.

Miriam grimaced and brushed the thought out of her mind. Other than Kai, who would Scott have gotten to know in the city in the last few weeks?

To her surprise, he gave a weak shrug.

Her eyes narrowed. It wasn't Kai; it couldn't be. Miriam would've caught on if there was anything. So who? Who would Sam know? Did Sam meet anyone else while she was away on missions? Her stomach clenched for a split second and then relaxed. She would've known. Sam was easy to read, at least for Miriam. But that wasn't completely true. Sam spent whatever time she had outside of work, the gym, and the apartment in the Altered Sector.

"You're not going to say?"

He shrugged again before his hands hesitantly spun and stuttered their own speech.

Miriam's face fell. They'd been getting along fine with her pointed questions, but now that she was intrigued and wanted more information, their communication was stunted. His hands stopped when he also seemed to remember his sister wasn't there to translate and the only person on Echo who understood sign had gone off to the bathroom. Miriam pinched her lips, uncertain of what their next course of action was. She drew out her commcuff and held it up, but to her surprise, Scott pulled himself up onto his elbows.

He whispered in a rough voice, "It just...happened."

Miriam shifted to the edge of her seat, closer. Having seen the man use his hands to talk and knowing he spoke little, this was too precious, too important to not miss out on. She composed herself and said nothing further, hoping he would provide more.

He didn't, his eyes on the floor.

"We don't have to talk, we can chat with this." Miriam tapped her cuff, but Scott shook his head.

"Sam... I'm worried..." His mouth drew tight.

"I won't say anything about this to her. That's for *you* to tell whenever you're ready." She wanted to know more—push more —but she held back.

Scott puffed air out his nose.

"But," Miriam added. "If you're going to share anything, now might be the time. Sam's distracted with the MED appeal, but I'd tread carefully. I don't know if I have enough bandages and jabbers to fix whatever she'll probably do to you."

Scott smirked, but their shared moment was brief as they fell back into an awkward silence.

Miriam stared off at the mock compound and its modular containers. "She needs something good right now, but a distraction like this works, too."

Scott gestured at her and her stomach tightened. The woman's insecurity had flared up, vaguely similar to when Miriam had run into her months before. And the anger... There was so much of it. It was never blatant like it had been when Sam lost her limb, but Miriam could feel it, an undercurrent constantly running.

"I don't know how to help her."

Scott moved his hands first, but then his lips cracked open. "She just wants to belong."

Miriam said nothing but nodded slowly. Those five words meant different things: an opener, an explanation, and a warning of sorts. Five words from an older half-brother, a guardian, and a man with the callsign "Mute." The last time she had overheard spoken words from him, it had been in the South, and Sam had broken emotionally. They hadn't talked about it since, but Miriam remembered the little she had garnered: that Sam and Scott's father had hurt Sam when she was a child, and Scott had killed him in self-defense. The both of them had sequestered that trauma for almost a lifetime. *Scott had held that secret for so long, and it had eaten away at him.* Miriam thought it sadly admirable. He was trying to protect her; he didn't want to hurt her.

"She worries about you, you know. She thinks it's her fault you renewed."

His cheek twitched, and his gray eyes turned upward to the cloudless night outside the door. One hand traveled to his neck and fiddled with a light chain. Little tics. The siblings were so similar.

She waited.

"When our father... When Sam..." He stopped and tried again. "The first time I joined, it was out of anger."

She held her breath.

"After the attack..." Scott paused then sighed. "I wanted to kill them all. And I couldn't sit this out. Not with everything..." His hands rotated around each other. "A cycle. I can't..." His fingers closed into fists, then splayed out, and his voice cracked. "I can't break it."

Miriam nodded.

"I regret it—bringing her there. To Ursus."

"Did you have other family? Did you have another option?"

He shook his head.

"You were, what? Sixteen? And Sam was a kid. Shit, I don't know what I'd do if I were on my own at that age. UMF has its faults, but structure was probably good for you both."

His index fingers curled, and he brought them together. "Complicated."

"Complicated," Miriam repeated. She leaned back onto her hands and stared outside. "I think you did your best."

Scott didn't respond.

"I know she's thrilled to have you here. You mean everything to her."

He huffed, then pointed a finger at her.

Again, a simple gesture seemed to carry more meaning. There was a hefty weight behind the motion, and Miriam couldn't help but feel it compound in her gut. She was glad when the others stirred, their break over.

21

UNFORESEEN DEVELOPMENT

"GIVE ME GOOD NEWS," Sam muttered as she paced the apartment. This had become her new routine: a run, administrative bullshit, time at the SOG gym, and then endless refreshing of her appeal case on her commcuff. She had already submitted the recommendations, references, and data MED wanted. She had done rounds of their additional tests, including the most frustrating psychological evaluations. They told her they'd get back to her in a few days.

It had been a few days. She had long missed the cutoff to train with the SOG teams for whatever mission they were on—Sam knew it was important—but she could be on reserves. She badly wanted her diamond tab back.

She refreshed the display, but it showed the same.

PENDING

Fuckers.

She opened a channel to her brother but stopped when a notification window popped up.

M. TANNER: Heading back.

Sam double-checked the time. It was much earlier than expected.

S. RYAN: Everything okay?

M. TANNER: All good. Released early. I'll stop by the base. Don't wait up. Are you going to your brother's?

S. RYAN: Not tonight.

They had been missing each other the past week. She'd show up at the studio and he'd be out, or he'd message her and she'd be with Miriam. But that was something to be addressed at another time.

S. RYAN: Updates?

She waited for a minute, staring at the display. She hated being in the dark.

M. TANNER: Have you been in the apartment all day?

Irritation burned within Sam, but she swallowed it back.

S. RYAN: No. Just got back from the gym.

It wasn't entirely truthful. Her damp top hung on a kitchen chair, and she had been half-undressed for at least an hour. It wasn't a complete lie.

S. RYAN: Updates?

Another long pause before the next message populated the screen.

M. TANNER: Brief's tomorrow.

Sam stared at the two words that Miriam had conceded. That meant Echo and the other recognizable faces from Ursus SOG were leaving soon. The mission, whatever Scott had come back to Station to do with the team, was approved.

Anger speared. *She* was supposed to be on this mission.

Her bad mood spiked as her cuff trilled. Sam stabbed a finger at her wrist. "What."

"Good evening to you, too, Ryan."

"Shadid." His surname came out in a grumble.

"How are you? Oh, I'm fantastic. You? You're doing great, too? Lovely." His saccharine mocking tone flattened. "That's how normal people usually talk. Sometimes I wonder how Jace did it, and how you convinced an Altered to actually talk to you."

"What do you want?"

Static riddled his loud sigh. "BigInt wants a last check with your contact."

"I sent in notes from the last one."

Her last meeting with Kuan-Lin had been weeks before, and it hadn't been much, especially with the unexpected run-in. Sam had left out her brother's presence and her quick departure after. She had been dealing with her own fallout from a delayed clearance. Part of her knew it had something to do with Densaned and her time in the temporary company. Too late for that now.

"Right. And they want a last check. Don't kill the messenger, okay? I'm just doing my job."

"What's the point of this if you can't help me with my appeal?"

More static came with another sigh. "We already sent in glowing recs about your sunny disposition. If MED's holding your case hostage, that's on them."

Sam sneered. What was the point of BigInt and SOG leadership if they had no further influence or pull on another UMF division?

"So are you gonna get me in trouble or are you gonna see your contact?"

"The Royal doesn't have anything else. She would've reached out if she did."

"You already know what they're going to say to that."

Sam pulled up her notifications and refreshed the window again.

PENDING

She had a sudden thought. "Shadid."

"What?"

"Is this for tomorrow's brief?"

"How'd you—" He paused on the other end, but the hesitation was enough of a confirmation.

Sam's attitude changed. "Shadid, I'll go right now and get your last check, I'll get you a fucking report of whatever you want, but you get me in that brief. I want to be in the TOC." It was her team, her brother, her mission. She would've been involved if not for her blunder with Densaned. She quickly added, "I'll be quiet. They won't even know I'm there."

"That's not up to me."

"You owe me," she pressed. "I've been making you look good, that's what you said, right?"

He sighed on the other end. "I don't know. I'll try."

"Try. Try really hard."

She disconnected from the call with new motivation and an incentive, no matter how disappointing it was in the overall scheme of things. She sniffed herself, slipped on a clean shirt, then sent a quick message. The shower would have to wait. She had enough time to go find the Royal and secure her involvement in whatever big mission was happening before Miriam returned.

◊

Sam normally preferred walking, but this time she made it past Oldtown to the Altered Sector in record time with the use of shuttles and transfers. She considered stopping by the embassy, but with the later hour, she was counting on the Royal being home. At her preferred side entrance, Artem wasn't there, replaced by an unfamiliar face who required more convincing to allow her into the residential area. Her patience wore dangerously thin before another legionnaire recognized and waved her through.

By the time she exited the lift on the Royal's apartment floor, Sam was panting. She smoothed down her shirt and composed herself before she walked the last meters to knock on the door. She didn't need the Altered hearing her desperation.

The wait was excruciating before the door slid open and Sam's eyes dropped to the Royal girl, whose shirt was covered in white smudges of powder.

"Oh," Xiaoling said, disappointed.

"Hey, kid. Is your aunt—"

The girl had already walked away.

Sam waited another second before she darted her head in. "Kuan-Lin?"

"Come in," the mellifluous voice sang back.

Sam turned the corner where the Royal was at the counter with Longwei. An assortment of dough and a large bowl of what looked to be mixed meat and herbs sat in front of them. Kuan-Lin's niece climbed into the chair.

"Hello, Sam, this is unexpected. Is everything alright?"

Sam waved the question off. She had run into the Royal several times without notice and this wasn't the first instance she had showed up unannounced. "I wanted to check if you found out anything more about..." She lowered her voice. "The North. Beric or Kartik."

Kuan-Lin patted her hands together and stood.

"Did something happen?" The Royal tapped the two

children on their shoulders and gestured a finger down the hall to the other rooms. She then turned to wash her hands.

As Xiaoling and Longwei departed with mild grumbling, Sam reined herself in. She was being sloppy. There was a reason UMF and SOG were being secretive about this mission. Though she wasn't on it—not officially at least—Scott, Miriam, and the others were. She wouldn't endanger anything for them.

"No, sorry. I know I could've—should've messaged ahead."

Kuan-Lin hummed, and then her focus seemed to falter. One ear turned toward the flat's entrance and gold eyes flashed at her. "Sam…"

"Has Legion provided any other information?"

The door opened in the other room, and Sam glanced back to acknowledge Dmitri. Everything erased from her mind as she did a double take.

It wasn't the bodyguard.

"Scott?"

Her brother froze, his expression suspended.

Sam's face fell as she tilted her head. "How…What are you doing here?"

He winced, then tucked a small bag with fresh greens poking out under his arm. His hands started, but any comprehensible sign stopped as he balled his fists, nervously knocking them together. His cheek pulled to the side and his eyes lifted to someone behind her.

Sam spun. For the first time, she saw a hint of color in Kuan-Lin's cheeks. The Royal opened her mouth, then closed it. Another first. For once, the Altered woman didn't have anything to say.

"Sam."

She turned back to her brother's voice. Under her confused glare, Scott placed the packet of herbs down on the nearby accent table. He lifted his hands slowly, palms out.

An impossible idea pieced together, and Sam's eyes

narrowed, widened, then squinted. "Outside." The word came out with an exasperated exhale.

Kuan-Lin called out behind her, but Sam ignored it.

"Now," she demanded, clearer and more pronounced.

When Scott showed no intention of moving, she marched forward, grabbed his arm, and pulled him to the corridor outside. Her left hand jammed into the panel, and the door shut.

"Why are you here?" Sam didn't bother lowering her voice. The Altered inside could hear her if they wanted.

"Sam."

"Did UMF—"

"You're hurting me."

The anger and frustration released with his words, and she dropped her eyes, relaxing her prosthetic. She mumbled an apology and took a breath. "I don't understand. Are they having you—" Her gut clenched. Useless. She couldn't do one thing correctly, so they had to send in another to do the job.

Her brother inhaled and rubbed his arm, a reddened mark where her alloy fingers had dug into. Ashamed, Sam avoided his eyes and watched his hands unravel, waiting.

IT JUST HAPPENED.

Sam shook her head. None of it made sense. "Did Shadid—"

Scott watched her with bated breath, bracing.

And then it hit her. The packet of fresh greens. The shared look between the two. The Royal blushing.

"You're fucking kidding me."

He shrugged.

"Seriously, Scott? She's my—" Kuan-Lin was her contact, but the Royal wasn't just that, was she? Suddenly, Sam was conscious of their conversation and the probable eavesdroppers on the other side of the door. She moved her hands aggressively. ARE YOU KIDDING ME?

He gave her an expectant look.

ARE YOU SERIOUS? She threw her hands up in exasperation. He was never supposed to meet the Royal. It was just happenstance, but with the initial course of shock and confusion waning, Sam rubbed her temple with her left hand. YOU'RE NOT...

Scott deadpanned.

She groaned. YOU ARE.

A muscle in his cheek twitched.

ALL THE PEOPLE IN THIS CITY, AND YOU WENT AFTER A ROYAL. WHEN DID THIS HAPPEN? ARE YOU SLEEPING WITH— Sam waved her hands. "What the fuck?" she sneered. She groaned again. "Actually, I don't want to know." Sam loved her brother, but she didn't want to talk about this with him. Her hands pumped furiously as she switched back to sign. DID YOU REPORT IT TO UMF?

He furrowed his brows and shook his head. IT JUST HAPPENED.

HOW DOES THIS JUST HAPPEN?

It wasn't the first time Scott dated someone she knew, but this was different. This was an Altered. A *Royal* Altered. This wasn't one of those flings, casual or not, to be had. Kuan-Lin wasn't their enemy, but that's not how a growing population of Station City and UMF viewed it. What Sam was doing was sanctioned and only barely. What Scott was doing was not. It was reckless.

"I can't—did she—" Sam tongue stumbled. "What the fuck? Seriously, Scott. What the fuck?"

Too many thoughts were swirling in her head and she grasped for something to ground her. She pushed past her brother and stormed back into the flat, where the Royal stood inside the main room.

"The Apostates. Do you have anything new on them?" Sam gritted out.

"You're upset."

"I'm not." Her jaw clamped. Was she? She wasn't upset.

She was irritated to all hell, but upset? That didn't seem like the right word. "Is there anything else about Beric? About Kartik?"

Kuan-Lin's lips set into a thin grimace. "No."

"Fine."

Box checked.

Sam didn't want to stick around any longer, not with her growing annoyance with her brother, with Kuan-Lin. Anger coiled, ready to pounce.

"Sam. Stay for dinner. Let's talk."

She glared at the packet on the tabletop next to her. Green. Like Scott's apartment garden back in the North—which was probably withered and yellow by now. Her reaction, the whole thing was stupid, she knew it. Her brother and Kuan-Lin actually had something in common; she had always thought they'd get along from the start. And that realization made her more annoyed. In that moment, she didn't want them to get along. She didn't want rationale.

"I'm good."

She felt a small breeze from the hallway through the open door and then her brother's presence behind her.

"Sorry for showing up without warning."

And then she backed out, careful to not bump into Scott. His hand lingered on her prosthetic as she passed and she paused, one foot out the door.

"Sam," he whispered.

"You have my fucking location. You knew I was here. So why the fuck did you come?" she hissed. "Was this your way of telling me?"

He shook his head incredulously.

Sam swiped at his hand, but he held firm. "Fine. It's fine. Enjoy your dinner."

She tugged again and his hand loosened. She felt a discomforting reminder of their last mission together and the conflicting emotions she had felt then. This was nothing in comparison. This was stupid. Silly. She was just surprised—angry at being surprised.

"It's fine," she repeated. "I'll talk to you later."

With that reassurance, his hand dropped from her arm, the delayed feeling ever present.

◊

Even with a night's sleep, Sam was still in a foul mood. It had lessened with Miriam's company and distractions, but her scowl grew when she received notifications on her cuff.

> S. RECKERT: Are you going to be at the brief?
>
> S. RECKERT: Let's catch up after.

The messages had been sent minutes before. If she responded, her brother wouldn't get them. He was already inside the building, inside the SOG special-use Tactical Operations Center. And this was the kind of brief that didn't allow any outside devices.

A hand waved in front of her face, and Sam flinched.

"Sorry. I called a few times, but you didn't answer." Miriam pulled her jacket closer to her throat and shivered. "Want to try your luck inside?"

Sam blinked as an SOG marine wearing the Ursus gray uniform with a Titan team indicator passed them. She didn't recognize her; there were so many new faces she wasn't familiar with. Sam glanced at Miriam, and her stomach roiled when light brown eyes followed the marine until she was inside.

"Yeah, sure." Sam looked away.

A waft of cinnamon touched her nose first, before the woman's hand grazed her cheek. "Hey. It's a hiccup. You'll get your clearance, okay? It'll all work out."

She ignored the placations but relaxed into the touch before it was gone. Though traffic around the compound was light, they were in the public's eye. "Okay," Sam replied half-heartedly.

Miriam prodded her into the building. "Come on. It's getting close."

"Mir." She stopped just inside, readjusted herself, and tried to keep the whimper out of her words. She hated how weak and insecure she felt. "If they don't let me in…"

"It's a big room. How much have you already done for UMF? Sending you into the lion's den over and over…"

Sam gave Miriam a questioning look.

"Hell, that's something Fox would've said," the medic mumbled. She shook her head. "They'll let you in. Come on."

But as they maneuvered down the hall and stood in front of the SOG TOC door, Sam wasn't so sure. She scratched at the side of her prosthetic thumb, unsatisfied with the delayed throb and sensation.

The door opened, and a watch officer peeked out. "You're cutting it close," he said to Miriam. "Rest of the teams are already in their seats."

Miriam nonchalantly shrugged and deposited her cuff into a lockbox on the wall. "And Command?"

He scowled. "Just get in." The door widened and Miriam stepped forward. As Sam made to follow, he held out a hand. "You're not on the roster. TOC's only open for those on mission."

Miriam frowned. "Price, she's SOG."

Sam's eyes flitted toward the small black diamond etched into the door. She wasn't. Not until her appeal went through.

"Tough shit. Is she on any of the assigned teams?"

Miriam's arms folded across her chest. "There wouldn't be a mission if she hadn't gotten UMF information."

"Is Shadid here?" Sam offered. "He can vouch for me."

Price eyed her up and down, weighing his tolerance and investment. In the end, he shouted over his shoulder.

It took five painful seconds for the intelligence warrant officer to trot up behind the watch officer. His jovial face dropped as he acknowledged Sam. "Shit," he murmured. "I forgot."

Her core churned, an edge sharpening.

"Mission-essential only," Price punched each word apathetically.

Shadid stammered, "I'm sorry, Ryan. I can try to get you in on the next one."

Her prosthetic fingers crushed into a fist at her side.

"Do we have a problem here?"

Sam turned and a woman in officer blacks gazed back at her. The aide behind her rolled his shoulders back, his chin out as if he weren't the lackey to the actual authority.

"No, ma'am. The room is ready," Price said, suddenly straight as a line, his voice dropping an octave.

The officer made no intent to move. "And this?"

"Doing what you requested, ma'am. Roster only."

Sam stepped back, out of the officer's path, and braced herself.

A thick eyebrow raised. "You're Valkyrie. From Ursus."

Sam swallowed. "Yes, ma'am."

"It's too bad what happened to you." The officer's eyes rolled over the prosthetic. "But I'm sure your recovery is progressing and you'll be back with us soon." She stepped into the doorway and gave Price and Shadid an impatient look.

The intelligence warrant officer weaved himself in front of Price. "First Officer Shaw, Ry—I mean, Valkyrie, collected information from the Altered POC. We've been using her connection to verify other sources."

The officer's eyes flashed over Sam and then she nodded. "She can stay." There was nothing more as she walked past Price into the dark room, her aide following haughtily on her tail.

The watch officer waited as the two moved out of earshot

before he hissed, "Fucking throw me under the bus. What's the point of a secret if everyone's invited? This is my fucking TOC." He pointed a finger at Shadid. "This is on you. We have processes for a fucking reason." And then he turned back toward the room, leaving the door open. Sam caught more of his grumbles as she hurriedly threw her cuff into one of the boxes before she followed them in.

Inside, Sam exhaled between her teeth and gave Miriam a wordless acknowledgment as they split: the medic toward Echo sitting at the front of the room and herself in the back row. She tucked herself in as best as she could beside Shadid.

As the first officer finished speaking with one of the team leads and strode to a podium, the room settled.

"Don't say anything," Shadid whispered.

Sam hadn't planned on speaking up, anyway.

At the front of the room, the officer cleared her throat then eyed each team. Titan-4, Titan-6, and Echo clustered together in the first three tables. Other uniforms Sam didn't recognize sat at the last one. She eyed the back of Scott's head and glared at Ace's next to him. She should've been in that seat, next to her brother. Sam caught Miriam watching and forced a smile.

"Marines, this is it."

The officer's aide worked the console and sent a map up to the front holoscreen. Sam studied the contour lines and structures, trying to make sense of what she was looking at. So far, she made out a compound nestled within a pocket of a mountain range. She had no context, but it had to be in the North, especially with two Ursus SOG teams present.

"The op's been confirmed for the EarthTek plant in three days. Event time hasn't been set, but we have high confidence the site visit will occur between 1600 and 2300 hours."

EarthTek? Sam never cared much about the different organizations or happenings outside UMF, but she vaguely recognized the name.

"It's a large spread, but you've all waited in longer lines at the DFAC on steak night."

Scattered chuckles dotted the room and someone hooted in the back row. Another muttered, "Fuck yeah, fake steak."

The officer gave a thin smile. "The plan remains. Three teams: Titan-4, Titan-6, and Razor-Echo along with a recon unit. Thanks to Intel, we have a good image of our target."

A window opened over the map, revealing a dark-haired man who stared at Sam from the display. His tri-colored eyes were sharp, his expression plain and serious. It reminded her of a profile shot UMF took for personnel files at recruitment and indoctrination. She leaned forward with the others, studying his face. The man was younger than she'd expected.

"Kartik Finlay. Strategist behind the assault on Temunco, the attack on Ursus, and what we believe was the successful coup of Arshangol. Priority number one."

The room let out a synchronized breath.

"One Kartik Finlay will visit the EarthTek plant in Bonford."

The room collectively held their breath.

Sam's face scrunched. That mountain range was north of Domovoy and far northwest from the outpost. She had only been out there once, but it held no wealth of familiarity or memories. It was pensioners' land, a series of terrain overlooking long stretches of farms. A high-value target like Kartik wouldn't just go relatively near a UMF post and past multitudes of pensioners trying to live their retirement from the military.

At Echo's table, Nas's hand shot up, then lowered as Yuri kicked him hard in the shin.

However, it was a marine from Titan-4 that stood, his chair squeaking out from behind him. "Impossible. The Apostates haven't made it that far." He stared at the officer, and when she didn't budge, he looked around to the other Ursus marines.

"They will. As of tomorrow midday."

An uneasiness stirred in Sam. She crossed her arms, digging her fingers into flesh and alloy.

"But the last reports from Ursus—"

"It was a controlled risk and sacrifice."

"The people—"

"Have been evacuated."

Knowing the demographics of the region, especially how stubborn UMF marines were, even if retired, Sam doubted the claim.

The officer's dark eyes flashed at Titan-4's dark-haired lead who pulled her teammate firmly back into his chair, but the news was running its course. The Ursus marines in the room shifted uncomfortably and exchanged looks.

"With the incoming storm, the location is ideal. We had to give up something to draw Kartik in, and Intel says he has his eyes on our factories, farming, and infrastructure systems."

Sam straightened as her memory sharpened. EarthTek. She remembered the branding and name on the sacks of garden equipment in Scott's apartment. The location in Bonford was similar to a soil remediation plant.

"We created an opportunity. Let's make sure it's not in vain."

A different marine from Titan-6 spoke up. "They'll know it's a trap. He'll know."

The officer blinked, and Sam stiffened at the realization of unsaid words. "It's not the only location they've given up," she mumbled. As she said it, she wished she was wrong—that UMF hadn't been that desperate.

Next to her, Shadid pretended he hadn't heard her, but his teeth bit into his lower lip.

The officer cleared her throat. "We've done as much diligence as we can. He'll take the bait, trap or not. And you've been training on similar layouts and structures. Bonford is only different in its route in. The site will be abandoned, of course, but EarthTek has provided us access through the southern pass.

It'll require a trek, but we've built that time in." She crossed her arms. "The incoming storm will provide additional cover, but it's a double-edged sword. As awful as it'll be for you, it'll be just as bad for them. Use it to your advantage. Any clime, any place. You know what to do."

She thumped the podium. "First priority is capture. That man holds all the knowledge, every thought and strategic point for the Apostates. If we can't get that, they can't either. You either leave that site with him or you leave the site with his head in a bag."

The sentence hung over the room like a heavy cloud. The officer didn't ask if anyone had questions. There were none regarding their objective.

"Let's break it down by teams. Razor-Echo?"

Krill stood, his hand extended to the map. "We approach and breach with Titan-4, secure Building A, and set up cover here and here. Recon will provide kill contingency and overwatch."

"Good. Titan-6."

A burly man stood, and his voice carried out. "We'll route around and enter from the north, clearing Buildings C and D. On signal, we'll shift to new positions and hold the gate and the main building." He sat back down.

"Titan-4?"

"Approach with Echo from the south. Secure Building B, and on Echo's signal, collapse on the main building. From there, breach, flood, and secure the HVT." She glanced at the officer and then the table of uniforms behind her. "Should we expect enemy reinforcements?"

One spoke up. "Our sensors show a settling camp in the northern clearing at the mouth of the range, but we believe this will be a low-profile visit. The Apostates won't alert his presence by rolling in full force. At most, we're expecting a couple patrols and perhaps an advance."

Where and how had they gotten this information? Sam's

forehead wrinkled. It hadn't come from her and Kuan-Lin. How many sources did BigInt have? She felt small in that room. Inconsequential.

The officer tapped the podium again and talked more about their risks, specifically the issue that if any alerts, alarms, or communication made it out of Kartik's detail, the entire camp of Apostates would be upon them in twenty minutes. Maximum. She discussed meticulous plans of exfiltration, emphasizing primary, secondary, and tertiary avenues. "Everyone gets out. Air will be waiting for you at Domovoy. Regardless of the outcome, the FOB is already breaking down and pulling further inland. Ships will be on standby for expedited EXFIL, but remember, we won't be able to set down within the range. Sensors have shown mobile proximity air cannons on the way."

Murmurs filled the room, but the officer continued. "Questions?"

A few scattered arms shot up.

"Proximity air cannons, ma'am?" Nas asked.

"We figure they've been repurposed and mobilized from captured Legion assets."

"ROE?" a marine from Titan-6 said.

"It'll be dark. If the eyes glow, shoot it. Preferably in between."

"If the HVT doesn't come quietly?"

"He won't. MED has provided knockouts." Her eyes pierced the room. "And if that doesn't work, kill the motherfucker. We'll make them pay. Starting with him."

Smirks filled the room.

"Shuttles to the airfield depart in a couple hours. If you haven't already taken care of what you need, you're SOL. Talk with your leads. Ursus TOC and Command Ops will track everything. Make us proud. Get this done."

Seats pushed back in a clamor and conversations burst as the brief ended. Scott turned to find Sam and after Krill and

Yuri excused Echo, he made his way back to her, weaving between uniforms. Thankfully, Shadid had already ventured away to find his own peers in ducked post-brief whispers.

I'M GLAD YOU'RE HERE.

She crossed her arms and nodded, although she let her attention sit beyond him, on Miriam, who was conversing with the medics from the other teams. The Titan marine who had passed them earlier was in their huddle, and something stuck in Sam's gut. The woman was pretty, her uniform sharp and neat. Sam's heart jumped into her throat.

ABOUT YESTERDAY.

She drew in a breath, then slowly counted it out.

I DON'T WANT TO LEAVE LIKE THIS.

Her eyes pierced his. "Were you going to tell me?" she snapped, hushed enough between themselves. "Do you know how fucked up this is?"

IT JUST HAPPENED. I DIDN'T KNOW I'D— He frowned, then bobbed a fist up and down.

YES, WHAT? Sam signed back angrily.

YES, I KNOW IT'S…MESSED UP. BUT…

Sam searched his face. He was actually nervous, but there was something more to it—he was excited. The heat of her anger cooled, aided by the brief and knowing her brother and Echo were headed off on a big mission—a dangerous one— without her. She sighed hesitantly, but in temporary resignation. In the overall scheme of things, this was something she'd dig into later.

"Are you going to be okay?"

His brows pinched together, and he studied her for a second before he shrugged. YOU'RE NOT UPSET?

She scoffed. "I don't want to talk about this right now. I'm *not* talking about this with you right now. I can't believe…" She made a sound of annoyance. "You're the worst. You'll explain this to me when you get back, I'll yell at you, and you'll make it right—everything."

Scott's brow lifted in skepticism.

"What?"

He smirked.

"Stop it. You're the fucking worst."

Her hand lifted to push him away, but he wrapped his arms around her, pulling her into an embrace. At first, Sam stiffened, surprised and conscious of their surroundings, but she relaxed into its comfort.

His gravelly whisper tickled her ear. "When did you grow up?"

She gave him an intentional squeeze, and his soft yelp was satisfying.

"Shut up," she said into his chest. "Be safe, okay? Make sure Acehole covers your six."

"No one covers it better than you," he replied, a pointed knuckle into the top of her head before he let go. A Titan-4 marine called out for him, and he gave her another look before he hurried away.

Sam rubbed the back of her neck with her hand in an attempt to hide the warmth and color from the surprise sibling moment. The public display of intimacy was strange. He was right. Getting out of Ursus, getting away from their usual lives and grind was changing them, as bizarre as it was for her to comprehend.

"Hey." Miriam approached and glanced back at Scott. She leaned against the wall. "That was something. For a second, I thought I'd have to jump in. You alright?"

Sam drew her finger across her cheek, pulling the skin up. "That asshole."

"He told you?"

Her attention snapped to Miriam. Was there something else he had held back?

Miriam's eyes widened at her intensity. "Or not. I thought maybe he mentioned he was seeing someone—"

"You knew?"

The medic winced. "I found out yesterday. You weren't exactly in a good mood last night, and I wanted to tell you, but —I don't know, it didn't seem like my place to tell."

"But he told you."

That *asshole*.

"Kinda, we had a little chat." Miriam's smile faltered, before it perked back up. "Your brother, he's quite…quiet."

Sam huffed. The woman seemed much calmer about the news than she would've expected. "He told you about the Royal?" she whispered.

Miriam's face froze then scrunched. Her lips opened, closed, then opened again. "What?"

She hadn't known the full story.

Sam softened, relieved by Miriam's shock and confusion. A small smile crept into her mouth as she watched the realization spread through Miriam's features. It took Sam out of her own thoughts about the entire thing, and she adored the woman for it—even if it was unintentional.

Miriam puffed out a sharp exhale. "Well, that's unexpected."

"You're taking it better than me."

"I mean, I don't understand how—" Miriam shook her head, then lowered her voice. "I'm shocked you haven't throttled your brother."

"I'm not thrilled about it." Sam paused. "But he seems—I haven't seen him like this before." She frowned. "It can't be more than a fling, right?"

"Does it matter? You're growing soft," Miriam teased.

Sam watched Miriam as the woman murmured a quick farewell to passing colleagues. Was she growing soft? She pondered the comment, probably more than the medic had initially intended. Put all the bullshit with MED, UMF, and her fucking clearance aside, she could argue she was in a positive place—content even. But the feeling fell and cracked. How could she be content if she wasn't with her brother, Miriam, and the others on this mission? If she wasn't there, how could she make sure they were safe?

"Are you set?" Sam touched Miriam's arm. "Everything taken care of?"

Light brown eyes grazed hers.

"Enough ammo? Visor synced? If they're on stims, make sure you get them in the head. They'll move fast, but torso shots won't do anything. Don't get caught one-on-one either."

"Sam." Miriam pivoted her shoulder on the wall and turned fully to her. "I was SOG when we met. You don't need to worry about me. You said you wouldn't do this, remember?"

Sam exhaled, then apologized. "I don't like—"

"Sitting on the sideline is shitty, I get it. I'll be okay. Scott will be okay. We're not spending the little time we have doing this, alright?"

Sam swallowed and nodded. The woman knew her. Grounded her.

"Come on. I want to get out of here." Miriam winked. "We have a bit of time before I'm due back."

A grin spread across Sam's face. There were perks of Miriam's apartment being nearby.

22

RUPTURE

ECHO ARRIVED at Ursus in the early morning, the second cohort of a staggered arrival, and Miriam had gotten little rest between pre-mission nerves and the rough flight in. Nightmares lurked around the corners of sleep, and she avoided them as the team made its way to FOB Domovoy. When they landed, the small base was noticeably emptier, just as the officer had mentioned, with only a skeleton crew and minimum services. Equipment and other items of value had already been moved or tagged for relocation.

What was left of the short day had dematerialized behind the rolling dark clouds. With last checks, inspections, and additional briefs, the others had turned in much earlier than their usual bedtimes. Their next movement would be late or early, depending on who was asked, although it didn't seem to matter much with the cloak of darkness instilling night for the next twenty-odd hours. Unsurprisingly, Miriam couldn't sleep. After what felt like an eternity, she rose, tiptoed past the others, and escaped the light snores into the cold air. Her boots crunched loudly against the rough ground as she found a position hidden in the shadows of the base's floodlights, watching as a shift crew whizzed around on the other side of the base, boxes and items in their arms, working until the end. Their responsibility was destroying what couldn't be salvaged.

She hoped the legionnaires did the same before they were overrun… Being there now, Miriam understood UMF's decision to withdraw their numbers from the forward operating base. There simply weren't enough countermeasures for whatever Apostates were carting this way. Whatever seized Altered technology would decimate the place. It hurt, knowing humans were giving up their territory, but with the inevitable horde on its way, FOB Domovoy would, at best, have only held them back for a day or so.

She blew warmth into her already chilled hands. She needed her mind to slow, to shut her eyes and rest, but here she was, outside, the hours before their trek into Bonford and the devils within.

The sound of liquid swished to her side. She wasn't alone.

"Fancy meetin' you here. Tryin' to call your girlfriend?"

"She's not—" She turned to find Fox, then walked the short distance to where he sat on top of a table, his feet square on the accompanying bench. A small metal container, a flask, dangled between pinched fingers. She eyed it but said nothing. Instead, she gestured, and he shifted so she could join him. She turned her gaze up at the cloudy sky. It was a shame; Sam had told her about the display of colors and the glint of satellites— but they were hidden now.

"I don't need you checkin' up on me."

She wrapped her arms tighter around herself. "I wasn't."

Fox grunted, and she could feel his stare. "Still can't sleep." It was more a statement than a question.

Miriam wasn't certain if it was a self-confirmation or directed to her, so she didn't respond.

His fingers played with his flask, screwing and unscrewing the top.

"There are rules, Fox."

He waved the now-open flask underneath his nose.

"I'm serious," Miriam warned, an eye on the container. She could smell the harsh alcohol from it.

He screwed the top back on, sealing it. "And I haven't broken any." At Miriam's scowl, he rolled his eyes and pocketed the item. "Don't give me the lecture. I'm doin' my part, ain't I?"

She sighed. "You're not making it easy."

In the distance, a worker dropped a box, scattering its contents. Miriam and Fox watched as others assisted the individual.

"How much time before we head out?"

Miriam shook her cuff. "Three—maybe four hours."

"Should we try?"

It meant they'd lie awake, their own anxieties and nightmares accompanying them until their alarms sounded. It wasn't a good start to any mission, especially this one. The gravity of it would have normally threatened to crush Miriam, but her own surmounted fears were already doing an excellent job. Miriam patted Fox's knee and forced herself to rise.

"After you."

◊

Her expectations were already low from the briefs and training, but when it came to the actual day, Miriam found it much worse.

And wet. Everything was wet.

Though miserable, the start of the mission was straightforward—almost easy—with everything going as planned and as briefed. Aided by their visors, Echo trudged and scaled the terrain through EarthTek's southern passage with Titan-4 and held their positions, watching as the first wunby patrol arrived. The SOG teams' breach and entry into the dark compound was flawless, stealth afforded by the heavy rain and light number of alties as they rotated—their perfunctory checks a flaw, a mark of arrogance. Miriam had expected more.

Now, as the wunby patrol stalked the ground in a cycled and optimal path shielding them from the gales of the thrashing storm, their hunched bodies looked the same as humans from afar, small and insignificant to nature. Miriam shivered, gritted her teeth together to prevent them from chattering, and lowered herself back behind cover. The cold and wet seeped through her clothes despite the resistant heatwear she wore underneath.

Misery. For both sides.

After hours spent holding inside their designated buildings and avoiding the scant patrols, Miriam had thought UMF spent all this effort for nothing, that the wunbies had actually selected one of the other opportunities provided. She, like the others, perked up and rejuvenated with an advance unit's arrival at the compound gate, a lone vehicle with its lights disengaged. Echo relocated and burrowed into their temporary positions as three individuals exited the vehicle parked underneath the overhang of the main building, their silhouettes barely visible at the edge of their visors. After a brief conferral with one of the patrol members, the three newcomers disappeared into the building and had not resurfaced since.

Miriam figured they were waiting. Regardless of their genetic engineering and environmental adaptability, the alties did not differ from them in this situation. Given the option, most everyone would choose comfort and dryness.

For Miriam and the other SOG marines, it wasn't a choice.

Her attention snapped to Ace's hand motions in the window above her. From his and Scott's perch hidden inside the two-story apartment building, he made an articulate movement with his fingers to Echo below.

Two sentries nearby.

Miriam cursed to herself. It hadn't been long since the last patrol; the enemy rotations around the compound were increasing, and if not for their recon teammates, she wouldn't have noticed. The storm effectively hid the SOG presence on-site, but it also meant that it effectively covered the enemy's movements as well.

Careful to not expose herself, Miriam peeked around and blinked the rain out of her eyes, scanning the slow motions of two growing silhouettes. As they neared, she dug into her nook and held her breath. She could make out the distinct sound of rain pounding on their bulky armor as they closed within meters of the half wall she and Krill were at. The lead motioned his hands silently in warning to the rest of the team and then Titan-4 across the way.

Another motion above, and Miriam glanced up at the splayed palm and fingers.

Stay down.

The sentries had stopped. She fought the urge to burrow deeper, worried that any noise would alert the two Apostates beside them.

A wave of fear washed over her as a wunby spoke in a deep, gruff voice. They were words she either couldn't understand or were distorted by her heart beating in her ears and the surrounding storm. At her side, Krill's weapon lifted, ready to engage.

It was too early to be detected. They had invested too much time, effort, and sacrifice to get to this point. Miriam willed them to keep moving. Leave.

And then, another voice called out, and she could hear their heavy footsteps recede. Miriam exhaled as she looked up for a confirmation from the window. She turned and peeked back out, watching as figures jogged away, back toward the main compound entrance.

Lights from two vehicles punctuated through the downpour as they sped toward the gate. Miriam focused her visor as far as she could, following the small motorcade as it slowed at the front of the building, two of the advances already there to greet the newcomers.

And hopefully their high-value target.

Miriam blinked as her visor stuttered, its lines glitching, and she dropped back behind cover. Krill tapped his own device, a deep frown underneath, and then grimaced. Their night optics were fuzzy but usable. He stiffened, nudged her with an elbow, then visibly keyed his comms. What would have normally come across as a click was nonexistent.

Her gut plummeted. Whoever had arrived had brought countermeasures. SOG still had their eyes, but they had lost their ears. The use of their cuffs and visors were last-resort contingencies but losing that safety net in a stealth mission was terrifying.

Krill waved up to Ace and made a quick motion. No comms. The lead then relayed it down the line and over to Titan-4. If Titan-6 was in range of whatever was scrambling their line, they'd know it and have to adjust from there.

At the muffled sounds of commotion, Miriam peeked out again. Her visor was unstable, but she caught doors opening and a flurry of bodies as they deposited into the building. From her angle, she couldn't make out how many in the quick deployment.

Barring the sloppy patrol, the arrival operation was swift. She was taken aback by how organized these so-called terrorists were. The ones they had come across before had not shown this kind of efficiency. It was almost military-like. Professional.

Ace's hand gestured four.

Drivers in both vehicles.

Standby on target visual.

Which brought the total of enemy wunbies to fourteen. Against SOG's twenty-two, who were now conveniently cut off from each other with their primary communications. For now, Titan-4 was within range where they could exchange hand signals, but once the teams split, each would be on their own, trusting the others to do their jobs. It wasn't ideal, but they were here now. And they wouldn't back down.

For a second, Miriam closed her eyes and raised her face to the downpour as they waited for confirmation. She knew Scott was upstairs, an eye behind his marksman rifle, waiting for a visual on their target in the several windows of the building. She thought to open her eyes, and look at the sky, but didn't. There would be nothing there but storm and rain, a reminder they had no air support, no reinforcements. They were on their own.

When Krill tapped her, she opened them. He was up, crouching behind their cover, and already passing information to the others.

Positive ID.

Miriam glanced over at the main building, where lights had turned on like multiple eyes perforating the darkness. The brunt of illumination came from the third floor, and she caught shadows moving.

With a last signal, it was time to move. Titan-4 had already relocated and staggered their approach toward the main building. She trusted Titan-6 was maneuvering to their new positions on the opposite end of the compound.

Aware of the roving patrols, Miriam pulled herself into a squat and quietly followed Krill, joining the rest of Echo. Together, they staggered their movement to the southeast corner, where bulky structures made up a water treatment plant just south of an administrative building. Miriam took her place behind cover. From this new vantage point, she could barely make out movement across from them, at least a hundred meters off near a small utility building.

Two Altered sentries. The tiny glows of their tapetum lucidum were evident through the curtains of rain. Miriam's jaw clamped down, and she raised her rifle, its attached suppressor augmentation sticking out over the small wall. It was a far shot, but if these Altered were on stims, they could close the distance within seconds.

But the situation never materialized. Her exhale cut short, suspended as swift hands and calculated strikes took down both shapes in a synchronized movement. The figures were drawn back where she couldn't see anymore. Titan-6. They had made it look so easy, taking the targets down.

Twenty-two marines. Twelve enemies.

Considering the situation, Miriam settled as best as she could into her position and watched her sector, the compound gate. She familiarized herself with its shape and its position and forced her visor to continue a seamless scan despite the slight static from whatever countermeasures the Apostates had brought. If they were back in Station City, in training, Titan-4 would be ready to breach the building soon, taking out whatever Apostates they could with stealth. She didn't hear the staccato of gunfire or shouting and took it as a good sign.

Something shifted in her peripherals, and she narrowed her eyes, willing the visor to focus. At least she had thought there was movement. Miriam held her breath, watching.

And there it was again. Another horizontal blur.

Shit.

Without shifting her eyes, she moved her left hand from the barrel of her weapon to get Yuri's attention next to her. She bladed her fingers in the gate's direction. Was there another patrol there? Were they outside the compound where the SOG teams had less visibility? Miriam resisted glancing back as the team second passed along the information.

Bait. What if Kartik was bait to draw UMF out? SOG had gladly taken it. Three teams, exposed for quick elimination.

Static hissed in her ear.

"Titan...unknown movement..."

Krill had broken the silence. His words barely made it through to her own visor, and she was close behind him.

"Tita—"

Piercing booms ripped through the storm noise. At first, Miriam thought they were sounds of thunder, but they were too intermittent and coming from the other side of the main building.

"What—" Kai said, all semblance of stealth gone.

Miriam shifted her attention away from the gate. Where and what were they shooting at? And who was doing the shooting?

Shit shit shit.

Miriam glanced back at the main building entrance, where a sentry swung his weapon forward, his back turned to Echo. Her eyes slit trying to make out what he was looking at, but there weren't any muzzle flashes or any semblance of motion from Titan-6's position. She turned back to the gate and her breath hitched as figures—she counted five—stepped out of the darkness into the bordering faintness of light from the main building. Her mouth opened to warn the others as strange rifle-like weapons were raised, but the words caught in her throat.

Bursts of light exploded from the ends of the shadowed firearms. The suppressed cracks of Titan-4's weapons responded immediately, their own small starbursts opening up, revealing their positions outside the main building.

Nas and Krill shouted in front, but their words were minced by the tumult. Fox's rifle added to the mix with streams of bullets, forcing the sentry and the drivers down.

Mayhem.

Chaos.

One figure in the rear turned toward Echo, its ominous weapon lifted. Before it could fire, Miriam squeezed her trigger, pounding rounds at it, but it seemed to either absorb or deflect her shots. It didn't fall.

Shit. Stimmed.

Miriam let another concentrated spray hit the individual before she realized its weapon was lowered, a dark hand splayed out in front. The figure staggered back and crumpled.

"Move!" Krill shouted. "We can't let them get out!"

"Where is he?" Yuri hollered.

"Take out the vehicles!"

Miriam shifted to find the other four shadows, who had since staggered apart, the furthest one nearing the first vehicle. She swiftly changed out her magazine and fired more rounds toward the entrance along with the others.

Everything had gone to shit. There were too many players, and these wunby reinforcements had scrambled everything. However, doubt bubbled when one newcomer launched a device at the motorcade vehicles. The projectile sailed then latched like a magnet onto the hood of the car.

The figure cocked its arm back again, but a barrage of bullets from Titan-4's position pushed them to the side. By then, Miriam and the rest of Echo had traversed as close as they could without putting themselves in friendly fire. They slid and ducked back into cover as a volley of shots came from the main building.

Miriam felt the pressure before she saw it. By the time she looked up, any semblance of a vehicle could only be known by its remaining tires. Its sides were crumpled in as if some invisible hand had squeezed it. Individuals darted out of the building entrance and slid into the two other automobiles: a bullet-ridden advance car and the second from the motorcade.

"Target moving! Target moving!" someone shouted next to her.

Engines roared and tires squealed on the slick pavement. The advancing car barreled toward figures who scattered, jumping out of the way. A shadow twisted, throwing another projectile at the passing vehicle. Miriam watched as the car drove wildly toward the gate and then hit an invisible obstacle. Its walls expanded like cheeks blowing out, and then metal crunched as it imploded, twisting and turning on itself, reducing to a fraction of its original size. Whoever inside was trapped in sharp torture, and if they weren't dead, would wish for it.

She didn't have time to gawk longer as another vehicle raced dangerously past her. Miriam threw herself to the side, her hip smacking into the wet mud. Pain shot through her body, but she was already scrambling up and away, aware the others had turned, their focus split between the vehicle getting away and the other wunbies and marines shooting in every direction. She hugged the wet ground as bullets chased the car, and then something squelched in the mud at her side. She stared at a shaking puck-like device, a red light blinking.

Every muscle in her body screamed as she pulled herself up and threw herself behind the nearest cover, a raised curb that wouldn't be enough. She felt the same pressure she had experienced before, but with nothing to contort and rip into, the blast blew mud toward her. Her breath was rough, almost hyperventilating at the near-miss, and she scrambled back to her feet, her rifle fumbling in her hands.

Someone grabbed her and Miriam swiveled around, her rifle up, but it was only Kai, with Fox behind her.

"Are you hurt?" her teammate yelled into her ear.

She shook her head.

Krill called for Fox and the man started forward. He threw his voice over his shoulder and over the noise. "Stay here! Make sure that one is down!" He didn't have to explain. Stimmed Altered had a way of not dying when they were supposed to.

Miriam found the subject of Fox's order: the wunby she had previously shot. She and Kai neared the body and held their sights on the armored figure. Closer, now in the dim lighting, she saw a helmet covering most of the wunby's face, a square jaw underneath, a dark substance oozing down its cheeks and chin.

Miriam flinched as blood geysered out of its mouth.

Shit. Still alive.

Her finger twitched on her trigger, but something was

wrong. Through the dim lighting, elements, and stains, she could make out patches of white through punctured plating.

Legion.

"Kai," she breathed.

"Oh, hell," her teammate groaned as she came to the same conclusion. Kai shouted after the others, but they were firing, caught in the chaos. The engineer keyed her visor, "Friendlies! The armored ones are friendlies!"

Miriam shook her head. Scrambled and cut-off words came through her visor. Whatever countermeasures were still in effect. "Go!" she ordered.

Kai sprinted off.

A hand flopped, trying to find something at its beltline before it reached up, weakly prodding its helmet. Miriam couldn't look away as the material folded back upon itself, the face shield pulling into some unknown technology beyond them. Green glows reflected faintly, and she flinched again.

"Help...m—" The legionnaire gurgled before it choked.

Miriam's stomach bottomed, and it took her another second before she swung her rifle to the side, dropped, and grabbed at the legionnaire underneath his armpits. She pulled, but her boots slipped in the mud. He was too heavy. With the conditions and the armor, as light as it looked, she wouldn't be able to relocate him to better cover. Miriam would have to work on him there, under the threat of ongoing fire. She scrambled back up and moved to the figure's side, clawing at the legionnaire's strange armor. Her gloves passed over dents and chips, but she couldn't find a clasp.

"I need you to help me," she said frantically.

His hand flopped to a latch she hadn't seen, and his breastplate loosened. Miriam didn't wait before she pulled it off, and her breath caught as she surveyed the damage. There was too much. A jagged hole ripped along the side of the man's neck, and with the armor gone, two areas on the legionnaire's undershirt immediately soaked in dark color. She swung her pack around. She grabbed bandages with one hand and thrust the other to the man's neck, applying pressure.

The young legionnaire opened his mouth, trying to say something, but only a wet gurgle came out.

"Don't talk. Shit, don't talk." Miriam's fingers worked his wound, trying to cover as much as she could. It was too much. The blood escaping was too much. She called out for Kai, for help, but the woman had gone.

She cut the legionnaire's undershirt. She had to see what she was working with. What she had done. Her eyes then searched her pack and flitted to the exposed torso as she simultaneously pushed against another injury. Would a patch work? A blood congealant? What did she have that could stop this, or at least delay it? Bloody fingers dug through her compartments and came up with a membrane applicator. She ripped the packaging open with her teeth and brought it back down. She wiped at the legionnaire's chest, drawing blood away, and glimpsed two vertical scars, almost like bars at his manubrium, above his breastbone. More blood covered it.

And then a hand covered hers, holding her back.

She pushed, resisting.

"Tan."

She tried to shake off the other hand on her shoulder.

"Tan."

Miriam looked up at her friend, her teammate.

"You need to keep this for the others," Yuri said.

Weren't alties supposed to be genetically engineered for faster healing? She just had to hold it together, delay so the legionnaire could heal on his own.

"We have to leave. We have to leave now."

In her focus, Miriam hadn't realized that most of the shooting had ceased. She looked over to the legionnaire. His breath had already fallen, and his eyes gazed up, rain splashing every crevice in a baptism of death.

Her ears plugged and unplugged as the surrounding mud

oozed with something thicker than water. She could make out familiar words and they ground into her, bringing her back into the world.

"Go. They're calling for you." Yuri lifted Miriam up, then thrust her pack into her hands. "Titan-4 needs you. Go!"

She ran off, her boots squishing into the mud and rain trailing down her cheeks like tears she couldn't produce for herself. She made to turn back toward Yuri, to ask him, but she stopped herself and stumbled toward her next patient. There was no need for the question; she already knew the answer in her gut.

They had failed.

Kartik had gotten away.

23

IMPLOSION

THE MESSAGE BLINKED on her cuff, its glow stark against the dim hallway.

MEDICAL CLEARANCE GRANTED
OPERATIVE STATUS REINSTATED

Sam stared at the words, turning her wrist over as if they might vanish. She should've felt relieved—thrilled, even—but the emptiness gnawed at her. She checked her private channels again. Nothing. Only silence.

The lines on her display cycled back, taunting her. Clearance granted. Status reinstated. She was back, officially. But back to what? The mission should've been over hours ago, but here she was, stuck in purgatory, waiting.

Sam paced the narrow hall. She dug her fingers into her arms. It hurt, but it served its purpose, a good and distracting pain. She'd bruise, and Miriam would fuss over her, breaking out her topical ointments to fastheal the blood vessels, break up the blood clots, or whatever the medicine did. Sam thought of how soft the medic's fingers would brush over her skin and then she kicked herself for letting her mind wander. Her leg stuttered as she glanced at her cuff.

The door opened to the SOG TOC, and Sam straightened. The watch officer startled, his body rigid, before he regained his composure and strode with long steps toward the building door.

She followed him. "Price."

He ignored her, his speed increasing as they left the building into the cool twilight air.

"Price," she repeated. "What's going on? No one is telling me anything."

"Good."

"My clearance came through. I can—"

"I thought you went home," he drawled. The compound lights cast long shadows across his face, and she couldn't make out his expression.

"No." She had spent the entire night pacing the corridor, badgering the watch officer whenever he stepped outside for a break. "There should've been news by now. I haven't heard from any of them."

In the military, no news was usually good news. But this was something else. Sam watched Price's shoulders tense then drop. She braced for his next tirade.

But it didn't come.

To her surprise, he said in a soft voice, "They just landed."

"In Ursus," Sam replied. She hurried to match his cadence as they passed a couple of marines on foot patrol. Her face quirked. "Were they held up at Domovoy?"

"No." The officer shook his head. "Here."

"What?"

"They landed here."

The clarification caught her off guard and her feet slowed, only for her to stagger back into a matching pace. It didn't make sense. The teams were supposed to exfiltrate back to

Domovoy, and then airship out to Ursus. They'd regroup at the outpost. Unless…

Fuck.

Unless there had been severe casualties, and the outpost medical center couldn't provide the needed services. Her stomach flipped. Neither Miriam nor her brother had messaged or called.

"What happened?" she asked, a slight tremble in her voice. "Who?"

He didn't answer. Sam looked around and recognized the gray windowless buildings. She and Price were walking toward Command.

And he was going in person.

This was bad. Really bad.

He was going in person to Command—something only warranted in the worst situations.

Casualties.

"Price, who?"

"Titan-6 got it the worst."

Sam exhaled in relief that it wasn't Echo, but guilt washed over her soon after. SOG casualties. More Ursus casualties.

"And the others?"

"Transport's already heading to Station General. The rest are at the airfield, waiting for shuttles." He turned to her without breaking his stride. "Are you going to walk me all the way?" It was a rhetorical question, but still the nicest sentiment the man had given to her since they met.

She slowed.

"North gate." He tossed the words over his shoulder.

She nodded, but then called out before he moved too far, "Price. The mission?"

He paused and turned. A vein feathered in his temple as his eyes dropped before he whipped back and hurried off.

It was enough, and Sam tried not to think further on it. She started into a jog in the opposite direction. When she reached the north gate, she touched her cuff several times, pacing alongside the wall and sentry station. The teams would have been able to communicate via the network, especially if they had been on the way back to Station this whole time.

But her channels were empty of anything recent. It wasn't a comm-silent mission, so something had either happened or the SOG marines had been instructed not to say anything. Her prosthetic kneaded painfully into her left arm, but Sam wanted the hurt. It was better company than the anticipation.

Sam counted an hour, seventeen minutes, and forty-seven seconds before a lone shuttle turned off the main street and down the side road. The compound's white lights reflected off the windows and Sam couldn't see or count who was within. She followed its trajectory and planted herself near the door, willing it to open so she could find out what had happened, to make sure Scott, Miriam, and Echo were okay.

As the door accordioned, familiar faces from Titan-4 trudged out. Some acknowledged her while others turned their eyes down as they sorted by. Then, Nas and Kai emerged, their movements heavy with weariness. Sam's eyes darted over them, scanning for injuries. None—just grimy kits and streaks of dry mud smeared across their faces.

Her breath hitched, but before panic could take hold, she spotted a flash of blond hair behind them. Her brother. Relief surged, and she exhaled shakily, her shoulders sagging as tension drained away. He shuffled down the steps, moved his long rifle to his other hand, and gave her a quick sign.

I'M OKAY.

She clasped his hand, but let go as Fox pushed by, alcohol wafting off his breath. Behind him, Miriam stepped out, the last one on the shuttle. Her rifle dangled off her shoulder, her pack and kit from the crook of a bent arm. Mud and stains streaked across her neck, and though the SOG marines' uniforms were dark, Sam could tell Miriam's pants were stiff and stained where mud or something else had dried.

Sam wanted to hold her, pull her in, but she refrained. She touched Miriam's cheek gently, uncertain of the glossy look in the medic's eyes as they slowly focused. "Are you hurt?" Sam breathed. From her cursory scan, none of the blood seemed to be Miriam's, but she had to make sure.

Dry lips cracked open, but before the woman could respond, a scuffle and voices broke out behind them. When she wheeled around, Kai had thrown herself between Fox and Nas, her hand reaching up, barely covering the top of the larger marine's fist. Nas's shirt bunched within it.

"Say it again," Fox growled.

Nas's expression remained flat, his arms still at his sides. "Let me go, you fucking drunk. Had to start early, didn't you?"

"Fox, let him go," Kai tried.

"I'm real tired of your fuckin' mouth, ya little shit."

Words of mitigation did nothing to defuse the situation, the two Echo teammates in their own world of anger. Sam looked for the Echo lead or second, but they hadn't been on the shuttle.

"If you weren't drowning and pissing yourself, maybe you would've noticed what was going on in your fucking sector. You're fucking pathetic."

"Nas, stop." Miriam took a giant step forward.

"You might not be drinking on the job, *yet*, but if you weren't such a fucking mess, we wouldn't have lost—"

Fox slammed his forehead forward with a bony crack.

Nas's hand shot up to his face, and when he pulled away, a curtain of blood flooded over his lips and chin. His eyes flashed. "As I said. Pathetic."

A large fist lifted and wavered dangerously in the air.

"Benjamin Fox. Let him go. Now." Miriam bared her teeth.

Fox shook Kai off and shoved Nas away.

The intelligence specialist opened his mouth, but Miriam snapped to him, a finger up in his face as she stepped between the two. "You." Her eyes glistened with fire. "Shut the fuck up. Go to MED and get that set and cleaned up."

"I'm right, and you know it."

Before Miriam could reprimand Nas again, he stormed away.

"Kai," the medic gritted.

The engineer nodded and ran after their teammate.

Miriam turned to Fox and glared.

Sam stifled the urge to pull the woman away, his frame looming over her. He was volatile, and though he was a friend and colleague, she was worried about what he would or could do.

"What the fuck are you thinking? You're already on thin ice."

With a scowl, Fox hefted his pack off his shoulder, and dropped his gear and rifle on the ground. "Take it. Better now than later." And then he turned on his heel and left.

Miriam flustered. "Hey! Are you serious? We're not done here!" She stomped after him, but Sam reached out and set a hand on her arm.

"Let him go."

The medic shrugged her off, and the rejection pierced Sam.

"Fuck." Miriam threw up her hands. "I can't. I can't with this shit. I'm not their babysitter."

Sam tried to catch the woman's eyes, but the medic turned away. What the fuck happened? The cohesive Echo she knew was breaking down.

Scott's boots scuffed as he walked over. He hitched his rifle bag further up his shoulder and reached down for the abandoned weapon.

"No. Leave it."

He froze mid-bend.

"Mir?" Sam said, uncertain.

"That dumb bastard," Miriam muttered. "He's done it now."

Sam shook her head. "We can't leave this here."

The medic frowned, but she didn't protest as Scott grabbed Fox's rifle and handed it to Sam. She heaved it up over her shoulder, its weight tugging her muscles.

With another sharp exhale, Miriam shook her head and led the way toward the SOG building. It was a tense walk back, and the three remained silent as they stepped around Nas and Kai's mess and tucked away their gear. Sam set Fox's weapon into the rack and helped place his kit in front of his locker. She grimaced at Miriam's heavy motions, her kit thrown into her locker. Sam held her tongue, although she desperately wanted to ask a million pressing questions.

Scott waved a hand at her and chucked his head toward the door. GIVE HER SOME SPACE, he signed.

She obliged, following him outside the team room, with a glance at Miriam as the locker door slammed shut. The sliding door severed and muffled a yelled expletive. Sam winced and gave her brother a questioning look. WHAT HAPPENED?

His blue-gray eyes were heavy, and his teeth gnawed on the inside of his cheek.

"Scott," she whispered. "Tell me."

KARTIK ESCAPED.

I KNOW. HOW?

He rubbed the back of his neck then motioned again. LEGION SHOWED UP. IT WAS A MESS.

"Legion?" Sam lowered her voice although no one else was around. "What were they doing there? How did they know?"

I DON'T KNOW, BUT THEY WERE THERE. WE DIDN'T KNOW THAT IT WAS THEM. I SHOULD'VE... Scott's hands wavered in the air. He looked up at her and whispered, "I should've known."

Sam reached out, but he pulled back into himself.

I HAD A SHOT. KARTIK. AND THEN, I DON'T KNOW. I TRIED, BUT I—

Sam grabbed her brother's hands. "It's not your fault. We'll get him again." The sentence fell off. Even as she said it, she didn't truly believe it. UMF's attempt, capture or assassination, had failed. If the Apostates were smart, the strategist would already be speeding back to the other side of the sea. He'd be hidden and stowed away.

She tensed. SOG had missed their one chance, but she was back in operative status, she was back with her brother and Echo, and they'd figure something out.

Scott pulled away and sunk into the wall, his legs barely keeping him up. His palms rubbed into his eyes as she stood there awkwardly, searching for something else to comfort him.

"Scott, we'll get him again. I got my clear—"

"I think I killed one," he rasped, softly.

Sam's own news fell to the wayside.

She shook her head incredulously. "They would've killed you. It's not your fault."

"No," he said, his eyes still squeezed shut. And then his hands began moving furiously. I KILLED A LEGIONNAIRE. I SAW THE HELMET, IT WAS DIFFERENT, I SHOULD'VE KNOWN. His fingers suspended in the air, trembling.

A mess. Everything was a mess. And there she was, sitting to the side while it had happened. Useless. She tried to push the thought away. Not anymore. She was back.

"Scott, what can I do?"

Sam approached him again, but he recoiled. WHAT CAN YOU DO?

Her chest panged. She knew he didn't mean it *that* way, but she had set herself up for it. What could she *do*? She couldn't get her clearance in time. She couldn't figure out what the Charonites were up to, if they were even up to anything. Her jaw clenched. Her brother didn't mean it that way.

Before she could try to tell him about her reinstatement— some good news as a beacon of hope—his eyes opened, sad gray-blues dropping to the side. I'M GOING TO HEAD BACK. I NEED TO... His lips pressed together.

"Do you want me to stay with you?"

He shook his head, and the lines on his face multiplied as he finally looked up at her. I'M SORRY. I JUST— His hand reached out then retracted. IF IT'S OKAY, I'D LIKE TO BE ALONE.

Her gut constricted, then released. She hated that he and the others were experiencing this, that she had been impervious to it all. She hadn't been there with them—to commiserate in their shared pain—and though she wasn't envious, she hated it. Sam swallowed, hoping the knot in her gut would untangle itself. "Yeah, no, of course. Give me a second, and I can walk you back at least." She placed her hand on Echo's team door.

NO. YOU SHOULD STAY WITH HER. I'LL SEE YOU IN THE MORNING, I PROMISE. He squeezed her shoulder, then lingered for a second as if he wanted to pull her into a hug. Instead, he lightly mussed her hair before he walked off.

She didn't complain. Not this time.

Sam watched him walk the long hallway and depart the building. Whatever clusterfuck the mission had become, everyone needed their own space and time. She sighed and leaned into the wall, waiting. She had wanted to tell her brother and the others that she was back in SOG, back in the fight, but with them dealing with their own emotions, it didn't feel right. When the door opened, and a bedraggled Miriam stepped out, Sam swallowed and held her tongue.

They slowly walked away from the building, away from the compound, and back to Miriam's apartment. As they entered the flat, the scent of cinnamon comforted Sam. She knew the others were taking the failed mission harshly, but she was glad they were all relatively okay. Something kicked in her chest as she observed Miriam in autopilot mode. She stared at the blood, the mud, and the stains. Things could've been worse, much worse. Sam didn't know what she'd do if they'd been hurt.

The door closed, and Sam gently took the woman by both shoulders. "Mir?"

Miriam rubbed her eyes with a splayed hand and blew out a shaky breath. "I don't—it's not you, Sam. I—can we not right now?"

Sam nodded. "What can I do?"

Light brown eyes hung on her, and even as they stared into Sam's, the woman wasn't entirely there.

"Mir, talk to me," she pleaded.

Before Sam could register it, Miriam crashed into her, mouth eagerly pressing forward, hands planting on the sides of her face. Sam tensed at the aggression but didn't pull back. She met the frantic motion, a desperation intertwined, and something unlocked inside her. When they separated, three words swept out of Sam's mouth with a breath.

The silence would have been deafening, if not for her heart pounding in her ears. Her breath hitched in the absence of warm hands on her skin. She followed Miriam's eyes as they darted, widened, then narrowed. Her heart sank as the woman pulled away and turned.

The door opened then closed.

It had slipped out. She hadn't meant for it to, but now that it was out, Sam knew it was the truth.

24

INFECTION

HER FOOTSTEPS VIBRATED *through the floor, each thud echoing down the corridor. To her right, the walls curved, and on her other side, floors dropped down in a deep silo. She came to a stop in front of three identical doors. Avoiding the first, she pushed into the second. In the middle of the room, a figure lay on the ground, shackled and unmoving. She started toward it, but froze. Even though she couldn't see its face, she knew who it was. She looked away, knowing she'd only see her own face the closer she got. She stepped back, her hands behind her, searching for the door, but it was gone, nothing but a cold and smooth surface. The lights extinguished, and then she could hear the walls clicking and whirring, moving in on her.*

Miriam woke up with a start. An ache ricocheted in her skull, and she groaned and rubbed the palm of her hands into her eyes, trying to ward off the growing throb.

I love you.

She flinched.

Those three words twisted and stretched, inflating and crushing herself out of her own mind. An unintentional added weight on top of everything else as the remnants of emotions ruffled through her. The failed mission, the legionnaire she killed, Fox's asinine destruction, her team's implosion, all her nightmares had come to life.

I love you.

Sam.

Trying to piece everything together with a throbbing hangover was like trying to walk through thick mud. She groaned. What a mess.

Miriam braved one eye open, and the world swam in blurred shapes and muted colors. When she forced the other open, her heart skipped. A low ceiling and dark walls loomed around her. This wasn't her apartment. The smell was off, the sheets too silky, and something pulled at the back of her mind, too slow, too hazy. There was something familiar about the place.

In hesitation and uncertainty, she turned to the side.

In horror, she sat up.

Blood rushed through her ears.

Her movement didn't affect the woman next to her, whose long dark strands of red-dyed hair flowed this way and that. Miriam's breath caught in her throat and her stomach tightened into a knot. She extricated herself from the binding sheets and her skin prickled at the coldness of the apartment. Her lungs burned at its inability to fill with air. A flash drowning in dread.

What happened? What did she do? The thoughts, slow before, now shredded through her mind.

Oh hell.

She stood, mouth agape at the mussed bed and the naked woman in it. Her jaw trembled as she looked down at herself, partially clothed.

Shit.

She grabbed at her commcuff and turned it on. It was early in the morning.

The *next* morning.

Shit shit shit.

Lines of notifications came through as her device reconnected to the network. Each one was a cut through her soul. What had she been thinking?

The last one came through, time-stamped hours before.

> S. RYAN: Please be safe. Take whatever time
> you need. However long. I'll be here.

Miriam doubled over, her stomach clenching so tight she thought she'd be sick. Her hand crushed over her mouth to hold it back in, to stay quiet. She had to get out. She could make it back to her apartment before Sam woke up.

Sam.

She and Sam weren't like that. They hadn't put any labels on anything. It didn't matter, did it?

Sam would be destroyed.

Miriam's soul compressed at the thought, but she had to leave first. As she searched for her clothes, nameless emotions passed through her, each excruciatingly winding her chest tighter, each lodging in the back of her throat, heavier and heavier.

Her hip bumped into a side table and Miriam froze, before taking a glance back at red hair. She couldn't afford to wake Ana. She couldn't deal with that on top of everything else.

Miriam wouldn't do this again—she couldn't. She just wanted to go home. Home where Sam was. Home to Sam. Sam, who looked at her like she was the world and everything beyond it. Sam, who, for some reason, wanted her and only her. Sam, who told her those three words.

I love you.

Why did she do it?

She found and donned her clothes, gagging from the fumes of alcohol, dried mud and blood on them, and she slipped back into the waking city, cursing herself, wishing she had never left her apartment, wishing she had never left Sam.

◊

When she returned to the flat, Sam was asleep, curled in a blanket on the loveseat. Miriam paused and stared. The woman's face somehow bore peace and worry at the same time. She thought to reach out, stroke a cheek—a physical apology—but she pulled back, conscious of the stench of alcohol, whatever dive bar she had gone to, and worst of all, Ana. She silently stole into the kitchen, found her hidden stash, and dry-swallowed an enzyme nanocapsule. Despite her already sobering state, she felt the leftover traces of alcohol break down in her system as she tore off her clothes and made her way to the bathroom, set on scrubbing herself clean of everything in the shower. The guilt and regret stayed regardless.

She'd tell Sam. She had to, but what if the woman left? Miriam couldn't lose her. In endangering everything, she now possessed immediate clarity. Sam wasn't an arrangement. Sam had always been something more.

When Miriam came out of the bathroom, a towel wrapped tightly around her, she heard stirring outside. She braced for the confrontation and reality she'd have to face. This fear was different. She didn't want to lose Sam. She couldn't.

The woman looked up, her movement deliberate as she folded the blanket. The faintest smile curved her lips, but her eyes held a quiet sadness that hardened Miriam's stomach and made her hands tremble.

"I'm sorry," Sam said first.

Miriam shook her head fervently. "No. I'm sorry. I shouldn't have left."

"I shouldn't have—I'm glad you're okay."

No. The woman was being too nice. She wouldn't be this kind if she knew what Miriam had done. She didn't ask where she'd been, what she'd been doing. *I slept with someone else.* The words caught in her throat.

"You needed your space, and I didn't—I wanted to help—I should've..."

Miriam shook her head again. Whatever she had wanted last night after everything, after those unexpected three words, whether she wanted space, physical exertion, an outlet, a loss of abandon, none of it mattered now. She didn't want any of that now. She had made a terrible decision.

"And I know you haven't been sleeping well, I just—"

Miriam closed the distance and took Sam in a firm embrace. She breathed the woman in as arms pulled her closer, one warm and one cool—a strange balance. This was right. They fit together. Why did she do it?

When Sam pulled away, Miriam whimpered softly. Blue eyes watched her with concern and something else. Guilt and regret pierced Miriam and she glanced away, enough to notice a uniform folded out on the kitchen counter. It wasn't hers. She caught the prominent display of the collar and its diamond tab.

"You—"

Realizing the focus of Miriam's attention, the woman cracked a smile.

"When?"

"Yesterday. It didn't seem like the right time..." Sam swallowed. "I'm sorry. What I said—"

Miriam shook her head. Everything had just gone so wrong. Her cuff buzzed on the bathroom counter, but she ignored it.

"Mir?"

"It's nothing," she mumbled as she reburied her face back into Sam's neck. She ignored the rattling of her cuff against the hard surface.

"It's early. It could be important. When is your debrief?"

Miriam shook her head. She didn't want to think about the previous day.

Sam pulled back again and studied her.

She could tell her now, but Miriam didn't want to ruin the moment.

And then something buzzed into her back. For a brief second, she stiffened, afraid that Ana had somehow gotten Sam's information. Would the woman be that desperate?

"Don't," Miriam blurted. "I don't want to rush back into everything, even if it's just for these few seconds."

But the cuff vibrated angrily into her skin, demanding attention. Sam's arm lifted and Miriam held her breath, pursing her lips into the woman's shirt and collarbone.

She could tell her now, before Ana did.

"Sam, I—"

"It's Krill."

Miriam swallowed the rest of her sentence.

"Hold on, I'm going to answer."

The commcuff connected.

"Valkyrie, is Tan with you?"

"Yes."

"Tell her to get over to base. SOG TOC. We have a situation."

Miriam perked at the edge in the lead's voice. "What's happening, Krill?" Her skin cried out as Sam separated from their embrace.

"Tan, answer your damn cuff. Just get over here."

The call ended and Miriam's eyes connected with Sam's.

"You should get dressed," the woman said.

Soon. Miriam would tell her soon.

◊

Miriam could hear the ruckus from a couple blocks away, and she and Sam broke into a run. They rounded the corner, and she startled, taken aback at the sight in front of the SOG building. SOG marines from Titan-4 and Titan-6, many of them bandaged up, were to one side in a leering and shouting match with three abnormally tall figures in white uniforms.

Legionnaires.

Miriam halted and stared. What were they doing on the UMF compound? It would have been comical—the ratio of humans to alties four to one—if not for the knowledge of how deadly the soldiers were. Thankfully, no one was armed or armored. She located the rest of her team, Yuri and Nas on the fringes, busy holding back some of the bigger marines while Krill and Kai stood in the middle of it all—their arms outstretched trying to distance and placate both sides. A dangerous position.

Hell.

Miriam hurried forward without a thought. She didn't want to deal with any injuries, especially her own team's. She passed by First Officer Shaw, her aide, and another officer standing to the side, their own anger evident.

"Why the fuck did you bring them here?" Shaw snapped.

"I'm the fucking escort, Shaw. You think they'd listen to me? I don't know how they knew you were here. We're supposed to have gone straight to Command."

"Whose bright idea was it to let them on in the first place? Get this under control. Before MP is called. We're not going on the front pages of the network feeds."

As Miriam moved forward, she caught a full view of one Altered soldier—a familiar face from what felt like a lifetime ago. The legionnaire from the South. The senior one, Hadeon.

"Varya?" Sam said, behind her.

Another short-haired Altered turned her head. She could somehow hear them over the shouting. Miriam cringed as heterochromatic eyes flashed in their direction.

The young legionnaire gaped up at her, his mouth opening and closing, but nothing came out.

Blue and green eyes burned into her. Did the legionnaire know Miriam had killed one of theirs? Her mind stuttered. She wasn't the only one who had shot at them. It had been confusion and chaos.

He pawed at his helmet and neck.

Miriam steeled herself, but Varya turned back to the SOG marines in Hadeon's face.

"You say it like we aren't allowed on our own land. And where have *you* been hiding this entire fucking time? Watch your fucking tongue, rat."

"Castle, cool it," Yuri snapped.

"You here for an apology tour? Here to take responsibility for fucking up?"

"Kartik got away because of you!" another marine from Titan-6 yelled, a finger pointed dangerously close to the legionnaire's chin.

Hadeon inched forward, and it was either immense bravery or stupidity that the marine did not take a reciprocating step back. "You were in our way," the senior said in an even voice, almost drowned out by the rest of the marines. "The blame is entirely on you."

"Oh, sure. Bet you rats couldn't stand us getting Kartik ourselves. Couldn't help yourselves, could you? Our teammates are in crit because of you."

Varya's shoulders squared, ready to match the sea of contorted faces. Krill placed a hand on the man's heaving chest and tried to push him back, but the others shifted behind, ready for a brawl.

Miriam moved closer. The other medic from Titan-4 was confined to a series of MedJets in the hospital. She'd be the first one to mend inevitable broken bones.

Hadeon blinked owlishly. "Count your blessings. Your comrades are still alive."

"We lost two to your incompetence," Varya growled.

It took a second to register what the legionnaire had said. Miriam's stomach dropped, and the situation combusted simultaneously. SOG marines surged forward. Miriam lost sight of Krill before he emerged, shielding himself as he and Kai were caught between the gnashing teeth and clawed hands.

A loud crack punctured the mayhem. And for a split second, everyone froze.

Miriam raised a hand to where she had last known Sam to be, trying to find her. Her breath seized as the crowd parted down the middle to reveal a Titan-6 marine, gun in hand. He leveled it at Hadeon.

"Castle," Yuri said, his hands hovering.

"Put the gun down, marine," First Officer Shaw added.

The sidearm did not waver.

"What's the difference? A rat's a rat. We gave up all that land, *our* land."

Miriam saw the motion in the corner of her eye, but she was too slow to realize, to stop it. In the lull, Sam briskly moved forward and placed herself closer to the legionnaires. A noise—a mix of a gurgle and squeak—escaped Miriam's lips.

"They're not the enemy, Castle." Sam displayed her palms outward. "Put the gun down."

Anger flashed in the marine's eyes, but then a delayed recognition seeped in. Hands trembled then fell to the side. Miriam breathed in relief when Yuri pinned and stripped the marine of his weapon.

"Everyone, get back inside," Shaw growled.

But no one moved.

"I said, get the fuck back inside," she ordered again. "I swear if I don't see your asses moving right now, I will strip you of your tabs myself." Her face flushed and with the heat of the moment diffused, many reluctantly backed up, shuffling begrudgingly.

Krill turned. "Hadeon, I think it's best you leave now."

The senior's expression remained a stony wall, but Varya blinked in acknowledgment. The legionnaires looked around once more with a mix of apathy and disgust, then started to walk away, the UMF escorting officer trailing after them.

"Varya," Sam called out.

The UMF officer's eyes flashed back, irritated.

"You were in Nakuan?"

The soldier stopped and sharply turned.

"They said Nakuan was lost."

"We did not *lose* Nakuan."

"But it was overrun?"

Varya's eyes slitted, and Miriam braced herself.

"We were ordered to destroy what we could and abandon the port."

Sam's face dropped in confusion.

"Abandon and go where? Back to Station?" Nas said, but Hadeon called out to Varya, and the three legionnaires moved on, their officer escort trying to regain a semblance of control.

Nas craned his neck. "Hey! Back to where?"

Miriam turned back to Sam. The woman's jaw clenched, her expression hardened.

"What, Sam?"

The woman ignored her, eyes darting around the remaining and scattered SOG marines. She whipped around to Yuri. "Where's my brother?"

He shook his head, just as baffled as Miriam. "He didn't answer when we called."

Miriam reached out, but Sam pulled away, already marching toward the base's gates. She called out after her over the second's protests and raced to catch up, just in time to hear Sam's growl.

"She lied to me."

25

EXPOSURE

"SCOTT, ANSWER YOUR FUCKING CUFF."

Sam stepped off the people-mover and re-engaged her device, impatiently trying her brother again. Her skin bristled as she looked around the stop, scowling at the government buildings and reorienting herself. She set off with another mutter. "I should be the one tracking you. Where are you?"

"Hey, slow down," Miriam said. "What are we doing here?"

Sam stabbed a finger at their private channel. "Call me back, asshole. You better not be at her place." She glanced over her shoulder to Miriam. "You didn't have to come." She winced as the medic's eyes narrowed. Sam looked away, her voice softening. "She might not even be here, but it's on the way."

It wasn't much of an explanation.

They rounded the corner, and Sam marched up to the front gate, side or back doors be damned. She heard Miriam's hesitant warning behind her, but didn't heed it, already slamming her right fist into the metal with a clang. And bolstered by the satisfying feeling against her prosthetic, she didn't wait before she banged the gate again.

White dashed into view and Sam measuredly held out her other hand. She thought she recognized the legionnaire from her time in the Alley—although she wasn't completely certain —they all sported the same two hairstyles: short or shorter. She wasn't here to fight her counterparts. They were just soldiers, after all.

Like her.

Used.

"No trouble." She backed up. "I only want to talk to—"

"You are Valkyrie."

Sam's mouth hung open for a second before she closed it.

"Artem's friend."

The comment threw her off, and the rush of anger and impatience disappeared. "Yes. Is he here? He can sort this out. I just need to talk with Kuan-Lin."

His cheek quirked, either at the casual way she said the Royal's name or the audacity of showing up unannounced. The legionnaire eyed Miriam behind her then returned his gaze to Sam.

"Artem is dead."

The words smacked her through the barred gate. Sam blinked hard, trying to make sense of her already derailed focus. "What do you mean? I just saw him—was it the Charonites—how? I don't understand."

"Path to glory."

Sam's face scrunched and she shook her head, the news still processing. What did that mean? Before she could start, a hand grazed her shoulder, and the medic stepped closer to the gate.

"Did he have—" Miriam whispered. She held up two fingers then brushed them under her throat.

The legionnaire's horizontal eyelid blinked, and Sam frowned. She didn't understand. To her surprise, the Altered tugged at his collar and pulled it down. Three pale scars lined next to each other like a tally.

Miriam inhaled sharply and Sam turned to her, confused. The medic shook her head. "He was at EarthTek, at Bonford. I'm sorry, Sam."

The stone in Sam's gut sunk heavier as she registered the new information. Her eyes squeezed shut and anger coiled from her toes, through her legs and up every muscle. All of this could have been avoided. Her vision tunneled and her hands trembled at the energy growing inside her.

She felt Miriam's touch on the small of her back, but it was too late. She had come here for a confrontation, and this additional information only added fuel to the fire.

Sam called out, her voice projecting up toward the building. "Kuan-Lin!"

She was pushing, but fuck the boundaries. The Royal had softened her, and Sam had completely fallen for it.

"Kuan-Lin! I know you can hear me."

Unless she wasn't there. Unless she was back in her flat with her brother. She should have never gone on that detour with Scott. She should have run the opposite direction and never introduced the two.

The door opened wide, and the Royal stood in the middle of the embassy entrance. Her cheeks were a shade of pink and behind her in the grand foyer, a small crowd of gold and silver eyes stared out.

"Did you do it?" Sam exclaimed.

Kuan-Lin shut the door firmly behind her. She gave a terse nod to the legionnaire who moved back to his station without a word, then walked down the entrance steps toward the gate.

Graceful, always so fucking graceful.

"Sam, you shouldn't be here. This isn't a good time." The Royal made no motion to open the gates. "Let's meet back at my place later. In an hour?"

"No," Sam sneered.

Golden eyes found something beyond Sam and Miriam, and Kuan-Lin shook her head sharply. Miriam gasped and Sam turned. Behind them, Dmitri had soundlessly emerged, his hands on top of each other at his beltline, his red eyes slitted.

Sam's muscles tensed. She pulled Miriam closer, stepping in

front of her, then steeled her voice. "I'm not leaving. You can sic him on me, but I won't go quietly." Her free hand lifted, open and prepared. The words and motions were injected with confidence spurred by anger, even if doubt was creeping in. It was a thin bluff. She knew the Altered knew it.

But she heard the Royal take a deep breath.

"Go around back."

She didn't wait for Sam's response, and by the time Sam peeled her eyes away from the bodyguard, the Royal had withdrawn into the embassy. Sam glared after her, then turned to face Dmitri again.

"After you."

He didn't budge.

Sam set her hand protectively on Miriam again. "You should go back to base."

"We should both go," Miriam whispered, an eye on Dmitri. "Sam, what are you doing?"

Antagonizing and burning her bridges. But not before she understood why Kuan-Lin had lied to her.

"I need to know why," Sam said.

"Why what?"

She shook her head. How could she explain that Kuan-Lin had lied to her, given her information that she knew Sam would send on to UMF? But she couldn't say any of it. It meant she had been duped. She was the piece that had started all of this. She could've prevented all the SOG casualties, the failure of that mission, and losing all that northern land in vain.

"I'm not leaving you," Miriam asserted when Sam didn't answer her question. She pulled her attention away from Dmitri. "I won't."

Something swelled past the shame in Sam's chest. "Okay." She stifled the urge to grab Miriam and kiss her right there in front of the Altered bodyguard and embassy. Sam took her hand with a squeeze and brought her around the corner to the entrance she had taken months before.

When they arrived at Kuan-Lin's office, the Royal leaned on her desk, waiting, a finger tapping the surface. Gold eyes glanced at Miriam, and then back to Sam, who glared back.

"We're all upset about what happened, Sam. Emotions are running high, and we should—"

"I'm not here about that."

Kuan-Lin's eyebrows pinched together in surprise. Miriam's head turned sharply as well.

"Is it because Sco—

"Nakuan."

The Royal blinked, then regained her composure, but not before Sam caught a quick frown. A hole opened at the bottom of her gut. It was confirmation enough.

"You knew." Sam scoffed. "You didn't just know, you decided."

The Royal's gaze dropped to the side.

"You told me you lost, that Nakuan was lost. But you conveniently didn't tell me you were the one who pulled the legionnaires out. You gave up the garrison and the port, didn't you?"

"We made a calculated choice. It wasn't sustainable, Sam."

"Bullshit. You led me to believe—"

"I told you the truth."

"Sure. Conveniently leaving out the important part."

"I never—" Kuan-Lin paused. "The garrison was surrounded, cut off from our supply lines. I wasn't going to let our people starve and die there."

"Surrounded. What a fucking convenient excuse. You had UMF support across the strait."

"But we didn't, Sam. Your military didn't support us, didn't support them."

Sam waved her off. She didn't want to hear the Royal's excuses. "You knew Kartik was interested in our land. You knew if you pulled the garrison, he'd cross over, he'd show his face. You dangled us in front of him."

The Royal shook her head and gave a placating gesture to Dmitri, who had moved closer. Sam glared at Kuan-Lin, waiting for a response, but she received nothing back. It enraged Sam more.

"Fucking politicians. Human, Altered, you're all the fucking same. Be honest for once. I should've known. Fuck, I'm an idiot. We're numbers to you. Whatever gets you what you want. And me? I was just another dumb marine who wanted so badly to do something. I was one of your game pieces, a pawn." She laughed incredulously. "And it didn't even work out. My own organization didn't listen to me. All your games, everything. It all failed."

"You know that's not true."

"You're right. Something worked out for you, didn't it?"

"Sam—"

"What do I know?" she snapped, voice cracking. "You could've told me, but you didn't. You had me pass along the story, the illusion. Why didn't you just tell me?" Sam stared at her, waiting, but she received no satisfaction from the Royal. "You offered us up. What, to give them an easier target while you regrouped?"

"No! We didn't know UMF would give up the land so fast. And so much on top of that," Kuan-Lin said. "The hindsight is there. It was a mistake. Yes, we should've worked with City Center, your leadership more, but no one wanted to listen, no one wanted to figure it out together. I didn't use you; I shouldn't have—"

Sam cut the air with a sharp wave. She leaned forward, her lip curling. "Did you ever give them a chance?"

The Royal's eyes narrowed. "You know—"

"No, actually. I don't. How many lies have you passed through me? How far back has this gone?"

"I never—please don't let this taint—"

"I don't believe that." Sam sucked air in through her teeth.

"Fuck, I'm an idiot. I'm an accessory. They told me and I didn't listen."

"You're not. You never were. I'm sorry, this isn't what I wanted. You're upset. I'm upset—"

Sam scoffed. The last time the Royal had been upset, it was a farce. If she was upset now, it was only because Sam had found out the truth and called her on it.

"Let's come back to this conversation when we've cooled off."

"Conversation?" Sam frowned. "No. No, we're done. I'm not your lackey anymore." She fixed her jaw. "Let's go, Mir. I got what I needed."

But no one moved for a moment.

The Royal studied Miriam, her nostrils flaring. "Sam—"

"No, actually, you know what else?" she interrupted. "Stop seeing my brother. You can make a fool of me, but—" She thrust a finger into the air and gold eyes flashed at her. "Stay the fuck away from my brother."

26

———

FEVER

GLOWING GREEN EYES SURROUNDED HER, *watching from both near and far. Miriam ran through the narrow alley until it became a hallway filled with doors. She looked back and saw nothing, but she knew something was behind her, was following her.*

She tried the first door, but it was locked.

She tried another. Locked, again.

Her fingers fumbled for the next and she stumbled inside and onto a bed, her limbs tangled in sheets as she rolled repeatedly. And then she was tumbling into wet, thick mud, sucking her down. She grabbed for something, anything, and her fingers caught on something cold. The body turned, and it was the legionnaire, the glow from his eyes gone. A metal hand grasped her wrist, and relief flooded her as it pulled her up, but then blond hair turned red and Ana's lips leaned in.

Miriam's stomach lurched. It had been a couple weeks since her mistake, but she could still smell Ana's perfume, potent from the nightmare. She rubbed her eyes and when she opened them, she watched the spots fade in her vision, merging into the dark void beyond. This part of the shore wasn't well-traveled, only accessible via a narrow walkway just north of the UMF base. She had almost forgotten the place existed, until her feet had automatically brought her there in the past week. It had become a new occurrence whenever she woke from her vivid dreams.

She breathed in the ocean and grounded herself in the waves lapping at the rock wall. Something scraped behind her and a shadow from the nearby light stretched in the corner of her eye. She straightened, ready for any trouble.

"You trackin' me?"

"Shit, Fox, you scared me." Her shoulders sagged in relief, and she turned back to the ocean and leaned on the banister. "What the hell are you doing here?"

"Could ask the same of you."

Miriam huffed. "I didn't know you were here." She hadn't seen her teammate since the night they came back from their failed mission, and he hadn't responded to any of her messages or calls. His silence was infuriating, but she bit back a comment.

"I come here sometimes when it gets real bad," he rumbled. "Can't sleep."

She hummed in response, again unsure if it was a question, an observation, or self-commentary. Miriam frowned as she tried to peer into the water below them, but it was too dark. The sporadic lamps lining the old boardwalk weren't strong enough to illuminate the hidden ladder down to the murkiness below. "When was the last time we were all here? Night dive training?"

Fox grunted. She could smell the alcohol before he leaned into the railing next to her. His flask dangled between the tips of his fingers over the edge. "Been a while. Forgotten. Like everything else."

She picked at the banister. It was another comment loaded with other meanings. Miriam looked up when Fox offered the

metal container to her. She took it and sniffed. "It's too late—"
She considered. "It's too early for this." But she took a shallow
swig then wiped her mouth.

He held out his hand, and she reluctantly gave the flask
back. He chucked it back with a long swallow, then smacked his
lips.

"You're a dumbass, you know."

"Always been."

Miriam rolled her eyes and pushed off the rail. "It doesn't
suit you, going quiet," she said. "Nas is fine, by the way."

He grunted again. "Fuck 'im. He had it comin'."

"Dumbass *and* asshole." Miriam gripped her jacket closer
around her neck and listened to the water below them. "Kai
misses you. I stopped by your place the other day, too. You're
suspended, not dead. Or have you actually decided to fuck off?"

"Jury's still out."

She scowled into the darkness. "Fuck you. I know you're on
this journey to destroy yourself, but did you ever wonder about
the impact on us? Me?"

He swung the flask between his fingers. "Didn't know I
mattered that much to you. Won't your bestest friend be
jealous?"

"Fuck you," Miriam repeated, softer this time. In fact, she
couldn't remember the last time she talked to Yuri like they
used to. The distractions were mounting.

Fox snorted. "Everyone's better off. You said it yourself—I
was bringin' down the group—"

"I never said that—"

"Didn't need to." He blew a puff of air past pursed lips, but
then quieted. They stayed like that, silent, as the darkness
swallowed them.

His voice came back, cracking in the middle. "I know I'm
not right."

A metal sign clanged softly against its post in the distance.

"When Jun—" Fox cleared his throat. "I'm not okay. I haven't been okay."

Miriam pinched the hem of her jacket.

The man cleared his throat again. "Y'all be fine." He drew the flask to his lips and pitched it back until it was empty. Fox capped the container and flipped it between his hands. "Why're you here when you should be layin' next to Goldilocks? You got someone."

She did. And she had been so terrified of what it meant that she had messed it up. She'd fix it. She would.

Miriam looked up. "You do, too. You have us."

"Avoidin' the question," he said, conveniently avoiding *her* comment. "You haven't told her?"

The truth stuck to the tip of her tongue. Fox didn't know about Miriam's terrible mistake. The question wasn't about that, but guilt regurgitated up and Miriam almost gagged as she tried to force it back down. She bent over, dropping her head below her outstretched arms to stop the shame from washing up and over her. It didn't, and she dropped into a crouch, her hands clinging onto the metal rail.

Sam.

Miriam had fucked up.

And she was fucking it up with every second, every minute and day she didn't tell Sam about what had happened. It wasn't like she'd had a lack of opportunity. With Sam and Scott working on administrative items, training with Echo, and preparing for defensive efforts, she'd had more time with the woman than the previous months.

"She doesn't know you're out here."

Miriam sighed.

"I'm surprised. She'll understand. She got it the worst."

The lump in Miriam's throat caught again. She knew Fox was talking about the loss of Sam's arm; he didn't know what she had done, but it was a delicate line. She swallowed again, trying to dislodge the feeling and steered the conversation away from ambiguity. "That's what I have you for," she said. "Who else would I talk with at zero dark whatever when everyone else is asleep? We get to be miserable together."

"Probably requires us talkin' about our issues." He snorted and then started into a chuckle.

Miriam joined him before they lapsed back into silence—only the noise of the water beneath them.

"Fox…" she said carefully. "Just do what MED says, get some help, finish your suspension, and come back. We need you on the team. Especially with all this shit happening."

He inhaled, then let it out harshly. "No, you don't. The Golden Twins are there now. They'll do fine."

She sighed again. "Whatever this is doesn't suit you. The old Fox would puff out his chest, pound it like a dumbass, and say something crude."

Part of her expected him to respond with a joke.

He didn't.

"We're fucked up, aren't we?"

The question hovered between them.

Miriam chuckled, and Fox joined in. After a long, freeing stretch, their laughs died down, and she wiped a single tear from her eye. She considered telling Fox about her mistake, but she held it in. What would saying it out loud do? It wouldn't erase what had happened. The one person she needed to tell, she couldn't.

"We're having another team meal soon," she said instead. "Before we head up for the long haul. You should come, apologize to Nas."

"Funny. And no, I'm not on the team right now, am I? But I gotta commend fuckin' boy scout on tryin' to keep morale up. His idea or Yuri's?"

"Mine, actually."

He dropped his head toward her, then rolled his eyes. "Always tryin' to fix shit."

She shook her head and checked her cuff. "Complete

dumbass," she muttered. "I should head back, but just go. Same place as usual."

He gave her a look that meant he wasn't planning on it.

"Am I going to see you before we head up?"

Fox shrugged. "Same time, same place tomorrow? I'll bring a bigger bottle." He shook his flask at her.

Miriam scoffed and threw a middle finger over her shoulder as she left. In a couple hours, the sun would rise, and she didn't want Sam to wake up to an empty bed.

◊

Why did it take a terrible sin to reveal a beautiful truth?

Soon, Miriam told herself. She'd tell Sam soon. It was eating away at her, and she was positive it was only making her nightmares worse. The leftover dread from the previous one haunted her like a lingering dark cloud. Miriam batted away the thoughts as she draped her jacket over the loveseat and made her way back to the bedroom.

When her eyes adjusted to the darkness and she slid into the sheets, they were cool on her skin. She brought herself as close to the sleeping woman as she could without disturbing her, despite the contact she desperately wanted. Her arm folded between her head and pillow, while her fingers hovered just above Sam's relaxed hand beneath the covers. Though the prosthetic conducted body heat differently, she could feel the contained warmth radiating from the rest of Sam's body and their proximity. It was just enough.

A slight hum sounded in the back of the woman's throat, followed by a whisper Miriam barely caught. "You're back."

She answered with an endearing hush. "Go back to sleep. I didn't mean to wake you."

Sam shifted closer. "You okay?"

No. Miriam's muscles tightened. *I have nightmares about the Apostates. I'm scared.* Her lips cracked open. *I slept with someone else after you told me you loved me.* Her gut contracted. *I fucked up. I should've never done it.*

Sam mumbled, her brows pinched together over closed eyes, and she shifted.

Miriam clamped her mouth, swallowed, then tutted softly. "I'm okay. Better now," she lied, but it was a strange lie. The clarity swirled through her, oddly relieving, but then she'd tear, ripping at every seam. *I'm scared that you love me. I'm terrified.*

"Sleep," she whispered. The back of her fingers brushed across a soft cheek and then moved up, stroking through short tufts of hair.

Sam's breath fluttered and Miriam continued to pull her fingers through, watching the woman's features relax, a smile pulling at the corner of her mouth. She continued like that for a while until Sam's breath slowed and deepened. Miriam didn't know how long she lay like that, time lost as she tried to buoy herself from her thoughts. She surprised herself sometime before the bedroom lit with the morning sun when she breathed out those three words as well.

◊

"Feels good to be back together, doesn't it?"

Miriam looked up, her attention returning to the group. Like the days before, she had told herself she'd tell Sam the truth, but every time she wanted to, something came up. Another administrative document, a training refresher, or weapons maintenance where they didn't get time alone. And when they were back in the apartment, she had never found the confidence to ruin the mood. She chewed on the inside of her cheek while Sam chuckled and shied away from Yuri's incoming nudge.

"Yeah, it does," Sam responded, bumping into Nas on her other side.

Unbothered by the contact, their teammate flicked lightly at her prosthetic. "Just remember, when shit goes down, save me first, okay? Don't play favorites now, just because you two are —" He made motions with his fingers and Miriam reached over to smack him. Kai beat her to it, and Nas rubbed his head with a scowl.

"Gross. You're seriously turning into F—" The engineer stopped herself and her expression hardened. She didn't finish her sentence.

Miriam stretched her neck to look around the street, but there was no sign of their suspended teammate. It was odd not having him there. When she turned back, her eyes met Yuri's then Kai's. They understood.

"When are you two getting hitched, anyway? Making it official with a ceremony? A ring?"

Miriam's eyes narrowed at Nas. Her body had gone rigid, a reactive muscle memory to any mention or comment implying commitment. But unexpectedly, the ensuing trepidation didn't come.

"It's not like that."

She glanced at Sam, her stomach bubbling. She knew the woman was saying it on her behalf, but coming from her, it stung. Or did Sam mean it? The doubt crawled up from her gut and sat heavily in her chest.

It's not like that.

Had something changed? Did Sam suspect something? Shit. Worse. Had Ana reached out to her? A whirlwind of potential scenarios stormed.

Just tell her.

No, Sam was saying it because everyone knew Miriam had been nervous about relationships. Right? That was the reason.

Kai pouted, then smiled. "Is your brother coming?"

Sam exhaled loudly, but Yuri beat her to the response, "He's running late, but he'll be here. I'm forcing him to. Gonna grill him—I personally think he has a lady friend." He chuckled.

Miriam felt the woman tense next to her.

"Told him I wouldn't calibrate his visor to our new channels unless he does. Unless you know something…"

Nas harrumphed grumpily. "How are the out-of-towners getting all this game? I've been here twenty-two, almost twenty-three years, and nothing!" His hands flailed up in the air.

"Yeah, cause there's nothing wrong with you." Kai chortled.

"Alright, this is fun and all, but after all that admin today? I'm hungry. Let's get inside," Yuri said. "Table's waiting in the back."

Nas chimed in as he led the way into Tsutsumi's. "I messaged ahead and ordered our usual apps—at least what they had available. Double for me, of course. We won't get food like this once we're back North."

The rest followed with Miriam at the rear. However, she stopped just inside the restaurant door. Sam paused and returned, ducking her face closer, her blue eyes concerned.

"You okay?"

Tell her.

She waved dismissively and took a breath, although it caught midway. "Are you?" Miriam said, instead. "Scott? I know you're upset with—"

"Not with him—annoyed, maybe, but it's not him…"

Tell her you slept with someone else.

Sam's words fell into the background as Miriam's chest constricted. She forced herself to maintain her composure, to keep her breathing normal.

"Mir? You look pale. What's going on?"

I love you. I slept with someone else.

"Sorry. My stomach doesn't feel great. I'm going to hit the head." Sam started after her, but Miriam shook her head. Her heart drummed in her ears, already drowning out the restaurant, and she forced out an even voice. "Sit. Order me a drink?"

Sam raised an eyebrow.

"It's fine," she said with a shallow chuckle. "Might've been that off-colored nutrient bar earlier."

Sam's brow raised higher as if to say, *I told you so*. And though it felt like her heart was about to burst, Miriam forced an eye roll. *Be normal*.

Sam didn't probe further, and she joined the others at the table with one more glance back. Miriam's smile dropped as she made her way into the back corridor and found the bathroom. Now by herself, she bent over the counter, willing her chest and muscles to relax. She focused on the cool surface through her palms and fingertips, the soft gurgles of the plumbing and pipes in the walls, the chatter of the kitchen staff nearby, and the light fragrance of artificial flowers coming from the little air freshener in the corner.

She'd tell Sam today after the meal. And if she had to get on her knees, beg, grovel, whatever to get the woman to understand how much she regretted it, she'd do it. It had to be done. Miriam looked at herself in the mirror and frowned at the bags underneath her eyes. It had to be done.

With the decision made, she exited the bathroom, wringing her hands. However, as she rounded the corner, she froze at Sam's hushed voice at the other end of the corridor. Miriam quickly ducked into the kitchen doorway. She didn't think either of them had noticed her—Sam with her back to her, and Scott invested in whatever conversation they were having. She hadn't meant to walk into the siblings' moment, and she wasn't sure why she had hidden, but now she was stuck. Miriam stood there but heard nothing. She peeked out.

They were still there.

Scott's right hand drew to his chin then pointed off.

"No. I don't want anything to do with her," Sam hissed. "She used me."

Miriam held her breath.

"And she's using you, too. You're just blind to it."

Miriam exhaled. They were talking about the Royal.

Scott's hands curled and turned outward.

"I don't know! But she is. She lied to me. What if you had gotten hurt? What if you had died?"

Scott clenched his fist and rolled it in front of the other. His hands animated, whipping around and fingers twisting. He paused and Miriam leaned forward, wondering if they had finished. She inhaled as his hands started up again.

"Yeah, trying her best for *her* people by sacrificing ours. She'll sacrifice you, too."

He shook his head and motioned.

"What? You discuss this at length with her? I told you to stay away. Why do I feel like I'm the older one here? Fuck, this is my fault."

He held up his hands and then turned them both down, his fists clenching and making the same motion.

"We're *not* fighting, especially not over her." Sam took a deep breath. "You really stopped by just to tell me you're heading over to hers? Fucking hell, Scott."

He leaned toward his sister, and Miriam couldn't see or hear anything beyond that. After what felt like a long minute, Sam pulled back.

"I can be angry at you if I want." The woman rubbed her hand into her face. "You are so fucking annoying, you know that, right?" But the woman sighed as her brother placed his hands on her shoulders, his lips moving. "Yeah, better than okay. Whatever. Just...be careful."

The corner of Scott's mouth pulled up, and he threw an arm around his little sister's neck, bringing her close in a half headlock, half embrace. Sam shoved him away, but they made their way back to the dining area together, the door shutting behind them.

Miriam breathed out in relief and stepped out of her nook with a mix of puzzlement and tenderness. She didn't have siblings, and she didn't fully understand what had happened, but it seemed to have mostly worked out.

She counted out a few more seconds before she followed, rejoining the laughter and conversation—Scott noticeably already gone. By the time the appetizers came out, Miriam had resettled and let the drinks and food warm her stomach and lessen her inhibitions. Despite the noticeably smaller portion sizes, she ate and forgot about her nightmares and her lack of sleep, basking in the company of her team, friends, and—she gazed at Sam—her lover? Her partner? Miriam scoffed to herself. The nomenclature needed work and though she didn't know what word fit, she didn't care. The feeling overruled any definition. And when Sam grinned, squeezing her knee, Miriam melted.

But then the woman's smile fell, her head angling slightly, ear toward the front of the restaurant. "Is that—" Sam started, her other hand lowering a piece of bread. "Do you hear that?"

The others quieted, and Miriam strained her focus. Past the ambient noise of the restaurant and its patrons, she could make out traffic and the occasional hollering from the city pedestrian. And then there were little noises, almost like something zipping.

She had just turned back when something boomed. It was as if something had either crashed or exploded a few streets down.

"What the hell was that?" Kai murmured behind her.

Miriam stood with the rest of the marines, their chairs scraping out from under them as they stared out the window. Prowlers and rabbits sped by like normal, although some pedestrians had slowed, their attention on something beyond the limits of the restaurant's walls.

And then the zips grew louder, followed by a succession of terrifyingly recognizable pops. Another boom sounded. Closer this time. The window tremored along with the plates and cups on tables.

One was an accident.

Two was the start of a pattern.

Miriam's blood iced.

More people rose, moving toward the front of the restaurant.

"No! Get away from the—"

Outside, the world exploded.

27

———————

INCURSION

It was a bizarre thought as Sam glanced at the unshattered windowpane while she hurriedly ushered other patrons to the kitchen with Yuri and Kai. Beyond the webbed cracks, blurs streaked through the dust and smoke in incoherent streams.

Sam impatiently tugged on a petite woman who tried for the door. *Are you trying to get yourself killed?* she wanted to hiss, but the words dissipated when the woman swung around. Panic edged in her face, and the whites of her eyes were large around dots of black. Shock. Sam loosened her grip.

"Not that way," she insisted, then passed the woman to Yuri, who all but swooped her into the back corridor with the rest.

Sam quickly scanned once more around the restaurant—its chairs tipped on their sides, tables and items scattered—then let the door shut. It'd be more cushion between the chaos on the streets and where they huddled now. With an ear angled outward, she crouched and listened for anything else. There had been screaming and strange gunfire before, but now she heard nothing.

"Kai!" Yuri whispered harshly over the shuffling and

murmurs. "Post up. Back door." He gestured for Nas, who joined them. "What do we know?"

The intelligence specialist swiped through his cuff. "There's nothing on the networks yet. Nothing from UMF."

"Attack?" Yuri uttered.

Sam hoped his question was rhetorical. It was definitely an attack.

"Who? And how many?"

"I don't know," Nas replied.

Sam's eyes scanned over the corridor filled with huddled bodies and found Miriam's hunched shape over a prone figure, then glanced at the kitchen nook. Regardless of who was attacking, the five members of Echo were unarmored with no weapons. There were knives and objects in the restaurant that could be used in defense, but against explosives and firepower like what she had heard, it'd be senseless.

"We have to do something. We can't stay here," Nas urged.

Yuri's dark eyes flashed back.

They could. Sheltering in place was an option—probably the safer one when they didn't know what, who, or how many were outside. Was it isolated to these streets or was the attack coordinated throughout the city?

Adrenaline coursed through Sam's system and she bounced on the balls of her feet in her stationary position. Part of her knew this was something bigger, and it wasn't in their SOG blood to stay down and hidden while the city was actively being attacked.

"Tell me if you hear anything," the team second ordered. He moved toward a young restaurant server and pointed past Sam. "Is there a way to lock this door?"

The boy shook his head.

"And the back? The alley?"

He nodded nervously.

"Okay. Come with me." Yuri jerked his head.

Sam, Nas, and the server followed him down the hall,

maneuvering around other patrons to the back door beyond Miriam.

"I don't think it's myocard—"

Sam touched the medic's back as they passed. "We're moving," she whispered.

Miriam nodded, then turned back to the man's family. "Keep him focused on his breathing. Nice, deep breaths." And then she followed Sam with the others around the corner.

"What's the plan?" Miriam asked as they joined up with their engineer teammate.

"Who's attacking us?" Kai started. "How many—"

"We can't sit and stay here," Nas interrupted.

"We don't know what's going on out there. What about these people?"

"We're meat shields without our weapons."

"SecTeam."

Sam shook her head along with Nas's reply. The city's security and police would be preoccupied and overwhelmed, if not confused by whatever was happening. Reaction was always slower than action.

"The nearest SecHut is eight, ten blocks down," Kai said. "We can make it."

"It won't do us any good if they're not there," Nas retorted. "We can't get into their vaults, can we? Worse, what if they shoot us? What about UMF?"

"Quiet." Yuri rubbed his forehead. "Any updates yet?"

Nas rechecked his cuff and shook his head.

The second muttered an expletive before he looked at the door. "UMF's a full sector away, but if we keep our heads down, take the back alleys and little streets, keep moving..."

Kai clasped her hands. "What if—"

"We adapt. There might be another SecHut on the way. If we need to shelter, if we need to rendezvous, we can use that."

Sam bobbed her head. It was motion. An action. Something. At least they weren't sitting to the side, helpless in the back of a restaurant, waiting for help to come—if there was help on its way.

Shrill sounds of device notifications cut through the air, and Sam quickly motioned to muffle her cuff.

EMERGENCY ALERT—SHELTER IN PLACE

Better late than never.

For a second, fear billowed. Scott. He was out there. She sent a quick message to him, but the network stuttered. As her message processed, pending delivery, she forced a slow exhale. Her brother would be in Oldtown, near the Altered Sector by now, behind the barricades and legionnaire stations. He'd be okay.

"If we're moving, we should do it now," Sam said, returning her attention to the others. Every second waiting was more havoc uncontrolled.

Yuri nodded. "Okay. Back to base," he affirmed. "Let's do this safely. Heads down, move fast." He turned to the wide-eyed server. "Lock the door behind us, and make sure everyone stays down and quiet."

The boy squeaked in acknowledgment.

With one last caution to the nearest restaurant staff and patrons, the five marines slipped out the back door into an alleyway lined with dumpsters—Nas first, followed by Kai, Yuri, Miriam, then Sam taking up the rear.

She felt naked without her visor, kit, and rifle, but Sam urged her eye implant to pick up any movement. As they moved, she noticed the air tasted off. Acrid. The back area and street were unaffected, untouched. Other than the sound of scattered footsteps, there was nothing hostile. Gunfire and explosions erupted far away like a passing storm, drifting further.

Toward the Altered Sector.

Sam's stomach clenched.

Scott.

She reminded herself of the legionnaires and the UMF company marines in the Alley. He'd be okay. She refocused and scanned the street they'd have to cross to pass through the next series of side roads.

Nas stopped at the corner, his fist raised up. His head swiveled, and then he gestured a bladed hand. Move.

They worked their way back toward the base, staggered and in bursts, much slower than Sam liked. She twitched at every distant boom, every little noise and movement, unsure of who or where their enemy was. The first sign of something nefarious came several blocks away from the compound's southern perimeter. Bodies lay in the broken street, their frozen faces contorted in agony with craters and detritus spread around them. The pavement bled and flowed freely.

This had happened recently.

Nas, Kai, and Yuri flitted across one by one to the other side of the road, taking cover behind a line of parked vehicles along the sidewalk. The second gestured. Clear. But immediately after, his body jarred stiff, and his hand clenched into a fist.

Sam heard the sound after. A boot or something heavy crunching on broken pavement. She froze and swept a protective arm across Miriam, pushing them both into the concealment of a rabbit vehicle, trying to make their profiles as small as possible.

Across the way, the other three carefully crept and disappeared into better hiding. Sam strained, listening for the footsteps. She figured at least two individuals, and whoever they were, they weren't talking.

Sam peeked through the rabbit's windows, and she saw exactly what she had surmised. Two figures lumbered forward, their steps slow and deliberate. Both wore what looked to be normal civilian wear and crimson headbands. They were armed, the first with a rifle-like weapon and a bandolier of small puck devices while the other carried a sidearm strapped to his leg.

The latter seemed oddly unequipped in comparison, and she eyed the broad metal pack on his back. It looked heavy, but the individual carried it as if it were another part of his body.

Sam ducked as their eyes—a mix of strange colors—swept the street, their ears tilting this way and that.

Altered.

And they were listening. Searching.

She recognized the way they walked—patrolled—the street. Had they been posted to this sector, this area, specifically? It was a wide avenue and almost a straight shot to the base. Were they waiting for the pending UMF response? Or exactly this? Off-duty marines trying to make their way back?

Cautiously peeking out again, Sam watched Bandolier motion to Backpack, and their heads remained on a swivel, their eyes watching their sectors. These Altered were trained. Legionnaires? No. Every legionnaire she knew was a certain build, their eyes a specific dark green and bright blue. Sam tried looking for any other sign of who these two were—brands, marks, emblems—but it was cut short as she pressed back into cover to avoid another sweeping scan.

The two Altered passed slowly between the separated marines—their sentry cautious, but their intention obvious and hostile. Sam held her breath along with Miriam. Could they hear her heart pounding in her chest? She clenched her fists, and her muscles tensed, ready to launch. If they were discovered, maybe surprise could buy them time—a second at least.

The Altered stopped, their boots shuffling as they pivoted.

And then Sam heard the flurry of commotion as it grew louder. Voices and footsteps clattered toward the main street.

Watching from a sliver of the vehicle's mirror, Sam's stomach dropped. Bandolier moved behind his partner and engaged the pack. Something within it pitched, then whined as a shell unfolded itself over Backpack's shoulders and down his right arm. As the material shifted and moved past his fist, it billowed out like a weapon barrel. The hair on the back of Sam's neck rose. She knew a weapon when she saw one, and she didn't want to be at the other end of whatever it was.

Miriam's hand curled around her bicep, and Sam instinctually clutched it.

Metallic bands and a claw-like mechanism stretched from the shrinking pack and anchored the Altered to the ground.

"What is that?" Miriam whispered.

Sam didn't know, but it wasn't anything good. In all her time in UMF, in Ursus, and in the South, she had never faced this kind of technology. Sam knew the Altered had better weapons, but the decades since the last Sovereign's reign of terror had seen no use of them. Was this a sample of the arsenal that the legionnaires, the Altered, normally had?

As the air shifted around Backpack, her skin prickled. And then a strange whoosh and zipping sound peeled from his raised straight arm. Sam followed its trajectory, but there was no projectile, at least nothing the human eye could see.

Down the street, the incoming group of five civilians—or off-duty marines like Echo—stopped dead in their tracks. The first two, burly men with high cuts, stumbled, then dropped to the ground. There were no punctures, no explosion, no blood. It was as if they had tripped over the same invisible obstacle and crumpled.

Behind them, a third man made a sharp noise between a squeak and grunt and slowed. Sam looked for the starting color of blood on his light-colored shirt, but there was nothing. He pawed at his chest then dropped to his knees.

The two others behind him unfroze, already trying to backpedal, but before they could scatter or leap into cover, another spray of zips sounded—different from the first. Sam watched in disbelief as blood sprayed out behind the two. As they fell, clean red lines stained their clothes as if thin strings or discs had sliced through them.

Sam's heartbeat rushed in her ears. She tore her eyes away

from the mirror, glancing down at the pressure in her hands, Miriam's whitened knuckles wrapped around hers, and she forced herself to control her own labored breathing.

After what felt like an eternity, Backpack disengaged his weapon, its bands, anchor, and plates receding into its original form. The two Altered walked nonchalantly toward their victims and the third man, still upright on his knees, as he feebly clawed at his torso, red spittle bubbling around his mouth. Sam's jaw set. The weapon had done something to their insides, and though the first men had died almost instantly from their internal injuries, this man had not. He was drowning in his own body.

Put him out of his misery, Sam wanted to shout. Her stomach turned as she hid from the dying man's sounds.

Miriam nudged Sam, then turned a wrist so that her commcuff displayed their team channel.

> Y. GREGOV: How do we get past them?

The main street was almost a straight shot to UMF. The closest detour would require backtracking, but even if they wanted to circumvent the area, the five marines were stuck. They were more fortunate than the other five humans, but they had stumbled right into the enemy's shooting lane. They could attempt to sneak past, but it was risky. The state of the street was a nightmare, and the nimblest step could alert and bring death.

Sam racked her brain, but nothing good emerged. The SOG marines were split, three on one side, her and Miriam on the other, and their cover was temporary.

She risked another peek at the Altered, who paced in the opposite direction but were within hearing and firing distance. Was moving worth the risk? What else could they do? They couldn't stay there. Panic threatened to choke her, but she forced herself to breathe, to focus.

Could they throw something, distract the Altered? Would noise divert their attention? It seemed so basic, so silly, but it was an option. What if it failed and it only drew them closer? Perhaps Sam could sprint out, draw their attention in a different tactic. She was quick; her incessant cardio training during recovery could be of use. She could distract the Altered and give Miriam and the others a chance. Backpack's weapon took seconds to gear up. The rifle weapon would be an issue, but there was an adequate amount of cover from the vehicles stopped and parked in the street. She just had to keep moving, and she was good at that.

Across the street, Yuri's hand waved and Sam and Miriam shifted around their rabbit.

DISTRACTION? she signed.

He shook his head and raised a hand—index finger and thumb curled—to his mouth.

Were the Altered stimmed? Sam had forgotten about that. She had forgotten the uncanny speed, strength, and general pain tolerance of junkie Altered, but it didn't matter. They needed to move.

I'LL RUN. DISTRACT. YOU FOUR GET OUT OF HERE.

His face warped, and his fists came together, wrists crossing.

Miriam squeezed Sam's tricep. "Whatever you're thinking," she whispered, "absolutely not." The medic didn't understand sign, but she understood the second's expression.

But whatever Sam planned to do, it didn't matter. Zips hailed out, and the SOG marines turned. The Altered had opened fire on another group of unknowns, but the direction was obvious.

Not theirs.

It was distraction enough.

Yuri quickly motioned forward, already darting away with Nas and Kai behind him. Sam prodded Miriam forward, crouch sprinting from one vehicle to a street kiosk to the next. Their shoes crunched loudly on broken pavement, plaster, and acrylic sheets, but they were moving. They just had to get across the street, out of the kill zone, and to the next intersection—it was close. As Sam and Miriam approached, the others slid and tucked around the corner.

Sam's feet slipped as a van between their intended destination and cover lurched to the side. It was as if something had slammed into it, but she saw nothing. The vehicle groaned as it settled back onto its wheels. Sam backpedaled, her eyes widening at the large caved-in dent in the metal frame.

What the fuck.

Pulling Miriam with her, she threw both of them into the cover of the prowler behind them. Sam's heart pounded in her chest as she peeked around the front bumper in time to watch Bandolier launch something into the air. It sailed up in a high arc, but its trajectory fell short, clattering against the street several meters away. She chanced a relieved exhale.

But then her eyes grew as it flipped to the side and slid, scraping across the pavement.

Straight for the van.

Straight for them.

Fuck.

"Mir!" Sam grabbed the woman as the puck zoomed toward the vehicle and lunged them both back into the open. She felt the heavy pressure of air as it compressed against her. Metal shrieked as the vehicle teetered to one side, then slammed back down.

This time she didn't hesitate. She pushed Miriam forward and the two sprinted, scrambling past a blown-out storefront, weaving across the pavement, dodging debris and bodies as sharp zips cut at everything around them. Something punched her in the back, and her breath wheezed out, but she stumbled forward with the added momentum into the safety of the intersection corner. Sam readjusted herself quickly, ready for whatever was next, ignoring the growing pain in her left shoulder blade. She fought to catch her breath. The firing had stopped, but it wasn't a relief.

"We're on the wrong side!" Miriam panted. She threw a hand at Yuri, Nas, and Kai, who were shouting at them across the way. Sam swiveled and her stomach dropped. The street cut short in a cul-de-sac, a dead-end space for dumpsters and a locked gate too tall for them to scale.

Fuck.

Another round of zipping shots turned her attention back to the others. Yuri leaped back into cover just as the pavement where he had just stepped out erupted with a splash of chipped concrete. More gunfire slashed out at the corner.

And then it stopped, the absence of noise so sudden and loud.

"—loading!" Kai yelled. "Reloading! Move, now!"

Sam peeked out. Backpack was a way off, his weapon anchoring him down. She quickly located Bandolier a block away, manipulating his rifle. His tri-color eyes bored into hers.

"Valk! Move!"

She didn't have to be told thrice. She propelled Miriam forward, and they dashed for the lone vehicle in the street. When the familiar scraping sound screamed in her ears, she urged her legs to push faster, further. She knew what was coming.

Miriam passed the car.

Sam sprinted right behind her.

And then the pressure came again, heavier than before. Her ears rang with pressure, and the world tilted violently. She lost her footing, her body spinning before slamming into the unforgiving ground. Sharp pain jolted up her spine as she rolled a few more times before coming to a stop.

Someone screamed, but Sam wasn't sure if it was real or in her head. Everything had muffled and her orientation was off as she tried to pull herself up. The ground meant death. Staying still meant death. She had to get up.

And then rough hands tugged at her, and Sam found herself swimming in light brown eyes. Miriam's mouth opened and closed, but she struggled to make out her words.

"—up! Sam!"

Her hearing gradually returned, a dull hum in the background before the unmistakable whine sliced through the fog in her mind. Whatever dregs of remaining adrenaline sparked, and she pushed herself up to her knees. She and Miriam were out in the open, and Bandolier was closer now.

Fuck. Fuck fuck fuck.

Suddenly, tires squealed and an engine roared. Before Sam could register anything, a dark prowler screamed around the intersection between the two Altered. Its weight teetered on its outer wheels before it lurched back and straightened. Bandolier whipped around, a barrage of zips flinging toward the incoming vehicle, but it did nothing to stop or slow its path. It plowed into the Altered, pinning him with a loud crash into the destroyed rabbit next to Sam. Bandolier's weapon continued its stream of fire and the windows shredded apart.

Sam scurried back but then froze at the sight of blond tufts as the driver dropped behind the dashboard. Metal groaned as the vehicle backed up and Bandolier fell forward, his hips and legs in a mangled heap. Before he could rise or lift his weapon, the prowler's engine growled and the vehicle lurched forward again.

Sam stared as the passenger door kicked open and the driver slipped out, blood coating one side of his face. Her knees buckled, a sudden lightness in her chest. Scott. His eyes met hers for a split second.

"MOVE!" Miriam shouted.

Sam didn't hear the whoosh, but she recognized the onerous zip as it ripped out. Miriam tugged her and she fell back at the same time that Scott dove to the side. Her knees locked as she watched the prowler twist and warp. The airgun, or whatever that weapon was, didn't just kill people from the inside. Whatever setting Backpack had increased it to could also destroy heavy equipment like it was thin aluminum.

Her brother pulled himself up and darted toward her. He said nothing, only grimacing as he briskly herded them toward the others. In the safety of the corner, their reunion with Yuri, Nas, and Kai was brief, hands clasped and backs thumped as they scurried down the perpendicular path.

"Won't ask why you're here, but it's damn good to see you. We're almost there!" Yuri pitched.

As they neared the next intersection, the six marines slowed.

Miriam glanced back and spoke between pants in a hushed voice. "What if there's more ahead?"

"We have to keep moving," Nas whispered loudly. "What if that one catches up?"

Sam focused on the intersection behind them. She could see the crushed vehicles, but there was no sign of Backpack. Or anyone.

"We can't run into the next street like we did before," Kai replied. "We got lucky."

Yuri bobbed his head and deliberated. "Dammit. Nas, you and me. We go first. Wait for our signal. Stay spread out. You saw what that thing did."

And then the two were off, moving toward the corner, then bounding from cover to cover methodically. Sam took the chance to turn to her brother, her eyes scanning over the gash above his eyebrow and the curtain of blood below. Scott leaned forward, resting his hands on his knees to catch his breath. After a couple seconds, he touched her hand before dropping it to clutch his side.

"Are you okay?" Sam had more questions, but her body ached—whatever had hit her in the back now seared with a burning pain—and everything she wanted to ask was too low a priority at that moment.

He nodded.

"How did you know where we were?"

He raised his wrist.

Right. Her location. Sam had forgotten.

"You're welcome," Scott rasped. He shot her a winced grin.

His face was pale under the sheet of blood and Sam reached out, but her hand stopped midway.

In the near distance, rifle fire ripped out, and Sam perked up with the others. Those were UMF-issued weapons. Reinforcements. She exhaled in relief before movement caught her eye. Yuri and Nas waved at them across the intersection.

Cross. Cross now.

Miriam stepped forward, then glanced back, her eyes flickering between Kai and the siblings. Before Sam could say anything, her brother nudged her.

Go. I'm right behind you.

She cupped his hand and squeezed, then moved next to Miriam. They both peeked around the corner to see an empty street, and with no signs of life, Sam and Miriam dashed through the open space to an abandoned van. When nothing happened, they darted to the next, leapfrogging their way across the intersection. A check behind showed Kai and Scott setting themselves in position, ready to sprint to the first vehicle.

Sam had just reached the next corner when ice flashed through her spine. She heard the whoosh and zip before metal crunched behind her. She turned, her muscles tightening. Down the block, Backpack stood, framed by a massive hole through what had previously been a shuttle bus. Her vision tunneled as she swiveled back to where her brother and Kai had last been. But they weren't at the corner. Her eyes drew to the crushed van and her heart dropped.

Ignoring her teammates' shouts and Miriam's flailing hands,

Sam's legs moved of their own accord. She ran into the open, directly toward the warped metal, and slid behind the broken frame.

Her heart dropped. No one was there.

Discombobulated, Sam pulled herself into a crouch, the sharp edges of the destroyed vehicle poking into her side.

Where were they? Where was he?

Shouting snapped her out of her distress and her head whipped back. Kai's dark hair swished around another vehicle parked further away, but closer to the corner where she had just been. They were safe. Kai and her brother had taken a different route; they had been faster than Sam thought. *She* had panicked. She had come back for no reason.

Footsteps slammed toward her, and blond hair flashed in the corner of her eye as her brother yanked her up a second time. Her feet stumbled but finally remembered their purpose as they sprinted into the open. Embarrassment jettisoned from her system as her legs pumped and she soon overtook him.

Her heart drumming in her ears, she registered another whoosh and zip too late. Heavy pressure slammed into her, and she tumbled forward into the gravel. White color flashed in her vision as her forehead smacked into the ground. She blinked, then blinked again, trying to push past the pain erupting in her skull. Sam groaned and tried to lift her head, but it was too heavy.

No. Something was on her. She was pinned.

She groaned again, and whatever was weighing her down shifted and rolled off her. Sam gasped for air and subsequently choked on dust and city ground.

"Get up," a voice rasped in her ear.

Her brother.

"Get up, Sammy."

The reserved name woke her already tired muscles and she whimpered. She found her hands, one of flesh and the other not, and tried to push off the ground. As she did, yelling and shouting burgeoned around her, but it was all a blur of noise. Her eyes focused, unfocused, and refocused on kitted marines, their weapons and armor as they poked in like a regimented hive, lancing out with rifle bursts at the faraway assailant with his pack weapon. Blood blossomed out across the Altered's chest and limbs, his body rigid, still standing with the anchor and bindings in place.

Her hand raised in front of her as the air around the Altered shimmered and displaced. More shouts rang out as the first layer of marines pulled back in time for the entire weapon and its attached corpse to implode then explode in a flameless ball.

Her ears popped again as a gust blew past her, but nothing as painful as before. She watched as a couple marines whooped before their squad leader pressed them forward, already moving toward whatever muffled explosions were still happening throughout the city.

Sam slumped on her hands and knees before remembering where she was and what the airgun did to people. Her breath quickened as she patted her torso in a sudden burst, but she was fine.

"It's over," she croaked in relief.

At least, this part was over. The reinforcements had come.

"It's over," she said again, a dry wheeze.

They had survived.

She shakily pushed herself up, the gravel digging into her knees. She turned painfully until she found Scott behind her in a replicated stance—also on his knees, though his head slumped with his haunches back.

"We have to go," she murmured.

He ignored her.

Sam touched his leg. "Scott."

He didn't look up, didn't move.

Her mouth went sour.

Though his face turned downward, she could make out little bubbles of blood in the corner of his mouth. Her breath caught, suspended in her chest. She dipped her head, trying to find his eyes, and when she did, chills surged through her, her entire being collapsing. Her voice cracked as she tugged at him—his hands, his clothes, his face—but those gray-blues were empty and dull below hooded lids.

A whimper turned into something worse, a harrowing wail as it exploded from her gut, her throat, and past her lips. Voices and movement swept around her, but Sam's world and everything in it had fractured.

Worse.

Shattered.

She didn't care about the attack.

She didn't care if she made noise.

She didn't care if she drew more enemies to her.

She registered nothing.

Hands pulled at her and Sam fought them and every waking moment of reality as she wrapped herself around him.

She refused to let go.

28

DEPLETION

THE SERVICE WAS DIRECT, over in less than fifteen minutes. Its punctual efficiency was a disguised slap to the face.

Miriam stood in the second row and tried not to focus on the fake scent of incense and flowers. They sat heavy, unpleasant in her nose and throat, a terrible weight added with each additional breath, a reminder of the room's formality and purpose.

As a solemn string of music hummed from the room's speakers, she clutched her hands at her beltline. An honor guard presented a thin metal box to the uniformed woman in front of her, and it trembled in passing before it was tucked away, clutched closer.

When Sam turned, her face was dry and devoid of emotion. The life and luster in her blue eyes were gone, and Miriam tried to catch them, to provide comfort, but the woman turned again, drifting automatically toward the chapel door. Miriam followed—the row filing out behind her—and she stared at the back of Sam's head, trying to project whatever warmth, whatever condolences she hadn't already mustered before. She nodded at familiar faces in the other rows, fellow Station SOG marines who had shown up in respect and solidarity. She noted the empty rows behind them; too many were grieving, tending to their own loved ones in the aftermath of the city attack.

What had the network said?

Hundreds of deaths. Countless more injured.

And Scott, Sam's big brother, guardian, partner, was one of them.

Gone.

Miriam shuffled forward. Behind them, the chapel personnel were already setting up for the next service. The swift and smooth operation was a sobering reminder of how many UMF memorials had already come and gone.

Past the door and into the foyer, Miriam's eyes flitted to Fox standing at the far side. His shoulders hunched and his hazel eyes turned away. His jaw feathered and he walked out the other set of doors before any of Echo could speak or gesture. Kai broke away from their procession line in pursuit, but Miriam pulled her attention back to Sam, who hadn't noticed.

A walking husk.

She placed a gentle hand on the small of Sam's back and the woman slowed, then came to a stop. Miriam raked her mind, searching for words of consolation, of sympathy, or reassurance, but nothing was enough. Her lips pinched together in frustration. Nothing she said or did could heal that grief.

"I need to go to the flat," Sam muttered. "To pack his..." Her voice dropped off.

Miriam swallowed, her own thoughts receding. Her heart ached for the woman and the despair laced in every string of her words and posture. "I'll go with you," she whispered.

Sam didn't protest or acknowledge her response, but she moved out the door. A cool gust swirled as they stepped outside, and sharp voices carried along with it. Sam stiffened, and Miriam froze with her as they located the source: a group of five individuals surrounded by several gray and black uniforms.

UMF sentries and escorts. Two officers among them. And over their heads and shoulders, colorful eyes honed in on Miriam and the others.

Altered. A mix of unarmored legionnaires and a Royal.

Sam and Scott's Royal.

The golden-eyed woman broke free from the group, easily evading the surprised yelp and outreached hand from a marine escort. The anger previously torched into her face extinguished as she crossed the path to meet Sam. "It's over?" she said, her voice somehow lyrical even strained. "They wouldn't let me in, they held us at the gate."

Sam's body tensed, more rigid than before, and Miriam shifted closer.

"Is he in there—" The Royal looked past them to the other service attendees, who only stared and gaped back. Redness edged around golden irises. "I want to see him."

The glossiness in Sam's eyes vanished, replaced with something smoldering, something dangerous. The woman's cheek twitched and Miriam braced herself, inching forward.

"Why are you here?" Sam's voice was taut and precariously quiet.

The Royal rocked back. "I want to see him. He meant—"

"You can stop pretending. He's..." Sam's lip quivered, and she clamped her mouth shut. She inhaled sharply through her nose before she repeated, "Why are you here?"

"You really believe... Do you know how much it hurt waiting for news? Not knowing? You didn't tell me. You could've, and you didn't. I know you're upset with me, but I at least deserve more than that."

Sam's hands clenched into fists and she jerked forward. "He went to you. He chose you."

The Royal shook her head. "He chose *you*, Sam. He'd always choose you."

For a millisecond, agony flashed across the marine's face.

Her mouth flattened before her upper lip curled. "So why didn't you stop him? You could've made him stay."

The Royal's eyes were pained underneath furrowed brows.

"Or maybe if I never brought him that day, maybe he wouldn't have ever met you. Maybe he would've stayed with me. Maybe…" Sam scoffed. Her chest heaved up and down before her mouth set in a frown. "Maybe he'd still be here."

To Miriam's surprise, the Royal shrank. "That's not—" The Altered stopped herself, then added in a small voice, "That's not fair."

"I told you to stay the fuck away from him!" Sam shouted, a finger stabbed in the air. She stepped forward, straining against Miriam's grip on her shoulder. "I told you, and you didn't listen. You tricked him like you did me, however the fuck you did it—"

"No—"

"He's my brother!" Sam threw her prosthetic out.

The Royal staggered back and clutched her chest. In a chain reaction behind them, the four legionnaires stepped forward like an expanding wall, and the UMF escorts moved to counter. Miriam swiftly positioned herself in between Sam and the Altered.

A delicate hand shot up and the Royal straightened. When she spoke, it was flatter than before. "I'm not here to fight. I abused your trust, and I am sorry—I hope we can fix that someday—but if you think you're the only one hurting, you're wrong." She sniffed. "I'd like to see him and I'm not leaving until I do."

Sam's upper lip threatened to curl, but the fight dulled out of her eyes. "Do whatever you want. You're good at that. It won't bring him back." She walked away.

Miriam glanced at the Royal, whose face struggled to hold its composure. She then hurried after Sam, leaving the others in their tense standstill. She matched the woman's pace and silence as they rounded the corner toward the base's main gate.

Now out of line of sight, the woman stopped and took a shuddering breath. Other than the previous outburst, it was the only visible sign of grief Miriam had seen from her since the attack, since Scott's death.

But then it was gone.

Miriam cupped the woman's face. "Hey, stop. You don't have to do this alone, okay? I'm here. We're all here for you."

Sam's eyes shut as she relaxed into Miriam's hands, but when they reopened, she straightened, and blue eyes dropped to the side.

Miriam wrapped her arms around Sam, pulling and anchoring her in a deep embrace, but it was one-sided. The woman made no effort to engage, but she also didn't resist. Her arms hung loose, one hand clutching the thin box from the service. Its corner poked into her thigh, but Miriam ignored the discomfort.

"I'm here, okay?" she repeated into Sam's shoulder.

The response came quiet through her hair. "I need to go..."

Rejection jabbed in Miriam's chest, but she understood. It wasn't aimed at her, and most importantly, it wasn't about her. "Whatever you need, tell me and I'll be there," she replied.

When she felt the tiniest of nods from the woman, she released her hold. Miriam watched as Sam shuffled away then disappeared beyond the next building.

She sighed. She didn't know what to do—what more or less she needed to do.

"Tan." Yuri rounded the corner. "She'll be okay."

It wasn't a confident statement. It was possibly something to reassure them, but Miriam wasn't reassured. Sam was resilient, but something pliable, something constantly battered, only needed one crack to finally break. And once shattered... How could one come back from that?

"I didn't know that Scott...that Altered... Did you?"

She made a curt nod.

Yuri muttered underneath his breath, then exhaled loudly

before gesturing back toward the chapel. "We should get back there."

Miriam hesitantly followed, her eyes narrowing as she returned. The Royal was nowhere in sight, and most of the SOG marines who had attended Scott's service had since vacated the area. However, three legionnaires remained and were in conversation with her Echo teammates. Though tense, it seemed civil, so far. Two familiar faces glanced at Miriam and Yuri as they joined the group.

"It was largely her push," Hadeon said.

"Who is the meeting with?" Krill asked.

"Your leadership, but your sentries held us up at the entrance." The senior tilted her head at their nearby UMF escorts. "They would not let her praetorian in. Just us. We did not know she was here for something else. This." She motioned to the chapel. "It is…"

"Unprecedented," Varya finished.

"Yes. But this is fate, our meeting again. We should go. We can continue without her."

"We?" Nas challenged. "I don't know about you, but what *we* is there? So many marines here, the people in the city, my family…"

"The Apostates did not just come here for you. They came for us, too. We are not your enemy," the Altered said. "And this, none of this, can stand. We worked together before; we can work together again."

◊

Miriam was tired, but in a different way from her usual restless nights. Between the attack, the funeral, an unexpected potential of alliance, Ana, everything, it all compounded together in a heaviness behind her eyes. Her feet dragged along the uneven pavement as she returned to her apartment.

The rubble in this sector had been cleared, erasing scorched vehicles and blast marks, but dark stains littered the street like scabs, and the relative silence of her street was jarring, unusual compared to the teeming life it had contained a week before. Wreaths made of cloth, wire, and other personal effects layered the sidewalk in a stretched altar to those who had fallen in the sector. Small holos staggered throughout, displaying faces of strangers and neighbors she faintly recognized.

Miriam ducked her head as she crossed the intersection into her building, and at her door, she grimaced—its bold red an affront to her senses. She rechecked her commcuff. No messages. None from Sam, at least.

When she entered, the apartment was dark except for a small triangle of light puncturing her bedroom from the en suite bathroom. Inside, the shower ran. Miriam stared at the black uniform jacket on the ground as she took her own off and let it hang over the counter.

"Sam?"

No response.

She moved forward, calling out another time. One foot set in front of the other until she carefully nudged the bathroom door open.

The air sucked from her lungs, and her heart shattered next.

Still clothed, Sam sat underneath the stream.

Curled.

Drenched.

Miriam hurried to turn off the shower and winced at the cold, whatever heat gone a long time ago. She pulled a towel and tried to coax Sam out, but the woman wasn't there. Not mentally.

She tried to enter the stall, but its small space and the woman's position made it impossible. It was only big enough for one person and her solitary grief.

Reaching as far as she could, Miriam draped the towel around the woman's wet and shivering shoulders. At her touch,

Sam choked in a silent sob, her tears gone, mixed down the drain, already recycling for the next stream.

Miriam tried to squeeze her body in again, but she couldn't. She wanted to wrap her arms, her entire being around Sam. Past her own guilt, her own shame, her own regret, Miriam wanted to shield this woman, her love, from all the anguish and despair.

But she couldn't.

29

———————————

PRIVATE MESSAGE
[RYAN TO RECKERT]

S. RYAN: You should've stayed with us.

S. RYAN: With me.

Message delivered.

PRIVATE MESSAGE
[RYAN TO RECKERT]

S. RYAN: Why did you leave me?

Message delivered.

The addressed account will deactivate in thirty (30) days. If this is in error, contact the System Administrator.

PRIVATE MESSAGE
[RYAN TO UNAVAILABLE]

S. RYAN: I can't do this without you.

Message undeliverable.

A problem occurred and this message could not be delivered. Check and confirm if the addressed account is correct.

PRIVATE MESSAGE
[RYAN TO UNAVAILABLE]

S. RYAN: I'll kill every single one of them.

S. RYAN: I promise.

Message undeliverable.

The addressed account is no longer in service.

PART 3

SUBCUTANEOUS

HYPERVENTILATION

"BODIES AREN'T EVEN cold yet, and you're telling us we have to train with those lab rats? It's bullshit."

Mumbles of agreement scattered around the front of the auditorium.

The team lead stood, spurred on. "They'll turn on us. But by then, we'll be too dead to tell you we told you so."

The Command officer at the podium folded his arms. "Are you finished? You're welcome to your own opinion, but until you time out of your contract with UMF, you're doing what Command says, and Command says we're working with Legion whether you like it or not."

"The attackers came from their camp!"

"Fucking hell," Miriam muttered.

She immediately regretted it. All eyes swung to her as the stage mic amplified her comment. She shrunk into her chair—pointless, considering she had nowhere to hide from the rows full of gray uniforms. She silently cursed Yuri for forcing her to take his spot in this meeting of team leads and seconds. Miriam still didn't know why she and Krill had to be on the stage.

"Pipe down, Dense," a team second called out from an

unfilled fourth row. "You've been reading a lot of network conspiracies."

Miriam stiffened at the name. She had never met the man, but Sam had been vocal in her disdain of her former company lead. She tongued her cheek, the embarrassment less now.

"Densaned reads?" another marine chimed in.

Chuckles scattered around the room before the officer firmly tapped the podium.

"Funny," Densaned said. "You're all hilarious. But—"

"But nothing. The full report is pending. UMF, SecTeam, and Legion already confirmed the attackers that infiltrated *from the coast* were *wunbies*. Turns out attacking a city in broad daylight gets you a lot of witnesses." The officer furrowed his brow. "Sit down. We're not here to discuss this. That's why we have a joint investigative team. They're doing their jobs, so stay in your lane and do yours."

Densaned sat, but not before he gestured aggressively at Miriam, Krill, and the two other SOG marines next to them. "If we're staying in our lanes, what are they doing here? SOG doesn't have a big enough ego as is? Do they have to steal our thunder, too?"

Miriam restrained herself from glaring at the man. She didn't want to be there, and she was positive Krill and the others hadn't planned on attending a Division brief. SOG had better things to do, including training maneuvers and preparations. The Apostates were pushing hard in the North— harder since the retaliation attack on Station City—and every day, humans were losing ground.

"Shit, Dense. What crawled up your asshole today?"

The lead twisted around to the same second in the fourth row. "You know exactly what, LaRussa, shut your wise-cracking mouth. You really want to pick up the dirty work that these soggers won't do themselves? You really want to listen to what they have to say?"

"Yeah, actually. I do. Especially if it means getting out of here so I can see my husband and kids before we ship out, but your yammering keeps pulling us away from the real issue." The second crossed her hands behind her head and leaned back. "Now if your little puckerhole is done jib-jabbing, I'd like to hear the rest of the brief."

On the stage, the Command officer coughed to the side. Miriam caught a thin smirk behind his hand before he refaced the group.

"Alright, settle down." He cleared his throat. "As I was saying, each of your companies has been assigned a Legion squad. If you haven't already met the senior, make sure you do. They aren't under your supervision, so don't piss them off by assuming they are." He pointed a finger. "Think of them as augmentation units. You're all leads and seconds for a reason. Figure it out. You'll be expected to learn each other's lingo and movements. Integrate their unit. When we ship up, they'll stay with you. They'll eat, sleep, drink, and exist with you. The more solid your communication is with your alties, the more solid we are across the battlefield. And *that* brings us to your peers." The officer gestured to the other Station SOG lead.

Razor-Charlie's lead stood with his teammate. "Afternoon. I'm Herrera and this is Bretner on intel and comms. Charlie deployed to Temunco shortly after Echo..." He dipped his chin to Krill and Miriam.

For their audience, it was a trivial gesture. Miriam doubted the leadership at this level cared about SOG and Echo's previous role in the South. The military, like everything else, was segmented—intentionally or not.

"We worked down there with some of you and BigInt to push the wunbies out and keep recovery efforts moving. About one, two months ago, the alties all but pulled out of the region." He snapped his fingers. "Gone. Like that."

In the back of the auditorium, a door opened and a shadowed figure entered. No one paid any mind, their focus on the stage.

"Did they go back home?" someone called out.

"No," another piped. "They moved to the North. That's what you're going to say, right?"

Herrera inhaled, about to speak before the same lead cut in.

"But how? BigInt said they didn't have transportation."

"I can answer if it's fine with you, Herrera," the newcomer called out as he walked forward.

Miriam and Krill straightened in their seats.

The Charlie lead nodded, and Jace hopped onto the stage—a quick wink in Krill's direction. "Sorry I'm late. I wasn't sure I'd make it," he said jovially. He sat on the edge of the platform. "Iniko Jace, Command Intel or BigInt, whatever you want to call it." He hovered a finger until he found the marine who had asked the last question. "And you're right, that faction of Apostates *didn't* have resources of that kind. A lot of the Altered in the South seem to have migrated over the years, settling into stolen farms, and most of Legion's assets at their garrison were destroyed. However, it seems like the Apostates picked up a bunch of goods when their coup succeeded in Arshangol. With what—" Jace twisted back to Herrera. "Shit, I don't want to steal your spotlight."

The lead chuckled and sat. "It's fine. Have at it."

Jace shrugged and continued. "Right. With what we assess is a communications-jamming device, our fleet went blind. We don't know exactly how, but most of the Apostates left. As much as we hope they're calling it a day, we're confident they're regrouping, distributing more forces in the North."

"I thought they wanted the South," a team second called out.

"They did. They still do. But something's gotta give. Razor-Echo—" He tossed his head at Krill and Miriam. "—complicated their big plan, whatever it was, and with Charlie, a bunch of you, and others helping, we assess with moderate confidence that the Apostates' southern campaign is on hold. They want the land, you see. The climate in the South is great and the soil's fertile, but it's isolated from the majority of the Altered territories. That region isn't any good if they're cut off from their new castle, so what's the next best thing?"

"The North," a handful of marines mumbled.

Everyone knew that the wunbies were pushing an offensive front there, that UMF had been sending reinforcements, but this was the first time the reason clicked.

Jace swung out his leg. "Our land's right there. Just a hop, skip, and a jump away."

"But the climate and soil ain't as good."

"No, but that's not going to stop them. They have the bodies and they have the tech. Each remediation plant, each water filtration factory they gain in the North only builds on their supply chain and capabilities."

"We're fighting them, holding them back."

The Command officer jumped in. "Yes, but there've been more reports of comm issues throughout the companies. We're going blind, deaf, and mute out there. And that's not including the limitations with the dark season."

"So let's get them," a team lead in the third row called out.

"We're trying. Alty scientists in Station are working with the city *and* our engineers to figure that out. Regardless, comms will be an issue for whatever movements we make. We heard from Legion that wunbies are moving heavy equipment in. We won't be able to break their lines if those jammers are up."

"Precision strikes," the same lead chimed in. "If Legion's working with us, they have weapons for that, right?"

Another lead responded, "They lost their outposts, they don't have anything. Does Legion even have weapons? Or is UMF issuing them ours?"

Jace looked back, his mouth pinched. Miriam knew what it meant—he had, after all, been a teammate long before his injury and transfer to BigInt. He knew something that he wasn't divulging. The intelligence warrant officer gave a light shrug.

"Let's put that aside for now," the Command officer said. "That tech isn't our only issue."

Faces contorted in confusion—Miriam's included.

"We came across something in the South, after the Apostates left. Bretner?"

Charlie's second nodded and engaged something on her cuff. The stage holoscreen lit up and Miriam studied the display of a cylindrical device and its bulbous tank. The auditorium erupted in murmurs, unsure of what they were looking at.

Jace rubbed the back of his head. "We're waiting for a full diagnostic back from the labs and confirmation from our new *allies* in Oldtown, but SOG teams encountered this device in the South. This thing poisoned at least ten thousand square meters of farmland before we figured out how to shut it off. Arsynthetic. It set back decades of process and remediation. We're lucky the chemical didn't spread into the river."

No one spoke.

"We also had a confirmed sighting from Ursus recon, one of these units being trucked in," the Command officer said, breaking the silence. "We think they're bringing more."

A second's hand raised in the first row. "Why? You said they wanted the land."

"They do—"

To Miriam's surprise, Densaned spoke up. "If they can't have it, they'll make damn sure we can't either."

◊

Miriam kicked at the floor as she waited to the side of the auditorium—well away from the stage. Most of the company leaders had left, but some stayed in discussion with Krill, Jace, and the officer at the front.

Charlie's second ambled past. "Did Liu get a hold of you? I think he was looking for more jabbers, said MED was running low."

"Yeah," Miriam responded. "I spared a couple. Should be good to go."

"Solid. See you up there, Tan." Bretner tipped her head and departed with her lead.

Miriam watched them go before she glanced back to see the others' conversation breaking up. She was relieved, eager to depart. Echo had little time before they flew back to Ursus, and this time, it'd be for an unknown period. They'd only come back to Station when they either succeeded or, worse, retreated. Miriam wanted to find Sam and savor their privacy before everything started—they'd have none with Echo, the other marines, and legionnaires. She was particularly wary around the alties. Even though she knew it was silly, there was a feeling they could somehow sense her secret and guilt.

There hadn't been a good time to tell Sam about Ana, not with the woman still fragile. Sam had been leaning heavily on Miriam since her brother's death, and though part of Miriam savored the growing physical and emotional attachment, she was terrified of how the woman would react when she did tell her. It was a conundrum she didn't want to face.

"You look upset."

Miriam's gaze lifted as Jace joined her. She scoffed. "Yuri could've rescheduled his meeting and Krill didn't need me here; I didn't even speak. You and the others covered everything. Definitely didn't need a stand-in second."

Jace chuckled. "I'm guessing he's getting an earful soon."

"Oh, he is. Count on it." Miriam toed the floor. "I didn't know you were back."

"Yeah, sorry, I would've messaged earlier, but it's been a blur since I returned."

A team lead patted Jace on the back and he excused himself, turning to chat with a few departing marines.

With Jace's attention elsewhere, Miriam frowned. She hadn't thought about it when he was briefing, but the warrant officer's presence in Station now gave her pause. Would Sam be happy to see him? Miriam hated the insecurity that followed. Did it matter? Sam had said she loved her—even if neither of them had broached that moment or those words again.

Miriam thought she loved Sam, but she was worried. Sam had latched onto her in Scott's absence. What if it wasn't love anymore, but a different kind of dependence? What if not talking about it had changed things? Miriam knew Sam spoke with Jace before the attack. Were they still talking? What if the two hit it off again?

If she told Sam about Ana...

Insecurity. What a bitch.

Jace shared parting words with the others and turned back to Miriam. "Sorry. It's been nonstop, but I *am* glad y'all are okay. From the attack, I mean." He folded his arms. "How's Valkyrie?"

Miriam rolled and twisted her wrists. "She's managing."

It wasn't entirely a lie. Sam presented fine to the others, but Miriam knew she was volatile.

"And you two..."

Her jaw clenched as she swallowed. She hadn't talked to Jace since she last saw him in Station almost five months before. Maybe Sam had said something in passing, or he had learned about their relationship a different way. Rumor intelligence, they called it. He *was* in BigInt.

"We're good," she said.

Jace unfolded his arms. "Good, that's good." He rubbed the back of his head. "I guess I'm surprised, Tan. Never figured you to...you know."

Me too, she wanted to say, but she didn't.

"I'm just surprised, but shit, don't mind me. You're lucky to have her, to have each other. You both are." His shoulder climbed in a half shrug. "Sometimes I wonder if Command hadn't sent me on that assignment, perhaps..." He gave Miriam a sad but encouraging smirk before Krill and the officer joined them.

She swallowed again. She didn't want to think about Sam with Jace or anyone else.

"Sorry about Densaned," the officer said. "He's a solid marine, but a bunch of these guys have gotten a bit mouthy since the alties came on. We already have enough marines in the brig, suspended, or manning the rubber gun squad. If we weren't hurting for resources and bodies..." He waved his hands. "I have to run back. LOGS is having issues again, of course. Thanks for helping out."

Miriam echoed a farewell before the officer hurried off. She followed Krill and Jace as they walked slowly to the exit. Although Miriam wanted to leave, to move faster, she matched their casual pace. Neither of them seemed to want to return to their preparations.

"So what can you tell us?" Krill clapped their former teammate on the back.

Jace chuckled. "It's been pretty ridiculous. Apostate numbers are surging and the North is feeling it. Bad. They've pushed well past FOB Domovoy. UMF's had to evacuate more towns, but you know how the northerners are. Stubborn. Too many pensioners staying behind and a shit ton of mercs moving up."

"Charonites?"

"No, but that's not a surprise. Regardless, the ones who stay stall for one or two days, but that's it. What can bands of old marines and mercs do against People's Army Apostates? And if they're lucky enough to face the stimmed factions, well, they're ripped apart... Literally."

Miriam winced as they exited the auditorium and stopped.

"There's one bright side to all of this, at least."

She gave Jace a look. Everything he had relayed sounded like they were losing.

"I don't think Kartik or the Apostates realized their stunt in Station would create this kind of unity. You have to give the Royals some credit. They were the first ones to reach out, offer doctors, scientists, intelligence, you name it." Jace scoffed and fished out his nicosynth device from a pocket. He took a long inhale. "Guess the Altered here realized that if we're gone, they're fucked. We're both reaching across the divide now. Kartik pissed us both off."

That was all well and good, but she had seen the alties' weapons and the damage they did. If that was what humans and exiled Altered were up against, she wasn't sure they had any advantage or favoring odds. "Do we even have the numbers? We still don't have the arsenal, Jace."

"The generation before us figured it out. We stopped the last Sovereign's reign of terror before."

"No, the Royals stopped him, and we survived. And barely." Miriam huffed. "We were babies when it happened. And I wouldn't call what we were doing before *living*."

Jace's lips pinched together, the same expression from before.

"You're not telling us everything. Spill it," she said.

He took another long drag on his device, then sighed. "Everyone has secrets."

"Jace," Krill urged.

"The Altered have kept things—a lot—under wraps. Let's just say I heard Command's giving Legion clearance on airspace movement."

"Airspace? They don't have airships. I thought all the alties in Station came over by sea."

Jace shrugged. "Look, I don't know where they've stored their assets this whole time. Nas won't shut up about his theory, but the more we find out, I don't know. Maybe Baby Echo's onto something. The Altered apparently've been hiding ships, weapons, and equipment from us."

"Hell," Miriam breathed. It sank in. "Could they have stopped the attack?"

"I wouldn't accuse them of that. The Altered here are *pissed*. Some of them might be excellent actors, but I really don't think they knew. We figured there'd be retaliation after our attempt on Kartik, right? But at this scale and in Station City? They took some hits that day, too." Jace tapped the tube of his nicosynth device to his lower lip. "Regardless, bright side, remember? Looks like we have friends. It's temporary, but still, an alliance."

His cuff buzzed, and he glanced down. "Shit, I've gotta go. Too bad we don't have time for another meal at Tsutsumi's, eh? Think we knew how good we had it then?" He chuckled, but not convincingly.

Miriam's hand thrust out. "Wait. Last thing. Someone mentioned precision strikes earlier."

Jace's brow raised.

"SOG. We're the precision strikes, aren't we?"

He gave a weak grin and bobbed his head stiffly. "Gotta restore comms to progress and gotta take out the poisoners to aggress. I'm sure y'all will figure it out. See you on the other side." The man trotted off with a wave.

Miriam digested his response and watched him leave. Krill's face tightened. After a pause, she broke the silence, attempting for something lighter. "Are we heading up with Elly?"

"No," Krill replied. "Just confirmed with Command. We're flying out with some equipment first thing tomorrow. Elly's transporting a company out in the next days."

Miriam watched the traffic and movement around the base —marines hustling with a few white legionnaire uniforms scattered about. It was still a strange sight, but frankly, also a comfort. She glanced over at the lead. "You should spend time with her."

"Yeah. That's the plan."

Their eyes followed a series of prowlers as they rumbled by, their cargo bed filled with boxes and crates.

"I'll send another reminder to the team, but be at the airfield with full gear and all the ammunition we can carry. Let's not burden Ursus and LOGS if we can help it." In a softer voice, Krill added, "You should spend time with Valk, too."

She bit her lip.

"Don't be late. Pass it along, yeah? How is she?"

Miriam hesitated before she responded. "Better."

If better meant a disconcerting quiet and focus. She thought of Fox, who she hadn't heard from in a while either—he hadn't been at their usual spots.

Miriam shook her head. "Actually, no, she's not. I don't know if she's in the right mind for this. She hasn't had enough time to process."

"It's been more than a month."

She huffed. That was callous, and Krill knew it.

He sighed. "How do you know?"

"She's..." Miriam didn't know how to put the feeling into words. How could she explain the woman's uncanny compartmentalization, Sam's ability to shut off what Miriam imagined was an overwhelming amount of grief? The woman had lost her brother, who had been there her entire life. Miriam was an only child, but she felt she could empathize, if only fractionally. Miriam had Yuri and Echo. If she lost any of them or Sam...

Regardless, in between their physical distractions, there was something in Sam's eyes that made Miriam uncomfortable. There was a sharp edge that seemed ready to combust and blaze a fire that would only be extinguished at someone's death: Sam or another's.

Lines etched into the team lead's face. "What do you want me to do? We're heading out and we're already down one."

"I don't know, Krill."

He scoffed. "Who's talking right now? Are you telling this to me as team medic or are you telling me as her girlfriend?"

"Does it matter?"

"Yes. If you're telling me she's not fit for duty, if she needs to be—"

"No." Miriam squeezed her eyes shut then rubbed them with a thumb and finger. She'd be personally plunging the knife into Sam's back if she forced the woman onto the sidelines. For a medical reason, no less, especially after all that time and recovery. But what was worse? A physical or emotional wound? "Shit, I don't know."

"Is she a liability to the team? To the mission?"

"No." Miriam's voice cracked.

A direct liability to the team or mission? No. Sam was a liability to herself.

When she didn't add anything further, Krill sighed again. "We can't do this without her; we barely have the numbers as is. Look, if you're telling this to me as a medic, if you really want me to, I'll go and tell Command myself, but you know we need her."

"I know. Forget I said anything."

He stared at her with a grimace, but they didn't discuss it further as they split ways.

Now alone, Miriam checked her cuff and found Sam's location on base—a point in the outer sections where access was more flexible for non-military personnel, only overfill annexes and expansion buildings there. She sent a message that she was on her way, and by the time she turned the block corner, her legs were warm from the walk.

As she neared and made to cross the street to the old warehouse, Miriam made out the back of Sam's head inside the bay doors. The woman conversed with a legionnaire, and beyond them other white uniforms milled about, busy moving and building equipment.

You're lucky to have her.

She paused at Jace's words in her head.

Miriam watched Sam in her bout of socialization—unusual, but a relief. She was too far away to know what they were talking about, but even if it was about their next operation, it was still a step forward. Any movement, no matter how trivial or small, was good for Sam. It was good for them. Miriam's stomach fluttered and her chest warmed.

She *was* lucky.

"Tan?"

A nightmarish anvil plunged into her gut, whatever lightness she had felt now gone. Miriam glanced at Sam again then turned, a frown warping her face. She recoiled as the red-haired woman leaned in for a greeting kiss on the cheek, her floral perfume lingering.

"What are you doing here?"

Ana's brows peaked, but she didn't pull back. "Ouch. Hello to you, too. It's been a long time. Thanks for ghosting me." She draped an arm over Miriam's shoulder.

Miriam shrugged the contact away as her eyes shot to the warehouse. She took a few steps at an angle where she was out of view from the open doors. "Sorry," she blurted, "but what are you doing here? How did you get into the base?"

"Wow." Ana whistled and reclosed the distance. "I can't walk and stretch my legs?"

Miriam took another step back. "Ana."

The woman motioned down the street. "For your knowledge, I'm here for the hospital. UMF's hosting a symposium with the alty physicians and community. I'm surprised you don't know about it, your mother said she messaged. There's a lot of UMF and staff from Station General. I thought you might also be around."

Miriam shook her head and strained her eyes to where the woman had gestured. It was a way off, but she could make out several individuals—some in scrubs and coats—loitering outside another bland gray two-story building.

"I'm a team medic. I'm not important enough to be included with BigMED."

"Don't say that. You're important." Ana pulled out her nicosynth device and took a deep inhale.

Miriam shifted uncomfortably.

"I was worried when you didn't respond after that night—more so after the attack. I know you play hard to get, but it would've been nice for you to message, shit, to let me know you were at least breathing."

Dammit. Miriam turned back to the warehouse, unable to see into it anymore. She recoiled when Ana's fingers brushed her jaw.

"I miss you."

Coward.

Miriam pushed the woman's hand down and took a deep breath. She lowered her voice to a hiss. "Stop. You can't do this. I'm sorry. For all of this." She exhaled. "That night was a mistake. I should've never reached out, never involved you."

It was Ana's turn to flinch. The woman's face contorted. "No, it wasn't," she said, too loud. "Is this about the blonde I've seen you with? It's not a big deal, Tan. I know you keep things unencumbered, no strings attached. It's okay."

Miriam fanned her palms out. "No. It's not—" She stopped and started again. "Ana, she isn't like—"

You, she almost said.

Miriam steeled herself. "Our arrangement is over. *Was* over. I should've done this a long time ago, and I didn't."

Ana's dark eyes widened then narrowed.

"I made a huge mistake. I'm sorry, I should've never involved you."

"We're not a mistake."

Miriam cringed. She wished the woman would lower her voice. "There is no *we*." Her voice firmed, and she touched Ana's elbow, trying to guide her in the other direction. "I'm with Sam. I..." She paused. It was so certain. Miriam should've never doubted, should've never done so many things. "I love her."

The woman's body stiffened and pushed forward. "No. No, you don't. We've known each other longer, Tan. I've always been here."

Ana reached out, but Miriam grabbed her wrists and locked them to the woman's sides. They were dangerously close, and maybe in a previous life, Miriam would've felt differently, but now, only guilt and disgust wrapped around her. She wished she'd never messaged Ana, never left the apartment, left Sam. Hell, she should've done this a long time ago.

"I'm sorry, I'm choosing her. I *choose* her."

A heavy breath escaped the woman's lips as if Miriam had stabbed her. Ana's dark eyes flickered, and Miriam searched them, looking for any indications of an outburst. In the end, the woman's gaze stilled, the fight extinguishing as tears welled up.

The woman pulled away and let out a shuddering exhale. "You really know how to hurt people," she whispered before she stormed away.

Miriam held her breath, watching the other retreat. When the red hair was far in the distance, she waited a few more seconds to make sure, then released a long sigh. Though Miriam felt a lingering heaviness in her chest, something had also lifted. She should've done this much earlier, should've done a lot of things differently, but it was a step in the right direction. If she could say it out loud to someone else, she could surely say it to Sam.

She had said it, and it was real.

She loved Sam.

She chose Sam.

34

———————

DEPENDENCE

"IT IS healthy to discuss these things. There is no life without death. Your brother was a warrior, and he had a warrior's death."

Sam's mouth twisted. Altered terrorists killed her brother in a cowardly attack. Scott's death wasn't a warrior's death; it was a *pointless* death. Varya didn't understand. They had fought on the same side before, but the legionnaire didn't know her, didn't know who Scott was to her, and didn't know how she felt. Every emotion mixed with a sucking emptiness, but worst of all was the unexpected numbness—never enough to help but always enough to despise herself. Losing her arm had unintentionally prepared Sam, and though losing Scott was far worse, any tears had all but dried up.

Her brother had called her resilient before. She didn't want to be resilient.

Sam averted her eyes away from Varya's heightened stare and swallowed the knot in her throat. Further in the warehouse, white uniforms hauled containers off a UMF flatbed while others unpacked, setting up the frames of workstations. Kai's dark hair bobbed behind a set of boxes with another legionnaire.

"I will stay with Hadeon for this fight, and if I do not meet death herself, I go a separate way after."

Sam's eyebrows bunched. "You're leaving Legion?"

Could legionnaires leave? Did they have contracts like UMF?

"Yes, and no. It is a strike team open to those who are willing and able. I thought you would be interested."

Confusion and offense rippled across Sam's face. After everything, her arm, medical probation, Miriam, her brother, the last thing she would do was leave SOG. "What are you talking about? Is it a joint op between UMF and Legion?"

"No. There are necessary actions military prowess cannot be responsible for. In uniform, you and I are bound by rules. This team is unbound."

"So you're abandoning this for what? Mercenary work?"

"I cannot speak more to it—"

Her irritation sharpened, and Sam scowled. More secrets.

"—but there will be no rules of engagement to limit us. It is necessary to fight these abominations. And do not insult me, Valkyrie. I am not abandoning anyone or anything. The Royal family and Legion understand the work needs to be done. Your politicians and military may as well."

Sam scoffed. "You don't need humans."

To her surprise, Varya smirked—or what she thought passed as one. "Perhaps not, but I have seen you and your kind fight. There is a fire in you. You survive." The legionnaire's hand— still missing two fingers from their time in the South—rested on top of her sheathed dagger. "And you hate this filth as much as we do. Together, we can hurt them in ways the uniform cannot. We have established that we bleed the same—it is just a matter of who bleeds out first." Her grin curved into something predatorial.

A tendril of Sam's anger reached out, wrapping around Varya's words and the opportunity there. It was freedom to fulfill her promise to Scott, to kill every Apostate she could find.

Varya's ears twitched and angled toward the warehouse doors. Sam turned, the hair on her neck rising, but she saw and heard nothing but the empty street outside, the compound's ambiance, and the city noises beyond it.

"What is it?"

Another attack? Something else?

The legionnaire's head tilted, but she said nothing.

"Varya."

"Your medic is here."

"Miriam?" Sam relaxed. She glanced at the unnoticed message on her commcuff. Warmth flickered in her chest, but a flurry of familiar, discordant feelings immediately followed, twisting her stomach. How could she feel this comfort when her brother was gone?

Sam stepped back, opening her angle to the street, then froze. It *was* Miriam, but she wasn't alone. A red-haired woman stood too close, too intimate, with one arm over Miriam's shoulder. It was the same woman who had been in Miriam's apartment months before. Sam's mind went blank. Her stomach turned and the cesspool of emotions spiraled up, insecurity at its brim. She forced herself to move and divert her eyes as guilt heaved up like bile. Sam swallowed it back and tried to control the tempest inside her.

Miriam was with *her* and Miriam had been there at her side.

Sam trusted Miriam.

"I should go," she forced out.

Varya's face evened and her full attention returned. "Think about what I said. If we live through this, and if you are interested, find me after."

Sam ruminated on their conversation as the legionnaire left, distracting herself and suppressing the storm still brewing inside her. At least Varya was confident she'd live through their next step: UMF and Legion's first coordinated attempt to drive their shared enemy back. If she couldn't decipher anything else from their conversation, Sam would take that.

She counted out several more breaths before she moved toward the open doors and stepped out—the other woman was gone. Miriam's back remained to her as Sam approached, and when she touched her hip, Miriam startled.

"Shit, you scared me. How long have you been—" The woman's eyes flitted around. She composed herself then suddenly pulled Sam into an embrace.

Though surprised at the unexpected display of public affection, Sam relaxed into Miriam. The storm inside her stilled. For those seconds, the anger, insecurity, and grief dropped away, and she pulled further in, sheltering and latching onto warmth and tenderness.

I love you, she wanted to say. *I'm in love with you.*

But she didn't. Miriam was the only thing keeping her afloat, and she didn't want to risk puncturing her liferaft.

"Everything okay?" Sam mumbled into Miriam's hair instead.

Arms tightened around her before the medic's head moved in the crook of her neck—neither nod nor shake.

They remained entwined before a pair of uniforms walked by, and Sam pulled away. For a second, she thought hands lingered in protest and her heart swelled.

Miriam sighed. "Can we go?"

"Kai's still inside. I think they're setting her up with demo gear."

"Ah. Like a kid with sweets. I imagine she's more thrilled to be working on her diplomatic skills." The woman sighed again. "Did you get what you needed? Or were you just accompanying her?"

Sam huffed. "She dragged me."

Miriam laughed softly. "Of course."

"I ran into Varya," Sam said. She briefly explained what the legionnaire had told her, and now away from the conversation, she was flattered—giddy at Varya's consideration.

But her smile fell when Miriam tensed.

"This isn't with UMF or SOG? That sounds really dangerous. You're not actually thinking about it, are you?"

"She wasn't really recruiting me," Sam tried to reassure her, but irritation spurred within her. Part of her wanted the opportunity to hurt, *really* hurt the Apostates.

"You're with us, with Echo now. You're with me."

Her eyes locked onto Miriam's and her rage was smothered. *You're with me.*

Those words tethered her.

"Sam."

"Okay," she said after a beat.

Relief visibly flushed through Miriam's face, and Sam's eyes grew as the woman reached for her again. Warmth swelled within her, hope and love shimmering through the hurricane of shit. Miriam wanted her. Sam belonged with Miriam.

"Thank you!" Kai's voice chimed loudly. The engineer tried to raise a hand over her shoulder as she approached, two containers stacked between her arms. "Sorry I took so long!"

Sam took a box from her.

"Thank you, Valk." Kai smiled. "Oh hi, Tan! I thought you were at MED."

Miriam shook her head. "Covering some team lead meeting for Yuri. But anyway, it's over now."

"Did they talk about this new Team Suicide?"

"What?" Miriam's forehead crinkled, but then something clicked and her eyes fell on Sam. "This is what... Are they calling themselves that?"

Kai laughed. "No, I don't think so, but can you imagine? I overheard some legionnaires talking about it. Even if it were actually called that, I doubt it'd keep the complete crazies from joining. Those guys seem to think it's extreme, and well, if *alties* think that..." Kai continued talking, unaware the others had stopped listening.

Next to her, locked gazes held their own silent conversation. Miriam's lips parted and formed around Sam's name. She gestured her head in an infinitesimal but significant movement, and Sam forced a small, reassuring smile in return. Rage and fury clawed inside her, wanting the opportunity to be freed and untethered, but she forced the demons down.

Promise me, Miriam mouthed.

She nodded and silently promised. Sam belonged with Miriam.

The medic's shoulders lifted then dropped in a heavy exhale. Miriam's mouth curved into a gentle smile, and every vessel in Sam's body warmed.

Kai hefted her box onto her shoulder. "Well, knowing us, we'll probably give them some fancy new acronym. Everyone loves acronyms."

◊

Sam took in the dance of activity in the hangar and surrounding tarmac. Uniforms worked around two stout cargo airships that took up half of the indoor space, their noses sticking out in the open. She stood to the side, watching and recounting the previous hours as her Echo teammates performed their last checks or made small talk with other nervous marines. Sam had said goodbye to Miriam's apartment, breathing in its cinnamon and spiced scents and drawing her fingers along the love seat as if she could brand those sensations into her memory. Echo didn't know when they'd be back, and though Miriam would be with her, Sam wanted to capture as much of home as she could.

Her muscles grew restless as the minutes and seconds counted down. Prosthetic fingers dug into her skin and muscle underneath. This was the first time she was returning to Ursus.

And what was she returning to? She had teammates there—friends maybe, although they were arguably Scott's friends—but she wasn't close to them like she had become with Echo. For Sam, the thing that mattered the most was gone.

Scott was gone. Dead.

And he wasn't coming back.

Her brother's apartment likely sat unbothered, alone, and gathering dust. Or maybe it had been packed, cleaned, and released—she didn't know. Sam didn't have the courage or strength to find out. It was like her studio in the medical sector, which still had another month or so left on its contract. The last time she stopped by was after the service. She thought about the thin box she had left on her nightstand, the silver chain Scott had always worn inside.

Sam took a shallow breath then slung her carbine over her shoulder, where it clacked against her brother's long rifle. She adjusted her pack, its tight and digging straps a reminder of the indefinite time she and Echo would be gone. Sam glanced to her right, at the emptiness past her prosthetic arm and shoulder. A different phantom pain reared its head, a lasting asymmetry. She let her anger unleash and burn from her chest into her neck, and it felt good in the moment.

Until a firm but gentle hand settled on the small of her back.

"Ready?" Miriam whispered.

It was a harmless question, but her rage spiked and a sharp retort whipped to the tip of Sam's tongue.

Fortunately, before it could escape, Krill jogged toward the team. "Pilots are ready to go!" he shouted over the thrum of engines, workers, and other machinery. "The crew's doing their final walkaround. Let's get on board!"

"They won't leave without us," Nas called out. "We're important cargo! Just as important as that stuff." He threw his chin at the prowlers, rabbits, and provision crates waiting to be loaded.

Kai rolled her eyes but led the team's procession toward the closest airship.

Sam exhaled, grateful for the interruption and motion. She kneaded a finger into her left forearm until it hurt. Between routine, distractions, and Miriam, she had muzzled her grief and anger as best she could, but with the anticipation of returning to the North... None of her teammates deserved her unfair cesspool of emotions, especially not Miriam.

When the others filed up the ramp and staked out their seats along the walls of the ship's open belly, Miriam pulled Sam aside.

"You okay?"

Sam tensed, irritation rippling through her. She looked past Miriam and focused on her breath, letting the surge of emotion drain as she watched the line of city buildings far beyond the airfield. She hitched both her carbine and her brother's rifle higher on her shoulder.

"No one will judge you if this is too much, Sam. I know going back, it's a lot—"

"I'm fine."

Sam winced at the shortness of her response and clenched her jaw. It was a lie, but she was as ready as she'd be. Sam had been ready this whole time, despite all the administrative bullshit UMF had put her through. She wouldn't sit out this fight and she wouldn't sit to the side, useless, anymore.

Miriam's lips pinched. "Okay," she said, unconvinced. "Tell me what you need. When we get up there, if you want—"

"I want blood."

Sam loved Miriam, but she didn't want to hear the rest of what the woman had prepared. She knew Miriam was worried, but Sam didn't want the concern or the sympathy anymore. She was committed. She wanted to squeeze, hack, and slice the life out of their enemies for what they'd done to Scott—done to her. Sam was going to keep her promise to her brother. She'd kill every single one of them.

VECTOR HAV-Z5 SCOPE
[SETTINGS]

Sync Unsuccessful

Device cannot connect to S. RECKERT.
Reset the account and respective devices and sync again.

CANCEL

Delete User Profile

Confirm deletion of User S. RECKERT.

CANCEL

Add New Profile

S. RYAN

Sync Successful

35

DEHYDRATION

MIRIAM PRESSED her fingers to the tender skin around her eyes. Exhaustion clung to her, but she ignored the weight of her nightmares, letting her focus slip to Sam. Next to her, the woman's muscles and ligaments corded while her prosthetic fingers dug into her skin. Bruising dotted Sam's exposed forearm, and Miriam grimaced. She knew her glances weren't as subtle as she hoped—the reconnaissance specialist caught every flicker of attention. But how could Miriam stop noticing? Stop caring?

Shadows stretched and shrunk with the street and building lights as the two weaved through the outpost. Despite Ursus's reconstruction, Sam still seemed to know the paths less traveled, and Miriam followed her without question. She caught the woman's fingers extending and brushing a wall or a post, but each touch only lasted a brief second at most.

Around them, the compound buzzed with a frenetic energy. Sizable trucks and personnel moved to and fro. It'd be the same outside the perimeter; Miriam had seen the rows of tents and modular containers housing thousands of evacuees. Most northerners would stay as a compromise until they were forced to do something else. Where else were they supposed to go? A radiation zone sat a mountain range away to the northeast and another, kilometers to the south. This was their home. It was Sam's home.

By the time the two entered the training classroom, Sam's lips were clamped and pale. Miriam placed a reassuring hand on the woman's back, and Nas and Kai arrived shortly after. Nas pulled a chair, turned it around, and sat, immediately slouching.

"Hell," Kai said, "you two are fast. We left before you."

Miriam shrugged.

Nas smirked. "Yeah, thought you'd want to get a quick—"

Her eyebrows raised, but Krill and Yuri walked through the door, cutting him off.

The intelligence specialist leaned forward, his palms on his thighs. "Was it an eventful brief? Should we be sad we weren't included?"

"Hush." Kai flicked at the air and sat herself on the edge of the nearest table. "There are too many people and too many moving parts."

"Right, we're just one tiny cog of the big dysfunctional machine."

Yuri chuffed. "The brief would've never ended if you were there."

"Ha-ha. So what impossible stunt are we attempting this time, boss? Are we the cannons or the fodder?"

Krill ignored him and took off his jacket. "The others are coming over. It'll be easier to say it all at once." He then glared pointedly. "Be good."

"What are you talking about? We're always good. Isn't that why we get all the crazy shit?" Nas leaned back with his hands behind his head. "Why not wait a bit more? We apparently have all the time in the world. No rush while the wunbies keep advancing forward."

But wait they did, although it wasn't long before Razor-Charlie and Razor-Foxtrot strolled into the room, followed by Hadeon, Varya, and six unarmored legionnaires. The classroom was soon crowded, with each team naturally segregating into their own corners. Miriam nodded at her colleagues, although she noticed a handful of unknown faces in their Razor ranks. Her jaw clenched.

Fresh SOG marines. *Replacements.*

She gazed at her team. Krill, who had only been promoted in the last year, was now hardened, lines throughout his face. Yuri, whose chipper demeanor was consistent since they were children, was still Yuri, although his optimism had dulled around the edges. And seeing him now, Miriam hated to admit it, but their friendship had taken a hit, their talks less frequent. Nas had always been nosy and chatty—more so since Fox's decline—but there was a bitter callousness now, and Kai, sweet, diplomatic Kai, was still recovering from Fox's absence. Beyond the changes, Echo was the most intact team of the entire group. Sam was a new face, but she was no stranger. She had years of SOG experience.

The leads gravitated into the center of the room along with Hadeon.

Herrera from Razor-Charlie spoke first. "Let's skip the pleasantries. Gather round." He nodded at Bretner, who projected a holodisplay that stretched up to the ceiling. A regional map flickered its blue hues around stony faces. "As we speak, wunbies are moving on the settlements past the range. This place isn't like Station, it's sprawling and vast. Ursus and the surrounding towns are naturally protected by the mountains and the radioactive zones to the northeast."

"Alties can—" Nas started in a whisper, but his mouth smacked shut after a swift kick from Yuri.

"BigInt and Legion say the wunbies have taken over towns south of the big peninsula. They have supply lines through

Woodchik, and with that, they're bound to control the entire northwest. We know enemy movement will come from those points. Ursus says it'll take time for the wunby camps to move, but as it's mostly marsh and farmland, we expect they'll reach the outskirts of Koyukon and Susinuska by midday. Command's placing an entire division at each town and companies on the other ridges. If we lose this front, we've lost Ursus and everything else."

He gestured at different highlighted points south of the peninsula—what looked to be towns. "Recon and sensors showed full caravans and heavy machinery moving into three different sites. BigInt is confident these are communication jammers and Blightbringers."

Miriam exhaled along with a handful of other marines. She hadn't known the poison device had such an ominous name.

"Spartans will assist Titans to take on Sites One and Two, respectively. We have the closest and smallest one, Site Three." A dot appeared over a small town named Sunali. "Don't let that fool you; this town's more remote than the others, but it's a possible back door to Ursus. Command moved two companies to the range just in case. Titans wanted to spare us a team, but Ursus SOG is already spread thin. Everyone here has the surveys, maps, and reports already, but I understand we have a marine who knows the area?"

The group turned to Sam, and she gave a curt nod.

"Good. If you have anything to add, bring it up."

She didn't.

Herrera scanned the faces around him. "Each SOG team will drive across the range via prowler, and once we're past the companies, we split through the river. Except for…"

The leads turned to Hadeon, but she and the legionnaires said nothing.

In the pause, one of the new Foxtrot marines piped up. "So we take the river, hoof it to the wunby-infested camp without being seen or heard *and* without night cover or storm? And the closer we get to those jammers, the blinder we get. All of this while the alties eye-fuck us. Am I getting this right?"

The marine's comments invited Nas's own. "Oh no, they'll proper fuck us. Don't forget we have to disengage the devices with a camp of possibly stimmed wunbies around us." He pointed a finger up. "And then we have to get back out. Alive, preferably."

A handful of marines chuckled.

The Foxtrot replacement nodded at the Altered. "Heard Legion has fancy, secret airships stashed away. They can't swoop in, blow it up? Bing bang, done and done?"

Miriam rolled her eyes. Typical marine, solving things by blowing stuff up.

"No," Foxtrot's new lead, Marshall, said. His eyes flashed irritation and disappointment. "We're not risking any of the arsynthetic getting in the water or in the soil. Not until those devices have been secured."

"So, we're each going to babysit the blight monsters until backup comes. There's a lot of what-ifs here. I don't like it."

"You don't have to like it, Mitch." Marshall glared at his teammate. "It's happening. This is the job."

The marine looked around the room. "Three teams versus who knows how many wunbies with superior weaponry. It's a shit job."

"If you don't want to be here, say it. I'm sure the outpost brig has space. If you're not up for this, strip your diamond tab and I'll give it to someone else who won't let the team down instead."

Mitch shrunk back as his hands shot up. "I'm all in, I'm just making sure we understand the whole situation."

Krill cleared his throat. "We won't be facing an entire camp. Legion, along with Division and its companies, will coordinate maneuvers at the same time to draw wunby attention. Once that happens, it's game on and we secure our sites. If any of those Blightbringers does its job, it doesn't matter." He folded his arms. "And it won't be just us Razor teams. Hadeon?"

With her name called, the senior legionnaire stepped forward. A handful of the new SOG marines flinched, but Hadeon didn't seem to care. "While you secure the machines, my team and I will disengage their main communications."

Marshall nodded. "For the camp."

"Yes, but we can shut off their long-range capabilities as well."

Miriam's eyebrow lifted with Nas's. This was a surprise update. Though UMF and Legion had joined in an alliance after the Station City attack, the interchange of information was still strained. The entire operation felt drawn together last minute, but it was the best they could do when they were moving on their enemy's timeline.

"That's…good news," Herrera said.

And important.

"Anything else we should know?"

"We fly in."

Faces scrunched in the three corners of the room, although Miriam noticed Nas's did the opposite. His eyes grew then slanted with a smug grin.

Charlie's lead rubbed the skin between his brows. "Even if we have airships, the instruments will fail. Nothing can fly with those jammers up."

The senior legionnaire thumbed the knife handle at her side. "You depend too much on technology."

The others watched her, waiting for more, but she said nothing.

"Fine. But if you're not there, if any of us fail at our jobs, this whole thing crumbles. Not just for us, but for you, too. We'll lose."

Behind Hadeon, Varya's chest puffed out and the tension in the room suddenly thickened.

Krill stepped forward. "We'll all do our part."

Hadeon looked past her nose at the marines, but her face softened into something less stony than before. She nodded once.

Miriam exhaled and looked around the room again. Three Station SOG teams plus Hadeon's legionnaires against a camp of wunbies and whatever arsenal they'd have. Charlie's lead was right. If they failed, the North was lost, and it wouldn't be long before Station City was next. Humans needed the land and its bounty to survive, but the wunbies were also desperate for its potential. Desperation made people dangerous, and both sides were desperate.

◊

The issue with plans was that they fell apart. With how everything was going, Miriam should have expected it. However, the slap of reality was harsher when it came in the darkest hour after Razor-Charlie and Razor-Foxtrot had already departed the outpost.

Nas's pacing footsteps added an offbeat to the tapping of Sam's alloy fingers, a sad percussion of restlessness. "We should've left by now," he groaned from the other side of the prowler.

"The whole point is to not be seen," Kai said, prone in the back seat. "The route's compromised. We'd be screwed before we touched water."

"I knew we should've gone at the same time as the others. Staggered, my ass."

"Krill said they'd figure something out."

"Yeah, well, we should've left by now."

Miriam shot him a glare as he passed. They all knew the situation; he didn't need to repeat it. The longer Echo stayed in Ursus, the later they'd hit the river. Though no one could avoid the North's dark season, they had planned on traversing the longest section in the short period of daylight. No one wanted to navigate that dangerous route in the darkness, especially with no comms or working gear. Of course, UMF also had contingencies to proceed the mission with two Razor teams instead of their planned three. It'd be more difficult—near impossible—but the SOG marines would find a way.

Miriam pushed off from the parked vehicle. "Any word from Charlie and Foxtrot?"

Yuri shook his head. "TOC received comms right before they crossed through the pass. The long-ranges can only reach so far, but I'm sure they'll make it fine. They just have to divert much sooner than planned. They're carrying enough fuel and batteries to make up the extra distance on the river."

Either way, Echo wouldn't know until they were out there— if they ever made it out there. SOG prided itself on its flexibility; change and adaptability were part of the job. Plus, Echo had no choice. The only way out was forward, and *forward* came with the unexpected arrival of white armor.

Miriam's breath hitched at the sight of the unhelmed Hadeon, who stood a giant in her full plates with a large sheathed blade fixed on her back. The last time Miriam had seen a completely armored Altered, it had been at a distance in a burning southern settlement. More recently, she had seen hybrid armor on the young legionnaire she had killed at the EarthTek compound. His gasping mouth flashed through her mind, and she swallowed the lump in her throat.

"New plan, boss?" Yuri bobbed his chin to their approaching team lead.

Krill took a deep breath, and Miriam braced herself. Whatever he was going to say next, he wasn't enthusiastic.

"Our window's closing." Nas tapped his cuff.

"You will make it," the senior legionnaire replied.

More than a couple eyebrows raised at Hadeon. Echo should've been on the road more than an hour ago.

Krill grimaced. "Get your stuff. I've already worked it out

with LOGS. Additional gear will be waiting for us at the airfield."

"Airfield?" Miriam asked.

Krill shot a look at Hadeon. "Slight change of plans. We're hitching a ride."

◊

"Thought you'd be delighted, Nas! After all this time, you were right!" Yuri shouted down the passenger compartment.

Across from Miriam, the intelligence specialist's face twisted, and he shifted nervously in his seat. For once, he didn't look pleased that his theory was correct. He hissed at the closest Altered soldier, "You still haven't said how long this ship's been in the radiation zone!"

The legionnaire's horizontal eyelids shuttered, and Miriam forced an exhale out. She was pretty sure that was the legionnaire's idea of humor, but she didn't want to think about it further. There was already too much going on: the fact that the Altered still had access to certain resources, that they had been squirreled away in the radiation zone, and that Echo, as humans, didn't have the proper gear to be sitting inside an irradiated craft. What were the immediate and long-term effects of that? Miriam wasn't sure if she was imagining it, but she could swear her skin was unusually warm.

"One minute out!"

Her gut lurched as she felt the craft slow almost immediately. If not for the straps holding her down, she would've flown across the cabin with the sudden velocity change. A light blinked above them, and Miriam unbuckled and pulled herself to her feet, trying to stabilize with the airship's dipping motions. The turbulence at this speed and altitude was unforgiving. The legionnaires had a different understanding of comfort and safety.

"I can't believe we agreed to this!" Kai yelled as the hatch opened and the roar of wind overtook everything. The engineer lugged a large bag forward with Sam and Nas.

Miriam shared the sentiment, but it was already done. She ran through her mental checklist of every training she could remember on aircasting and riverine infiltrations, but it had arguably been some time. It had never been a feasible method for UMF with their aircrafts' communications jammed.

As the back of the Altered ship yawned open, the sun gaped, low on the horizon. Thin trees and brush lined the wide river below them, and Miriam could smell its earthiness. A tingling and constricting sensation started from her chest into her throat. The last time Echo had been on a river, it hadn't gone well.

She wasn't the only one who hesitated. In the corner of her eye, Yuri paused, and his fingers touched a small compartment on his kit. Miriam splayed out a hand and took a deep breath. "Not yet. You'll overheat."

The second squeezed her shoulder then stepped forward to the airship's open jaw.

"Good luck!" Krill shouted to the legionnaires.

Hadeon gave a single nod and looked on.

Shuffling forward with the others, Miriam grasped Sam's elbow. The woman glanced back, her eyes softening for a second before they sharpened again.

And then it was time.

Nas walked to the edge with Kai, the hefty bag between them. The two dropped without hesitation and Yuri followed in quick succession. Sam stepped off next, and Miriam moved forward, no sight of her teammates below—the current had already taken them.

Before she could think further, she plummeted. It was a short distance to the water, and its coldness slammed and swarmed upon Miriam. Her kit and gear pulled her down, and she briefly lost confidence in her own movements as her body acclimated and numbed. Her grip tightened around her dry bag, the only buoyancy she had, and as the current rushed around her, Miriam fought to keep her head above it.

A wave surged over her, and she kicked her legs hard to resurface. As another crested and then dipped, she glimpsed a shape, an inflating boat. Though Miriam lost sight of it as water pounded into her face, she kicked again, maneuvering with the current to bring her to the last known trajectory. Within seconds, she saw its dark hull and reached for a hold. She missed, and her head went under, water swirling into her mouth and throat.

Miriam stretched, her fingers slow in searching for a grip, brushing but not grasping. She kicked again, and she found it. With a burst of movement, Miriam strained and heaved her bag over the sidewall and quickly pulled herself over in a huge effort. She crashed against another body, gasping, but she was out of the cold and raging river.

Someone patted her. "Heads," they whispered hoarsely. Krill, maybe.

"Alive," Nas coughed.

"Here," Sam rattled.

Tired relief flooded Miriam before she ushered out her own response, followed by Kai and Yuri. They had all managed.

But the work wasn't done. Miriam flexed her fingers, willing blood and warmth to circulate as she and the others secured their packs and gear. Miriam braced herself against the river's choppy currents and loosened her dry bag to extract her visor and carefully secure it around her head. There was still enough light as the sun dropped beneath the horizon, but the headpiece was a relief when she could make out her immediate surroundings in a dim glow. She scanned the riverbank for any movement, but there was nothing but thick brush.

With no visible threat and the immediate peril of drowning gone, Miriam set on her next task. Her teeth chattered as she pulled at her kit, willing her fine motor skills to work, to open the dry pocket of her assortment of jabbers. She waved at the others, some still working their own visors and weapons, and pointed at her kit, a reminder to use their issued medication. After all, Echo was human. At this juncture, the cold was their enemy, and hypothermia would get them well before they arrived at their destination. She almost missed the radioactive airship.

As Miriam thrust a thermajabber into her thigh, the numbness in her body dulling its point, she watched the others' mirrored motions. Except for one. Yuri's hand flew to his rig but came up empty. In the dimming light, his frame violently shook.

Despite the medication's fire already spreading through her body, Miriam's gut clenched. Energy burst in her veins and into her fingers as she tore through her pack to find the one extra thermajabber—only a limited amount provided by MED and LOGS with the unexpected change. She could fix this. Miriam forced down her agitated state and willed her hands to cooperate, to find the right cylinder. When she did, Krill raised a hand across the boat, but with the churning waves, Miriam knew better. She had one shot. She braced and lunged herself over the others, stretching to thrust the last thermajabber into Yuri's thigh.

She stayed there, in an uncomfortable splayed-out position, her visor scanning Yuri's face until his features relaxed. He was still shivering, but less so. Miriam exhaled, Sam and Nas's knees digging into her hip and chest rig with the motion. The team was still wet and cold, but the medication would be enough to stave off danger. Their bodies wouldn't shut down, at least not until they were on to their next destination. With the immediate action done, Miriam felt Sam's grip loosen around her lower body. The touch and thought provided a bonus warmth.

Echo moved into their next motions, and Miriam shifted back into her seat. She tucked her boots underneath the secure foot ropes and watched the last remainders of twilight as the river roared around them. Its noises blended together, almost pleasing now that Miriam wasn't personally fighting its chaos. She glanced around at her team as they worked, then up at the darkening sky and its uncontained stars and satellites. For a moment, she leaned, reflexively gravitating until she found Sam's body next to her. If Miriam forced herself to not think about what lay ahead, it was almost calming.

36

SCORCHED

SAM FROWNED.

The North was her arena. Though she had grown up in Gould and Ursus, Sam had traveled and lodged in many of the towns in the North, Sunali included. She had rucked and trekked the mountains, trained in the marshes and flats, and ran the numerous hills. But now? She couldn't shake the dissonant feeling she was behind enemy lines.

Despite the night and long hours of painfully slow stalking, Echo hadn't met any resistance. Their largest concern had been convoys heading toward the town or past it to the range where UMF marines and legionnaires were fortifying, but no one was looking in their direction. When Sam's visor stuttered, its scanning jittery, she knew. They had made it.

Sunali wasn't one of the more populous towns in the area, but it was a decent size, roughly the same footprint as Ursus Outpost—if the UMF compound had a concentration of stores and local administrative buildings at its center. Sam had passed through years before, but she didn't recall anything outstanding. Despite its mediocrity, the town didn't deserve the scabs of war now etched into its features. Scorch marks and broken veneers were visible from afar, and around the perimeter, tires, furniture, and miscellaneous heavy equipment tangled together to barricade all of the streets except one.

Sam made the smallest adjustment, shrimping closer to the edge of the ditch. She ignored the static in her visor, and observed a cluster of shadows on top of one of the several four-story structures in the town's center—probably Sunali's government or SecHut building. She was certain it was what they were after: the jamming system. But even with that location and the knowledge of Legion's airships, they couldn't destroy those points—not with the Blightbringers a looming threat. The timing between the three SOG teams and Hadeon's legionnaires was paramount. And with communications interrupted, Legion wouldn't know when SOG had secured the Blightbringers.

Sam's mouth pinched. Baby steps. Focus on one action at a time.

A soft rumbling noise piqued her attention, and both Sam and Yuri flattened themselves into the ditch, hoping their position in the brush line was enough to hide their presence. Though they were a distance away, they still needed to avoid wandering Altered eyes.

Sam's eyes followed a line of four large vehicles as they progressed down the only open street. Beyond the drivers, she saw no one else. She strained her ocular implant and watched the trucks disappear around a corner into town.

No stops, no checkpoints, no sentries.

Echo had arrived from behind—where the Apostates would least expect an infiltration—but it still seemed too easy.

To her side, Yuri set down an old-generation scope and gestured past the tallest buildings to a thin pole sticking into the sky. Sam had seen something like it before—she couldn't remember where or why—but this one was more immense in scale. With the new structure identified, she made out the tips of others peeking between buildings in the town. Most were positioned on the other side, the Apostates' attack side.

Jammer relays, Yuri mouthed.

She'd take his word for it. *He* was the communications specialist.

Sam ducked her eye behind the scope of her brother's long rifle. The sync between it, her eye implant, and her visor was moot with the jammers engaged, but its manual settings allowed her enough magnification to confirm the lack of movement within the town from their current angle. She arranged her sight onto a two-story building, its slanted attic space looking over the main road. An extensive gash replaced its top window and though Sam could see nothing inside, the hair on the back of her neck stood. She pressed herself instinctually into the ground and reassured herself that their position—Echo further behind them—was concealed.

Yuri tapped his boot to hers, and Sam nodded. She took one last look at the shadows and they cautiously made their way back to their waiting team. The others had also seen the caravan of vehicles, but they watched the two now, waiting for their silent assessment.

The second bent his elbow and bladed his fingers perpendicular to the ground. He made another gesture to note the relays they had seen then turned to Sam. Did I miss anything else?

She stared at his hands but couldn't bring herself to sign back.

Anything else?

Sam shook her head.

Krill's lips parted and silently moved. *Options?*

The second made a fist with one hand and walked two fingers over it.

Kai's head moved side to side. *Traps*, she said in silence. She tapped her commcuff. They didn't have time to navigate that option.

The lead curved his hand around Yuri's fist. His eyes met Sam's.

Go around? From what she had seen, the blockades funneled all access to one point. Echo could try to find another entrance, but they'd have the same improvised perimeter to deal with. If they ventured further, the probability of sentries and other countermeasures would increase. Echo couldn't sacrifice more time to find another access point and they didn't want to step on Charlie and Foxtrot's routes, especially without ongoing comms. Each team had their designated sectors and each team's job was contingent on the others doing their part.

Sam tongued a silent no.

Mines? Kai mouthed. She zigzagged a hand.

Sam shook her head. The caravan had driven straight through the street. If there had been explosives, they had made no attempt to avoid them—unless there were other technologies in play.

Krill's lips pressed together, and he walked his fingers and flipped his hand.

Both Yuri and Sam shook their heads. They hadn't seen anyone beyond the convoy drivers.

The lead's shoulders sagged. In any other situation, less traffic was great news, but in this case, everything about the open route into the town screamed *trap*. Ambush.

Sam motioned to the attic she had identified before. *Sniper.* The others instinctively crouched lower though there was no line of sight to their location.

Krill's eyebrows quirked.

She wasn't one hundred percent confident of her assessment, but she'd go with her gut. If *she* were an Apostate, or if she and Scott had been assigned to cover this layout, that space would've been where they'd set up and hold. The question, however, was whether the Altered terrorists thought the same way and if they had the resources to spare. The Apostates' speed and ambition through the North had to limit their resources and assets, and Sunali wasn't as large in scale as the other sites.

"Shit," Miriam breathed.

Krill pondered, but Sam already knew what he'd say. There was no other way, barring a complete UMF division attack or an airstrike to bomb the Apostates to oblivion—which weren't viable options, not while the threat of Blightbringers existed.

And so Echo moved forward. The approach on the perimeter was easier than expected and the marines stayed in the concealment of the one- and two-story buildings. With her carbine in hand and Scott's rifle tucked behind her, Sam scanned horizontally and vertically. Though the main road was open, there was a narrow path along its sides with cover from the attic's angle, but it'd be a delicate dance. She hadn't seen anyone before, but Apostate sentries could be inside each structure they passed. Every door and window she cleared could have a stimmed Altered ready to pounce and kill. Her heart beat steadily, and she tried to maintain her breathing. It was slow work, but Echo made good progress, already more than halfway down the avenue.

At the front, Nas paused. A sizable stretch of distance sat between their current location and the next closest structure. Sam repositioned herself, peeking around the corner, her sights on the shadowed gash in the attic. Her gut churned as she stared, certain she caught faint glints of green.

There was no other way forward without cover or concealment, and if Sam was right, the team not only had to worry about their own lives in the sights of an Altered weapon, but its subsequent alert to an entire camp of enemies. Echo wasn't only risking their lives, but also their SOG and legionnaire colleagues, the land's fertility, and consequently, humanity's future and survival.

No pressure.

Sam forced herself to remain calm. She had been training for this, obsessively working hours and days at the range to bring her prosthetic to her standards, to understand how much pressure to squeeze with, to make the tiniest adjustments to strike something a hair to the left or right. It had been an obsession bordering on addiction to distract herself from her loss, his absence.

Sam flexed a different muscle memory. She had the same training as Scott, but she was never the designated marksman, always at his side to support, guide, and cover. But she knew how he had worked, what he had looked for, how he had thought.

At least most of the time.

She switched out her carbine and brought her brother's rifle up, leaning and bracing herself into the wall. She focused on the coolness of the weapon stock pressed to her cheek. It was the same place, the last touch *his* cheek had against it. She shut her eyes and inhaled.

A touch lingered on Sam's hip, and she reopened her eyes. Emptying her mind, she concentrated on the attic. When she gave a slight nod, she knew the others responded, passing ready signals down the line. She didn't dare take her eyes off those shadows, knowing she'd only get one chance.

Nas's boots scuttled across the pavement and Sam breathed out a smooth exhale, her wrist ready to make the smallest adjustment, her finger ready to squeeze. Time stretched and each millisecond elongated.

But nothing.

Another body moved forward and sprinted into the danger zone.

This time, she caught slight motion in her reticle. A sliver of darkness moved. Sam squeezed and the rifle flinched into her shoulder and cheek, her ears registering its suppressed shot.

She kept her eye on the scope, unblinking.

For a second, nothing moved. Had it been wind? Was she mistaken? But then something shifted forward. Slumped.

Yuri tapped her kit, but Sam held her breath and continued to watch vigilantly. If there was a second Apostate up there, there was no motion or sign. If anyone had heard the suppressed fire, there was no alarm or commotion in response. She exhaled and motioned her head again.

Sam recognized Miriam's quiet steps and then another's before the team second tapped her again. She watched through her scope one more time before she pushed off the wall. A quick stretch of her limbs and she was ready for her own sprint. With an eye still up, she crossed the distance, knowing Yuri would be behind her, taking up the rear.

Just short of the others, her ears pricked up at a low hum. It was a familiar noise, and her muscles tensed. She dropped to a knee, disregarding her own lack of cover, and raised the long rifle, trying to steady her prosthetic and shoulder as best as possible.

Something zipped, and she saw the dust billow out from the same void she had been watching. Her stomach plunged, but she squeezed the trigger. A wisp of her shot hit the side of the building, just below and to the left of her target. Dirt and pebbles sprayed her back and Sam forced herself not to look behind her, afraid of the possibilities.

She let out a harsh exhale and braced herself as the humming started again.

Breathe.

Calm.

Slow pull.

Slow breath.

Slow everything.

She squeezed and the rifle dug into her muscle.

This time, a shadow fell forward, crumpling into view over the ledge.

Yuri bumped into her, and his hands scrambled for her kit, trying to pick her up. As Sam rose into a last sprint, she glanced at the small crater in the pavement behind them. When the two joined the rest of the team, Miriam's eyes were wide but relieved, scanning over her and Yuri, searching for any injuries.

Sam waved her off and looked around their immediate surroundings. The commotion hadn't been loud, but compared to the relative hush of the area, it was enough to draw attention. Collectively, Echo held their breath waiting for the shouts, the alarm, or something following, but there was nothing but the drone of the Altered weapon coming from the attic.

A chill spread through Sam's skin as that pitch continued to rise.

And rise.

Her gut dropped when the inevitable loud and long zip sounded.

The following second of silence was deafening.

And then the building's frame groaned, and the facade cracked and crumbled. Concrete and plaster fell two stories down, a thunderous percussion.

So much for stealth.

Whatever timeline Echo had hoped for in securing the Blightbringers had shortened. The countdown started now.

"Comms?"

Krill's voice was an additional shock after the last hours of intentional silence. Yuri and Nas tapped their visors instinctually. Their frowns confirmed they had no communication. The legionnaires, Charlie, and Foxtrot would still be working their way into Sunali. It was too early to be detected. They were all supposed to attack at the same time.

From within the town, an alarm began to wail.

"Boss?" Yuri said.

"Dammit! We need to move, find the device."

Sam slung her brother's rifle over her shoulder and cinched its sling tight as she switched back to her carbine. She hoped the other teams were faring better. She also hoped the UMF companies and legionnaires had already done their job, enticing most of the Apostates in this camp to the front, kilometers away. The SOG marines and legionnaires needed all the distraction they could afford.

"Valk and Nas, in front. Kai, you've got six. Clear and move, people. No civvies left. Unless you see our uniforms, everyone's an enemy."

Sam led, making quick decisions on their route, watching for any movement, any glints of green in the shadows. Around the corner and down the street, she froze and raised her left fist to the staggered column behind her. Vehicles sped by a block over and Sam held her breath.

She waited another couple seconds before she dropped her hand, and Echo continued forward. Sam followed the sound of the alarm as it grew louder, its oscillation grinding into her brain. When it cut out, her pace slowed, unable to use its volume for audible cover. Despite the ringing in her ears, Sam noted a different sound. And then a slight thrum in her chest.

Rumbling.

"Smell that?" Nas hissed behind her.

He was right. The faint scent of earth and foulness pulled into her nose.

Though she had studied Sunali's layout, Sam didn't need it anymore. She maneuvered around buildings and streets as she followed the smell until it grew pungent, a mix of fertilizer and bitter chemicals. She stopped short of a clearing, taking cover behind a strip of two-story shops. A small neighborhood park or square lay across the road. Tents, containers, and stations replaced what used to be a playground, benches, and tables.

But Sam's eyes drew to its center.

Echo had found their Blightbringer.

TACHYCARDIA

"LOOK at the size of that thing."

Miriam shot Yuri a look, but it didn't matter. The amount of noise generated from the camp and the cylindrical behemoth in its middle was enough to cover a normal conversation short of shouting.

The Blightbringer's tank was the size of two prowlers, and it sat on a wide platform with what looked like four giant talons that sunk into the ground. Several tubes and cords hooked at its base, most leading to what looked like a raised module station. The device Miriam had seen in UMF's brief was conceivably a third the size of this one.

She peeled her eyes from its monstrous form and looked over the rest of the campsite. Four-story buildings stood several blocks past the clearing, looking over its new operations, and stations were set up on the two corners closest to Echo. The one to the north looked to be a cargo drop-off point with a series of stacked crates and containers, and the one to its south was an improvised L-shaped laboratory with transparent overhangs. Small light towers dotted the entire park, though they were shut off in the current hour of daylight.

Beyond that, closer to the far corner, a hefty truck—what

must've carried the device—was parked. Approximately ten individuals milled around in no state of rush. Miriam knew she couldn't count on that number; there would be more wunbies close by in the town. If the UMF companies and legionnaires had done their jobs, they would've pulled most of the wunbies away from Sunali, but a defensive force would still be left behind. From what she could see, the individuals wore different outfits, but none were heavily armed, nor did they look like soldiers.

At the Blightbringer's module, two wunbies were visibly in a shouting match, their body language and gestures apparent to the naked eye. One, wearing light armor, motioned in the direction Echo had come, then tried to reach for something on the console behind the other. The second wunby, who wore a strange version of a scientist's white coat, swatted the man away. Though Miriam couldn't make out anything over the din, it seemed like the two were at an impasse over whether to start the poison process or not.

It was good for Echo. So far, at least.

"Look," Kai gasped, "they've connected it to the aquifer."

Miriam had studied what she needed before the operation, but she didn't recognize which tube or apparatus the engineer pointed at. She trusted Kai's identification; it only confirmed their fears. All it'd take would be for the first wunby to get what he wanted and engage the Blightbringer. Miriam found herself rooting for the scientist—the first and only wunby she'd ever root for.

"Kai, can you turn that off?" Krill asked.

"I think so. I need to get to the controls or somehow disengage its power source."

"How much time do we have?"

"At that size?" Kai considered for a second. "Five minutes before it starts pumping."

"Shit," Miriam breathed. She eyed the two arguing wunbies again. It'd be near impossible to get to that module without alerting any of the Altered. And they'd have less than five minutes to secure the place—barely enough time to stop the Blightbringer from releasing arsynthetic into the town's water supply. If the chemical hit the irrigation systems, it'd spread to the creeks, streams, and rivers. There'd be widespread damage.

To make things worse, Echo didn't just have the dozen wunbies near the machine to worry about; they had the band of armed ones behind them as well. The camp already knew Echo —or at least some type of force—was there. Miriam had known this operation stacked the odds against them, but she was watching it slide closer to a suicide mission as their time and options thinned.

Krill turned to Sam, his eyes floating to the second floor of the strip building.

"No," Miriam cut him off before he could start.

It was an overstep. She was an SOG marine and a medic, but she wasn't the team lead. She didn't make the calls, but if Krill put Sam into a position to cover Echo, it'd leave her alone. If one of them stayed to cover Sam, they'd only have four to take on mostly open ground and unknown wunbies—who, despite their disposition, were not to be underestimated.

"We're not separating," she continued.

Krill glared.

"The power source, the battery," Nas offered. "Can Valk take a shot?"

"No," the lead snapped, but he considered. "Maybe. No. The risk—" He glanced over to Kai. "How many disc grenades did you bring?"

The engineer unclasped her pack. She tilted it and several pucks slid forward. "But we can't use these near—"

"I know." The lead turned to the others. "How many do you have?"

Between the six of them, they had quite a lot—Sam and Nas having packed their own stashes as well. Kai stacked two in Miriam's palm.

"Set them to ten seconds," Krill instructed, then quickly assigned lanes and sectors to each marine. "Stay in a line. They won't expect it. Get to the module and fan out."

Miriam quirked an eyebrow. The wunbies expected enemies, but she agreed, they wouldn't expect six SOG marines running straight in. Miriam didn't feel good about it, but she saw the plan. It was a thin one, but it would sow chaos, almost like the wunbies attacking Station City in broad daylight. Hopefully this mayhem would buy them enough time and space.

"Don't hit the device. But everything else? Make sure you don't miss." He nodded as he looked around the team. "We've got this." And then he broke off in a sprint.

Miriam and the others followed, matching his pace in a spread-out column. They had made it to the middle of the street when the lead threw a hand up and Miriam slung her disc grenades, aiming for the southern corner laboratory. She didn't watch them land, already transitioning to her rifle as her boots touched onto a patch of unpaved ground. She pumped her legs as they burst past one of the tents, four wunbies looking up in surprise, their faces frozen, watching from inside.

At the module, the two wunbies were the first to turn. The armored one shouted out and Miriam pointed her rifle, but between her movement and angle, she hesitated. If she missed, she'd hit the Blightbringer.

Someone else shot first, their UMF rifle stuttering through the ambient drone.

The armored wunby staggered back but didn't fall. He shoved his colleague out of the way and struck the console. He then reached inside his rig, and a thin metal cover glinted.

The pit in Miriam's stomach grew. The countdown for their Blightbringer had started. And worse, the wunbies had stims.

Past the laboratory, Miriam slowed and shifted to movement in her lane. She squeezed her trigger alongside Sam's own mirrored action, loosing several rounds into an armorless wunby until he fell. The individual didn't have a weapon, but

Echo couldn't let them get close; these alties didn't need weapons to be a threat.

Behind her, the tent exploded along with the northern corner the others had targeted. Six grenades would have been overkill for a temporary laboratory with unarmed scientists, but in this scenario, there was no such thing as *too much*. Echo couldn't afford to leave any of these wunbies alive, especially now that the SOG marines had announced themselves.

She heard the zips before she saw the armored sentry. He emerged from behind the truck in front of her, his rectangular weapon engaging Krill, Nas, and Kai on the other side. Miriam fired on him and he ducked back. More weapons sounded from the furthest corner she couldn't see.

"Get to the module!" Yuri yelled to the others as he, Miriam, and Sam moved forward.

They skirted the open space, capitalizing on their momentum and surprise. To Miriam's left, Sam dropped rounds into the truck's bumper where they had last seen the sentry retreat. Miriam stepped out to widen her angle on the vehicle and past the Blightbringer when her heart lurched. The armored wunby who had been at the module before waved forward two others armed with heavy rifles.

"Contact, ten o'clock!" She shouted before she fired in their direction.

One swiveled on her and Miriam threw herself toward cover, her back slamming into the vehicle's massive front tire. A staccato of bullets pinged against the truck.

"How many?" Yuri roared behind her, his voice punctuated by gunfire.

"Three!"

A body stumbled into their view then crumpled to the ground.

"Two!"

From her angle, something blurred forward and disappeared behind the Blightbringer and its platform. Miriam shouted to

Krill and Nas, who had taken their own defensive positions, but they were both too distracted and too far away for her voice to carry over. The wunby was too close to them, too close to the device.

Before she could try another warning, Yuri yelled out behind her. "I see him! I'm moving! Cover me!"

Miriam barely had time to acknowledge him before the second darted toward the others. She fired a few rounds at a head that popped up behind toppled containers. It dipped back down.

Something rushed above her and Miriam's eyes widened as a silhouette jumped on top of her. She grunted at the shooting pain and weight from both the individual above her and the ground below. She tried to raise her rifle but couldn't, her limbs tangled, trying to separate from whoever was thrashing against her.

And then she was free. Separated.

Miriam scrambled back on her hands and feet until her head banged into the truck's running board.

Next to her, Sam wrestled with the sentry who they had forgotten about—distracted by the incoming wunbies. Shots zipped from the sentry's rifle into the air as Sam tried to manipulate the weapon in any other direction but theirs.

Miriam's hands grasped for her weapon, but she didn't have a clean shot. Sam was too close, and their movements were too wild, too erratic.

"Mir!"

In a burst, Sam simultaneously eased her resistance on the weapon and pushed her body weight into the wunby. At the precipice of falling, Sam yanked back, ripping the rifle from his grip. In the separation, Miriam squeezed her trigger, her bullets ripping into light armor and flesh. Sam flung the weapon to the side, reached into her kit, and lunged forward.

Miriam quickly pulled back, afraid of catching Sam in her cross fire. The woman cocked then slammed her prosthetic forward, a fist crushing just below light armor, past a growing ring of blood. Sam's hand stuck *in* the sentry's gut and his face contorted. And then the woman pulled back with a sickening sucking sound.

Miriam froze. "What—"

But Sam was already moving, picking up her rifle, and pulling her away from the wunby and the truck. Miriam glanced down at the woman's prosthetic and the compartment she had previously reached into.

Disc grenades.

Hell.

They had made a few long steps into the open when the still-shocked sentry tore at his armor, clawing at his abdomen. Miriam was more than halfway to the Blightbringer and the others when she watched the wunby stiffen.

In a blink, the body was gone in a squelching pop.

She blinked again.

Legs remained standing before they finally toppled, the other half of its person flung a short distance away.

"Valk! Tan! Get over here! Incoming reinforcements!"

Miriam stumbled over her feet, still staring at the dead sentry before her attention drew back. Her eyes followed Krill's motions to the area Echo had initially started and attacked from. She could make out the rumble of vehicles as they sped toward the square.

"Kai!" the lead shouted again as the others adjusted their positions.

"Almost! Alm—" The rest of the engineer's response was lost in a growing hum.

The hair on Miriam's neck rose as the air rippled.

She and Sam were still in the open.

The whine climbed higher in pitch.

Miriam twisted and tackled Sam just as the ground ripped up where they had been. She huffed as the stock of a weapon poked into her side, but other than tangled limbs, they were both unscathed. She looked up to see the linear path of destruction from the incoming caged vehicle and its attached airgun.

Another modified rhino van skidded to a stop, its four light-armored passengers already jumping out. Krill, Yuri, and Nas laid down fire, but if they landed their shots, they weren't critical enough to drop their enemies before they dashed into the remains of the exploded laboratory and cargo crates.

Still on the ground, Miriam extricated herself from Sam and crawled to the nearest cover. The whine of the airgun started again, cutting through everything else. She peeked over and found the heavy weapon. Her eyes furrowed at the airgun's new upward direction and her stomach clenched.

The Blightbringer tank.

What were these wunbies thinking? Were they that reckless —this crazy? If they shot at the device, it'd poison the earth. If they targeted the tank, they'd release concentrated arsynthetic onto the immediate area. Echo was directly in the splash zone. They'd be poisoned, either ejecting all their bodily fluids, destroying their internal organs and cardiovascular system, or both in an excruciating and undignified death, but the wunbies were in harm's way as well. Even if the Altered were genetically enhanced, that amount of chemical would destroy them, too.

"Rhino! Take out the rhino!" Miriam shouted. She didn't wait for the others to acknowledge, letting loose a barrage of bullets toward the operator behind the gun.

A hail of zips and bullets rained back at her from the other corners and Miriam ducked back into cover. She tried to pop out again but was pressed down by another torrential stream of fire. She called out for Sam, but only the thunder of the firefight answered.

Miriam scrambled around and found tufts of blond hair slightly behind her, tucked behind a small light tower. Sam had transitioned to her brother's long rifle, but every attempt to steady it, to find a good platform and shot was interrupted. The small generator box that the woman used for cover was eroding with the constant pounding of bullets and advanced projectiles.

The pitch increased.

They had seconds before they were all dead. Even if Kai had disabled the countdown, had detached what she needed to from the Blightbringer, the tank of arsynthetic was there, a tangible target.

The impacts lessened against her partition.

"Sam!"

Miriam had a terrible, awful idea.

"Sam!" she shouted louder, her throat raw. She could taste carbon in the air.

Blond hair fluttered toward her.

"The airgun!"

A blue eye flashed, the understanding there, but delayed.

Miriam shut out any protest and before she could think of how stupid her idea was, she jettisoned out from cover.

Don't miss, Sam. Don't miss.

Her legs pumped at an angled trajectory—unfortunately closer toward the wunbies—and she held down her trigger, trying to delay any enemy popping out.

She should've told Sam.

The commotion of the battle fell away as her lungs screamed and her heart pounded, filling and muting everything else.

I love you.

Why hadn't she told Sam yet?

She should have said it by now, said it often, when there was time.

And then the air compressed around her, and Miriam felt her feet lift, her body following. Pressure smashed into her from all sides, disorienting and inundating her senses.

When the dust settled, Miriam found herself on the ground. She groaned but made no effort to get up. She patted herself, trying to make sense of what had happened. Had it worked? Or was she already breathing in arsynthetic? Were they too late?

Adrenaline pierced her initial stun, and she perched up, her body complaining and aching. Miriam was in the open, a meter away from her intended destination of cover. She dragged herself toward it when something grabbed her. She twisted, her rifle coming up.

"Mir, it's me. It's me."

Miriam exhaled and her head dipped forward into Sam's kit —she thought she could smell the scent of fresh linens past the dirt and earth. She snapped back and pulled the woman down to the ground with her. There were still wunbies, a battle around them, gunshots.

She tried to wriggle the last bit toward cover, but Sam resisted on top of her. Miriam stopped, her eyes narrowing, panicked and questioning, but as she regained her senses, she realized there were significantly fewer rounds of fire. She heard footsteps and swiping sounds cutting through the air.

More advanced weapons?

Miriam lifted herself onto her elbows and looked up. Her frustration at Sam's lack of hurry vanished. The airgun and its vehicle were gone—or at least almost unidentifiable. What remained was a spray of metal skeleton spread out on display.

"Was..." Miriam swallowed. "Was that you?"

Sam ignored her question and swept over Miriam's body, checking for any injuries or pain points. When she was satisfied, her hands planted firmly around Miriam's face. "Don't you ever fucking do that again." Her eyes blazed down.

Miriam leaned into the woman before Sam's hands dropped to lift her up.

Though the shooting had stopped in their immediate area, explosions and steady gunfire sounded from across the town. The other Razor SOG teams were still engaging their own Blightbringer sites.

"What happened to all the wu—"

Miriam cut off. To the side, a figure stepped out of cover, a rifle brandished. Miriam flinched closer to Sam and her heart leaped into her throat. She'd spoken too soon.

Before she could react, white color flashed forward, a large blade glinting in the air before it came down in a wide slash. And then the armored legionnaire pivoted, moving on to clear the next area.

The wunby's head lolled then fell to the side. After another wavering second, its body dropped.

"Friendlies!" Krill shouted. "Don't shoot, more coming in!"

Two more white suits of armor came around the truck, and relief flooded her system. The entire battle had turned. Echo had taken the site and the Blightbringer. Her body started to shake as it processed her crash of adrenaline.

"Valk! Help Kai out." The lead waved as the legionnaires made their way to the module. He then spouted out another set of orders to Yuri and Nas nearby.

Sam turned, but not before scanning Miriam over again.

"I'm okay." Aside from some nasty scrapes, Miriam had gotten through relatively unscathed. From what she could tell, her insides were intact as well.

For a second, she thought the woman would embrace her in front of the others, but it didn't happen. Sam squeezed her arm and hurried to find Kai, now near the base of the platform, already detaching tubes and cords. Miriam followed slowly, her body still aching. She meant to check on the others, to confirm if anyone was injured, but she stopped when the first alty soldier tapped their helmet and its faceplate folded back.

"Hadeon," Krill said. "What are you doing here?"

"You struck early. We were supposed to attack our sites at the same time. Together."

Miriam didn't attempt to smother a look at the senior legionnaire.

"The plan snagged, and we had to move." The lead scowled, but it fell as he winced at the sound of a distant explosion.

"That's one of ours now. Why are you here? Shouldn't you be destroying the jammers?"

"Plan snagged," the senior legionnaire mirrored, her voice flat. "There is more resistance than we anticipated." Her tone was almost accusatory.

"What are you—" Krill stopped.

Miriam stiffened as two individuals approached. One of the legionnaires limped heavily, leaning on the other. The injured soldier set himself down on the steps of the platform.

"Tan."

But Miriam was already moving, her kit out. She stared at the deep gash on his leg, blood seeping out above the knee. She furrowed her brows as she wiped at the area, ripped muscle and bone exposed beyond torn armor. Around the edges, white material melted into the soldier's skin in terrible hues of white and red. Miriam wasn't sure how the legionnaire had walked the way he had, or how he wasn't beside himself in pain. She ripped out a tourniquet from her small pack.

"Hadeon, what happened?" Krill said.

"Reinforcements."

Miriam gritted her teeth, but she kept her attention on the injured soldier, trying to figure out a way to work around the armor.

"They set up another perimeter. They know what we want. If they have not given up the other Blightbringers, they will soon. They will fortify their tower to keep their advantage at the front."

Meanwhile, the injured legionnaire swatted Miriam's hands away and gestured at his thigh before he fished inside his beltline. She exhaled, but she held the tourniquet capsule snug to the legionnaire's armor, then engaged the device. The straps snapped around and pulled taut. It wasn't ideal, but it seemed to put slightly more pressure on the leg. The legionnaire produced a thin pen-like applicator and for a millisecond, Miriam thought of the wunby stim she had previously held during another mission. The memory quickly faded. This was a smaller version of a medicated jabber.

"Our objective is to take down their system."

"What are you saying?" Krill said.

Hadeon met him with silence.

"We're not leaving our site. What if the wunbies come back? Set this off?"

"You have done the difficult part. I need bodies." The senior legionnaire looked over her team and then Echo. She motioned at the sitting legionnaire. "Perun will stay to hold this position."

Disbelief washed over Krill's face. "Your man is injured."

Perun grunted and gently pushed Miriam aside. He stood to his full height, his weight on his good leg, and glared down at Echo's lead. "My hands work. Would you like to try me?"

Krill ignored him. "Even if I agreed, what's your plan, Hadeon? We aren't your bait."

She pointed at one of the four-story buildings blocks away. "The base station is on the top floor, but there are too many. We can get close, but I need you to cover our exit. Ten, fifteen minutes. A distraction."

Miriam huffed. Still bait.

She pulled Perun back down and fumbled with the pen before sticking it in a patch of exposed and untorn skin. A few seconds passed before the legionnaire visibly relaxed, a contrast to what she had thought was normal before, a tension and stiffness she had assumed was part of his stature.

"Every second we dally here, more of our people die, your comrades and mine."

Krill's eyes fixed onto the ground, but Miriam knew his mind was turning. As long as the jammers were still up, Echo and the others were stuck. *Everyone* was stuck. On top of that, it was a rare moment where a legionnaire was asking for assistance.

From humans.

Krill's eyes landed on Yuri, Sam, then Nas. "I can give you three."

Miriam shook her head and stood. "Four. Me, too."

If Sam was going, she'd go, too. Even if it meant taking on more wunbies.

"No—"

"More is better," Hadeon interrupted.

Krill's lip twitched, but he looked around the square. "Ten minutes, Hadeon. Get this done." He called out for the others.

As Sam, Yuri, and Nas joined them, Krill filled them in on their new task. No one complained; the gravity of the situation was obvious. Yuri and Nas followed Hadeon and her squad as they moved, and Miriam waited for Sam as she left her brother's rifle with the Echo lead, her hand lingering before she let go. The recon specialist looked up and held Miriam's gaze before she dipped her head, tightening her grip around her carbine.

Krill turned. "Good decisions, Tan. No one gets hurt."

She swallowed. "I know, boss."

Miriam hurried off after the others, Sam at her side.

38

VANGUARD

THE FOUR ECHO marines and seven legionnaires met their first resistance a block from Sunali's central government building. The Apostate enemies tucked behind cover in an improvised checkpoint made of three rhinos; this time, at least, no weapons were mounted to them. However, beyond the vehicles at the top of the main entrance's steps, Sam recognized the anchored airgun.

The Altered already knew they were there, and Hadeon was right. Whatever reinforcements within the camp had congregated to defend the communication-jamming systems. Success for Echo, for UMF, Legion, and humanity would be twofold: not only securing the Blightbringers, preventing their land from being poisoned, but also in taking down the equipment hindering UMF and Legion's largest muscle and need. Communication. They needed it to win in the long run.

Watching the Apostates swarm around the barricades, skepticism and doubt inched at Sam. Hadeon had wanted help —bodies—but Sam wasn't sure if four additional SOG marines was enough. Without comms, they didn't know how Charlie and Foxtrot were faring, and they didn't have time to check, to buffer their numbers.

From the shadows, Yuri raised a hand from his weapon, tapping his thumb and curved fingers together. Pincer movement. Nas, Sam, and Miriam understood, but Hadeon and the others didn't. Or if they did, they ignored him.

Though Sam didn't feel that way herself, the legionnaires seemed emboldened. She looked around at their situation and then back at her teammates and the white-armored soldiers. Eleven. Against an array of heavy weapons and Apostates. The scientists and sentries they had encountered at the previous site had been easy in comparison. But here? Sam wasn't as confident.

"The system is on the roof and the level below it," Hadeon stated.

"We're going to fight our way through that?" Nas exclaimed.

"No," the senior replied. "Not anymore." She moved closer to one of her legionnaires—Varya? Sam couldn't tell them apart when they had their helmets on. The other soldiers joined, their heads huddled in. She leaned forward, trying to make out their discussion, but their passed words were too subdued.

"What does that mean?" Nas whispered.

Before anyone could answer with their own speculations, Hadeon separated from her squad. Behind her, four legionnaires hurried away, leaving the senior with two remaining soldiers.

"Well, bye, I guess. What is going on?" Nas said.

Hadeon nodded to the legionnaire next to her, who tapped their helmet, the front plate folding back. Varya. The Altered woman reached behind her, then held out both hands to the marines, two cylindrical pucks in each. They were the same devices Sam had seen used in the Station City attack.

Sam carefully plucked one and Miriam, Nas, and Yuri grabbed their own.

"Twist and throw. It will latch onto anything magnetic," Varya explained.

"And Porevit will stay with you," Hadeon said.

On cue, the other legionnaire stepped forward.

"You can take the first point with these. Make as much noise as you can." She clasped arms with Porevit. "Path to glory."

"Path to glory," the legionnaire repeated gruffly.

Yuri balked. "Wait. You're leaving?" He craned his neck, trying to find the others, who had already disappeared.

"Where are you going to be?" Sam asked.

Hadeon straightened, then closed her helmet. Her voice came through, slightly muffled but clear enough. "We will be at the top." And then without further explanation, she was off, Varya on her heels, leaving behind four disconcerted marines and a legionnaire.

"We weren't supposed to be bait!" Nas hissed.

Porevit chuffed. "We should go now." He adjusted his stance toward the checkpoint. "Use the gravnades when I signal." The legionnaire stepped out of cover, his rifle leveled at the checkpoint.

Shouts and gunfire erupted as their enemy spotted him.

"What's the fucking signal?"

Sam gulped. What was the plan?

But Porevit either didn't hear Nas or didn't care, already engaging and dodging, his movement liquid and savage. It was a harrowing dance, a one-legionnaire army against small-arms fire. There was the airgun beyond, but its use would have collateral Apostate damage.

Sam dipped back into cover when stray bullets lanced at the wall next to her, a ricochet catching and flicking across her cheek. She flinched, but from cover, she watched as the legionnaire risked one hand away from his heavy weapon and angled his forearm parallel to the vehicles. A compartment shifted in the soldier's bulky armor and something launched toward the checkpoint. The door of the middle rhino exploded. It was too small, too isolated, to do much damage, but it was enough for the enemies to cease firing for a second.

"I think that's the signal!" Miriam shouted.

Sam twisted the top of her puck, stepped out from cover, then launched it as far as she could. The gravnade sailed over the legionnaire, its arc ending with a clatter on the ground, meters short of the checkpoint. But then it tremored, clattering forward and across the pavement. It jumped into the air and latched onto the side of the middle vehicle, close to the same point Porevit had attacked. In quick succession, two more pucks attached to the other vehicles, and within seconds, a clash of screeching sounded as metal walls crushed in.

Gunfire resumed and Porevit pressed forward like a valiant tank, moving on the depleted checkpoint to meticulously eliminate stunned Apostates before he ducked back down. Sam and the others rushed forward, staggering their own approach.

When she slid into the cover of the first destroyed vehicle, careful of its jagged edges, Sam caught movement in the corner of her eye. At the building's periphery, armored legionnaires had taken advantage of the commotion, silently taking out enemies in their path—the Apostates' attention and reaction too slow, too late. Sam's eyes widened as the soldiers ascended the side of the building at an uncanny speed. She couldn't comprehend it. Was it by tool? More technology UMF didn't know about?

Rounds slammed into the hull around her and Sam tore her attention back to her situation. She could hear the hum of the large gun in the background. Were the Apostates still going to attack despite their own in the line of fire?

"We can't stay here!" Miriam's voice shook in her ears.

Sam peeked over the destroyed hood of the vehicle. A half wall sat between them and the town hall, but it was short in height and poorly positioned for cover. She turned to address the legionnaire, but he was gone.

Shit.

Porevit sprinted toward the building, his rifle zipping in no coherent manner. Sam's muscles clenched as she watched him. She had lived the horror of being chased by a fully armored legionnaire before, but now she was watching from the other side. What would this have looked like with a full squad of legionnaires? Terrifying. But with only one, it wasn't enough. Did Hadeon leave this legionnaire as a sacrifice so the others could reach their objective?

To her side, Yuri barked out commands, and Sam forced herself to refocus. As the airgun's whine reached its climax, she burst out with the others, splitting and sprinting toward the half wall. She flung herself into its shadow as a loud zip sounded. A wall of air blew past her and metal screamed behind her. Sam couldn't afford to look back, not with her own carbine up, blasting away. Even if she had, she knew they couldn't retreat or go back the same way. Their last cover had been reduced to tangled debris.

"Porevit!" Miriam shouted.

The legionnaire was almost to the steps, but stumbled, his rifle dropping. Sam wasn't sure what had hit him or where, but with the majority of the Apostates focusing their fire on him, she knew his armor had reached its limit. The man retrieved an uneven pole from his back—the heavier end already expanding out like a mace—and charged forward again, slower this time.

"Sam!"

Miriam rolled something toward her, and Sam snatched it. Another gravnade.

"Suppressing fire!"

And then the others drew up, their streams of bullets intensifying. Sam launched the explosive puck toward the concentration of barriers closest to the airgun then dove back into cover as the top of the half wall scraped with return fire. She hoped she had thrown the gravnade past Porevit, hoped that his armor wasn't magnetic, hoped that the airgun or something around it *was* magnetic.

Behind cover, Sam didn't feel the change in air pressure from the projectile, but from the shouting and lessened gunfire, *something* had happened. She waited before she peeked to see the first barriers had taken the hit. She could see what looked like twitching limbs wrapped into crushed metal.

On the steps, Porevit swung his mace in different directions, his wrath slamming into anyone within reach. Chaos had broken out and those in the front clambered past the double doors into the building. Others raced beyond in their own retreat.

Yuri shouted another command and the marines were up, advancing in a staggered line as they picked off stragglers. When they reached the steps and the first warped barricades, Sam and the others ducked at a sudden burst of zips and bullets their way. From a crack in the metal barrier, she watched the airgun operator remove the weapon from its stand. By the time the attacking fire stopped and she stood back up, Sam didn't have a clear line of engagement—Porevit in the way. The airgun escaped inside.

Sam rushed to the legionnaire in time to witness him crushing his boot into an Apostate's neck. Porevit's armored shoulders heaved with heavy breath, and his mace fell from his hand with a heavy thunk. The man faltered, leaning into the side of the building, before his legs crumpled. Sam tried to help, but the Altered was too big, too heavy to hold up. She crouched next to him and glanced at the punctures in sections of his plates. Bright red color had already started to seep from his armor's joints.

"Tan!" Yuri stepped past the downed legionnaire, his rifle on the double doors.

Nas moved with him and fired careful shots at the last Apostates running into the distance.

"No! Save your rounds! Tanner!"

"I'm here," Miriam said, already beside the legionnaire. She wrapped her hand around the Altered's waist, searching.

"Fools," Porevit muttered. He motioned at the door but failed to keep his hand up. He opened his helmet and sneered. Blood curtained into his eyes and face and his semi-transparent eyelids shuttered horizontally to clear his vision.

"What do you mean?" Sam's eyes flashed up at the sound of gunfire inside the building—it was muffled, distant, as if coming from the top floors.

"That weapon," Yuri answered over his shoulder. "If they use it inside, it could bring the building down."

Sam spared a look back at where the checkpoint—the three vehicles—had been. Between the gravnades and the airgun, she couldn't recognize the frames and the leftover metal.

"Comms still aren't up," the Echo second said. "The others..."

Subdued noises clamored inside the building and something rumbled at a heavy impact.

The legionnaire's breath rattled. "Go."

Dammit. Hadeon and the legionnaires were dealing with enemies on the top floors. And now there was a new wave of retreating Apostates swarming inside with a weapon not meant to be used in close quarters. The SOG marines were supposed to be the distraction, the bait, but now they were also the reinforcements and contingency plan.

"Are we going?" Nas inched toward the entrance.

Yuri glanced back, a frown cutting into his face. "Can he move?"

Miriam shook her head at the same time Porevit attempted to get up. For a second, he stood, before his body gave out and he doubled over in a coughing fit. The legionnaire slumped into the wall again. Before he could try to stand another time, Miriam injected a pen-like device into his neck. Porevit sighed loudly, but he didn't resist as the medic lowered him back to the ground. He gestured weakly at the discarded weapons around them, and Miriam piled what she could near him.

"Get them out. Finish this," the man rasped, his hand searching weakly.

Sam placed the mace into his hand and his fingers wrapped around it.

"Keep this on." Miriam tapped his helmet. "We'll be back, I promise."

Sam flinched.

I promise.

She expelled her brother's words from her mind as the four SOG marines flooded into the government building. Despite its clutter, the lobby was empty, but inside the walls, the noise of fighting from the floors above was louder.

They found the stairs, but as they took their first steps, a hail of shots rained down. Nas called for covering fire and without further thought, Sam burst toward the center of the stairwell, squeezing her trigger upward. Bounding past, Nas took two to three steps at a time until he was closer to the second-floor landing. His arm jerked forward and then he shouted. The marines pulled back as the section above them exploded. Sam's ears muffled, an incessant ringing within them, but she and the others pressed up in time to see Nas empty the last of his magazine into an Apostate who had been left behind—legs mangled by the disc grenade.

Yuri and Sam continued to the third floor as Nas reloaded. However, short of their destination, they stopped. Heaps of concrete and metal blocked the way, and above them, a section of stairs and the next landing were gone, completely sheared off. The door and sounds of fighting sat beyond, taunting them. The marines could traverse the rubble, rig something to climb to the door, but no one had the proper supplies or the time.

"We'll find another way," Yuri panted out.

"There should be another stairwell on the other side," Sam said. At least, that's how most of the North settlement government buildings were built. They all took on the same uniform layout—functionality over individuality.

In the back of the group, Miriam now took point with Nas behind her. They returned to the second floor, clearing and moving through the long hallway, but all the fighting seemed to be elsewhere. Toward the end—where the corridor turned to the left—voices reverberated. The marines' pace slowed before Miriam and Nas burst around the corner and their rifles cracked before fire returned. Sam and Yuri shifted forward in time to see the heels of figures scurrying away, their shouting retreating into the second stairwell.

"Nas!" Miriam cried out.

Their teammate gritted his teeth and gripped his gun arm. "I'm fine." He waved them forward, shifting his rifle to his other hand as he silently took the rear.

Sam took point. "Pushing," she hissed. They had to get into the stairwell before the Apostates could set up an advantageous position.

At the entrance, Sam flinched back as gunfire erupted and concrete chips danced around the doorframe. When there was a brief pause, she thrust her carbine forward and loosed a few rounds before pulling back.

Nothing.

No return fire. What were the chances she had gotten critical shots while firing blindly?

Slim.

Too slim.

But there was nothing but shuffling and muttered curses.

Sam inhaled. The Apostates above had run out of ammunition.

Without further thought, she burst into the stairwell, her carbine pointed up. Sam caught glimpses of feet and limbs as they disappeared onto the next landing and she took chase. At the third floor, she heard movement beyond the stairwell door, but Sam waited for Miriam and the others to catch up. When they did, she flung it open and immediately peeled in, the others surging behind her. The familiar sheen of the airgun flashed around the corner and Sam's stomach clenched.

She followed, worried the operator would get too far ahead, flip the weapon, and shoot down the corridor—an easy killing lane. But as she turned, something grabbed her rifle and pushed her back into Miriam. Sam struggled against the grip, but now tangled with the medic, they all stumbled and collapsed into an open office.

The Apostate stripped her rifle from her with a sudden yank and it clattered across the floor. It shoved her to the side and Sam's body twisted in the disorientation as she tripped and fell. She rushed to get back to her feet just as its hands clamped onto Miriam, wrestling with the medic's weapon.

Sam lunged forward and tackled the Apostate. It shifted its weight easily, despite their similar size, and clawed into Sam's left forearm. Sam yelped as its grip tightened. Any stronger and her bones would break. She freed her prosthetic from around the Apostate, but it grabbed at her right arm as well.

With both hands captured, Sam stared at the Altered in front of her. Its lips curled back, its teeth bared and its open mouth a cavern. Sam's eyes drew up its face and pools of oily black took her in.

Stimmed.

Fuck.

Something blurred and cracked over the Apostate's head.

Its grip loosened, but before Sam could react, it kicked her squarely in the gut and she slammed into the floor. She writhed and her muscles spasmed with each empty gasp. Sam helplessly watched the Apostate's next movements.

It turned, a throaty growl escaping its mouth. A line of blood started down its head where Miriam had struck it with a chair. Sam reached out, knowing what was coming next, wanting to stop it, but unable to do anything.

It leaped onto Miriam and knocked her to the ground. The woman tried to grapple, tried to defend against the incoming blows, but she had nowhere to go—the Apostate straddled her and pinned her arms down. A sharp elbow battered into Miriam's head and Sam silently cried out. Stunned, Miriam's ensuing resistance wasn't enough to prevent the Apostate from tightening both hands around her throat.

Panic, then rage flooded through Sam. It overthrew her pain, her need for oxygen, everything. She lurched forward, raining blows on the Apostate's head and face, but nothing fazed it. She pulled at its hands but its clasp was unbreakable. Her chest tightened. Miriam's face was now a dark shade of red and her hands, previously raking at the fingers and joints of the Apostate's grip, were weakening.

No.

Sam's muscles tensed as she wrapped her prosthetic around the Altered's neck. She squeezed as her eyes latched onto Miriam's. The vessels in the woman's light brown eyes ruptured and Sam's world broke with them. Sam squeezed with every ounce of anger, every ounce of fear, hatred, and vengeance.

This was for Miriam.

For Station City.

Something broke, something popped—a delayed and dulled sensation in her prosthetic—but she didn't stop. She clenched her arm tighter and tighter until the body underneath her twitched and flailed.

This was for Ursus.

For her arm.

Something tugged at her shoulder, but Sam wasn't done. Her fingers clawed at the side of the Apostate's head, looking for a catch and finding it. Bone. She flexed and ripped in.

This was for her brother.

39

ORGAN FAILURE

MIRIAM HALF PULLED, half fell out of the Altered's grasp and air splintered into her lungs—a pain and a relief. She grasped at Sam, tried to call the woman's name, but her throat was crushed, screaming its own anguish. The wunby had gone limp in the crook of Sam's arm, its face a shade of violet and its eyes bulging. She croaked out for Sam again, but the woman's face had completely hardened, her eyes dark and glazed.

Nothing registered.

Miriam struggled to her feet and touched Sam's shoulder. "Stop, Sam. I'm here. Stop." Her voice grated like sandpaper.

The woman finally released her hold, her gaze steady on a middle distance. The wunby's body dropped, its head at a grotesque angle, its neck strangely elongated. Miriam painfully swallowed as she stared at the corpse and its internal decapitation, a skull severed from its spine. The head and pinched neck only connected to its person by skin and muscle.

Something thundered upstairs, a violent crack followed by a rumbling echo. Miriam tore her eyes away and covered herself as the ceiling shuddered, small pieces raining onto her. Her attention returned to Sam, whose face was still contorted, glaring down at the dead wunby.

Miriam realized she was heaving, still gasping in shards of air. She was afraid. Not of what was happening upstairs. Not of the Altered. Miriam was afraid of Sam in that moment. She didn't recognize the woman at all.

"—cho. Echo. This is Foxtrot Actual. Come in."

The voice crackled in her ears.

Her visor.

Krill's response was crisp. "It's good to hear your voice—"

Next to her, Sam blinked, then straightened. Blue eyes found her, and Miriam swallowed roughly again. She smothered and smoothed out her expression as best as she could.

"—commandeered prowlers. Heading back to help the company—"

Sam touched her ribs and grimaced before she moved to retrieve her rifle. She found Miriam's and offered it out. Miriam took it, but not before wrapping a hand around Sam's. *Stay with me,* she tried to say with her eyes and touch.

"Echo, status?" Krill's voice chimed in her ear, but she ignored it.

Hadeon and her team had done what they needed. The jammers were down and communication was back up, but they weren't finished.

Outside the office, the whine of the airgun climbed.

Sam brushed past Miriam and took a defensive stance in the doorframe. Miriam followed, positioning herself next to her, and took a broken breath. Across the hallway, Nas fired shots into a body. On the ground to his side, Yuri let go of another dead wunby's arm, a thin metal box falling out of its grip. Relief sped through Miriam, but it was short-lived.

Someone shouted down the hall over the airgun. Miriam didn't understand—whether it was a call in a different language or names she didn't recognize. The shouts came again. Names. Probably the dead wunbies.

Sam peeked out.

And then Miriam was driven back, Sam pushing her into the room as a heavy pressure slammed by. She stumbled over the corpse but found her balance again.

Around her, the building groaned, a grating sound shuddering through the floor and up Miriam's legs. And then one second, the floor in the hall was there, and the next it was gone, swallowed up by the level below. Miriam's eyes widened as the office wall crumbled with it, revealing a heavyset column and the now-open office across—Nas and Yuri scrambling back, their own mouths agape. Something crunched and snapped like splintering sticks, and the column compressed.

"Shit," Miriam breathed.

Bits of the ceiling above the hall flecked out.

"Back up!" Yuri shouted. "Back—"

Miriam's gut keeled into her throat as the floor gave out. She and everything around her fell forward in a steep slide into the inner workings of the building. Her hands flailed for Sam, for something, but it was all happening too fast. A shadow slammed into her face and stars alighted in her vision.

When she finally opened her eyes, the world had settled and Miriam was on her side. Her armor wedged into her armpits and neck, and everything hurt. She choked then coughed on the dry dust lining the inside of her nose and mouth. Pain coursed through her head with each racking motion and she winced, her jaw on fire. She'd have a concussion at least, and her hand moved automatically for her pack, trying to find the capsules that would stem the symptoms and keep swelling down, but her bag was gone, had somehow been dislodged in the descent.

Miriam forced herself to sit up. She couldn't tell where she was—if she was on the first or second floor. Debris and rebar scattered in copious piles around her. She gasped, choking once more on the particles in the air. She had been lucky. Her dropping path had been ridden out on top of the colossal slab of concrete below her. She lifted her eyes to the hole in the floor—now ceiling—then regretted it, her neck and jaw despising the movement. Miriam placed trembling palms on the dusty surface to ground herself.

Somehow, she survived.

Her stomach hardened and Miriam twisted, pain momentarily forgotten.

"Sam," she croaked. The bones and muscles in her face protested, but she didn't care. She called out again, louder, willing her throat and mouth to cooperate.

Rubble clattered. At the bottom edge of the slab, a powder-covered Sam crawled on her hands and knees. After a brief movement, she collapsed, then rolled over onto her back.

Ignoring her body's pleas, Miriam pulled herself closer. "Are you hurt?" She swept her hands across the woman. "Sam? Tell me where."

The woman mumbled, but Miriam couldn't make out the words. She inched closer, checking Sam's neck, face, and head. Her fingers brushed through dusty tufts of hair.

"Fine," Sam finally breathed, her voice a husky rattle. Her eyes squeezed shut. "Just need a second."

Miriam's forehead lowered to Sam's, her muscles both tensing and releasing. She ignored the return of pain in her head and jaw as she closed her own eyes and held herself over the woman she loved, their heavy breaths joining with the grime and particulates.

"You are alive."

Miriam's attention whipped to the new voice, and she squinted into a sudden shining light. Her hands flew to her side, but her weapon wasn't there.

"Friendly," the voice came. "I am friendly."

As Miriam's vision adjusted, she made out green glints peering down at her. Her eyes floated to the white armor, smudged and scorched, but familiar.

"Varya," Sam exhaled underneath Miriam.

The legionnaire made a throaty sound of acknowledgment

and her focus drifted up to the hole in the ceiling. "You two are lucky."

Miriam sat up. Her response came in the quietest of whispers, more a breath than anything. She doubted the Altered legionnaire could discern it even with enhanced hearing.

"I know."

◊

"No rest for the wicked."

Miriam cradled her face. The pain in her jaw receded with the capsules releasing in her bloodstream, but she still grimaced. The saying was something Benjamin Fox would've said—but he wasn't there. Would things have gone better if their teammate had been with them? Worse?

"Definitely wouldn't mind one of those secret scientist wonder drugs right about now," Nas muttered. He leaned into the wall while the rest of the team rested in the shadows of what used to be a small store.

Miriam stared at the government building across the street. Its facade mostly disguised the partial collapse inside, but she could still see a slight sag, like the start of a stroke on its face. She was grateful to be outside. Despite the smell of earth and chemicals, the air was fresh in comparison to where she had just been, and Miriam lapped it in, desperate to flush the dust and carbon out of her system.

"The Blightbringer?" Yuri asked.

"Perun stayed behind," Krill replied. "Ursus said another Legion squad is arriving soon. Razor-Alpha's making their way here as well."

"And the other sites? Spartans? Titans? Any news?"

The lead flicked a small piece of soil off his kit. "Still too early to say."

Miriam tried not to think about it. If the news from the

other locations was bad, it could wait until Echo had fully soaked in their victory in Sunali. She tossed medication gel to Kai and one of her last jabbers to Nas before she turned back to Sam.

Sitting on a broken chair they had pulled from a destroyed shop, the woman gazed at the bodies strewn across the lawn. Miriam followed her sightline to Porevit's armor on the steps. Another legionnaire hovered before they crossed his arms, his mace in between them. Her heart sank, and she looked away to her team around her.

Echo was intact.

Or as intact as they could be considering the hell they had fought through. Each marine had their own assortment of scrapes, holes, and cuts, but they were alive.

Miriam's hand tightened on Sam's shoulder and she fussed with the woman's hair, pressing it back to clean the scrapes and cuts along her scalp and face. Her fingers lingered but she didn't care that the others were there, watching.

Sam was alive. And though she was terrified of what she had seen the woman do, Sam was there. Miriam would figure this out. She'd fix it. They'd figure this out together.

"Don't get too comfortable." Krill straightened half-heartedly. "We still have work to do. We need to clear the rest of the town, at least what we can. Who knows what these fuckers left."

Miriam arched an eyebrow and though she partially regretted the motion, it was warranted. The team lead rarely swore.

Nas piped up. "Like I said, no rest for the wicked."

◊

The first cluster of Sunali shops and flats were cleared with no issues, no resistance, and no wunbies. There was nothing but unlocked spaces where the Altered terrorists had lived the past weeks. After the fifth building, Miriam found her guard relaxing as her own medication ran its course. Her head still ached, but it was dull, and the fog of concussion would remain a short distance away until her next prescribed intake.

Yuri produced a small paint marker and noted the door from which they had exited.

Clear.

Echo moved on to the second cluster of buildings down the street—what looked like a school interconnected with small bridges and passageways.

"Last one in the sector. Let's do it right," the lead said.

The team was exhausted, but they pushed on.

Sam took point, Yuri and Miriam behind her. The door opened and they were in, moving through the hall, holding angles while they cleared each room. Some high-ceilinged classrooms were filled with desks, bed frames, and mattresses scavenged from other residences. Others had been cleared out to serve as improvised workspaces and laboratories. Whoever had taken up this space had been higher-ranking along with any intellectuals working with the Blightbringers and other devices.

When Echo arrived at the second-to-last room, they paused. The rattle of a door reverberated down the wide hallway. After an entire building of unlocked classrooms, this locked space was a surprise. With Yuri covering, the team reenergized and shifted to clear the remaining area before they routed back, and when they repositioned, the second touched the door's panel.

Nothing.

Miriam stiffened, her senses heightening.

Krill motioned and Kai fished something out of her belt. She maneuvered to the front of the waiting stack and pressed a thin line of Hush Detcord at the seam of the door closest to the console. Chemical notes fluttered into Miriam's nose as it sizzled, and then something popped.

The door slid open and Yuri was first in, hooking to the right. Sam immediately followed on his heels to the left, and

Miriam and the rest of Echo filtered in. The room opened out in front, its ceiling higher than the others they had cleared. Rifles and visors scanned for any enemies in their delegated angles.

No wunbies.

"Well, shit," Nas exclaimed.

Miriam took in the room. Desks and overturned chairs filled the room. An array of displays and drives sat in rows on top of tables along the back wall.

"Are you seeing this?" Nas's rifle lowered and he hastened toward a stack of devices, sifting through them with a free hand. "Where was this when we needed it?" he said, partially to himself. He raised his voice to the others, "Pick up anything and everything. This is BigInt's wet dream."

Kai made a face as she followed him to the back. She touched a datapad. "Legion will want a look at this, too."

At the first row of desks, the lead hesitantly slung his rifle and opened a drawer. He lifted a stack of thin drives. "Call this in, please."

Yuri nodded and motioned at his visor and cuff.

Even if Miriam didn't know exactly what she was looking at, it was obvious the locked door and Nas's enthusiasm were indicators of importance.

"Hey, where are you going?" Kai called out.

"There's something back here," Nas responded. "Guys?"

Sam's rifle twitched. Nas's tone hadn't been one of surprise or worry, but Miriam could tell the comment made the woman anxious. She tried to find those blue eyes, to give Sam a reassuring smile. Part of her knew Sam was itching for a fight and wanted to go after more wunbies, but Miriam was relieved. There were none here. This was a win on top of their other wins.

She trailed after Kai and saw what Nas had found: a hidden rusted ladder that led to a loft-like space unseen from the entrance. The intelligence specialist slung his rifle and slowly climbed with a pained expression.

"Nas, wait," Miriam started, her sidearm already out.

He didn't wait.

Her visor scanned for any movement above, but there was none. She couldn't hear anything either, at least beyond the ambient noise.

At the other end of the room, Krill's voice lifted. "Slow down. Let's get—"

"It's fine," Nas called down. "I'm already here."

Miriam stepped closer to Kai and the ladder, while Sam stayed back at a wider angle, her rifle raised. Looking straight up, Miriam could make out the lip of what looked like a small nook bordered by a broken banister at least a floor and a half above. Had they seen this part of the school from outside? She couldn't remember.

Just before the edge of the platform, Nas winced as he hooked an arm into one of the rungs. With the other, he shifted his weapon forward. He tiptoed to peek over, his rifle barrel up with him.

"Clear."

Miriam relaxed, and Kai audibly sighed next to her. Sam lowered her weapon.

"There's more up here! Something else." Nas clamored over, and then he was out of view. A couple seconds later, his face reappeared over the edge. "Come up."

Kai flashed a sheepish smile before she started her ascent.

Miriam holstered her sidearm. "Nas, I swear if we got through all of this just for you to fall and break yourself, I'll kill you myself."

"Chill." He flashed a toothy grin. "We won!" He held out his hand for Kai and they both absconded into the nook.

Shortly after, Miriam heard the engineer click her tongue.

"Kai?"

"Huh. Interesting." Her teammate's voice drifted.

Krill made his way toward them. "Guys?"

No one responded and Miriam glanced back. The lead chucked his chin and she gripped the first rungs, the rusted texture digging into her fingers. She gave it a shake, but it held. Sturdy enough.

"Coming up. Don't shoot," Miriam muttered loudly.

Neither of their teammates answered, their whispers ongoing.

As she climbed, she could make out Kai's voice, cautious and hesitant. "Nas…"

"What'd you find?" Krill called up.

Miriam startled when the engineer's face appeared above her. "I don't know. Should we get Legion here?" She crouched and offered a hand to Miriam.

Nas's voice floated out. "And let them take credit for this? No way."

"Alright, leave it alone," Krill warned. "Especially you, Nas. Don't play with anything."

"Why do you always think I—" He groaned. "I'm just looking. Didn't touch—"

The space became a plume, a deafening roar in Miriam's ears.

And for the second time that day, she fell.

40

INHALE

ONE ONE THOUSAND.

First, her arm.

Two one thousand.

Then, her brother.

Three one thousand.

Sam wouldn't allow the Apostates to take Miriam. Not her, too.

Four—

Fuck.

Breathe. Just fucking breathe.

41

———

SELF AID

MIRIAM'S EYES WERE OPEN—SHE was sure of it—but she saw nothing but darkness. Her head throbbed like an undulating block of concrete and her body hurt something terrible, like a building had fallen on top of her. Again.

She tried to sit up but something pushed her back. She tried again but couldn't; that same something was strong, holding her down. The fight left her with a cry as pain and pressure responded to her straining, and Miriam tensed against the heat, then cold.

Cold.

Her back was cold.

She was on the floor. She could feel the uneven ground poking at her.

It wasn't much, but it provided some semblance of orientation. Her vision slowly returned as she clamored for control and she could make out a couple of figures above her in a haze, like she was seeing through both water and smoke. She could taste blood, metallic and thick on her aching tongue.

The pressure on her arms and body eased and Miriam tried to perch up again. Immediately, rough hands pressed into her and a gurgle of frustration bubbled up her throat.

"Mir, stop. Stay still."

Sam.

She froze. She made out the blond hair, then roamed down until she found Sam's eyes. Through the pain and confusion, Miriam anchored herself to them. She wanted Sam to look at her, tell her what was going on, but the woman was preoccupied, her skin tight around her eyes and mouth. Miriam raised her head, but she didn't have to lift far to see it.

A scrap of metal protruding in the air.

From her body.

Miriam exhaled sharply.

Shit.

Liver? She couldn't tell. She strained further up to see, to touch, but hands were in her way, batting her own down.

"My kit..." Miriam muttered. Her head turned, trying to locate her gear, but her vision was limited—she couldn't see around Sam and the overturned tables behind her.

It could be her large intestine.

"I need my kit."

The woman ignored her, but Miriam realized she could barely hear herself. Had she actually spoken? Had she said it out loud?

The edges of her vision blurred and the face above hers transformed into a patchwork of light and dark strokes, the world around her a kaleidoscope of distress and discombobulation. Amidst it all, the throbbing resumed, a relentless drumbeat against the backdrop of her muddled consciousness.

Hell. This wasn't good.

"I can fix it. Just get my—"

"Mir, please—"

Sam's voice muffled or Miriam's hearing went out. The ceiling rotated and shifted. And then familiar voices echoed and shouted beyond them.

"—dic! Get a fuckin' medic!"

Medic. *She* was the medic.

Miriam tried to sit up again. "Sam, I can fix this."

She reached out, trying to locate her pack. It had just been on her. It couldn't have gone far.

"Fuck! Someone help!"

The rawness in Sam's cracking voice stopped Miriam, and then something pressed her down again. This time, green eyes glinted at her. Miriam studied them, entranced, as she made out the swirls of black in now green and blue eyes. Words came out and floated, spiraled around her, but she was oblivious to their meaning, their realities.

Miriam gasped.

Words.

She needed to say three words, but her mouth wouldn't work. She tried to force her lips to open, her tongue to curl. She tried to find the set of blue eyes, but everything was colliding, blurring together.

She just needed to fix

42

SEPSIS

A DULL PULSE throbbed behind Miriam's eyes, a persistent throb demanding her attention. She opened them slowly, wincing as harsh light stabbed at her. Her head and body were heavy, a leaden weight anchored to cool, crisp sheets.

Memories flickered like glowing embers in a dying fire.

The North.

Ursus.

The earth erupting around her.

Falling, and then, nothing.

Alarm gnawed at the edges of her mind, and as she looked around, confusion replaced it, twisting like a knot. These walls and equipment were familiar, but it wasn't enough to connect and explain why they *were* familiar. The realization was just out of reach.

"Welcome back."

Her head rolled to the side, and Yuri straightened in the chair beside her. The medication coursing through her system had made her sluggish, but his voice was a balm to frazzled nerves.

"Where..." she started. Her throat was sandpaper dry. She tried again. "Where are we?"

"Station."

The color of the walls, the furniture, all the familiarity snapped in, but it made little sense. She and Echo had just been in Sunali. Miriam tried to pull herself up, but Yuri placed a gentle hand on her shoulder.

"What happened?" she pressed, her voice barely a whisper.

Yuri's smile faltered, and languid panic rose again.

"Sam. Where—is she okay?" Despite her medicated brain, she wanted information. Details. She craved them, needed them like a sudden thirst.

"She's fine. She's headed back to your apartment. You just missed her, but I messaged, let her know you're awake."

Miriam's eyes narrowed. "What happened, Yuri?"

He sighed but relented. The words and sentences came out like running water and after a while, Miriam wanted it to stop, but it was already out—she couldn't plug it back up. She lay there as blurred memories pieced together with Yuri's recount. The Blightbringers and jammer relays hadn't been the only things left behind in the wunbies' retreat and defeat. The school site Echo had stumbled upon had been trapped, a bonus gift from the terrorists. With communications back up, Hadeon's squad had emergency exfiltrated Echo back to Ursus, but the outpost's resources were inundated with the other sites' casualties.

Miriam had questioned Yuri, pondered out loud why she couldn't have been seen in the nearby settlements—their clinics had similar capabilities. Her injuries in her hazy memory had been serious, but not terrible enough to evacuate to Station City hours away.

When Yuri answered, Miriam turned her head the other way, her eyes stinging. Of the three who'd been evacuated, her injuries were the least severe. Nas's spine had shattered in the blast, only made worse by his wild motions after. Their teammate had gone into hysterics, not because of his own state, but from Kai's broken body next to his. The doctors didn't know the full extent of the engineer's injuries, but her brain was swelling, an ample section of her skull already removed to relieve the pressure.

Yuri sniffled and cleared his throat. "They'll be okay."

He didn't seem convinced.

"I talked with your mother. She said she'd come by later when she's done with her meetings. And Fox stopped by before —he's with Kai now. Nas's family…" Yuri took a deep breath. "I'm just glad you're okay."

A tear escaped Miriam's eye, but she didn't try to wipe it away. She carefully touched her own abdomen under the sheet, feeling the padding of gel bandages underneath a thin gown. When she looked back at Yuri, her mind much clearer with the sobering updates, she found his eyes weary. Around the scrapes and cuts, his face was full of lines alien to his characteristic optimism. Or maybe that was an old version of her best friend. Maybe this was who he had been the past months and she hadn't been paying close enough attention. They were all injured and hurt. He didn't have to be in a hospital bed to understand or hold the full weight of that.

"Yuri, I—"

Hurried footsteps echoed into the room, and Sam emerged in the doorway. Her hair was unkempt, her eyes tinged with sleepless nights, and her breath was shallow, as if she had just sprinted an entire sector. Sam's hands fidgeted as she rushed to the bed, and then cool fingers brushed along Miriam's forehead.

A different kind of warmth spread from Miriam's core—a better one.

"I'm okay," she whispered into Sam's palm.

Yuri cleared his throat and stood. "I'm going to check on the others. You'll be alright?"

Miriam wasn't sure if he was talking to her or Sam, but she broke her gaze to give him a nod. She'd reach out to him, and soon. Between her own close call and the news of Nas and Kai, she couldn't take anything for granted—their friendship included.

He slipped away.

"I'm okay," Miriam repeated.

"What can I do?" Sam pulled away to bring the chair closer, but didn't sit.

Frustration gurgled in Miriam's throat, protesting the loss of physical contact. Her hand reached out, but her muscles ached and her arm dropped.

"Water. Are you thirsty?" The woman moved away, starting to rummage around the room.

Yes. At the mention, Miriam's throat was bone-dry, but no, she just wanted Sam to be near her.

"There's nothing here." Sam pulled at a drawer then poked at a cabinet. "Why don't they make things accessible? Do you have the console? No, never mind, I'll go find—"

"Sam."

The woman stopped, a foot already in the doorway.

"Just—just stay with me."

The woman's eyebrows raised then relaxed. She hurried back to the chair.

"No. Come here." Miriam weakly patted the side of the bed. Her little movements were compounding, and her body protested, already fatigued from the briefest interaction.

Sam's voice quieted. "I don't want to hurt you."

Miriam scoffed, then winced. "You won't."

The bed dipped to the side with Sam's weight. Gentle fingers fixed her hair and Miriam's eyes drooped.

"You need more rest."

Miriam shook her head, but it felt slow and clumsy again. "I've had enough…" She forced her eyes open.

Sam's mouth pulled to the side. "I can see you fighting. Listen to your body, isn't that what you told me before?"

A lifetime ago.

"Sleep. I'll be here, I promise."

Miriam's eyes shuttered, too heavy to keep open. "Fine." She felt a cool thumb brush her brow, down her temple, and trace her jaw. Drowsiness crept in with the comforting motion. But then the hand was gone, and the bed shifted.

"Coffee?" Miriam croaked in a last-ditch effort.

Sam chuckled. "Coffee isn't what you need right now."

Miriam forced her eyes to open halfway, a blur of blond hair and blue eyes smiling at her.

"And you say I'm stubborn. I'll see what I can find. Sleep."

Her eyes shut.

Sam's voice came again, more distant now. "Mir? Don't go anywhere."

"Wouldn't dream of it," Miriam mumbled.

Distant pain and heavy medication dropped over her like a mantle, and then she was out.

◊

Something fluttered against her cheek, and Miriam's nose wrinkled. She sighed as fingers brushed up and down her jaw. Without opening her eyes, Miriam turned into the touch, a kiss into the palm.

"That was quick," Miriam murmured. She floated in the grogginess of partial slumber and smiled as lips brushed hers. She returned the kiss—barely a peck—before it was gone. Miriam arched, wanting more, but her heavy body held her down.

A whisper tickled her nose. "I was so worried."

Miriam's brows furrowed and she fought the pull of medication to open her eyes. Dark irises in smudged outlines stared into hers. Confusion anchored her to the bed.

"Ana?"

"They said you were here—" The woman leaned in and planted her lips on Miriam's. "You weren't responding before and I—"

Miriam's muscles groaned as she pressed further back into her pillow. "What are you doing—"

Something shifted in the background, and Miriam swung her sluggish vision to focus on the doorway. Her chest tightened. Sam stood frozen, gripping a tray of covered plates and cups. Blue eyes held on Miriam and the woman leaning over her, above her. Too intimately close. Miriam's heart fell as Sam's face suspended, crumpled, then darkened in seconds both too long and too short.

"No, S—"

But the woman was gone, the door sliding shut shortly after.

Panic bolstering her strength and energy, Miriam raised herself onto an elbow, forcing Ana back. She inhaled sharply as she maneuvered herself from under the covers, whimpering at the tug of connected tubes and wires. Ana protested, but Miriam shrugged her off, fumbling with the needles and their shackling imprisonment.

On wobbly legs, she stumbled forward, leaning into the bed frame, the door, then somehow catching the swirling corridor wall. At the first intersection, Miriam called out for Sam with a strangled plea.

Something dripped, and she found a broken tray sitting on the edge of a nearby counter; a cup was on its side, its spilled dark liquid still steaming as it splattered on the floor. Despite surprised and sharp remarks from faceless figures, Miriam forced herself in the counter's direction—toward the hospital wing's atrium and the exit beyond it.

The floor, ceiling, and walls spiraled, but she couldn't pass out. Not yet.

She cried out again with a desperate gasp.

Her hand reached out to cling to the atrium door, but found it was already open.

"You shouldn't be out here."

Miriam halted and willed her heart to stop thumping inside

her head. She fought the unbalance of a swaying floor and stepped into the wide space, her sight anchoring on the blonde woman sitting on the steps. Miriam's legs trembled and she clutched a nearby pillar. The ache in her abdomen spread, and she shook away the thought of reopened stitches.

"Sam."

It came out in a broken whisper.

"Sam," she uttered, louder.

The woman didn't turn around.

Miriam's stomach contracted and twisted. This wasn't supposed to happen like this. None of this was supposed to happen.

Sam's shoulders lifted with a deep breath.

Miriam concentrated, bracing for the exhale.

"Do you—" The woman's voice caught, as if the next words would saw through every muscle and bone. "Do you love her?"

Blood drained from Miriam's face, and a coldness persisted in its place. She hadn't expected those words, that question. Why would Sam ask that? It had never been a thought in Miriam's mind. How could she think that?

The shock rendered her speechless. Paralyzed. The words she wanted to say—

I'm sorry.

It meant nothing.

I regret it.

It was a mistake.

I should've told you.

I love you.

Each phrase, each word curled up inside her, wanting to punch up and out, but nothing did. Her throat closed and she couldn't say anything, couldn't breathe.

Sam's voice dialed into something colder and distant. "How long?"

The question punched into Miriam's lungs and diaphragm. Black spots dotted her vision, and the steps and pavement threatened to swallow her up. She tried to shake her head, but Sam didn't see, her back still to her.

"No—"

"I'm so stupid. I thought you were—" Sam huffed. "I thought you couldn't sleep all those nights—"

The atrium shifted.

This wasn't happening. This was never supposed to happen.

"No, Sam," Miriam managed.

It was only one time.

One time too many.

Sam scoffed. "How long have you been lying to me?"

The serrated edge carved in.

"I didn't—" Miriam cracked. Her vision began to tunnel. If only she got to Sam, got her to turn around, to face her, see her. If Miriam could just hold her, Sam would understand what she couldn't say.

She pushed away from the concrete pillar and stepped forward, but her foot fell through the floor. As the pavement enveloped her, Miriam resisted. She clawed at air and ground, grasping to keep herself in the conscious world.

I love you.

Miriam had to fix this.

I love you, Sam.

Her hand reached out, but it was too late.

Darkness consumed her.

PRIVATE MESSAGE
[TANNER TO RYAN]

M. TANNER: Can we talk?

M. TANNER: Sam, please answer my calls.

M. TANNER: I don't want to do this over messages.

Message delivered.

PRIVATE MESSAGE
[TANNER TO RYAN]

M. TANNER: I love you.

M. TANNER: I should've told you earlier. I should've told you all of this before. I'm so sorry, I know I messed up.

M. TANNER: I love you.

M. TANNER: Please talk to me.

Message delivered.

EXPECTANT

MIRIAM RAPPED her knuckles on the studio door. She called out a few more times before she sank forward, her forehead resting against the cool material, willing her desperation through.

"Sam, please let me in."

When Miriam had discharged herself early from the hospital, her first destination had been her apartment. Though she had a feeling the woman wouldn't be there, part of her still hoped. She hoped she'd catch Sam, hoped to apologize, to explain, to make everything right. Though her body had protested her impatient motions, she had made it home.

But home was Sam, and though the woman's items—her clothes, her toiletries, her holopad—were still where she had last left them, Sam wasn't there. Miriam had waited, then messaged and called, even searched their usual spots in UMF, but the woman eluded her.

It was excruciating, the sudden absence, the sudden silence.

After a week, it was too much. She finally turned to Yuri, and her guilt and regret barreled out. It had been another wave of anguish when his face fell then hardened. Yuri was her teammate, her best friend, and they had known each other since they were kids. He'd laughed and teased her through uni into UMF for her womanizing, her flirtations and games. They talked about anything and everything without judgment. Or they used to. Before it all went to shit.

Before *she* made it all go to shit.

Yuri had sat in uncharacteristic silence, unable to look her in the eye. She knew she deserved it, knew she had taken a chisel to their own friendship, but she'd fix everything after she fixed things with Sam. She just needed to find Sam first.

Miriam struck the door with her palm, and the motion reverberated through her body, a dull ache spreading through her abdomen. Down the corridor, another flat opened and she reluctantly straightened. The neighbor eyed her suspiciously and she gave a curt nod in response. They had seen each other the previous day, and the one before that. Miriam pounded her fist one more time before she pulled herself away.

Defeated, she left the complex and stood at the shuttle stop outside. She was in no rush to get back to her empty apartment, and despite the growing throb in her core, Miriam walked away from the wails of ambulances toward the streets of laughing drunks and muffled club beats. The messages she had sent earlier remained a block of their own on top of a mountain of unanswered lines.

Someone stumbled into the pavement ahead of her, and Miriam stepped aside. The late crowd was spilling out, the first wave of ongoing frivolities. The city was capricious, either in celebration of UMF and Legion's success or tippling as an escape from their wartime reality. Rhythm leaked from open doors and Miriam hurried by, ignoring the reminders of another life and other gravitations before.

Before Sam.

Miriam tried to swallow but couldn't.

Without Sam, she was adrift.

It was obvious the woman was avoiding her. Could Miriam fault her? She had cheated. Even if Miriam had a different definition of what they were at the time, she had known the second she woke up. She knew how awful the betrayal was, had been terrified of confessing it, and of the potential consequences. Miriam still recalled little of that night, but she knew she had been a participant; she had pulled the trigger herself.

Do you love her?

Her throat tightened again. It killed her knowing Sam believed there was more to it, that Sam had thought what they had was a lie. Pain speared into her, but she quickened her pace. When her muscles screamed out in protest, Miriam stopped a few blocks from her apartment and leaned into a closed street kiosk. She clutched her abdomen and wheezed for breath.

In a nearby side street, containers clanked against the pavement and voices flurried out. Miriam wiped the sweat from her forehead and glanced over. Two figures loomed near another, a drunk woman from the look of it, doubled over in the shadows. Miriam scowled and pawed away her aches. She could do one thing right, this night at least.

She made her way closer, her steps soft and careful. The drunk woman slipped, barely catching herself before her face planted into the wall. In the movement, something caught in the streetlight and Miriam's breath seized.

Light and short hair.

Even in the darkness, Miriam recognized it and she gravitated forward.

Sam.

Of all places, Sam.

Miriam's posture tensed, and her lip twitched as the two figures—two men—alerted to her presence. "Back off," she growled, the ache in her body gone. Her muscles coiled.

One of the men raised his hands. "Whoa. We didn't do anything. We were walking by, I swear. She fell over. We're just trying to help her get home."

The other individual took a step back. "Look, this lady's drunk off her rocker."

"Yeah, she really shouldn't be out here by herself. She's lucky it was us who came by, not anyone else."

Sam straightened, then swayed forward, her prosthetic delayed but catching her before she fell into the wall again. Miriam darted closer just as the woman's legs folded and dropped to the ground, a knee in a puddle of her own sick.

What was Sam doing out here? Had she been coming back to the apartment?

"We were about to call SecTeam..."

Miriam touched the woman's shoulder carefully then waved the men off, a mumbled *thank you* on her lips. Sam pushed off the ground, and Miriam wrapped her hands around the woman before she slipped.

"You sure? Thought she was one of them alties at first—arm like that. Maybe SecTeam or the base guards can help—"

"No, I know her. We're..."

Together? Could they still be together?

"I know her." Miriam settled. She waited for the two strangers to walk off before she heaved the woman up, grunting as her gel bandages stretched underneath her shirt. She slid herself under Sam's armpit. The stench of alcohol and vomit hovered over them as Miriam moved carefully back to the main street, back to her apartment nearby.

She struggled; Sam's feet and weight were inconsistent, sometimes dragging along the pavement, sometimes working like those of a child who had only started to walk. Miriam's body ached and pulled at each movement, but she ignored it. She owed Sam this. She was committed.

When they made it to the lift in her building, Miriam was drenched in sweat, and she was grateful for the short break. She hitched Sam higher on her shoulder and tucked a strand of the woman's hair behind an ear. The warmth of intoxication radiated from Sam's skin.

Once inside, Miriam lowered the woman into the loveseat and caught her breath. She watched Sam's slackened face, the redness where she had hit the wall, and then the rise and fall of her chest. The woman's eyelids fluttered. Sam had been nearby, close enough to the apartment. After a week, was she trying to come home? Come back to Miriam?

She went to the kitchen and came back with two cups of water, a clean cloth, some bandages, and an enzyme nanocapsule trapped in her palm. After unsuccessful attempts to get Sam to take a drink, Miriam stared at the capsule, uncertain whether to use it or not on the intoxicated woman. After a few seconds, she put it aside and dampened the cloth, softly brushing at broken skin on Sam's face, palm, and knuckles. When they were as clean as she could get them, Miriam gently applied medicated strips along the scrapes.

Sam shifted, and her eyelids fluttered again. She took a deep inhale, then stirred as recognition crept in. "No," she breathed, barely a whisper. "Not here."

Daggers stabbed into Miriam's heart and she pulled away, but Sam had already stilled, her breath deepening. Miriam got up and took a step back, another glimpse at the nanocapsule. She had been right in her hesitation before. What would happen if Sam was suddenly sober when she didn't want to be —when she didn't want to be in the apartment? Near her?

Reluctantly, Miriam raised her commcuff. She wanted to keep the woman there, take care of her, hope that she'd listen to her pleas, but part of her knew it was wrong. She quickly sent a message before she could change her mind then returned to cleaning what she could, taking her time, holding on to however long she had with Sam, even if the woman wasn't fully there. With the hum of her appliances in the background, Miriam tried to figure out how she could turn back time and change things, change her decisions, her fear, and her actions.

She had lost herself in her thoughts and automatic motions

when a thin sliver of blue stared at her in a glimpse of consciousness. And then it was gone, a heavy eyelid shut.

Miriam froze as Sam exhaled, a murmur enveloped within. If Miriam hadn't been right next to her, she would have missed it.

"Did you ever love me?"

Her breath hitched as the question punched into her, impaling her. Time stretched as she stared at Sam's lithe face, lips slightly parted with each breath whirling alcohol and regret. Miriam exhaled shallowly. That question pressed upon her, a juxtaposing sharp and dull hurt.

Did you ever love me?

Miriam forced her throat to unclench. "I lov—"

Someone knocked on the apartment door.

She searched the unconscious face in front of her. "Sam, I've always—"

The rap came again and then her cuff buzzed angrily on her wrist.

Hesitantly, Miriam rose, her steps slow and heavy. Words hung heavy in her chest as she hovered a hand over the door's console.

"Tanner," a muffled voice filtered through.

She didn't want to open it, but the knock came, harsher this time.

Miriam touched the controls and stepped back, avoiding Yuri's frown. She wished she had taken longer to message him, wished he had taken a much longer route, wished he had given her more time. He slipped into the apartment, and by the time she turned, Sam had been effortlessly scooped into his arms, her head lolling into his chest.

Without a pause, Yuri grunted, "Address?"

"I'll send it to you. Her cuff—"

"Got it."

And then they were both gone.

Miriam stood, unmoving, watching the space where Sam

had been, the indent of her body and presence already disappearing. She touched the console automatically and the door closed, locking her in her own prison of consequences. Her arm dropped like a weight to her side.

Why hadn't she said what she needed to when they first met? Why hadn't Miriam told Sam to stay with her? That she had made a mistake, that she had learned how much Sam meant? Miriam wanted Sam. She chose Sam. She loved her. Why hadn't she answered, told her what she knew was true?

Did you ever love me?

The choke came like a cresting wave and a tearless sob shook her from the core out. Her knees buckled, and the cold, bare wall bit through her shirt, through every layer of skin as she slid down.

"I love you."

She said it.

"I'm *in* love with you."

A truth too quiet, too late.

Was it real if no one heard it?

$$46$$

CULMINATION

SOMETHING FLUTTERED in Sam's ears, in the back of her mind, but it was like a voice lost in the wind. Her stomach churned and she shot up, scrambling for anything to puke into. Pain exploded in smacked knuckles, and the shock shoved the bile back down her throat.

Now brutally awake, she squinted, adjusting her vision. Dark outlines of walls and scant furniture stared at her, too close and at wrong angles.

She was back in her studio apartment.

Sam had no memory of how she'd arrived, where she was before, or most of the night, but she was there now. The realization came accompanied by an ache threatening to split her brain and body apart. She clutched her head but winced at the motion. Her hand, her face—everything—felt raw.

With a groan, Sam pulled herself to the edge of the bed, her bare toes curling before she resigned them to the tile beneath. The coolness grounded and soothed the growing throb in her muscles and she took a deep breath, but cut it short. The place faintly smelled of herbs and plants.

In the corner, the shadowed frame of an empty vertical

garden sat where she had last placed it—on top of a small box of her brother's uniforms and city-bought clothes. She had never gotten around to bringing them to the reclamation center or to the nearby dumpster.

Sam mumbled a command and blinked as the studio lights engaged. Now illuminated in the spartan space, Scott's possessions looked sparser—his life reduced to a small square meter in a city he had barely lived in. Her brother had had hobbies, aspirations, and people who loved him, and this was all he had left.

What did she have?

Even less.

It was a sobering thought. Sam squeezed her eyes shut and rubbed her fingers into her forehead, trying to physically press the ache away. Something flapped on the back of her hand, and she stared at the bandage on her knuckles.

Recognition flickered, but before she could try to process it, something winked in the corner of her eye. She straightened. In her violent awakening, her brother's thin memorial box had jarred loose on the nearby end table. Sam touched the lid before she retrieved Scott's necklace, letting its cool links spill and pool into the palm of her left hand. For a long minute, she stared at the chain before she closed her hand around it.

She looked up, finding herself in the wall mirror, and glared at how simultaneously small and giant she was in its reflection. Her eyes turned away from the person staring back and her jaw clenched. She hated the mirror's false projection—an attempt to make the room something bigger than it was.

This studio wasn't her home. It was a dead space with empty remnants and husks of someone who had once existed during a fleeting visit. It was just a room in a city where she had nothing to tether to. Not anymore.

Sam swallowed the lump in her throat and engaged a new channel on her commcuff. With a last look around the apartment, she pocketed the last memory of her brother and cleared her throat, instructing her device to prepare a message.

"I want in."

◊

"You look like shit."

The Altered woman had learned new vocabulary, probably from her time with UMF and SOG marines. Sam grumbled a sarcastic response and pulled her forearm from Varya's grip.

"But you are in good company. We do not look much better."

She wasn't wrong. A dark welt sat over one eye and synthetic staples lined what looked to be an already healing gash along her jaw.

Metal clanked against metal and Sam shot a glare at the screener as he turned her carbine in examination. He didn't notice, his eyes scanning meticulously along its parts, ridiculous spectacles magnifying bright orange irises.

"I didn't know you were all back," Sam mumbled.

"Only me. Hadeon and the others are still out there." Varya blinked at Sam's raised eyebrow. "There is more work to do; the enemy is already refortifying elsewhere."

"And your team won't miss you?" Sam's question pricked at herself, but she shrugged the feeling away.

"Legion understands the importance in this initiative. I have their support," Varya responded. "Your timing was impeccable. No problems from your team and leadership?"

"No."

Whether it was because of her previous poster child reputation, the spotlight from her experimental prosthetic, or something else, someone had pulled strings with UMF Command and SOG. As for her team... Sam's stomach knotted.

Before she could identify the onset of emotions, the

screener fluttered his fingers at her head and outstretched an open hand. Sam placed her visor in his palm. Without examining it, he tossed it into a bin behind him then held out his hand again.

"What? I need that."

Orange-ringed pupils stared back at her. Indifferent.

"Those are my eyes. It syncs with my weapon, my implant. We don't all have your genes." She turned. "Varya, am I not getting any of this back?"

The Altered woman smirked. "You can hold on to your weapon for now, but we will have to visit one of our armorers. You will want adjustments—better features, better rounds. As for your other items, do not worry. We will fit you with something better." She motioned an impatient finger at Sam's wrist. "Svaroz wants your device."

Sam cradled her wrist. "Don't I need it?"

"Not where we are going. You will not be able to contact anyone for a while. Nor will you want to."

Hesitancy and doubt hovered, but before Sam could consider anything further, she unlocked the clasp and shoved it into Svaroz's palm.

"Are you certain about this?"

Sam avoided Varya's intense gaze and watched her cuff clatter against her visor in the bin. She held out her prosthetic hand until the screener pushed her carbine into it. "Tell me what we're doing again."

The Altered woman's chin lifted. "We will find Kartik and everyone else responsible. We will make them all answer for what they have done."

Sam closed her fingers—flesh and alloy—around her rifle. She could feel the scratches, scuffs, and blemishes along its sections and grip.

"Then yes, I'm certain."

"Good," Varya huffed. She led the way out of the room and

into a sweeping, open hangar. Two short-winged airships sat staggered, the engine of the furthest one already engaged and whirring as a mix of people milled about in purposeful motion.

Sam noted the first ship was smaller than the one she and Echo had taken with Hadeon and Varya. As they passed, she smothered the ache in her chest and the voice whispering in her thoughts, distracting herself with a long gander inside the passenger compartment. It had two rows of seats facing each other, and could easily fit ten people—maybe seven or eight legionnaires crammed together. Her eyes widened at the turret-like weapon in the open side door and the sizable gash around it across the ship's surface. Metal gnarled, like teeth in a terrifying grin.

"Varya, where exactly are we going?"

"Wherever it hurts the most." The woman flashed a smile— or what Sam thought was one. "Come on. We need to get you a skullhelm."

Sam wanted to ask what that was, but Varya had already slipped around the second aircraft's wing and pulled herself through the side door, squeezing past its turret. Sam eyed the buzzing propulsion device along the wing and thought it better to approach the ship via its open ramp in the rear. She caught a glimpse of the Altered woman before she disappeared in the front cabin and reemerged a few seconds later, lobbing something dark and compact at her. Sam grabbed it from the air and studied the item. Its matte texture was almost a perfect match with her prosthetic's material—smooth to the touch— and it was essentially a square, thick and flat, but surprisingly light in her grip.

She turned it over curiously. "What is it?"

Varya weaved around the turret and plucked the square out of her hand. She lifted it and Sam flinched—a memory and flash of someone else reaching out. Sam shook her head, cursing and apologizing under her breath, then forced herself still as the square touched and covered her left ear. Before she could recoil, the device unfurled itself from its sides and she felt a strange sensation as the light material expanded over her skull then framed around her face. Her breath caught as the material flexed over her jaw in a flash of claustrophobia.

"This is new," Varya said, her voice now somehow clearer.

A visor-like shield shuttered over Sam's face and her eyes flitted at the strange symbols and gauges in the display before the Altered legionnaire tapped against the helm.

"A new generation of technology, and far better than whatever your military has." Varya motioned at a spot behind her own ear. "Until we fit you with an embed, this will be the best way to communicate." She then touched another spot on her jaw for Sam to mirror. "Disengaging clasp."

Sam held two fingers over the approximate location and the helmet folded back into itself and dropped into her waiting hand. She stared at the square in her palm.

"We will fit you with better armor when we get back to camp," Varya said. "And your weapon…"

Sam gripped her carbine.

Someone called for the Altered woman outside the aircraft, but Varya observed Sam curiously before she continued. "The rest of the team is on the way. We will head out soon. In the meantime, you can store your pack in one of the empty cabinets. Do you need anything else?"

Sam forced her fingers to relax. "No, this is fine."

After Varya jumped out of the ship, Sam wrapped her mind around the new technology and the suddenness of everything around her. She brushed her hand along the wall of the cabin, and looked over the individual cubbies above each seat until she stopped in front of one with no nameplate. She peered down at the diamond on her T-shirt. After months of trying to return back to SOG status, she was willingly giving it up. For what?

UMF was her life.

Sam set her pack on the chair and thrust her hand into her

pocket. Her fingers rubbed along the links of her brother's necklace.

Scott and UMF had raised her.

But Scott was dead and UMF had held her back.

Her hand clenched into a fist, as if the motion could close the gaping hole in her heart.

You're with me.

Sam's stomach hardened, her muscles tense.

Lies.

So many fucking lies.

She had no home in Ursus and she had no home in Station City.

Her hand pulled out of her pocket and Sam flexed both flesh and prosthetic. Fuck it all. She'd make her home in relevance, in doing what she was trained to do.

Sam took a deep inhale. She cared little about the scant details in joining a strange, hybrid team. Its adamant promise of effectiveness was all that mattered.

"Psychin' yourself up?"

Sam shot a glare toward the ramp and the voice's owner.

"Oh, if a look could kill. You s'posed to be the one-armed wonder?"

A stocky man trudged up the ramp, a huge bag slung over his wide shoulders. He heaved it over his head into a nearby nook, then slapped a piece of tape haphazardly in the nameplate below. When his meaty hand drew away, Sam read the scrawled letters: ALPHABET. The "alpha" had been bolded in a repeated outline.

The man sucked hard on his nicosynth device before he pushed out a steady stream of vapor from the side of his mouth. A pink scar on his opposite cheek stretched with the motion. "Not so one-armed, are ya?"

Sam lifted her chin as he sat diagonally across, his gaze blatantly roving over her. When his dark eyes met hers, he didn't look away, only settled into an unimpressed stare. The man tongued his cheek then adjusted his scuffed chest plates. Sam took a glimpse at his kit—not UMF issue. It was customized and well-made despite the scorch marks tinging the edges of his shoulder straps. Mercenary. Sam looked for any identifying patches or emblems along his outfit, trying to figure out his background, or where he was from, but she came up short. A discomforting glimmer danced within his pupils.

Unstable.

Did Sam have the same look?

Team Suicide, Kai had called it.

Promise me.

Sam scowled at the silent words.

"Don't talk much, do ya? Y'mute?"

Her teeth gritted together before she snapped, "Get your callsign cause you can't spell?"

Alphabet's eyebrow twitched before his face cracked with a crazed grin. "She bites." He took another inhale of his nicosynth then exhaled.

Sam bristled.

"Vengeance said you're alright."

Her lip curled. "Vengeance?"

The man sucked his teeth, then softly whistled to the side. Sam looked down the ramp where Varya stood with two other Altered in dark outfits, their heterochromatic blue and green eyes flashing.

"Your pal."

Varya? Sam hadn't realized legionnaires had callsigns.

He raised one hand, clawing in the air. "Have y'seen what she can do? She's a beast. She might tell ya she rescued us over yonder in the taints of hell. Vertex left us a bit high and dry, but we would've been fine, we dint need any rescuin'. Looks like you've dealt with them—Vertex, I mean." He bobbed his chin toward her prosthetic. "Looks like summa the tech they do."

Sam continued to stare at him. Definitely a mercenary hire.

"We've been runnin' with Vengeance and summa these

fancy-ass soldiers for a week now. We'll see if ya can keep up." His attention shifted and he jerked his head as another individual lumbered up the ramp past the Altered.

The incoming man was slim, his hair shaved down on both sides, emphasizing swollen, enlarged cartilage on both ears. As he passed between them, he slowly peered at Sam and regarded her with the enthusiasm of a rock. Sam steadied her breath. His eyes were pools of oil, both seeing and not seeing her. If not for the minuscule rings of brown irises, she wouldn't have been certain if the man was human or Altered. He lowered himself carefully into the seat next to Alphabet, directly across from Sam.

"This's Brute, but on special occasions, you can call 'im 'Princess.' He likes that." Alphabet slapped his hand on the man's knee and chuckled to himself, before he hollered out, "Oy, superfreaks! We gettin' a move on?"

Sam stiffened, ready for the ensuing confrontation with the Altered. To her surprise, Varya and the others calmly headed toward them. When they had all boarded, Varya tapped the hatch, and the ramp raised, sealing the back of the aircraft.

"You are mouthier than usual," said one of the Altered as he passed, a hearty pat on Alphabet's cheek. "I prefer you stimmed."

Across the aisle, the man grinned and playfully kicked at the Altered as they passed. Both former legionnaires gave Sam a nod before they found their own seats closer to the open side door. She looked around, waiting for introductions or Alphabet to chime in, but there was nothing. It was a dynamic she'd have to get used to. She felt the aircraft dip slightly as two pilots entered from the front—Altered, from the brief glints of their eyes. This was an Altered ship, after all.

Varya paused and towered in front of Sam. "Is he bothering you?"

She shook her head.

The Altered woman scoffed. "No need to lie. He bothers all

of us." She smirked to the side. "Alphabet, how did your other colleague say it?"

"Eh. Fuck 'im. He's a pussy. Too afraid to join the real fight."

"Ah. Psychopathic motherfucker," Varya chanted, quoting someone from their battles the week before.

Crazies, Kai had said.

"Fuckin' right, Vengey-poo."

"I would love to kill you someday." The Altered's mouth widened in a predatory grin.

"Git in line, love."

The airship's engine purred, and Sam felt the mechanics inside the aircraft shift.

Varya turned back to Sam and shouted over the increasing noise, "It is good to have you with us. Get comfortable, it will be a long ride." The Altered woman pulled herself forward and sat on the other side of the open door.

Sam watched past her and the others as they left the hangar onto the tarmac. By the time they were in the air, Station City's structures waved goodbye in the heat entrails of the airship. The sudden introduction of new technology and new people had been a keen distraction, but now, as she watched the shrinking city, she was reminded of everything that had happened. Her throat tightened as emotions slammed into the barriers she had thrown up in her hasty departure. She focused on her breaths, counting and recounting them, in, then out. She was grateful for the wind in her face as she blinked back the hurt, the anger, and the bitterness.

When she returned her attention back inside the ship, Brute watched her intently. Sam gave him a nod, then reached her hand across the aisle. "Valkyrie," she shouted.

The man eyed her prosthetic before he gingerly took it with an oddly soft grip. His voice surprised her, a higher pitch than she'd expected. "What's past is prologue. Baptize in fire, greet death, rise and be reborn. We shall see what name suits you then."

With his other hand, he pulled a narrow box out of his kit and placed it gingerly in Sam's prosthetic palm. She closed her fingers over it and her mouth cracked open, the question on her lips, but Brute had already leaned back into his seat, staring past her, in a world of his own. Next to him, Alphabet gave her a wink before he draped his legs over the neighboring perch.

"Welcome to SRAF!"

Sam squinted.

"Special Requirements Allied Fuckers!" the stocky man shouted, then shrugged. "Who fuckin' knows? Does it matter? We're gonna have fun." He leaned against Brute and pulled a hood over his eyes, tucking his chin into his chest. And that was that.

Baptize in fire.

Greet death.

Rise and be reborn.

Sam settled into her seat and watched out the opening a bit longer, her thumb rubbing the edge of the thin box. When she was certain no one was watching, she unraveled her fingers carefully, as if whatever Brute had given her would fall or fly away. She opened it, and two interconnected triangles greeted her, lasered on the inside of the hinged lid. Below, small letters were stamped out: AXIOM. Sam didn't recognize the term or know what it meant, but her eyes fell to the smooth cutouts. Within them, a circular white pill and a thin pen-like syringe sat. They stared up at her, like a pale eye and a thin smile.

Waiting.

Whispering.

Sam gasped and closed the lid. She spared a glance up at the others, but no one paid her any attention. She carefully reopened the box and caressed the strange pen and then the tab, her alloy fingertip too big to trace the imprinted triangles on its surface. Though her prosthetic's sensation was numb and delayed, Sam could feel the beckoning, the pull, and gravity.

A stimulant.

A temptation.

An opportunity.

Rise and be reborn.

ACKNOWLEDGMENTS

I couldn't have refined this story without the support of the incredible people around me. This acknowledgments section is a thin shadow of all the thanks they truly deserve.

The biggest THANK YOU goes to my wife, Claudia. Everyone else deals with my frustrations and emotions when I choose to reach out—but you live with this every single day. This entire journey was only possible with you beside me. Thank you for your unending patience, for grounding me in reality, and for always believing in me. *Te amo.*

Katie P. and Robin G., thank you for being my sounding boards. You see my weaknesses and challenge me to rise above them. And no, I'm still not writing a spicy scene—I'd like to look my colleagues and family in the eye, thank you.

To my alpha/beta readers, editors, and proofreaders: Christine H., Nicole J., Jessica L., Lauren H., Eric M., Rob M., Hal, Brittany, Alicia, TJ, Sarah I., Lee T., Ian Y., and Brett B. Thank you for helping me clean up this story. To best practices and lessons learned!

To my cover designer, Jason Arias, and my audiobook narrator, Savannah Gilmore, thank you for your talents and bringing this book to life in ways I never could have imagined.

To Cody S., my siblings, in-laws, Amy and Olivia T., Aron G., Liv L., and all my friends and readers who have cheered me on throughout this wild ride—thank you for your unwavering support and encouragement.

And finally, to everyone who picked up this book and let it be a part of your world, thank you.

OF IMPERFECTION
BOOK 3 OF THE ALTERED EARTH SERIES

Every beginning must have an end.

GLOSSARY

Alty—Human slang for Altered in the Station City region

Apostates—Also known as The Promised

AOR—Area of responsibility

Arshangol—The capital city of the Altered; where the Royal Court resides and governs

Arsynthetic—A toxic synthetic chemical

AWOL—Absent without leave

BigMED—Informal moniker for UMF Medical Services

Carbine—A long gun with a shortened barrel

Charonite—A member of the Children of Charon

Children of Charon (COC)—A prominent human-supremacist group

Command—UMF's leadership charged with overseeing the military's operations

Commcuff—A wrist-worn technological device used to communicate and connect to the network

DFAC—Dining facility; (pronounced dee-fak)

Duncan's—Compound bar in UMF Station

EMP—Electromagnetic pulse

ENDEX—End of exercise

EXFIL—Exfiltration

FOB—Forward operating base

HVT—High-value target

Intel—Intelligence

Jabber—An injection device

Legion—A company of Altered soldiers

Legionnaire—An Altered soldier

LMG—Light machine gun

LOGS—Logistics services

Matam—Large human population center located in the South (Andean region)

MED—Medical services

MedJet—A large medical support device

MedPort—A portable medical support device

MP—Military police

New Zapala—Southernmost human population center (Andean region)

OpSec—Operations security or operational security

POC—Point of contact

Prowler—A large utility task and terrain vehicle that can carry at least four passengers and cargo

The Promised—A prominent Altered supremacist group

Rabbit—A modular all-terrain vehicle that can carry at least two passengers

Recon—Reconnaissance

RF—Research facility

RHIB—Rigid-hulled inflatable boat

Rhino—A vehicle with a boxy shape and a high roof used for transporting goods or passengers

ROE—Rules of engagement

Royals/Royal Court—The governing body of the Altered population; legacy of original genetically engineered Altered

RUMINT—Rumor intelligence

SecHut—Security hut; a SecTeam's office

SecTeam—Security team; a local security force

SitRep—Situation report

SOG—Special Operations Group

SOL—Shit out of luck

Sovereign—The highest authority of the Royal Court

Station City—Largest human population center located in a central location

Station General—A prominent medical center in Station City

Sunali—A small town in the North

Tapetum Lucidem—A reflective layer of tissue in the eye that assists in low light vision

TDY—Temporary duty

Temunco—UMF's southernmost outpost, which overlooks Matam, New Zapala, and other regional settlements; borders Altered territories

Tsutsumi's—A restaurant in Station City

TOC—Tactical operations center

UMF—United Military Federation; the unified human military that oversees the defense and security of the entire human population

Ursus—UMF's northernmost outpost, which overlooks Gould and other regional settlements; borders Altered territories

Visor—A head-worn technological device used to communicate and assist with tactics

Wunby—Human slang for The Promised/Apostates based on their mantra, "one blood, one promise"

Yoomy—Slang for UMF

CONTENT WARNING

This fictional novel is meant for adults only. It contains material and scenes with:

- Profanity and explicit language
- Graphic violence
- Alcohol and substance abuse
- Death
- War and terrorism

ABOUT THE AUTHOR

S.J. Lee is currently in the foreign service and holds a master of science in security and intelligence and two bachelors of science in different business fields. She has lived and worked in Iraq, Mexico, Chile, India, Brazil, Guyana, and all over the United States.

instagram.com/sjleewriter